A Beautiful and Terrible Murder

By Claire M. Andrews

Daughter of Sparta series

Daughter of Sparta

Blood of Troy

Storm of Olympus

A Beautiful and Terrible Murder

CLAIRE M. ANDREWS

LITTLE, BROWN AND COMPANY
New York Boston

This book is a work of fiction. Names, characters, places, and incidents are the product of the author's imagination or are used fictitiously. Any resemblance to actual events, locales, or persons, living or dead, is coincidental.

Copyright © 2025 by Claire M. Andrews

Map illustration copyright © 2025 by Virginia Allyn.

Distressed floral wallpaper © Annmarie Young/Shutterstock.com; floral vector © RODINA OLENA; vintage frame © AKA_KerKer

Cover art copyright © 2025 by Elena Masci. Cover design by Jenny Kimura.
Cover copyright © 2025 by Hachette Book Group, Inc.
Interior design by Michelle Gengaro-Kokmen.

Hachette Book Group supports the right to free expression and the value of copyright. The purpose of copyright is to encourage writers and artists to produce the creative works that enrich our culture.

The scanning, uploading, and distribution of this book without permission is a theft of the author's intellectual property. If you would like permission to use material from the book (other than for review purposes), please contact permissions@hbgusa.com. Thank you for your support of the author's rights.

Little, Brown and Company
Hachette Book Group
1290 Avenue of the Americas, New York, NY 10104
Visit us at LBYR.com

First Edition: August 2025

Little, Brown and Company is a division of Hachette Book Group, Inc. The Little, Brown name and logo are registered trademarks of Hachette Book Group, Inc.

The publisher is not responsible for websites (or their content) that are not owned by the publisher.

Little, Brown and Company books may be purchased in bulk for business, educational, or promotional use. For information, please contact your local bookseller or the Hachette Book Group Special Markets Department at special.markets@hbgusa.com.

Library of Congress Cataloging-in-Publication Data
Names: Andrews, Claire M., author.
Title: A beautiful and terrible murder / Claire M. Andrews.
Description: First edition. | New York : Little, Brown and Company, 2025. | Series: Irene Adler ; volume 1 | Audience term: Teenagers | Audience: Ages 12 and up. | Summary: At Oxford's All Souls College, Irene Adler, disguised as student Isaac Holland, navigates a cutthroat competition and a series of gruesome murders while working with Sherlock Holmes to uncover the killer.
Identifiers: LCCN 2024034762 | ISBN 9780316575355 (hardcover) | ISBN 9780316575379 (epub)
Subjects: CYAC: Mystery and detective stories. | Characters in literature—Fiction. | Murder—Fiction. | Great Britain—History—Victoria, 1837–1901—Fiction. | Oxford (England)—Fiction. | England—Fiction. | LCGFT: Detective and mystery fiction. | Novels.
Classification: LCC PZ7.1.A53274 Be 2025 | DDC [Fic]—dc23
LC record available at https://lccn.loc.gov/2024034762

ISBNs: 978-0-316-57535-5 (hardcover), 978-0-316-57537-9 (ebook)

Printed in Indiana, USA

LSC-C

Printing 1, 2025

*To my friends, far and wide—
my greatest champions.*

CONTENTS

CHAPTER 1
The Curious Cadaver 1

CHAPTER 2
A Mercury Heart 8

CHAPTER 3
Charles's Law 20

CHAPTER 4
A Moriarty by Any Other Name 30

CHAPTER 5
A.W.M. 34

CHAPTER 6
Communing with the Dead 39

CHAPTER 7
Moriarty Knows 51

CHAPTER 8
Claws Made of Ice 65

CHAPTER 9
A Pipe That's Not for Smoking 67

CHAPTER 10
Eau de Soleil 87

CHAPTER 11
The Treachery of Moriarty.................100

CHAPTER 12
Bartlemas Chapel........................117

CHAPTER 13
Mumely.................................126

CHAPTER 14
Life of a Mayfly........................131

CHAPTER 15
Ghosts of Oxford.......................141

CHAPTER 16
A Disingenuous Smile....................150

CHAPTER 17
The Bullingdon Club.....................155

CHAPTER 18
Black Embroidered Roses.................165

CHAPTER 19
The Haunting of the Bodleian............169

CHAPTER 20
A Bloody Initiation.....................176

CHAPTER 21
A Scorpion's Sting......................190

CHAPTER 22
The Red Negligee........................196

CHAPTER 23
A Single Good Lord 208

CHAPTER 24
Oxford's Dirty Laundry. 215

CHAPTER 25
His Weakness. 224

CHAPTER 26
A Rosewood Pipe 236

CHAPTER 27
A Matter of Dignity. 251

CHAPTER 28
His Golden Hair. 261

CHAPTER 29
The Orchard and Bend 265

CHAPTER 30
Teeth Stained Red 278

CHAPTER 31
A Bed Full of Dresses. 284

CHAPTER 32
A Rare Luncheon. 293

CHAPTER 33
The Mask Falls 306

CHAPTER 34
Eden's Papaver 310

CHAPTER 35
To Waltz with Brilliance 319

CHAPTER 36
Dangerous Assumptions 325

CHAPTER 37
A Great Mind 330

CHAPTER 38
The Framing of Sherlock Holmes 337

CHAPTER 39
Feminine Wiles 341

CHAPTER 40
The Ripper of Oxford 348

CHAPTER 41
To Dance with Death 365

CHAPTER 42
A Steady Heart 373

CHAPTER 43
Her Beloved 377

CHAPTER 44
A Grave Mistake 384

CHAPTER 45
Never Trust a Moriarty 388

CHAPTER 46
A Smoking Gun 394

CHAPTER 47
All Souls Triumphant 398

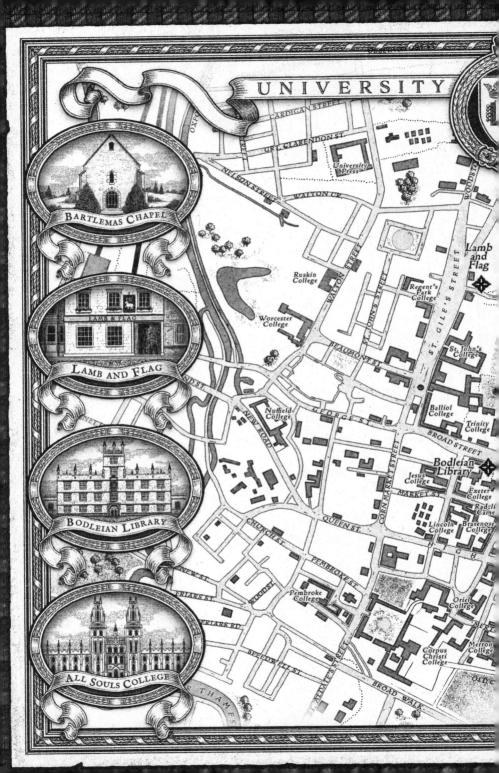

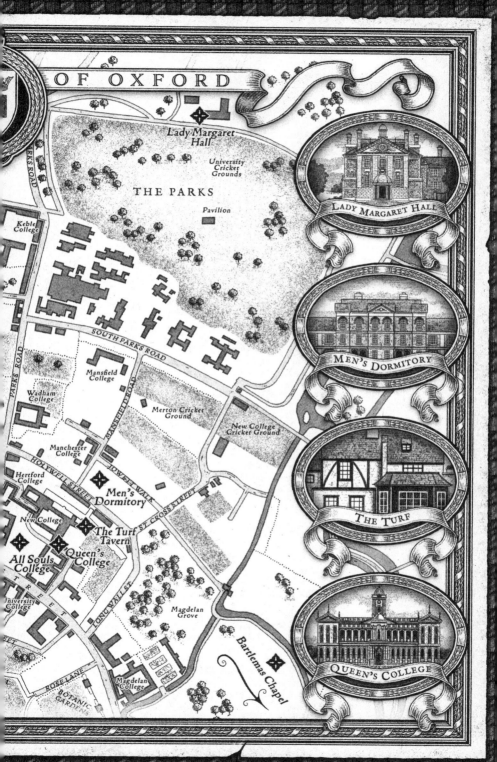

He used to make merry over the cleverness of women, but I have not heard him do it of late. And when he speaks of Irene Adler, or when he refers to her photograph, it is always under the honourable title of *the* woman.

—Sir Arthur Conan Doyle,
A Scandal in Bohemia

CHAPTER 1

The Curious Cadaver

Blood beaded and dripped, from body to table and eventually to the floor, pooling like a ruby mirror. The growing stain on the flagstone floor isn't my pressing concern, nor is the body lying a scant ten feet before me. I'm more concerned with why a cadaver, whose supposed time of death was more than two days ago, would still be bleeding.

I cough, raise a tentative hand, and make sure to pitch my voice deep and gravelly. "Forgive me, Professor Stackton, but when did you say the time of death was?"

My question elicits chuckles from my classmates, and from my steepest competition, a few raise their eyebrows and turn their rapt attention on the professor laboring above the body.

"Very good, Mr. Holland," Stackton says, elbow-deep in the chest cavity. "You should all have noticed, from the blood now soaking my best shoes, that the time of death was wildly incorrect. This body wasn't found yesterday. It was brought straight here, just this hour."

My bushy eyebrows, drawn dark and thick like fuzzy caterpillars, shoot high. If a body's blood starts to congeal somewhere between six to ten hours after the time of death, and the bell for the ninth hour has yet to toll, this man's death occurred sometime in the earliest hours of the morning.

Darkest hours before the dawn takes on a whole new meaning now.

The cadaver is splayed across the table at the front of the classroom, with the victim's absolute horror written across his face, split into a curdled scream.

What could have killed this man in a way to evoke such a response?

Despite my better judgment, I lean forward in my seat. The wood creaks with the movement, drawing more unwanted attention my way as a few of my classmates turn their gazes toward me. On reflex, I hunch my shoulders and bow my head. Ever the image of a meek boy. A nobody, not worth even a passing glance.

"*Rise in the ranks, but not too quick.*" My mentor's voice echoes through my mind. "*Draw no undue attention, for they cannot know what you are hiding.*"

Yet.

They can't know what I'm hiding *yet*.

Morning light filters through the stained-glass windows, catching on the centuries of dust floating in the air. I always dread our anatomy classes here, in one of the oldest classrooms in All Souls, where the ghosts of Oxford seem to moan the loudest. I'm not a superstitious person, but my mother raised me to have an appreciation and respect for the supernatural.

Just because I don't see it, doesn't mean it doesn't exist.

The classroom is silent, ghosts and students alike waiting with bated breath for Professor Stackton's next words. The wizardly old man toddles around the table, spectacles pressed high on the bridge of his nose and wiry beard threatening to drag along the body.

"And who will tell me the cause of death?" He glances about the classroom, ice-blue eyes jumping to each of my classmates, whose backs all straighten. Stackton's gaze lands on the worst of my peers. "Ah, Mr. Moriarty. What is your hypothesis?"

James Moriarty stands, flicking pale blond bangs from his eyes, and strides to the front of the classroom. With quick efficiency, his gaze sweeps the naked corpse from head to toe. His narrow nose scrunches, top lip curling back to reveal very sharp canines that never fail to make me shiver. His voice is deep and insufferably assured when he finally says, "One would rightfully assume overindulgence in drink, judging by the smell and vomit still lingering on his chin, but that could have easily hidden his other symptoms."

Moriarty then moves on to the abdomen, tripping his long fingers just above the body's pale skin. "Judging by the bloat, his stomach was considerably swollen before death and"—he takes Stackton's knife, peeling the incision farther apart—"his appendix ruptured. With fair certainty, I would tell this man's loved ones, if he had any, that he died of untreated appendicitis."

I bite my tongue to keep from arguing aloud, clenching my pen tight so that I don't raise my hand.

"All clever deductions," Stackton says. Moriarty's smile of pleasure is quickly swiped from his face as the professor continues, "But incorrect. Anyone else?"

Snickers fill the classroom as Moriarty's face flushes a lovely shade of maroon.

"Professor"—another of my peers raises his hand—"I would like to, for lack of a better word, take a stab."

A guffaw rips the air from the back of the classroom. Bertram Elmstone has more pomp than a preening peacock. Being the son of an earl would do that to the egos of most men, I suppose. "Don't kid yourself, Holmes."

Sherlock Holmes stands without Stackton's approval and walks slowly toward the table. His dark eyes linger on the man's hands and feet, tracing up the body's legs to his knees, and then travel to his gaping mouth.

"Myocardial infarction," Holmes says without blinking, almost too low for me to hear.

Stackton nods. "Very good. Now, share with your peers how you made such a quick and shrewd deduction?"

Holmes straightens his cravat and plucks the knife from the simmering Moriarty. Using the knife to peel back the skin of the man's chest, he says, "The heart shows asymmetric left ventricular hypertrophy." He lifts the man's arm. "And the scrapes on his knees and hands suggest he'd been crawling around before his death. He keeled over from the pain."

I can't sit quietly any longer. My hand rises seemingly of its own accord.

Stackton's brows narrow. "Yes, Mr. Holland?"

Against all my better judgment, I ask, "Where was the body found?"

Holmes, Moriarty, and every single one of my classmates swivel in my direction. I will the blush rising up my throat to cease.

I'm a blasted fool.

"Why would that be relevant, Mr. Holland?" Stackton demands, voice as sharp as a knife.

"It is entirely relevant." My own ego threatens to maim me. I push my spectacles farther up the bridge of my nose and take a deep, steadying breath, pitching my voice lower, more manly. "Both Holmes's and Moriarty's deductions could be correct, depending on the victim's whereabouts. Perhaps a substance ingested at a pub caused the victim to have a nervous breakdown, leading to cardiac arrest. The time of death could point to the closing time of most pubs, or brothels. And both Holmes and Moriarty are ignoring an obvious tell."

The gazes of both men in question sharpen. I really, *really* should have kept my mouth shut.

"Which is?" Stackton's voice has lowered. His patience with me is nearing its end.

Now it is my turn to stand. I walk toward the front of the room with my chin high, acutely aware of the fisherman's cap atop my head, marking me as lower class, and the itchy fuzzy worm stuck to my upper lip, likewise marking me as barely more than pubescent—despite the nineteen years to my name. I take the man's hand, so cold and firm, and splay his fingers.

"Opiates." The word is barely a whisper. "Commonly found in pubs and brothels, depending on where our man was found. The blue tingeing his fingernails points to poor blood circulation at the time of a potential overdose. They can also cause vomiting and cardiac arrest. And"—I turn his head toward the classroom, displaying for all the abject horror in the man's expression—"hallucinations."

Holmes's mouth presses into a firm line, and even Moriarty takes a step back, assessing me anew.

"An interesting hypothesis, Mr. Holland," Professor Stackton allows. "But unlikely. This man was found in a field."

My classmates chortle, the sound making my skin crawl and itch.

All but Holmes, whose shrewd eyes pierce me. I shiver under the weight of his focus.

The bell tolls in the distance, signaling the end of class, and I'm the first out the door.

I don't make it far before the force of a battering ram slams into my spine, flinging me against the cold stone wall. My books and glasses clatter to the floor. My pen rolls down the corridor after a shined boot sends it flying.

Bertram Elmstone's hideous face presses mere inches from my own. "You think a little upstart like yourself would know better than the greatest minds of All Souls?"

I force my shoulders to quiver as I look anywhere but in his eyes. Pleased with my apparent cowing, Bertram straightens and takes a step back. He flicks a disgusted glance at my moth-eaten tweed suit. None of my classmates say a word of reproach, the whole lot of them nothing but nameless faces leering from the shadows of the classroom door.

"Your kind," he says—*poor, of no class, with nothing to their name,* he doesn't add—"do not belong at Oxford." He raises a knee and slams his heel into the thick lens of my glasses, shattering them. "*You* do not belong in the All Souls."

Bertram takes another step back and I immediately duck to collect my things, abandoning the broken remains of my spectacles and hustling away. The barking laughter of my classmates chases me down the corridor. Let them think I flee with shame. Another day, another face, and I might have shown him exactly why I belong here.

Storming into my dormitory on the opposite side of campus, I ignore the cluttered chaos on my roommate's side of the room and take a long, grounding breath. The moment the door clicks behind me, the fake mustache is peeled away, and the buttons of the corset binding my chest pop open one by one, revealing a figure far fuller than that of my male cohort. My roommate's schedule memorized, I know I only have thirty-four minutes left to shed the tweed, the pants, and collect a corset of...a different sort. A dress is donned over the flattering—and painful—Victorian corset that emphasizes my figure, my lips painted rouge, white makeup washed away, and lastly, my wig tossed aside to let my hair, a red so dark it's almost black, tumble down my spine.

With twenty-six minutes left before my roommate finishes his post-class stroll that he takes every day to "clear his mind"—which I'm fairly certain is a cover to smoke from that pipe he tries to hide in his jacket—I move to the window, picking at the iron mullions and watching my classmates rush to their next classes. Another bell tolls in the distance, and their footsteps speed up, quick breaths catching in the air and trailing behind them like a line of smoke. I'll be late for my class, but it's better to not risk being seen.

Because none of the students passing below, kicking aside fallen leaves and stumbling over the cobblestones, know that every day I'm masquerading as someone else. That I'm not Isaac Holland.

My name is Irene Adler.

CHAPTER 2

A Mercury Heart

UNLIKE THE TENSION THICK ENOUGH TO CHOKE ON IN THE men's classes, the Lady Margaret classes are duller than watching rust form. My head cocks to the side. Watching rust form might actually be interesting, as long as the process was sped up. In the margin of my notes, I jot, *research rust formations in the Bodleian*.

Not exactly riveting, but it could prove crucial to the report I'm supposed to draft for my All Souls chemistry class.

The All Souls competition. A cohort composed of only the most prestigious and brilliant students in England, selected by hand once a decade to compete for the favor of Queen Victoria and to become one of her advisors. Some of the young men—ranging mostly in age from twenty to twenty-six—have been training for this competition since they could first hold a pencil, while others are gifted with a seat simply because their parents were wealthy enough to buy it for them. All must have a faculty sponsor, and mine...well, I hate to admit it, but I'm a bit of both. My grandmother did indeed have to bribe my sponsor, but not because I'm not brilliant or talented enough.

No. She had to bribe my sponsor because I'm a woman.

I am the youngest of the All Souls cohort. Of course, this only makes my face appear even more youthful to my male classmates. Bugger.

A moan echoes down the hallway before a door slams, interrupting Professor Chatham's monotonous lecture and rattling the classroom's windows. My classmates titter, whispering about Oxford's ghosts and demons. Even my friend Geraldine Hayward shivers in her seat beside me.

Mouth quirked to the side, I nudge her gently with my elbow. "Superstitious hen. The sound was obviously from a draft."

She hisses, "I knew that."

I chuckle softly and tug gently on one of her golden curls when the professor's back is turned. "Of course you did."

I purse my lips, debating topics for Isaac Holland's reports. Professor Chatham, sensing my wandering mind, queries me. Even half paying attention, I answer correctly, and he begrudgingly moves on to his next victim.

Lady Ermyntrude's head snaps up from her notes when Chatham's attention turns to her. "Yes, Professor?"

Chatham repeats the question. "What are the four chambers of the human heart called, Miss Bedford?"

I roll my eyes. The women's medical classes are so elementary compared to the men's. Even though we would, ideally, be expected to deal with dead bodies in a medical field post-graduation, the upper echelons of Oxford have deemed our sensitivities "too fragile" to even let us look at a body.

Ermyntrude twirls a cobalt nib pen expertly between her long, elegant fingers. The expensive piece likely costs more than my entire tuition, the pearl-and-gold casing a flagrant display of wealth. Cobalt ink is something likely even Queen Victoria would use only for the most important of signatures.

The lady must be equally annoyed with the easy question, as she—rightly—snaps, "Do you pose such simple questions because you can't think of anything else to ask, or because you believe I'm daft and can't handle a true challenge?"

My eyebrows rise as high as my hairline; the girls in the front of the class whisper. I can't help but admire Ermyntrude's gall. I wish I could react to the professors with such brassiness. My seat at this college—both of them—is tenuously held at best. While my All Souls grades are flourishing, I can't be bothered to spend the time on my Lady Margaret studies enough for them to be more than middling.

Ignoring the professor's indignant sputtering, she continues. "If the former, perhaps you should find another profession. I'm sure that Oxford expects much more of their professors. If the latter"—she leans forward in her seat, ebony mane falling over her shoulder—"I'm sure my father would love to have a chat with you."

Even from the back of the classroom, I hear Chatham gulp.

Lady Ermyntrude, daughter of the esteemed ninth Duke of Bedford, is decidedly not one to be trifled with.

The chalk in Chatham's hand clatters to the floor as Ermyntrude stands. She gathers her things, wiping the ink from her quill on a silk handkerchief. "I think the bell has tolled, Professor. This *lesson* has ended, and it is time for you to dismiss us."

The bell has done no such thing, but Professor Chatham can only nod, and the rest of us file out the door behind Ermyntrude. She wears a fine silk blouse tucked into a black skirt, accentuating her statuesque figure. Her porcelain skin and elegant coiffure mark her as the finest of gentry, and my classmates know it. They press close to her heels, hoping for her to deign to notice them.

A tug on my sleeve spins me around.

Honeyed eyes look up at me through dark lashes. Geraldine hands me a slip of paper.

"You were late to class," she says by way of explanation, and shrugs. "I thought you might want to copy my notes. You probably don't need them, though...."

She's right, of course; I don't need the notes. Nonetheless I say, "Thank you, Gerry."

"Please," she says, dimples deepening around her shy smile. "Call me Geraldine here."

A startled laugh cuts through me. "I hope you're not actually worried what these girls think."

"You know how ruthless they can be, Irene," Geraldine says, tone equally motherly and laced with warning.

I nod and tuck her notes in with my own. "Should we walk to the Bodley together before—"

"Hayward!" Ermyntrude's sharp voice cuts down the hallway. She gives us both a pensive look, dismissing me quickly in favor of my wealthier friend. "Come along, darling. I need to ask your opinion on something."

"What the hell does she want?" I ask my friend at the same time she arches a brow and says, "What could Ermyntrude Bedford want with me?"

Ermyntrude waves her forward, turning without waiting for my friend to follow.

It's an effort not to sneer. "Well, you two do run in the same circles. It was only a matter of time before she—"

"Deigned to acknowledge my existence?" Gerry lifts a shoulder. "I guess I should learn why."

I watch the two of them go, disappearing around a darkened corner and whispering to each other. My curiosity is truly piqued. Gerry has never mentioned an acquaintance with Ermyntrude, let alone a friendship. The two are of the same social standing, much higher than I as a daughter of one of Oxford's deans, but my friend has never said a word about the duke's daughter before. What could have changed since the semester began, not even a month ago?

Anyway, I have other things to worry about.

Alone, I make my way to the Bodleian before I have to revert back to Isaac's clothes; I have enough time to do some reading before my next class and would rather not fight with an itchy mustache and wig while I do so.

I prefer the Bodleian to anywhere else on campus. The lighting in the library is perfect, the shelves welcoming, and it's so blessedly quiet. Before I was accepted to the school, I used to hide in the seldom-used upper levels as a young girl.

I can now go over some alchemical experiments in its abandoned corners without drawing suspicion. Though my mentor had the foresight to book me a second dormitory room in the male wing—easier to sneak in and out of, away from ladies prone to snoop and meddle—I can't practice my experiments there while my roommate stews in the corner. Any discovery could give me the needed leg up against the lords that already have the money and prestige necessary to catch the queen's eye. I also have neither the money nor prestige to garner my own laboratory, like many of my All Souls classmates. Rich bastards.

Many of said classmates are perusing the Selden End's shelves, balancing piles of books to their tables. Some men look up and glare when I enter. Women are only recently allowed to study in the Bodleian, a point of much resentment among the students.

Moriarty, all sharp angles and hateful looks, sneers as I pass his table, leaving no uncertainty to his feelings about me using the sacred study space. He's surrounded by a handful of our All Souls peers, each vying for his favor much like the ladies do with Ermyntrude.

Smiling to myself, I continue past his table to the stairs. Above, on the first floor, hidden near the theology section, is a small reading room in which I have hidden my experiments.

A mercury heart.

I climb the spiraling metal staircase. A shadow jerks backward, and I nearly collide with the firm chest of Sherlock Holmes.

He recoils, pressing as far away as possible, against the black iron handrail. Exactly the opposite of how men usually behave around me.

"Milady," he says, sputtering slightly. So unlike the assured, confident, *arrogant* Sherlock Holmes in class.

I cock my head, smile widening, catlike. "I don't think anyone has ever called me that before."

"Would you prefer *Irene?*" His dark voice lingers over my name.

He knows who I am, and without proper introduction. Whether he says my name to intimidate or impress me, I haven't the slightest. The corner of his mouth curls upward. His behavior dances between curiosity and trepidation in my presence.

I like it.

"Pardon me, but I don't think we've been properly introduced before." I dare a step closer, suddenly glad I wore my favorite dark red lipstick, the same color as my hair. He smells of horses and an underlying hint of smoke, and on his thumb is a thick pewter ring. "Would you prefer to be called Sherlock, or simply Lord Holmes?"

A myriad of emotions spread across his face. His eyes widen in surprise, eyebrows rising. His mouth pops open a fraction—to say what? I don't think even he knows. His nostrils flare, undoubtedly taking in the scent of lemon-and-honey soap that I use to wash my clothes, so far removed from the oak-and-moss soap I've squirreled away from my family butler for Isaac's jackets and the floral scents that are fashionable among the ladies my age. Silence stretches between us for a few heartbeats.

"I do so enjoy our chats," I joke with an airy laugh. This isn't the first time we've come face-to-face, but it is the first time that I've ever spoken to him as Irene. I reach up to pat his cheek gently with my gloved hand. But not before I catch the heat rising in his tan cheeks, and the pair of icy eyes staring daggers at us both over his shoulder.

Moriarty tries to pin me with his gaze. He clenches a quill hard enough to snap the thin wood. His friends, curious about what has drawn his attention, have all turned to stare as well.

Ignoring him and the others, I continue up the stairwell. When I reach my hidden reading nook, my heart trips. The doorway, a single panel of wood without handle or keyhole, is ajar. Perhaps not quite so hidden after all.

A quick look around confirms that I'm alone. Pressing a

handkerchief to my nose in case the experiment is no longer contained, I dart into the room.

Chemistry is a meticulous field. Which is exactly why I kept the mercury, sulfuric acid, and potassium in distinctly separate vials before I went to my classes this morning.

The metallic-colored substances and dark liquids stream in narrow, shining lines to pool together in the center of a rapidly disintegrating table.

A table that could catch fire at any moment and burn this entire library down.

I leap into action. Pulling out the assortment of beakers and droppers, I suction up as much of the sulfuric acid as possible and deposit it in a dish. Smoke begins to form, and I pray for my eyesight and lungs to remain intact. The wood of the table groans, the mercury burning a hole through it.

I drop to my knees and whip out my last beaker. The mercury lands in the glass.

A soft sigh of relief escapes my lips. I place the dish on the floor beneath the hole to catch any remnants.

So much for that experiment. The last of my allowance for the month went into those supplies. I could always ask Grandmother for more, or steal some of my brother's allowance. With a huff, I blow my bangs from my eyes and rescue what remains of my mercury heart ingredients, taking stock of supplies as the cogs in my head begin to whirr.

I'm not nearly as concerned about replacing the experiment as I am with how—and why—it was tampered with in the first place.

Someone, likely one of my fellow All Souls pupils, must have seen Isaac Holland enter the room, either last night or the night before. I thought I'd been sure to cover my tracks. I'll have to find a new spot to practice my experiments and take extra precautions when making my changes from Isaac to Irene.

Stepping from the nook and making sure the hidden door is shut completely this time, I move to the balcony and survey the Bodleian, searching for suspects.

Other than in class this morning, I've been quiet as a dormouse, riding the coattails of my classmates. They couldn't know that my grades far surpass theirs.

Unless they are mentored by someone with direct access to our grades.

One such young man, Lord Hugo Davies, lingers by the checkout desk, waiting for the Bodley's librarian to return. He peeks over the counter, reading the list of books checked out by his classmates. Davies, rich enough to garner a seat at Oxford but by no means clever enough to rank in the top. Yet he still managed to swindle a seat in the All Souls competitive class because his uncle is Dean Markham, the Archbishop of York.

There's Edgar Hayward, Geraldine's brother. Not direct royalty but his father is a favorite of the queen, as well. Noticing my attention, he flashes me a brilliant smile, which I return in kind. He's handsome in a classical way and has not a single malicious thought in that beautiful head.

I give him a friendly wave, and his answering smile lights up his entire face. He takes a step toward me, but an unwelcome figure stands, stopping him with a question I cannot hear. Moriarty gives Edgar a not-so-friendly jab in the arm, chortling about something. Edgar nods, replying to whatever he asked, far too polite to brush the younger lord aside.

Then there's Sebastian Moran, sitting beside Moriarty. Moran peers over his friend's work while Moriarty talks with Edgar, and dots the answer on his own sheet. No, not clever enough. Especially not when Moriarty sits back down, scratches out the answer with his quill and writes another the moment Moran's attention is elsewhere. All in a matter of moments before returning to his conversation with Edgar.

Moriarty is no fool by any stretch of the imagination, but I know his concerns are elsewhere. That, and his ego is large enough to never consider Isaac Holland a true threat. Or so I thought before this morning.

As if my gaze burns a hole atop his repulsive head, James Moriarty turns around. His pink lips peel back in an almost feral smirk, revealing pointed incisors and eyes depthless with malice, and winks. The bastard has the audacity to bloody wink at me.

His face has haunted my nightmares for far longer than I've attended Oxford. Shivering, I force my gaze away.

Holmes's dark gaze catches mine. He leans against the railing of the second floor, not the flustered man from only moments ago. He's watching me to see what I'm going to do next. Either I'm a curiosity or he expects me to reveal the alchemical mishap.

None of my other classmates in the library give me any cause to suspect them. Not the surly Evans fastidiously writing notes in his journal, nor the meek Oliver stacking a pile of thick books on top of his table. None but perhaps my two biggest competitors for the All Souls prize.

I suck in a deep breath. Ever so aware of both men following my every movement, I collect a random book from the shelves and begin a turn around the upper levels of the Bodleian, seeking a new nook for my experiments.

I flip errantly through the pages, thoughts of Holmes and Moriarty tumbling through my mind like Alice down her rabbit hole. If Holmes really is the one who ruined my experiment, then he must know, or have a hint toward Isaac's true identity.

I click my tongue, refuting the possibility. My ruse couldn't possibly be up already. We're not even a month into the term.

The narrow hallways are dark, sconces low to minimize light damage to the ancient texts kept here. A low, hollow moan echoes through the lines of shelves. They say that the ghost of a widow still wanders the stacks, searching for the husband she lost at war. She will attack any veteran she finds, furious that he is not the soldier she's looking for.

A superstition, obviously, but sometimes I find ledgers and lists pulled randomly from shelves detailing the men lost at sea and in battle.

Another soft moan trails my steps, prickling my arms with goose bumps. When I reach the upper reading room, it is blessedly devoid of students, but also much colder. My breath fogs before my face in warm tendrils. I turn, peering around the dimly lit room for the chill's source, rubbing my arms brusquely.

I'm kicking myself for not wearing a heavier shawl when a slight breeze teases my hair. It seems to whisper my name. I spin around, tiptoeing deeper into the reading room. My heels click on the floor as I walk between rows of wooden tables toward the history section. There's the breeze again, tickling my nose.

And with it, impossible to miss, comes the coppery stench of blood.

I jerk to a halt.

Slowly, carefully, I lean down, taking off my shoes and setting them on a table. My footsteps are near silent as I continue toward the history section. I hold my breath as I pass through the reading room, more to avoid the smell than from fear. The breeze is much stronger in here, the call of autumn's last songbirds and the church's teatime toll leading me to the far corner of the room.

I gasp and jerk backward, my hand shooting to cover my mouth. Despite the staggering amount of bodies I've seen compared to most ladies of my station, this one still takes my breath away.

His body hangs halfway out the open window, one arm draped above his head, the other on the sill. Blood drips from his fingers, pooling on the floor.

I swivel around. There's not a single other soul in the room. The light from the open window turns amber as the sun begins its descent beyond Oxford, filling the room completely. Leaving nowhere to hide.

Moving closer, I recognize the body's face, once so obnoxious and now filled with abject horror.

Bertram Elmstone's mouth gapes open, pale eyes popped wide, and his throat open with a crescent-moon slice. Blood pours from the gaping wound. There's another wound on the bleeding hand, a cut deep enough to reach the bone.

And, above the smell of blood, there's the undeniable stench of scorched flesh. Curiosity begs me to examine Bertram's body further, but common sense wins out. I would disturb the scene of the crime, and anyone could walk into the room at any moment.

Now, what would a lady do when stumbling upon a body?

I return to the reading room and grab my shoes, then walk into the history room once more. After returning the shoes to my feet and checking my dress for any blood, I open my mouth.

And I scream.

CHAPTER 3

Charles's Law

There is no laughter in class. No rumbling chortles or breathy guffaws. There's only the scratching of pens.

I grip my pen hard, gritting my teeth until my jaw begins to ache. The noise reminds me of the mice in my father's walls. Grating and incessant. My All Souls classmates are bent over their desks, hurriedly taking notes before Professor Ruminton erases the board again. Holmes, sitting in front of me, is the only one who doesn't bother. He gives the board a mere cursory glance before gazing out the window.

Either his memory is astounding or he's just as distracted as I am.

Or both.

My mind drifts again to being relentlessly questioned by the Scotland Yard. The lies had come easily to me, and so had my own questions.

"Who would do such a thing?" I faux sob into the handkerchief handed to me by the nearest officer.

My mother would have applauded my performance.

The officer reaches out as though to rub my back consolingly but stops himself, hand lingering above my shoulder. "That's what we are trying to find out, miss."

He is young, much younger than the rest of the officers and perhaps only a year or two my senior. His hair is a vibrant blond, his skin pale, and his eyes red-rimmed, all signs of a night-shift officer. I return the handkerchief, and his hand shakes as he grabs it. The initials J.H.W. were sewn with royal-purple thread in the corner.

I had thought he, the youngest, would be the easiest to beguile into revealing answers to me, but I obviously underestimated him. I tuck this tidbit into my growing satchel of secrets.

"Can you tell me the circumstances of discovering the body?" He replaces the handkerchief with a notepad.

The other officers crowd the normally vacant history section, searching for answers in all the wrong places. My respect for the Yard drops substantially when one knocks over a chair and tries to surreptitiously put it back, and another nudges the corpse with his knee while leaning to look out the window.

Hiding my annoyance with some pitiful sniffling, I reply, "I needed an escape from the crowded Selden End. Hardly anyone comes to the reading room on the top floor because of the stories."

"What stories?"

"Of the ghosts." I pitch my voice low. "There are rumors that a maid, after being romanced and promptly discarded by a viscount, flung herself from that exact window." I nod in the direction of the body still being examined by the officers. "Her ghost is said to roam the top floor, still searching for the lord in question."

"And these... stories didn't deter you from exploring the floor?" He coughs. His eyes crinkle slightly in the corners. To him, I am nothing but a superstitious girl. Exactly the character I intended to portray.

"Well, that's all they are. Stories." I flash the officer my loveliest smile. "Wouldn't you agree, Officer...?"

His pale cheeks flush. "Oh, I'm no officer. Not yet. I'm just getting in my hours of training and grunt work." The smile he offers me, though forced, is kind. "You can call me John."

"There are a lot of Johns in the force, I'm sure."

"Ah, but there's no other John Watson." His smile falters. "Not anymore."

I want to ask more, but don't. The lad looks beaten down enough as it is.

"I'm relieved that they allow ladies to study here," he says, surprising me by the turn in conversation.

My mouth pops open. "Oh?"

"They're quite...prickly...about who they admit to Oxford," John continues without looking at me, scribbling more notes down on his pad. "I applied once."

And didn't get in, he doesn't need to say. Because I know all too well how the upper echelons of Oxford stick their noses up at the lower class.

I snort in a definitely unladylike fashion. "Prickly seems to be an apt description of the deans. What did you want to study?"

John opens his mouth, then closes it again, pen hovering over the notepad as he taps the top of his nib pen against the worn paper. Finally, in a voice so low only I can hear, he admits, "I wanted to be a doctor. But my father thought the dream was too lofty. He said I would better serve society in the Yard." He shakes his head, lips pinching. "I never stood a chance of being accepted into a school like this anyway."

"Is your father an officer?" The question bursts from my lips before I can stop it, remembering his earlier words too late.

"He was." He brusquely tucks the notes away in his back packet. His movements are rough and jerky. "He passed recently, actually."

I should give him my condolence, or offer comfort somehow. An honorable lady would. Instead, I am struck speechless, and somehow I know that he wouldn't want to be consoled or coddled in front of his colleagues.

So I whisper, "I know the pain of losing a loved one. Take comfort in the knowledge that your father must have been so proud of you."

Another officer taps him on the shoulder, and John readily takes the excuse to leave. With an apologetic smile at me, he joins his fellows crowding around the body. They peel back the man's shirt, and some take a step back. The men go deathly silent, but my sight is blocked from whatever stole their breath.

The deans are called to the Bodleian for questioning. They all glare in my general direction but otherwise ignore me. They still resent being forced to accept women into their ranks. Perhaps they'll find some way to blame the murder on the influx of women in the school.

Murder. The thought jars me. I look again to Bertram's body. There's no denying that he was a pompous ass, but if I went around slitting the throats of every insufferable man at Oxford—tempting though the thought may be—there'd be no one left by the end of a fortnight.

Speaking of insufferable men, the worst of the bunch arrives in the doorway of the reading room. Moriarty easily talks his way past the officers, moving to stand beside his father. Dean Richard Moriarty's chest puffs up with pride at his son's appearance, despite the dead body in the room, and he claps the young man on the back.

James Moriarty nods in my direction, but the dean only scowls. He will deal with me later.

I sniff, still the shocked and heartbroken student to everyone else *around me, and turn away. John Watson leaves his fellow officers and walks to the doorway. He says something, leaning over to whisper in a student's ear.*

Gone are the dress and fake tears. Cloaked in the disguise of Isaac again, I stare now at the back of that student's head, silently willing him to reveal what Watson said to him.

Sensing my attention, Holmes turns but my gaze has already moved on to the board above his head. I squint as if struggling to translate Professor Ruminton's illegible handwriting. Though the writing is nearly unreadable to the point of being another language, the formula isn't. Chemistry, easily my strongest subject, comes to me as effortlessly as breathing.

"It's Charles's Law."

It takes me a moment to realize that Holmes is talking to me. I blink, returning my attention to him. I'm painfully aware of the way his eyes linger on my lips. If I didn't have Isaac's fake nose and mustache, I would be flattered. But I do, and I can't help but wonder if Irene's—my—lips are somehow memorable.

"Yes, I know what Charles's Law is," I say, struggling, and failing, not to sound snippy.

Holmes's dark brows pull down into a heavy frown. "It looked like you were struggling to read the board."

"Thanks. I was. My glasses are missing." Not missing. Just broken beyond repair beneath the late Elmstone's heel. Whispering, I add, "I was frowning because the notes seem superfluous."

"I couldn't agree more." He chuckles, turning back around. I notice a scar on the back of his neck, like an upside-down V.

I tap the end of my pen on the paper. "Do you think he hides the equations between the unnecessary verbiage on purpose?"

Grinning now, he whispers, "You're not so common as our classmates believe."

"There is nothing common in this world." I jot down Ruminton's latest note.

Holmes turns sharply to face me. I shake my head and ignore him. What a bizarre interaction.

Professor Ruminton makes sure to close out the class with a few kind words about Bertram. My classmate's absence is keenly felt. I never thought I'd miss his tactless remarks or near-constant bullying, but I would rather hear him insult Isaac's ill-fitting suits again than to remember the gaping maw of his slit throat. A shiver steals up my spine.

"The deans have agreed with the Scotland Yard that, until the murderer of our fine young Master Elmstone is apprehended, there is a need to limit foot traffic in and out of Oxford. Students, staff, and faculty are the only ones allowed on campus. Do not linger in the halls. Go straight to the classes from your dormitories, the lecture halls, and refectory. Walk in groups no smaller than three, whenever possible. You may be questioned at any time, so be sure to state your class year, faculty sponsor, and dormitory."

"The Ripper has Oxford looking like a prison," Moriarty announces. His associates all chuckle.

"The Ripper?" Holmes turns in his seat to face Moriarty. "The murderer has a nickname? Wouldn't that imply that he's killed more than once?"

"Maybe not yet," Moriarty allows. "But your kind should be next."

The skin beneath Holmes's nails suddenly pales as he grips the wood hard enough to make the chair groan. The bell tolls in the distance. I'm rising to pack my bag when the classroom door swings wide, revealing three men wearing familiar high-collared, blue-and-black greatcoats. One face is now also familiar to me.

When John Watson surveys the sitting class, Holmes straightens, chin rising as a wordless exchange passes between them. I'm not the only one to notice, either.

Moriarty leans back in his seat, crossing his arms, icy eyes dancing between Holmes and Watson.

The officers assess us, squinting long enough to make us all squirm, until Professor Ruminton finally coughs.

"Can I help you gentlemen?" he asks.

The officers ignore him, continuing to survey the class, before one announces, "Which of you is Isaac Holland?"

Isaac's timid expression is hardly a mask as everyone in the classroom turns to look at me. Holmes's gaze is only the second heaviest fixed to me, as the officer who spoke ushers me to the door.

A barked command stops us all from going into the hallway.

"Don't let the little weasel off easily." One of my classmates stands. Lord Jude Wilson, a tall, pinch-faced son of an earl and friend of Bertram. He'd never deigned to acknowledge my presence before, as either Isaac or Irene, but the venom with which he beholds me drips like poison down my veins.

"He was the last one to speak with Bertram," another classmate, Avery Williams, pipes up, making me grind my teeth.

"Do not"—Jude Wilson points to each officer, then slowly raises his finger toward my face, which must be as white as a sheet—"let him go. Those gutter rats infect our school like the plague. Every year, they come, chittering in our walls. Their dirty claws ruining our streets."

My nostrils flare, everything in me screaming to stare him down. Good sense wins out, and I turn my gaze to the floor.

His next words are like the lash of a whip on the back of my neck. "A rat can hang from the gallows just the same as anyone else."

"Justice is in the hands of the law and God now," says the elderly officer before peeling from the room.

My gaze meets Holmes's as Watson and the other officer usher me through the door. His black eyes are completely blank.

Wordlessly, I follow the trio of officers down the corridor to an empty classroom. The cold stone walls seem to close in around us, the only light in the room the fading amber of sconces gasping for life on the walls beside the chalkboard. The eldest of the trio indicates for me to take the seat behind the front desk.

"I am Inspector Gregson." I look up into the wizened face of a much-too-old-for-this-sort-of-work man. He leans down, grimacing as his hips protest, to make his face level with mine.

"I'm not going to mince words." His pale eyes watch my every reaction. "We have it under good authority that, as one of your classmates proclaimed, you were the last to speak to Bertram Elmstone."

Watson steps forward. "What do you say to their claims that you had an altercation with the young lord?"

A myriad of words dance on the tip of my tongue. What would Isaac do? I—Irene—would demand the presence of a solicitor and her guardian. But Isaac? He has no one to protect him, left speechless and absolutely petrified.

I stammer. "Not in the library, sir. He shoved me in—"

"The corridor. Yes, we heard." Inspector Gregson straightens.

My shoulders curl forward as if in response. "I don't see what this has to do with his death. I haven't been to the Bodleian since Feast Day."

"Is that when you lost these?" Gregson reaches into his pocket and pulls out my broken spectacles. The glass has been removed from the silver frames and the temples are bent at ungodly angles. "They were found on the top floor of the Bodley."

The air leaves my lungs in a great whoosh. Those had fallen off my face when Bertram slammed into me in the corridor. If I admit they're mine, it will only open the doors for further questioning. They will dig deeper, seeking any excuse to throw a lowborn lad like Isaac Holland into prison instead of one of their precious lords. I can't afford to be taken into the station for further questioning. They will find out who I truly am, which is a fate arguably worse than a prison cell.

The cell my father would make for me would make prison look heavenly by comparison.

"Those aren't mine, sir."

"No?" Gregson's eyes bore into mine. "That's not what your classmates say."

I would tell him that none of Isaac's classmates have ever paid enough attention to recognize his glasses, let alone the color of his eyes. But Isaac can only repeat, "Those aren't mine."

The other two men shift behind their superior. With an impatient edge to his voice, Gregson asks, "Where were you between the hours of eleven and two yesterday?"

I expect they already checked Isaac's schedule and discerned that he has no classes during that time. It's an effort to not raise my chin and instead keep it pressed close to my chest. "Studying in my dormitory."

The inspector's next question is immediate. "You must know we will be asking your roommate to confirm this?"

My answer comes just as quickly. "He wasn't there."

One of the younger officers pipes up. "Is there anyone who can confirm your whereabouts?"

"No one." I press my lips together, fake mustache tickling my chin. If I don't say anything more, they will take me in for further questioning, and there's no way my disguise will hold up in front of a hundred officers. "If you want to take me away, it will be a waste of all our time. You'll find no record of crime in my file, nor family and friends to question. I am nothing but a poor, humble student seeking a degree. Murder would get me nowhere but a fetid prison cell."

Gregson opens his mouth, then snaps it shut again. His gaze dances about my face. A drop of sweat slides slowly down the back of my neck. He turns to the other two officers and gives them a curt nod. Both march down the corridor without further direction, leaving me with the inspector.

"If I have further questions, then"—his icy eyes linger on the spot below my right eye, where my birthmark should be covered with pale makeup—"I know where to find you."

I sag into my seat when he leaves after his fellow officers. My heart pounds so hard it threatens to rip a hole in my chest. The echo of their thudding footsteps fading down the corridor will haunt me for a long time.

Not only was my secret so nearly undone but now I know that my movements will be watched with even more scrutiny.

Because someone is trying to frame me for the murder of Bertram Elmstone.

CHAPTER 4

A Moriarty by Any Other Name

On the Lady Margaret side of campus, the ladies are all atitter about the murder, and I can't blame them. They whisper amongst one another while we wait for the professor to arrive. Some are louder than others, but no whispers are loud enough to drown out the roar of my thoughts. Not until the duke's daughter speaks.

"My father almost didn't let me attend class today," Ermyntrude announces, sashaying into class. She carries one of those fashionable fans from France, waving it in front of her face despite the steady autumn chill filling Oxford's halls. "Bertram was a cousin of mine. What if the madman who murdered him has it out for our family? I could be next!"

The ladies gasp. I shake my head and return to my notes. Though not outside the realm of possibility, the idea is a bit farfetched. Elmstone was a distant cousin, at best. The movement catches Ermyntrude's attention.

"Irene, you were the one who found poor Bertie's body, correct?" She zeroes in on me, her dark eyes piercing. The other ladies in the class turn, faces ranging from curiosity to distaste, and whisper amongst one another. She doesn't refer to me as *lady* for a reason, after all.

I allow a curt nod. Today seems to be the day for irritating interactions. "Correct."

The whispering heightens.

She leans forward in her seat. "What was it like?"

I hesitate, warring between giving in to her morbid curiosity and casually dismissing her. It would be better, I think, to have her as an ally than an enemy. And perhaps her curiosity is a blessing in disguise. I lean forward, grinning wickedly, and whisper, "Just as horrid as you'd imagine."

Now all the girls are leaning in, surrounding the two of us. All except Geraldine, whose skin has taken on the pale green tinge of one about to toss up their breakfast.

Swallowing, I continue. "The smell was ghastly, and a chill hung in the air." My eyes widen for effect, and my voice pitches lower. "And I could have sworn I felt another presence there, like his ghost still lingered in the room, begging me to catch his murderer."

One lady's cheeks pale. "That's impossible."

"Who's to say?" I shrug, turning back to my notes. "His ghost could have been pointing at the murderer waiting behind me before I screamed."

"Have you no respect for the dead, Miss Adler?" Professor Stackton's voice is like the crack of a whip. He stomps into the classroom and slams a stack of books on the desk. "The coroner has just ruled Lord Elmstone's death a suicide, so the mass hysteria overtaking you all must immediately cease."

Impossible. There's no way Bertram Elmstone could have inflicted those wounds upon himself. Of course, I am one of only three students able to argue that fact. Moriarty, Holmes, and myself.

There's no body on the table this time. They would never let the students dissect Bertram's body to prove otherwise.

Stackton's following lecture falls on deaf ears. I don't deny the overwhelming relief that soars through me, with the red circle of suspicion around Isaac's head erased, but what could have scared the deans enough to take part in this charade? Dean Moriarty also knows personally that I'm no fool; he'll come to me sooner rather than later to demand I comply with the secrecy and lies. I lean back, twirling my pen. Perhaps I could use this to my advantage.

"That was quite a show," Geraldine murmurs, matching my steps down the wide corridor. "I had no idea you were so prone to theatrics."

A startled laugh escapes me. "You've told me to take up opera on more than one occasion."

"For your voice, silly." She nudges me.

A tall shadow steps around the corner in front of us. We leap backward, my heart jammed in my throat. The lady who crossed our path laughs as if our fear is the funniest thing in the world.

With wide, innocent eyes, Ermyntrude asks, "Did I frighten you two?"

Obviously.

Geraldine hooks an arm through mine. A silent warning to refrain from biting the lady's head off.

Straightening the cuffs of my sleeves, I reply a tad too sharply, "I'm still a bit jumpy after finding the body."

"Why were you even up on that floor anyway?" Ermyntrude squints at me, eyes like black jewels in the hallway's dim light. "We don't have any history classes this term."

I answer honestly. "It's the quietest place in the Bodleian for that very reason. There are no history classes offered for any section this term."

Ermyntrude's lips pinch, like my words are a tart lemon.

Geraldine's eyes are lovely and wide. "I'm so sorry you had to be the one to find him, Irene."

Ermyntrude frowns, glancing between us. "What did your brother have to say about it?"

It takes me a moment before realizing that she is speaking to *me*, not Geraldine. My heart stills. "What?"

"What did James say about Bertram's death?" Ermyntrude takes a step forward.

My palms are suddenly clammy.

Enemies and murderers are nothing when you're the half sister of the narcissistic sociopath James Moriarty.

CHAPTER 5

A.W.M.

I HALT ON THE THRESHOLD OF RICHARD MORIARTY'S TOWN house. Rapid breaths escape me as the color drains from my face.

Shadows reach long, gray fingers from the darkness inside the wide-open doorway. My heart flutters more rapidly than the wings of a hummingbird, but I'm not given a chance to turn on my heels and run away before an impatient hand shoves me by the back of my neck and I stumble inside.

The foyer is as cold as my mother's grave. I wrap my thin arms around myself, gazing about the room with a gaping mouth.

A tall figure cloaked in shadows stands at the top of the spiraling stairs. Though I can't make out his face, I know he watches. I know by the cold, heavy weight of his eyes.

"I expect my payment," says the man who shoved me inside, straightening his plaid bow tie. "Or I can dump the wee lass in the Thames before you'd have time to descend those stairs."

My trembling begins anew. My tiny fingers catch in my frayed cuffs as I hug my arms ever tighter around my too-thin waist.

The shadowed figure's voice could cut through a battlefield. "There's no need for threats. Your payment is awaiting my signature in my office."

"Shall we adjourn there?" *The broad man takes a step up the stairs, and then another.*

"Indeed." *The figure gazes at me once more.* "Irene's brother can show her to her room. James, make the girl feel at home."

Brother? I flinch, then nearly leap from my shoes when another figure steps from an alcove to my right.

Danbury didn't wait for our introductions, sweeping up the stairs with the eagerness of a husband on his wedding night. I watch him ascend, torn between the devil I know and the devil stalking toward me.

James sneers. "You are no sister of mine."

My lips curl back to match his revolted expression. "I'm not in the market for a sibling anyway."

"She speaks?" *He chuckles.* "And I thought you wouldn't have half the cognitive abilities of a gutter rat." *James cocks his head.* "But you'll have to lose the accent."

"Accent?" *I'm not familiar with that word. At least not in English.*

He ignores my question, walking around me, eyeing every stray thread and hair, every smudge of dirt from the long passage to Britain. "Grandmother will have to pay off the gossip rags. And whatever nosy ninnies watched you slouch through the door."

"I don't slouch," *I hiss.*

"A tutor will be another dip in Grandmother's coffers." *James continues assessing me, and I itch to tell him that someone with such messy hair has no ground to stand on to be so judgmental.*

I raise my chin. "I'm sure I could whip you from toe to nose in linguistics and mathematics."

James's mouth presses into a line. "I doubt that."

"I see the introductions are long past and you two are already falling into the sibling rivalry stage."

We both whip toward the stairs as a man, dressed in a pristine three-piece navy suit, descends. His heavy heels echo around the foyer with each step.

"Where is Danbury?" I demand in a high, tremulous voice. Perhaps I could bribe him into returning me to France.

"He got his payment," the man says, reaching the final step and stopping. I have to crane my neck to look up into his gaunt, pale face.

"He left me with you?" My voice cracks on the final word. "I don't even know you."

"It's about time you did." He doesn't come any closer, remaining on the final step. "I am your father, Lord Richard Moriarty."

The ground threatens to give way beneath my tiny feet. "Impossible. Mon père est décédé."

"Is that what your mother told you?" Richard shakes his head. "That woman will have a shawl of lies wrapped around her in the grave."

Tears spill down my cheeks. "My mother was no liar."

"Nobody will believe this, this"—James waves a hand through the air—"this charade! She looks nothing like us. Grandmother will have to empty our coffers to even present her to the public."

"That's enough, James," Richard snaps, making James's chest puff out. His thin lips curl in a sneer as he looks me over. "The people will believe what the Moriartys want them to...."

After I had been brought kicking and screaming from France, where my mother had squirreled me away, Dean Moriarty had taken a single look at me and known that preparing me for my introduction to society—as a bastard, no less—would be a feat fit for an entire army. But for a Moriarty? Where my improprieties, faults, and curiosities could be excused as a by-blow of my bastard blood? A welcome challenge.

All is right in my room when I step inside, careful to keep my footsteps silent and light, mindful of the seconds ticking away before my roommate returns from his regularly scheduled row on the Cherwell. My disguise is ripped free before the door swings shut behind me, one hand peeling away the mustache as the other slides the lock home. I'm unbuttoning the jacket and sliding my arms free when a large, pale envelope on my desk gives me pause. Jacket forgotten, I stride to the table, continuing to undress with a single hand as the other reaches for my letter opener.

The door had been locked when I returned this evening, the echo of the chamber clicking open still a sharp memory, and my roommate only ever drops by in the afternoon between the hours of four to six p.m.—so how did this get on my desk, which was empty only three hours ago?

The answer comes to me as soon as I slice it open.

Out tumbles a pair of spectacles, a perfect replication of Isaac's before Bertram crushed them beneath his heel, and a short note on heavy ivory paper.

> *Looks like you've misplaced these.*
> *Continue to make me proud.*
> *A.W.M.*

I rub my eyes with the back of a hand, smiling to myself. Of course she had her own key made.

A movement out the window catches my eye and immediately freezes my spine. "Bloody hell."

My roommate, soaking wet and steaming in the cold, twilit air, strides across the green. I have less than two minutes to get my costume back on or *this* charade will be entirely at an end.

I rush around the room, retrieving the discarded garments, throwing them on as I rush from corner to corner. The letter is tucked into a breast pocket, glasses shoved up on my nose, curses streaming from my mouth as I desperately tighten the stays of the corset keeping my curves unrecognizable. I'm just pressing the mustache to my tender upper lip when the lock clicks on the door and it swings open.

My roommate strides into the room, unbuttoning his soaked shirt. Black curls plastered to his tan face. Bare chest taut and dripping. He throws his head back, spraying the closing door behind him as he pins me with his ebony gaze.

My heart thunders in my ears, mouth hanging open as I take him—all of him—in. He does the same.

Holmes's dark brows narrow. "What the devil are you doing here?"

CHAPTER 6

Communing with the Dead

I GO AS STILL AS A DEER SPOTTING A HUNTER.
Holmes takes another step inside, shrugging out of his ruined shirt and tossing it unceremoniously to his cluttered side of the room. Bare-chested and dripping on the flagstones, he braces large hands on his hips and looks me up and down.

"What are you staring at, Holland?" he demands.

I drag my gaze from his chest with considerable effort, swallowing. "What are you doing here?"

"I live here, too," he says, reaching for the buckle of his pants, before hesitating. "Do you have my schedule memorized?"

Oh god.

It takes everything in me to not turn around or drop my gaze to his...hands. A man wouldn't be embarrassed, or likely even care. I think. Oh god. Oh god. Oh god...

"Well, I live here, too," I snap. I give a brusque wave toward the pile of his belongings. "Me and the laundry monster that slowly encroaches on my side of the room."

Holmes scoffs, the sound grating on my last nerves. His pants drop to his ankles and he kicks those to join the rest of his clothes in a heap on the floor. "Don't worry. I'm only here to change into something dry. It seems that someone thought it would be funny to dump me in the river. Likely that prat *Lord* Wilson." His lips curl with distaste around the title.

I hide my smirk behind a textbook. I'm sure I also have James to thank for this half-naked display right now. At least he's good for something.

"Besides, it's not like you'll be sleeping here anyway."

My smile drops alongside my stomach. I keep my face as carefully blank as possible. "Have you been following me, Holmes?"

"No, that would be a waste of time." Sherlock cocks his head, watching me. "Only a fool would take a look at your bed and think that someone had ever actually slept in it."

I refrain from looking over at the bed in question, which he is painfully correct about, and cough. "I'm a tidy person."

"Undoubtedly." He says the word slowly, enunciating each syllable.

"Where do *you* go, then?" I blurt, unable to control my tongue, and unable to keep my wandering eyes from watching as he buttons up his new shirt. "At night, I mean."

His crooked grin begs me to slap it. "Don't be too eager, Holland."

He tosses on a jacket and tips an imaginary hat before leaving me with his pile of stinking clothes.

"Bastard," I mutter. Only when his tall figure cuts across the green below the window do I yank up the bag squirreled away beneath my bed.

It's been a long day, and now there's only one place on campus I feel comfortable tearing away this disguise.

Night has fully settled across Oxford, a blanket of black covering the spires and roofs by the time I finish sneaking across campus to the Lady Margaret dormitory.

Holmes was right. I don't sleep in the men's dorms—because I don't dare to. Not only do I not trust that bugger to leave me alone in my sleep—my most vulnerable moments—but I also don't trust my disguise to hold firm through the wild thrashing I'm known to do.

Here, in the Lady Margaret dorm booked for me by my grandmother, I worry less about someone learning my secret.

There's a firm knock on the door just as I'm slipping the mustache beneath my pillow. "Irene, darling, it's Ermyntrude."

"Oh, bloody hell." I curse softly under my breath, rushing to stash Isaac's remaining belongings throughout the room. "Just a moment!"

I can hear her heavy huff through the door. "You don't have anything I haven't seen already."

Oh, I very much doubt that.

My doorknob rattles, and this time Ermyntrude does more than huff. She snaps, "Why would you lock the door?"

Makeup wiped away, hair atop my head in a bun, and Isaac's prosthetic nose safely tucked into the pocket of a gown, I whip the door open. "In case the murderer comes back."

"But the coroner already ruled Bertie's death a suicide, darling." Ermyntrude's silk dressing gown slithers across the cold floor as she strides right into my room, an ivory color pale enough to rival snow. "I wonder what could have inspired poor Bertie to take his own life."

She sets down her lantern, a great big porcelain monstrosity, on my desk and peeks around the room. "This is quite...cozy."

"You mean quaint?" I shrug, pulling the curtains open. Lanterns streak the darkness below with orange silhouettes.

She not-so-surreptitiously peers at the anatomy notes I have on my desk. "Lady Augusta Moriarty can't afford a better apartment for you?"

"I'm sure she would oblige if I asked." I've always been my grandmother's favorite. "But I prefer how *cozy* this room is."

Ermyntrude looks up from my notes. Her grin, like a cat with the cream, matches mine.

What are you really doing in my room, Ermyntrude?

She very well might have the cream, but this game of cat and mouse feels dangerous *and* delicious. It calls to something dark in me.

"Why are these in...*êtes-vous francais?*" Her gaze returns to my notes, dragging a finger down my flourished scrawl.

I shrug my narrow shoulders. In an effort to keep myself and Isaac even more differentiated, I take my Lady Margaret notes in French, and his in English. Besides, it feels good to write in the language that I spoke the most with my mother. "*Plus que la plupart des Anglais.*"

"But not more than most Englishwomen?" She snaps my notebook shut. "I came to see if you would like to join the girls and me for a game."

"What game?" I look her over, my distrust no doubt written across my face. "I'm rather tired and have a lot of studying to do."

"Oh, please," she says, waving a hand dismissively. "You and I both know that you, of all my classmates, need to study the least for these ghastly, boring classes."

She's not wrong in that regard. But I do need to study for Isaac's classes. Badly.

Ermyntrude grabs her lamp and swings to the doorway, then jerks to a halt. "What is that?"

My stomach drops. Isaac's jacket, of all the blasted things to forget to hide, hangs on the back of the door.

"Why do you have men's clothes?" She peers more closely at me. "Are you sneaking men into your dormitory, Irene?"

The laughter comes easily to me. As if I would bother sneaking a man into my room. "That's James's."

"Your brother comes by the ladies' dormitory often?" Ermyntrude's mouth pops open. I don't miss how, despite the nightgown, her lips are still painted a rosy pink.

I nudge her toward the door. "Would you love it if James visited *you* in the wee hours of the night?"

"How scandalous." Ermyntrude hardly sounds scandalized. "No more excuses. I've set out a glass of wine just for you."

She doesn't see me clench my fists as she turns to lead me to her rooms.

They're the most luxurious on campus, short of the deans' and male lords' rooms—well, except for Sherlock's and mine. We've been shoved together into a veritable shoebox. While the other ladies and I have been sequestered to single rooms and a shared lavatory, Ermyntrude's dorm consists of a living room, dining area, personal bath, and the most enormous four-poster bed I have ever seen. In the hearth—easily larger than my tiny bed—a great fire blazes on the far side of the room. The fire fills her room with an amber glow, illuminating shelves of great tomes, a white vanity, and a low oak table.

Three more of my classmates surround the table, and between them is a circle of candles and crystal glasses of dark red wine.

"Irene!" Geraldine squeals with delight and leaps to her feet, flinging herself into my arms. She guides me to a cushion on the floor. A hint of hurt flickers through me that it was Ermyntrude, not Geraldine, who invited me. That my friend didn't even make an effort to tell me the ladies were gathering at all.

"Have you ever been to a séance, Irene?" Ermyntrude's grin is laced with mischief.

My eyes widen despite myself. Of all the games I imagined Ermyntrude had in store, this would have never made the list.

"We're going to call on the dead," she says, handing me a shimmering glass of wine. "Together."

I shiver as, despite all the candles lit around us, the room darkens. The fireplace beside the low table spits and hisses, as though hell itself forbids such foolishness.

"Perhaps Lord Arrington will deign to speak to us tonight." Edith, one of Ermyntrude's closest confidantes, giggles into the shoulder of the girl beside her.

Despite myself, I ask, "Lord Arrington?"

Ermyntrude answers for her. "The Murderous Fiend of 1748. He killed eight of his classmates before being caught. Perhaps his ghost murdered Bertie."

Of all the preposterous ideas... "There's no such thing as ghosts."

"Weren't you just talking earlier about the ghost in the Reading

Room?" Ermyntrude sits, every move as graceful as a dancer's, across the table from me with her own glass of wine. "Shall we find out what exactly Bertie's ghost has to say about that?"

I pretend to drink from my glass. Either Ermyntrude believed me when I said that I felt Elmstone's ghost in the room or this is part of some elaborate plan to humiliate me in front of my classmates.

I will be no one's fool. A frown of resolve settles between my narrow brows. I guess it's time for a show.

Rolling up the sleeves of my nightgown, I say, "Let's see if Lord Arrington is interested in a game."

Ermyntrude's smile could rival the Cheshire Cat's. Her friends—the pedigree dancer Edith and watchful Roslyn—sit on either side of the table, reaching eagerly for the matches to begin lighting the candles. I haven't spoken five words to either of them before this evening. Geraldine sits to my left, her pale legs stretched out toward the fire to warm up her toes.

Roslyn astutely ignores me; I'm neither offended nor shocked. She is one of the gilded gentry, her family exceedingly wealthy. So much so, I don't see the need for her to attend Oxford. Women like Roslyn, Gerry, and Ermyntrude have no need for further schooling beyond what a governess provides, so I'm surprised that their families even let them attend school instead of securing husbands. Geraldine's parents only acquiesced to her begging because her brother agreed to keep an eye on her.

"What shall we ask Lord Arrington?" Roslyn asks before taking a hearty gulp of her wine.

All the girls' eyes are glassy, Geraldine's included, their movements fumbling. How many glasses had they indulged in before Ermyntrude pulled me from my room?

"What about if Hugo Davies will again call on our dear Ermyntrude?" Edith releases a high-pitched giggle.

"That dolt." Ermyntrude rolls her eyes to the ceiling. "Never in a million years would I stoop to his level."

Roslyn's eyes clear of the wine's haze long enough for her voice to ring with a moment of clarity. "And Bertram?"

Ermyntrude scoffs before smiling at me over the rim of her wineglass. "Let's ask Bertie's ghost something."

Edith crosses herself. "That's terrible."

Ermyntrude only shrugs. "Why? Irene said that she felt his ghost up in the library. What if he was trying to tell her something important?"

Something in me yearns for her approval. As a bastard, I'd never been accepted among the ton, other than by the Haywards. Their grandmother was a dear friend of my own. So I spent my childhood watching, as if through a looking glass.

A shiver rolls up my spine. Brushing aside the feeling with a grimace, I roll back my shoulders. "Maybe Lord Elmstone could tell us why he took his own life?"

"You don't really believe the coroner's statement, do you?" Ermyntrude frowns, her pert nose wrinkling in distaste. "Just last week, Bertie was planning on proposing to Lady Henrietta Bennett. He had the permission of his parents and support of Henrietta's. He had a manse full of money and more friends at Oxford than even me. Why would Bertram Elmstone take his life with all of that?"

Why would someone kill you, Bertram? The question dances on the tip of my tongue. "I guess we can always ask to find out."

"Yes." Ermyntrude sets aside her glass of wine, reaching for a ruby candle. "Let's."

"How about an easy question first?" Roslyn drums the table with her free hand.

"Like what color knickers you have beneath your nightgown." Edith laughs, nudging her blond friend with an elbow.

"Don't be such a prig, Edie." Roslyn shoves her friend hard enough to spill the wine all over themselves.

Geraldine glances between Ermyntrude and me. With a clear, ringing voice I rarely hear, she says, "Let's start with whether or not Bertie killed himself."

"You're no fun, Geraldine." Ermyntrude winks to soften the words.

"You wanted an easy question." My friend shrugs. "The Yard declared it a suicide."

Ermyntrude raises her candle and brows, wordlessly indicating we follow suit. Her face is so serious, pulled in a frown of such abject assuredness, at the ridiculous nature of what we're about to do. The flames in the fire gutter. The hair on my arms rises. I hesitate, the illogical nature of speaking to ghosts rebelling against my rational mind. But, as each of the other girls raises her candle in salute, my own hand seems to rise of its own accord.

Geraldine gives me a grateful smile, the cold fingers of her free hand joining mine beneath the table's edge.

Ermyntrude asks the room, "Lord Bertram Elmstone. Cousin Bertie, friend and companion, did you take your own life? Blow the candles out if you did not kill yourself."

For a split second, nothing happens. The ladies all hold their breath, candles still raised to the ceiling. The only sound is the fire crackling softly behind me.

And then, a long, cold wail echoes down the hallway beyond Ermyntrude's room. The ghosts of the Lady Margaret dormitory have awoken.

I keep my face neutral. A draft licks my upright arm with frigid air. One of the girls, likely Ermyntrude on purpose, must have left a window ajar.

Then the candles sputter out, one...by...one.

The girls gasp as my head whips around. The windows are all actually closed, as is the door.

"How in God's name...," Geraldine mutters softly, eyes impossibly wide.

"Looks like I was right," Ermyntrude says with a gleeful smile that bares all her perfect white teeth. "And the coroner was wrong. Bertie would never take his own life."

"If you're to believe this superstitious nonsense over the word of a licensed professional," Geraldine says, arching an eyebrow.

"Then let's ask the ghosts something that only Bertram would know." Ermyntrude turns to my friend. "Light your candle again and ask away, Geraldine."

Ermyntrude may be queen of the flock, but Geraldine outranks her in society, and I know from experience that my friend does *not* like to be bossed around.

Spine straightening, she opens her mouth to argue but snaps it shut again. Something passes between her and Ermyntrude, something silent and strange, before Geraldine jerks her chin toward the matches. A wind outside begins to rattle the windows, and a branch taps against a single glass pane.

Ermyntrude notices my ignored glass and inclines her own. "Drink up, darling. The wine will ease your nerves."

Edith practically guzzles her own, and Roslyn refills her glass with a trembling hand, dripping red liquid on the board. It is so much like the blood that had dripped from Elmstone's hand. From his neck and down the rooftop. Shivers run up and down my spine.

Candles once more lit, Geraldine's words are curt and begrudging when she asks, "Who killed you, Bertram?"

Ermyntrude's face goes slack. "Yes or no questions only, darling."

This was obviously not part of the plan. I allow the corner of my mouth to curl in a half-smile.

It's quickly wiped from my face when Edith releases a blood-curdling scream.

"Something touched me!" Her eyes roll into the back of her head, flashing white like a full moon. We leap to our feet as she begins to shake. A gurgled moan erupts from her chest.

"What's wrong with her?" Roslyn drops to her friend's side and reaches for her face.

"Don't touch her! Go get help," I command. "She's seizing."

Glasses of wine are kicked across the floor. A howl of wind rises outside the dormitory to a high-pitched, keening wail.

Geraldine leaps for the door. She gives it a short jerk and yells, "It's locked!"

Ermyntrude drops to her knees and grabs Edith's shoulders. I open my mouth to protest, just as the lady's pale hand slaps Edith across the cheek.

Her body stills, mouth hanging open. Edith takes a great inhale, looking to each of us in turn. Her eyes land on me last.

"I s-saw him," she stammers, voice shrill. "I saw his dark figure in the library."

Cold sweeps over me.

Her eyes, like warm chocolate, are watery and rimmed with unbroken white. "He was with Bertram in the library."

She gasps as Ermyntrude's hand flies again.

"Get a grip," the Bedford lady snaps. "Enough of this nonsense."

Edith's mouth opens and closes, her once pale cheek now red as a rose. "You're the one who made us—"

A click of the lock echoes through the room and the door bursts open. Screams tear through the air. The ladies fly about the room and the bottle of wine shatters on the flagstone floor.

"Girls!" Headmistress Allen stands in the doorway. Her gaunt face is partially illuminated by the candle she carries. Shadows fill the hollowness, rending her face a pale skull. "What is the meaning of this? You must return to your rooms at once!"

"Do you police the boys' dormitory in this way?" Ermyntrude demands.

"We do now" is Allen's tart reply. "Clean up this mess and return to your rooms at once."

"What do you mean, 'now'?" I ask.

The girls have stopped their frantic movements and are as still as statues. Ermyntrude is the only one who moves, grabbing her lantern to hold up to Allen's face. There, we see nothing but fear.

The headmistress swallows, lantern in her hand trembling. "We do now, Mistress Adler, because there's been another death on campus."

CHAPTER 7

Moriarty Knows

The All Souls cohort is as quiet as the grave. No student cracks a joke, though all often look to the back of the classroom to stare at the two empty seats lurking there.

I keep my eyes on my notes; I have forty pages of reading to get through in less than an hour, and Bertie Elmstone's and Jude Wilson's ghosts are unlikely to help.

Jude Wilson was mid-ranking in the competition, a middling lord at best. He had no debts, as far as my meager research tells me, nor enemies.

Nothing about the lad ever stood out until he proclaimed me a murderous rat before all my classmates, and nothing sure as the damned ever made me think he would be murdered last night.

Professor Edwards, the oldest and most crotchety of Oxford's deans, glares from the desk in the front of the classroom, daring us to complain about the arithmetic assignment. Nobody does. We're all too preoccupied with our thoughts.

Except for Holmes, apparently. In record time, he hands in his paper and exits the classroom on long, swift legs. Annoyance swells within me, but I'm not far behind him. Third to only Moriarty, I hand in my work and leave. Isaac's wig itches to all hell, but I can't pull aside the costume just yet. Isaac has another class in under an hour, just enough time to set up my new lab in the Queen's College Chapel and return for class.

Despite the unseasonably sunny afternoon, the Queen's courtyard is desolate as I cross the perfectly manicured grass of its quad. No students linger beneath the covered walkway, nor fill the hallways.

One death is bizarre; two deaths is suspicious. And, once again, Isaac Holland has no alibi.

How many of my classmates question the nature of Elmstone's death, I wonder, and what exactly happened to Jude Wilson?

I sequester myself in a forgotten closet in the chapel, brushing aside cobwebs. I used to hide here from my brother when Dean Moriarty brought us both to campus with him. I'd been ordered to *"sit in the pews and pray for my mother's sins,"* so I'd quickly sneak off, each and every time. Especially once James discovered how easy and delightful it was to torment me.

From my rucksack, I pull out a candle and quickly light it. There's already a table and chair in the room, hidden beneath a stack of ancient papers, tomes, and about a century's worth of dust.

After cleaning the room, I take the ingredients for my next experiment out of Isaac's rucksack. I've had my theories about how exactly to melt metal, but the possibility of trying it out makes me giddy. If I'm correct, this discovery would put me leaps and bounds ahead of my classmates. It wouldn't just secure me the top seat, it would make it impossible for the deans to not select me as the winner.

I'm practically bouncing on my toes as I pull out aluminum and a vial of iron oxide. My grandmother had an account made specifically for me, which James cannot touch. I use it to buy all my chemistry supplies—and my brother's account to buy all my clothes.

It really is too easy to dip into James's ledgers.

Voices beyond the door yank me back to reality. Hurriedly, I finish unpacking—making sure that everything is separated and unable to spill together—before creaking the door open just a smidge.

Roslyn and Edith sit in the pews, heads bent in prayer. Perhaps they felt it necessary to ask for forgiveness after this weekend's indiscretions. Not that I'm judging.

But I'm sure someone is.

Beside them are two young men from the All Souls cohort. Not particularly sanctimonious, I note, as all four take the opportunity to gossip.

"I heard that they found Jude's body in a similar fashion to that prig Elmstone," one man says. I recognize him as one of Moriarty's toadies, Avery Williams.

Edith titters. "You shouldn't speak of the dead that way."

"Where did they find him?"

"In the Cherwell," Avery says, flipping through a Bible before tossing it onto the bench beside him. "The deans are claiming that, because the murder wasn't on campus, there's no need for heightened security. Probably only because they don't want the students to flee en masse."

"And was his"—Roslyn gulps, her voice dropping to a whisper

as a priest walks down the hall, glaring in their direction—"his, um, throat. Was it cut open, too?"

Hugo Davies nods on her other side, making both girls gasp.

"They can't both be suicides," he says, putting my thoughts into words. "Any suspects yet?"

"None that they've shared with the students, obviously." Avery leans back, resting his feet on the pew in front of him, causing Roslyn to titter. "My money's on that Sherlock Holmes character. He'd do anything to secure the All Souls seat."

"Even murder?" Davies shakes his head. "You go too far. But what of Holland?"

"That meek little boy?"

A bell tolls in the distance, signaling the start of my next period, and I'm saved from having to hide much longer in the closet by the priest's return. After he berates Avery for having his feet on the pew, and the girls for being without a proper escort, even in a church, all four flee the Queen's College in a fit of laughter.

I arrive in my next class just before Stackton can lock the door— his way of deterring delinquency—and shuffle to my desk with my head bowed. His glare could burn a hole through the back of my wig. I'm pulling out my books when someone taps on my shoulder.

Holmes leans across the aisle. "Do you have a quill I may borrow?"

His face is polite and surprisingly earnest. But is it also the face of a murderer? I realize belatedly that I've been staring and blurt, "I've never seen you take notes before."

Chagrin quirks the corner of his mouth. "Today is the quiz."

"Oh, right." Cheeks flushed with the fires of hell, I hand him my spare pen.

I glance sidelong at him as surreptitiously as possible. His hair, dark, unkempt curls, falls before his tan face, obscuring it from my view. I can see from here that his hands are not the soft, coddled sort typical to gentry. Calluses dot his palms, and his knuckles are nicked with an assortment of pale burn scars. Shaking my head, I return my focus to the questions written on the board.

Even half distracted by the possibility of sitting next to a murderer, I'm the first to finish my quiz. I wait, though, for someone else to turn in their answers first.

I hear my mentor's voice again in my mind. *"Draw no undue attention, for they cannot know what you are hiding."*

Even if the others can't know I'm faster than them, my chest swells with pride. I deserve to be here. But it would be *delightful* to see their faces when they realize that a girl has been excelling ahead of them this entire time.

Moriarty stands, flashing Holmes a smug smile before turning in his answers first, and my pride pops like a balloon. I regret not turning in mine sooner. I hate being shown up by that pompous ass. I stand at the same time as Holmes, but let him go first, gathering my belongings into my bag before handing in my quiz. When Stackton turns his attention back to my classmates, I make sure to swipe a quill from the professor's desk for good measure.

The crowd in the Turf may be raucous, but the beer and food are as delicious as ever. The hearth roars, filling the tavern with the scent of smoke and burning cedar, though I can barely smell it behind Isaac's mustache; his wig itches naggingly on my head, but I daren't remove it yet, enjoying this blissful moment free of Oxford's academia.

Sure, more than a few of my classmates have also chosen the Turf for their evening meal, but Irene Adler could never dine here. A lady alone would never be welcome here if she wished to show her face in proper society ever again. And my father still wishes to marry me off—eventually. So I continue to wear Isaac's face, his irritating mustache sometimes dipping into the evening's stew. I doubt I'll ever get used to having facial hair.

The Turf also makes for the best people watching. My mother used to take me to taverns just for this purpose.

She would point out the man with too much money for his pockets, and the one sipping water but pretending it was beer. *"See how the men flock to some but ignore others? How some men seem to hold court, even here in a pub, and others can only watch with awe? Which of these men can you bend to your will, Mumely? The ones with all the attention in the world, or the ones desperate for it?"*

The memory is joined by an intense wave of pain. The cavern in my chest, where my heart once was, is an aching maw. It's been so long since I thought of her, recalled the sound of her voice, allowed myself to long for the warmth of her arms around my shoulders. I roll my neck and will my lips to cease their trembling. Isaac should not look like a weeping fool in front of his classmates.

I push my mother from my mind but continue studying the people around me. Moriarty sits with his usual entourage in a booth in the corner. The table groans beneath their collective mugs and fists. He raises his beer to me when he notices me watching, a smirk twisting his face. I turn my gaze without reaction, pretending not to have noticed. But Moriarty knows.

He always knows.

Skin crawling, I watch Hugo Davies at the bar, passing a coin across its surface for another drink. He's well on his way to pissed, having indulged far too much already.

"You don't know my father," he blathers when the barman pushes the coin back. He sways on his stool. "He could buy this blasted dunghole and sell it to shine his shoes."

He tries to stand. His foot catches in one of the stool's rungs and he slips forward, chin cracking on the counter. The tavern erupts with laughter.

Despite my better judgment and my mentor's warnings, I rise, ready to help him back to the dormitory.

My view of Davies is blocked by a familiar tweed jacket. I look up into the dark eyes of Sherlock Holmes. A pipe hangs from the corner of his mouth, and in his hands, he carries a pair of mugs. "You look like you could use a drink."

Uninvited, he sits across from me, sliding the drink and my pen across the table until both gently nudge the textbooks I brought to the tavern.

"Thank you...," I say with Isaac's low drawl, accepting the dark frothy beer. I peek over Holmes's shoulder and Davies has disappeared. Hopefully, someone walked him back to the dormitories and he didn't dare the trek by himself. "...roommate."

"Imagine my surprise when your bed was yet again impeccably made." He spins his beer on the table.

Holmes's shrewd eyes pass over my textbooks, all chemistry,

almost too quickly for me to notice. They linger on my notes, and I realize belatedly that my scrawl is decidedly fluid Irene's, not Isaac's blocky chicken scratch. I push a textbook over my notes with an elbow. "What brings you to the Turf, Lord Holmes?"

"Please, call me Sherlock," he says, lips wrinkling in distaste. "I'm not a lord."

I incline my head, taking another drink of beer. He might not be a lord, but he has expensive taste. "Neither am I. How did you find yourself among the preening prigs of the All Souls cohort?"

"How did *you*?" Holmes's voice is like velvet.

"I asked first."

He leans forward, black eyes pinning me to my seat. "Never before has the All Souls accepted anyone below the status of lord. And now they've accepted two." Every word is carefully enunciated. "You and I."

I swallow another rapid mouthful of ale, struggling to find the words. Or even admit them out loud.

His nostrils flare. "I'll tell you why I joined the cohort if you tell me."

Why does he care so much? Another panicked swallow of beer passes my lips.

I feint. "Is this some game of 'I'll show you mine if you show me yours'? Because if so, this is a roundabout way of asking to see my—"

"Quit avoiding the question, *Holland*." He says my name—my fake name—like the lash of a whip.

I pop my lips. "Fine."

Holmes leans back, his heels landing on the edge of the table. Waiting for me to continue.

I set aside the ceramic mug. "It won't come as a surprise to someone with your particular"—my eyes sweep over him—"skill set to learn that I am not a natural academic. My memory is unparalleled, and it gave me many advantages. Puzzles are my bread and butter." His mouth drops open, and I point a finger in his face. "Don't you dare interrupt me."

He snaps it shut, but with a smirk that says he wasn't chastised enough. "So bossy."

Glaring, I continue, "My sponsor saw my skills."

"When?"

I pointedly ignore his interruption. "He recognized the potential in me, and something else. I have...a family I need to prove something to. That I'm more than my blood. I think that my sponsor wants to prove that, too."

His mouth twitches. Sherlock no doubt takes in every morsel of knowledge about myself I give him with the ravenous appetite of the starved. Puzzle pieces click into place for a board I cannot see. I wish I could be myself with him now, see if his candor would remain in the presence of Irene, and if he would find me half so interesting as he does Isaac Holland.

I balance the mug on its side, spinning it with a careful finger, making sure not to spill a single drop. Holmes watches with avid interest. Coughing, I ask, "And you?" He raises his brows. "What made you join the All Souls?"

"You like puzzles," he says, waving a hand to the table. "I like games."

"What kind of games?"

"We're not lords like them. Money will never buy us the blood they inherently possess." He leans back, throwing a glance over his shoulder at Moriarty and the growing crowd of our classmates. "We're nothing but pawns to them. Rats. Prey, if you will."

All the noise in the tavern seems to dim until I'm only aware of my own shallow breathing. Holmes turns back around, leaning across the table and whispering, "Here at Oxford or in London, we are nothing to them. They are a pack of wolves, and we are their game." His eyes widen, teeth white and sharp in contrast to his dark, tan skin. "They would feast on our bones."

My mug stills with a heavy thud. A match to my thundering heart.

Slowly, Holmes leans back. "I will prove to them that I am more than some fleeing prey. I am the lion they never saw coming."

He grins, effectively breaking whatever spell he had me under. The raucous noise of the tavern seems to come flooding back as well.

"Do you think of me as one of the 'preening prigs' of All Souls?" The light of the fire dances in his eyes.

It takes me a painfully long moment to find my voice again.

"I used to," I admit, leaning back in my seat, balancing the chair on a single leg. "Until that pile of clothes in the corner of our dormitory just kept growing and growing... and growing. And the smell. Nothing short of a sty."

"Touché." Holmes raises his mug in a salute, dark locks falling over his brow. "And I thought you were simply an upstart with too-big shoes, thrown into a lion's den without the smarts to even tie a cravat."

"*Your* lion's den?" Despite the darkness lingering behind his gaze only moments before, I'm enjoying this version of Sherlock Holmes. It seems that there are multiple sides to us both. I take another drink to hide my smile.

"You're trying too hard to go unnoticed, Holland."

I choke on my beer, coughing and spitting it across the table.

He grins triumphantly as though my reaction answered some unsaid question. "Why do you make a point to not be seen?"

"If that's what I'm doing, I'm obviously not doing a good job at it." I have half a mind to shove my books in my satchel and flee for the dormitories, but Holmes's interest in Isaac Holland is intriguing.

Quickly, he says, "I notice everything."

Obviously not everything, or he'd have a lot more to say about my peculiarities as a roommate.

When I don't dispute his *very* incorrect claim, he continues, "And from what I've noticed, I think a partnership between the two of us would be useful."

Thankfully, I don't have anything in my mouth to choke on this time. "Beyond being roommates?"

He gives a flippant wave of his hand. "Our classmates are now starting to partner up, leveling up their odds. Although I do loathe having to share credit with anyone"—*hardly surprising*—"I think that you and I could be a good match. You're insightful, like myself, but more of a strategist. You always score perfectly, despite taking such a long time to read anything through, proving you have an impeccable attention to detail. And despite your obvious inclination to avoid conflict, you have a way of riling up that ass James Moriarty."

I'm sure there was a compliment in there somewhere. I open my mouth, ready to deflect Holmes's backhanded praise and overtures of false camaraderie when Moriarty's blond head catches my eye.

"A toast, then, to our fallen classmates. The colleagues that have passed." He's standing, raising his pint. "To the All Souls who are still here, and the All Souls who should have known better than to even try."

Something cold and bitter settles in my stomach. Could James have been the one to attempt to frame Isaac Holland? The idea is so ridiculous, I nearly slap myself. He would stand to gain nothing from either death. My brother's apparent flippancy about their deaths leaves me queasy and furious all at once, ready to storm across the tavern and smash my pint across the back of his head.

His friends cheer, raising their mugs in salute before downing their contents. Beer spills down their chins, dribbling on their lace frocks and velvet doublets. Holmes turns in his seat to watch, his face falling the same as mine.

And in his eyes, I see a spark kindle. Loathing lingers in their depths, and something more. A challenge. There, it flickers again.

A flame I can stoke.

"I'll be your partner," I say, raising my chin.

Holmes's attention swivels back to me, eyebrows high. "Why?"

I down the rest of my dark beer in a single gulp and stand. He gazes up at me, a roguish half smile quirking his lips as though he already knows my answer. I nod to Moriarty's table and, with a voice so low only he can hear, I say, "Because you hate James Moriarty just as much as I do."

Tossing a handful of coppers on the table, I turn without a backward glance to either Holmes or my brother.

The streets are dark, a late-evening fog rolling in from the rivers to slick the cobblestones and make the walk even more treacherous. I regret the last gulp of beer, my steps wobbly on account of it.

I drag a hand along the rough walls, bowing my hat at the occasional passerby. The night is still young enough to not appear suspicious. Even if it was, a man walking alone at night is hardly the cause for gossip that a woman seems to be. God forbid we leave our rooms for anything other than prayer and shopping.

I bite back a sigh, cutting through the lingering fog like a knife. The closer I get to the school and the bridge I must cross to get there, the thicker it gets, and the closer I get to campus, the emptier the streets get. Rumors abound about the deaths of the two students.

I slow, suddenly unsure. No time of day, no place, is completely safe. Beneath the arching bridge, the dark water of the Cherwell gurgles, making me shiver. A shadow appears in the white fog, leaning against the railing.

"That you, old fellow?" Hugo's face is suddenly clear in the fog, and he sways dangerously over the stone railing. "I thought we were meeting there."

Curiosity piqued, I ask, "Meeting where?"

Hugo squints, nostrils flaring. "Who the devil are you?"

"Isaac Holland. Your classmate."

"Oh." Hugo sways and shakes his head, turning back to the river. "You don't belong here."

"Yes, you lords have made that very clear." I move to stomp past him.

His hand, as cold as the grave, whips out absurdly fast for someone so pissed. He latches around my upper arm. I jerk free, ready to slap the lord silly, but pause when I see the blatant terror blanching his features. Even in the fog and night, the whites of his eyes shine bright.

Hugo croaks, "'There is no fouler fiend than a woman when her mind is bent to evil.'"

A chill sweeps over me. I struggle to find words.

"Homer," I say around an awkward cough. "Though I don't think he'd yet met some of the crueler men who roam the earth."

Hugo turns again to the river, effectively dismissing me. His words linger in my ears long after sleep claims me that night.

CHAPTER 8

Claws Made of Ice

In class on Monday, I'm the first to arrive. The seats begin to steadily fill. The hangovers have worn off. A few cough, the fall chill settling thick into their lungs, but are otherwise silent. Even Moriarty, usually chortling with Moran, is quiet when he arrives. He takes the seat before mine, completely ignoring me.

Holmes takes the seat to my left but does not acknowledge me, either.

It isn't until Professor Stackton arrives, his face long and ashen, do I realize that there are now three empty chairs among our number.

Heart hammering in my chest, I spin in my seat. I search for whoever could be missing. Their names all run like an endless tally in my head.

"It is with a heavy heart that I have to share this news with you all." Stackton doesn't look up from his desk. His old, wizened hands clench and unclench a piece of paper. "Two nights ago, Hugo Davies was found dead."

Hollow silence fills the classroom. My classmates look anywhere but at one another. I look down to my own hands, gripping my nib pen so hard it threatens to snap. My face jerks up when Moriarty's sharp voice breaks my thoughts.

"Where was he found, sir? The Bodleian again?"

I watch as a single drop of sweat slides, ever so slowly, down the nape of my brother's neck.

"Queen's Chapel," the professor says. Claws made of ice dig into my lungs. "They're searching the college now for more information."

I'm suddenly lightheaded. I will my face to betray nothing but the barest hint of remorse for my fallen cohort. When I turn, Holmes stares directly at me.

CHAPTER 9

A Pipe That's Not for Smoking

My mother taught me many things. How to mend a torn skirt. How to write in French, English, and Latin. And how to steal wallets and forge any signature in the world.

First, though, she taught me how to flirt.

A man will never spill his secrets—unless perhaps he's an idiot—to someone he considers to be his competition. But he might just reveal his entire hand to someone he hopes will join him in bed.

The Bodleian has been decidedly less crowded over the last couple of days, many families having pulled their sons from classes, in exchange for the occasional officer wandering the stacks with a hand on their hip, but everyone I want in attendance is here.

Wearing my loveliest dress, a fashionable pale green, with my hair half-up, half-down in artful dark ringlets, I lean against the librarian's counter and give him my most pleasing smile. "I can assure you that an anatomy textbook is exactly what I need for my classes, sir."

Mr. Charles, old and squishy like a mushroom, looks disbelieving. God forbid a woman know her way around the human body, even one studying medicine at Oxford. With a huff, he turns and shuffles from the desk and into the shadowed halls of books.

He's not the focus of my interest, though. No, I've thrown a line out to another individual in Selden End by popping out my hip, shrugging my lustrous hair over a shoulder, and releasing one long, suffering sigh.

Edgar Hayward takes the bait, just as I knew a man would. Geraldine's brother strolls over, hands hooked behind his back, and smiles at me. His hair is the same golden blond as his sister's, skin just the same shade shy of never-seen-the-sun, and his eyes a pale blue. There's never anything untoward in his face, just bald, honest affection.

"Geraldine struggles with that man as well." Edgar leans an elbow on the counter.

I very much doubt that. Geraldine is so pretty, she could sneeze and a dozen men would pop out of the woodwork holding out their handkerchiefs.

"Mr. Charles really is ghastly, isn't he?" He holds up a hand to his mouth and faux whispers, "Would you like me to check out a book for you, Irene?"

"That would be lovely, Edgar," I say, matching his posture. "But first, answer a question."

"I offer to do a polite thing and you demand more of me. Moriarty has taught you well." He holds up a hand to his heart and pretends to be affronted.

Ignoring the queasiness that sweeps over me from that last sentence, I look up at him through my dark lashes. He can distract Mr. Charles so that I can peek through those ledgers and learn what books my fallen classmates recently checked out. Perhaps they were looking into things they shouldn't have. With so few clues available to me, I'm stuck looking in a shallow pool for answers.

"I'll let you check out a book for me," I say, daring a step closer. His eyes widen. "If you guess what book I want to check out."

I just happen to know that Edgar is so enamored with me, he would have proposed years ago if his father would have allowed it.

I continue to look up at him through my lashes, blinking ever so slowly. He'll have no idea, but that's fine. I'll let him guess and proclaim him brilliant. Another trick I learned from my mother.

"She was hoping to check out Calvin Cutter's book," a deep voice says from behind me.

Edgar's face falls. The delicious shivers running up my spine tell me who exactly is behind me without having to turn. I do so anyway. Holmes saunters up to the counter, giving me a smug look.

I sniff. "That's not actually what I was hoping to check out."

That is *exactly* the book I was hoping to check out.

"No?" Holmes's dark brows rise as he peers over the counter. "Then why is that the title you passed to Charles?"

Damn him.

Holmes leans forward. "You can read a copy in the Radcliffe."

A perpetual hint of stubble grazes the sharp cut of his chin, and his shirt is unbuttoned at the top, giving me a teasing view of the taut, tan chest beneath. Not too much, but just enough to stir a prickle of heat in my core. I hate admitting it, but Holmes is far too handsome. Even more so than the angelic Edgar standing beside him. It simply isn't fair to be both handsome *and* brilliant.

It's an effort to not grind my teeth. This will not do. For a multitude of reasons. Not the least of which is, if Holmes gets even a whiff of Isaac in my face, he'll blow my cover to the deans. There's no way he would pass up any chance to take out a member of his competition for the All Souls seat.

I lean out of his way and give Edgar an apologetic smile, lips tight. "I need to get to my next class."

Holmes catches my hand. "Let me escort you."

I gently pry away, keenly aware of Edgar watching our every movement. "There's no need. I know this campus far better than most."

"I'm not worried about you getting lost." Sherlock's sharp chin rises. "There's a murderer on the loose, and this place isn't safe for ladies to wander about as they please, all alone."

My mouth snaps shut. I'm at a loss for words. I search his face for any signs of malintent or forced gallantry. There's nothing but earnestness in those dark eyes and that tan face. He reaches for my hand again.

"But it's perfectly safe for men to do so? It's men who seem to keep dying." His hand drops to his side, face darkening, and I continue, "I thought you were above such sexist beliefs, Mr. Holmes. Besides"—I turn to Edgar and hold out my hand—"Lord Hayward can escort me just fine."

Edgar is silent for much of the walk, a tic in his jaw as he chews on the inside of his cheek. The autumn winds moan against the panes of stained glass outside, making me shiver despite the warm shawl around my shoulders. Or at least I tell myself it is the wind.

"Remember when you coerced Gerry and me into helping you sneak pigeons into your father's study?" Edgar asks suddenly, grinning as he watches the familiar gray-and-white birds fluttering above us.

"Coerced?" My mouth drops open. "It was your idea!"

He chuckles. "An idea only. You're the one who went and actually caught the birds."

"And you were the one to set them loose in my father's house."

We reach the equally drafty lecture hall of my next Lady Margaret class, and he squeezes the hand I have on his arm.

"Will you"—he swallows—"and your family, of course, come over for supper soon?" The question tumbles from his lips.

I can't help but notice how cold his hand is in mine. How, despite having felt it before, the hold is like an extraneous limb. I can only nod.

"Excellent! I'll tell Father, and he can arrange it with your grandmother." With a smile as shining and brilliant as a midsummer sun, Edgar kisses my hand and turns to leave.

A figure over his shoulder catches my eye and keeps me from walking into the classroom. Holmes, with hands in his pockets and chin tucked into his chest, stands at the very end of the corridor. Even from this distance, I can feel his black gaze.

Yes, I was a fool to take up his offer of partnership with Isaac.

Sadly, my mother never taught me what to do when someone might be trying to frame me for murder.

I typically spend my Saturdays with my nose in a book in my Lady Margaret dormitory, but it's the only day Holmes could make work to study with me. After trading my silks for tweed, I would give up tea for an entire year if it would make Isaac's wig stop itching. And that's no small sacrifice. Cursing Holmes's *supposedly* busy schedule, I'm digging my nails into my scalp and ruminating about the deaths over some physiology books in my dormitory when the door swings open and Holmes strides inside. He brings no books, no paper, and no quill, only plops unceremoniously on the edge of *my* bed.

"Am I expected to do all the writing?" I ask, fighting to keep my typical tartness from my voice. Isaac isn't "tart." He's reserved.

"You said so yourself that I never take notes." He yawns, leaning back on his elbows. "It distracts me. I find it easier to simply read things."

His shirt has been unbuttoned farther, revealing more of his smooth chest. His hands are large, gripping either side of my bed. His dark hair falls over his brow and shoulders, begging me to brush it back so I can better meet his onyx gaze.

Coughing, I turn back to my notes and resolutely ignore how delectable Holmes looks on my bed. "If everyone refused to take notes, you'd have nothing to read."

"It's a good thing I am not everyone."

"That must be nice," I say, with more than an ounce of sarcasm. Either he doesn't catch it or ignores it. "Speaking of distractions, why did you want to meet here and not in the library?"

Holmes bounces a foot over his knee. "Everyone's afraid that they'll be the next body."

"But you're not?"

His eyes assess me, sweeping over my rough-spun jacket to the mop of Isaac's brown curls atop my head. "No."

"That was a rhetorical question." It's a struggle akin to Sisyphus and his boulder to keep the myriad of emotions that assail me from showing on my face. Such confidence. Either he vastly overestimates his ability to keep the mad murderer at bay... or he is the killer himself. Though no person with half as much intellect as Sherlock Holmes would actually admit it.

I should return our focus to the work we need to do, the projects we need to design to impress the professors more than our classmates, but curiosity rankles me like a burr beneath a horse's saddle. "Why are you not afraid?"

"So much for rhetorical." Holmes releases an aggrieved sigh. "Because the murders are of no relevance to me," he says, picking a piece of lint from his sleeve. "Hugo, Jude, and Bertram, though in the All Souls cohort, have never spoken a single word to me. My family has no relation to theirs, and I gain nothing from their deaths because their grades were so much lower than mine with no hope of overcoming me. I have no motive. Nor do you."

And yet the bodies still seem to be piling up around Isaac Holland—me. I was one of the last to speak with Hugo, half of our class having seen me leave the pub only moments after him. If anyone saw him and me speaking atop the bridge, the inspectors will be pounding on my door before the week's end. All their deaths are an itch I cannot scratch, a thirst I cannot quench.

"Your friend in the Yard couldn't tell you more?"

"My friend in the Yard?" Holmes sits up. "In the Scotland Yard?"

I realize my mistake too late. It was I, not Isaac, who watched Holmes speak to John Watson. I'm playing a poor game today.

"I would have assumed you'd have a contact in the Scotland Yard," I say as airily as I can, flipping a page. "All the gentry seem to have a particular contact to get themselves out of legal trouble at a moment's notice."

"I'm not part of the gentry, remember? But that would make

my life a lot easier." Holmes shakes his head. "I know of only one student to have seen any of the bodies. The others were found by a priest and a professor."

"I'm glad you're not amongst the growing number that believe I'm a suspect." Hopefully. "What student saw the bodies? Do they have access to the morgue?"

"One body, and no, she's one of the Lady Margaret class," he says with an impatient wave.

"Is she pretty?" I ask, setting down my pen and puffing out Isaac's chest.

It quickly deflates when he replies, "No."

"What a shame." Did my voice just crack? Why do I give a damn if he finds me pretty?

"No, she's not *pretty*." Holmes falls back to stare at the ceiling. "She's stunning."

"Oh." My voice is pitched low and accompanied by a dark chuckle. I dare not smile, even as pleasure from his words thrums deep through me. "Sounds like she's done a number on you."

Holmes drums his fingers on his chest, ignoring my statement. "There are four things we must do if we hope to catch the killer."

I roll my eyes, knowing full well that he expects me to ask, "And they are?"

"First"—he holds up a finger—"we must observe the nefarious fiend's tactics."

I shake my head and let him continue.

Another finger rises. "From that, we deduct his next steps."

Likely murder me or frame me again. Or both. "Go on. Out with it already."

"And third," he says, holding up three fingers now. "We gather all the facts we've learned to reveal our killer."

"Riveting deductions, Holmes. It's a wonder they haven't handed you the All Souls seat already. And the fourth?"

He leans back up onto his elbows. "We need an inside man."

Something about *this* man piques my interest like no other. I am compelled to ask, "Why are you so concerned with our classmates' deaths?"

He leans forward in his seat and asks, "Why are *you?*"

His deflection doesn't go unnoticed. I incline my head. "There's a target on my back. I need to remove it."

A half truth, one which he no doubt sees through. He considers me as I wait for him to give his own answer. Even the ghosts of Oxford seem to huddle closer, eager to hear whatever Sherlock Holmes has to say. An eternity stretches between us, a world without words. I don't have time to wait.

"Well, if neither of us has contacts in the Yard," I say with a long, aggrieved sigh, "and neither of us seems interested in studying at this moment, I guess there's only one person who can help us find answers."

Holmes grins. "Who do you suggest, Holland?"

I snap my textbook closed. "The late Hugo Davies."

Sneaking into a mortuary should not be this simple. The coroners of Oxford's medical wing hold the same hours as the staff, leaving once the tea bell tolls. There are no guards, though judging by the bodies piling up around me, there should be. Something drips at the end of the long, dark hallway, and a chill seeps through my clothes, down to my very bones.

"Why are mortuaries always located in basements?" I mutter, rubbing my arms brusquely.

"To keep the bodies cold and to slow their decomposi—"

"It was a rhetorical question, Holmes."

We reach a set of doors at the end, bound together by a single padlock. If my hair was bound up in Irene's typical fashion, I could have easily picked it with a pin.

"Have you been in many mortuaries, Holland?" Holmes brushes me aside and pulls from his pocket a pipe.

"Planning on burning through the lock?" I lean against the wall. "It's too bad I didn't think to bring some iron oxide. I'm beginning to suspect that it has the potential to burn through metal."

"I knew I selected you as a study partner for a reason." He flashes me a lopsided grin, dark hair flopping over his brow. "Though, I believe iron oxide would only burn through aluminum." Holmes pulls off the end of the pipe, revealing a pair of wires suspiciously like a hairpin. He jangles the wires in the lock. "And under heat."

"Well, then, I would say that it's a good thing you brought your pipe." I move forward, watching his technique. "But it's obviously not for smoking."

The lock clicks open and clatters to the floor. He leans back with a satisfied smirk. "Just for sport."

I follow him into the dark room, my words echoing in the wide space. "Funny, I would have thought it was because you think it makes you look dashing as it hangs from your lips."

I give my cheek a sharp bite. That was something only *I* would say, not Isaac Holland. I dig my nails into my palms. I need to watch my tongue. Soon, I won't have to worry about Sherlock Holmes removing my mask if I continue to tug it off myself.

"You really think I look dashing, Holland?" Holmes asks with a short laugh, his eyes gleaming even in the shadows.

"You would if it wasn't so obvious that you've never smoked a pipe in your entire life."

This time his laugh is hearty and deep. I slap a hand over his mouth, checking over my shoulder to make sure nobody is in the hallway, but barely restrain a chuckle of my own. His tongue pokes my palm, and I snatch my hand away just as quickly.

"You're an impertinent wee thing." His eyes dance with mirth.

I don't like how closely he's examining my face. Swallowing hard, I say, "We should find a light in here."

"Already done." Holmes turns the burner of an oil lamp, and soon the room fills with a sickly pale glow. The smell of kerosene makes my temples throb.

I do the same with two other lamps in the corners as Holmes shuts the door behind us with a soft click. When we turn to the center of the room, though, we both stop short.

The bodies are all naked, covered with only white sheets pulled back to reveal three faces in ranges of decomposition and horror.

"Why would they not release an official statement about Hugo's death?" Holmes muses, leaning over our classmate's body for closer examination. "And why has Bertram's family not yet collected the body?"

"Perhaps the Yard is hoping it will reveal more answers." My words sound false even to my own ears.

Their chests have all been carved open, then meticulously stitched back together in a Y-shape pattern, stretching from collarbone to navel. Stitches also cross their necks like black chokers. But only one shares Bertram's split palm.

"There's dirt beneath Hugo's fingernails. A substantial amount of it." Holmes points to the lord's fingers.

There's a flicker of memory through me as I take Bertram's hand, the corpse we examined in the classroom flashing before my eyes. I pry apart his pale, stiff fingers to examine the gash. Despite the coroner's stitches, I can see that the cut went deep enough to touch the bones. I drop the hand when I notice Holmes's attention fixed on my own. Isaac would never be so dainty and handle something so gingerly. Even a corpse.

Jude and Hugo are littered with stab wounds across their abdomens. The only other immediately noticeable wound on Hugo's person is the dark bruise on his chin, probably from his spill in the Turf, and Jude has none.

"These two"—I point to Davies and Jude—"did not have a chance to fight back." I hold up Bertram's hand. "He did."

Holmes nods, distracted by something on Bertram's shoulder. "Davies was drunk enough to confuse the Thames with the Nile. There's no way he could have fought anyone, let alone walk in a steady line."

And yet, as delirious as he'd been that night on the bridge, he'd been cognizant enough to quote bloody Homer. Shaking my head, I walk over to the first victim and, even more than a week after his death, the stench of scorched flesh still hits me like a punch in the nose.

Burned into Bertram's shoulder is the single letter *B*. My head snaps toward Jude where, on his forearm, a horse and rider have also been branded. "What in the world?"

Decency of the dead be damned, I pull back the sheet on Davies. On his right thigh, the letter C is branded.

"Could B and C be the killer's initials?"

"Only a fool would brand their own initials onto a person they've just murdered." Holmes shakes his head with a grimace. "No, these are all pieces of a much larger puzzle."

"To which we don't have all the pieces yet," I finish for him.

He nods.

"The killer will strike again."

My proclamation settles heavily in the cold room.

Discoloration in Bertram's arm draws my attention. I walk slowly to his side, my fingers drawing down his forearm, tracing the tendons. There, on the inside of Hugo's elbow, is a similar puncture. I'm leaning down to examine the wounds further, Holmes pressing close behind me, when a steady click echoes in my ears.

Footsteps.

I snap up, the back of my head colliding with Holmes's jaw, but I slap a hand over his mouth again before he can cry out. I point to the corner where more bodies lie, side by side, on tables, and toss him one of the sheets.

"Leave the lights," I whisper. "They'll have already noticed them."

Holmes and I rush to the corner and climb atop a table. We press up tight against each other, lying flat on our backs. He has just pulled the sheet over our heads when the door groans open.

I breathe slowly and silently. Beside me, a body reeks of chemicals and mildew, cold as ice against my arm even through the thick tweed of Isaac's jacket. I will my hands to cease their trembling. On my other side, Holmes is as still as the dead.

"Blasted Abraham," an unknown voice says. "I'm always having to remind him to lock this place up when he's through."

"That old bat left the lights on, too," says another. The hair on my arms rises at the voice. I must know him from somewhere. "Perhaps he just went to the lavatory and will be back soon."

"No." The other clicks his tongue. "Abraham will be home by now nursing a pint of warm rum in bed."

The boots clip across the floor; I trace the sound of their steps toward my classmates' bodies.

"What a waste," says the unfamiliar voice.

"I wouldn't go that far." That other voice is so familiar. I can see his face as though looking through a frosted window. It begins to thaw when he continues, "Do you still believe these are actually suicides?"

"Only a fool would believe that these lads killed themselves. That's only the story put out by the school to keep the rich families from pulling all their sons and daughters out of classes, taking their money with them."

"So how are these deaths related?"

"Well, aside from the slit necks and impeccable bloodlines, they're all your classmates."

"Groundbreaking deductions."

I can't help the visceral reaction that sweeps over my body. I flinch as the wind is knocked from my lungs as surely as a punch to the gut. The voice, that low, honeyed tenor, could only belong to one monster.

James Moriarty.

Holmes must recognize the voice at the same moment I do. His breath is suddenly timorous, and the hand beside me clenches into a fist. My fingers find his and pry his hand open, taking it in my own and willing it to stillness.

"I must get to the bottom of these murders before any more of my classmates are murdered," Moriarty says. His footsteps clip in a circle around the tables and in our direction. "Or before the murderer moves on to other, more delicate victims. The Lady Margaret class."

"How noble of you, sir," says the other man, voice dripping with cynicism. "There are some lasses with impressive families among that lot, too."

"My sister among them." Moriarty's distaste is evident in the way he says my name. "Irene Adler."

Holmes flinches. I dig my nails into his palms.

"You needn't worry about the ladies, I'm sure. The Scotland Yard must nearly have the case solved."

"I doubt the Scotland Yard has even the slightest lead. They couldn't tell the head from the ass on a horse even if astride one," my brother says with a low chuckle. My brother's tone is cold, reproachful even. I know it too well. The man should stop asking questions.

Moriarty's footsteps stop just short of our table. Silence stretches in the mortuary. Somewhere beyond the room, water still drips. I hold my breath and clench my eyes shut. Even the other man in the room is quiet, his breath a dull rasp.

I don't even breathe a sigh of relief when Moriarty turns, marching back to the bodies.

"Bring me answers," Moriarty says. "And you will be well rewarded."

The man scoffs. "I have no need for money."

"I wasn't talking about money." I can practically hear Moriarty sneer. He begins to walk out of the mortuary, lingering at the door. "Bring me answers when the Hunter's Moon hangs low in the sky like a mother's tit."

Who even talks like that? I roll my eyes beneath the sheet. What a pompous, son of a—

"What in God's name does that mean?" My brother's opponent stomps around the room, heavy, slightly dragging footsteps suggesting someone older, with a limp. "And where are we to meet next?"

Moriarty starts down the hall, his voice echoing down to us. "'When nations are to perish in their sins, 'tis in the Church the leprosy begins.'"

"Moriartys and their damn riddles," the man grumbles to himself when the sound of my brother's steps fades into the distance.

I couldn't agree more.

He snuffs out the lights one by one. When he reaches the corner where we lie, he stumbles into the table. The breath exits my lungs in a sharp gasp. He doesn't seem to notice, though, leaning across us and putting out the light.

We lay there in the dark for a long time after the man leaves. My chest shakes, the binding I have wrapped around it threatening to snap. Holmes's breathing is ragged. I jerk my hand from his and fling the sheet from our bodies.

"That was"—I swallow, remembering to pitch my voice low—"that was too close."

"Really, *Holland*?" Sherlock eases himself off the table. "Not just another day for you?"

I cannot make his face out in the dark, but the tremors in his voice are unmistakable. My mind is awhirl with potential meanings behind his words.

"What was Moriarty doing down here?" I ask, though more for myself than for him, having not the slightest inclination as to why my brother also seeks the murderer. It definitely isn't for fear for my life. In fact, I'm sure my death would be a relief to him. It rules him out as a suspect unless he's playing a long game. "Does he truly fear for his life?"

"No," Sherlock says, circling the bodies once more. He sniffs once, then twice. "But I'm sure he knows something that we don't."

I resist the very Irene urge to stamp my foot. "And who was that with him?"

Holmes shrugs. "The only way to find out would be to listen in on their next meeting."

Obviously, but I have no intention of bringing Holmes along when I find out exactly where that is.

Holmes straightens his jacket and checks his buttons, oblivious to the strange disappointment inside me. My eyes have adjusted to the dark well enough to make out the form of him. His hands tremble as they pat down his front.

"Why do you hate the Moriartys so much?" I dare to ask. "When James spoke, it was like your body had become possessed."

"Why do you care?" Sherlock's question is like the lash of a whip.

I struggle for an answer that Isaac would have at the ready, because my initial query was all me, not him. I understand why I hate the Moriartys so much, but in all my years behind the dean's door, I never heard of a quarrel with the Holmes family.

Finally, with a clear, deep voice, I answer, "Because it could make you a liability in this competition."

Sherlock Holmes grimaces, an odd expression on a face that shows little other than knowing condescension and derision.

"The only liability here is you." He gestures impatiently to the door. "Shall we go? Moriarty is long gone by now, and I'd rather not have to pretend to be a corpse again if the constable decides to take a round here."

I follow him from the mortuary, keenly aware of the newfound stiffness to his gait. Holmes's eyes refuse to meet mine, and his hands can't seem to still.

We walk, side by side, until we reach the statue of Queen Anne. At the foot of the pale stone, Holmes jerks to a halt.

"Where are you to go now?"

"Bed," I say exasperatedly. "It's late, Holmes."

He watches me carefully, and I know then that the question was twofold.

"Where?"

"Under the watchful, ever-seeing eyes of our dear Lord, of course." I chuckle. "Where do *you* sleep, Sherlock Holmes?"

He returns my chuckle. "I have an apartment in town."

"Quite the commute for only a few hours' rest." My smile is crooked beneath the scratchy mustache. "You needn't fear my snoring. I can find somewhere else to rest."

"Let us not avoid each other any longer." Holmes steps forward suddenly, towering over me. "There's no need to find other places to sleep when there are two perfectly acceptable beds with our names on them."

I know, deep in my gut, that he only proposes this because he doesn't entirely trust me. This ruse, this partnership between us, was to use my knowledge as well as keep me close enough to spy on. I am the leading suspect, after all. And while I would normally sleep in the Lady Margaret dormitory, the guards patrolling across campus make it exceedingly difficult to do so.

There is nothing I can do but sleep in the men's dormitory, across from the all-seeing Sherlock Holmes.

The room is frigid by the time we arrive, and unbuttoning Isaac's jacket is much harder than it normally is. My fingers are stiff like icicles. Cold air slaps my bare skin like a crashing wave, but when I shiver it has nothing to do with the chill.

I toss Isaac's cap in a corner before climbing beneath my heavy quilt. The blanket does nothing to warm me, my mind spinning like a storm-tossed sea.

"You're not washing your face?" Holmes grimaces. "Or, at the very least, changing your clothes?"

Because you'd see my bare face and ass. Why do you ask so many questions, Sherlock?

"It's too cold." I roll onto my side, facing the wall. "And I'm too damned tired."

I feel, rather than see, him shrug. "Suit yourself."

Soon enough, Holmes's breathing, steady and heavy, echoes about the tall-ceilinged room. Unlike him, I have no ease slipping into dreams. The corset makes it hard to breathe. I'm sure to wake up with a hitch less than an hour after sleep claims me.

I roll onto my other side to face the window. Clouds partially obscure the moon, so close to the moon's full glory that I imagine celebratory bonfire smoke floating through my window.

My mother used to love this time of year. Her grandparents

were from the north, where they still paint their doorframes with blood and create altars to their dead for Samhain. The thought fills me with an ache that sleep could never hope to chase away.

Beneath the window, harsh features painted white in the moonlight, Holmes sleeps as though death has claimed him. His mouth hangs open slightly, midnight locks splayed across his brow, a bare arm resting on the pillow above his head.

When my eyes finally close and sleep overtakes me, it's not me the murderer hunts in my dreams. It's my mother, with her throat sewn shut and chest branded with the initials *BC*.

CHAPTER 10

Eau de Soleil

Holmes is gone when I wake the next morning, and half the Lady Margaret dormitories are empty when I slink down the corridor to my room. My disguise is hidden away across campus and my eyes are pinched from a poor night's sleep. I reach my door just as another at the end of the hallway swings wide, and my hand halts above the doorknob.

"Adler? What were you doing out so early in the morning?" Ermyntrude steps into the hall, white satin nightgown kissing the flagstone floor. Uncommonly tall, Ermyntrude towers over my meager height. "*Veux-tu m'accompagner à l'église ce matin?*"

Will you come with me to church this morning?

The demand—definitely not a request, coming from her—leaves me speechless. I don't often visit the praying section of the Tories, or ever really, and definitely not of my own volition.

I must look as dumbstruck as I feel, because she gives an exaggerated roll of her eyes. "I asked if you would accompany me to church."

"I know very well what you said. I just don't understand why *you* would ask *me*."

"Because we're friends, darling," she says, batting her eyelashes. Without invitation, Ermyntrude shoves open my door and flounces into my room, the scent of roses trailing her. "Now, let me pick out your dress."

I sigh through my nose, eyes rolling to the ceiling. "Be my guest."

She pops her lips, flipping through my wardrobe. Her nose wrinkles as she presses aside my finest dresses. "You really do favor darker colors even though it does absolutely nothing for your complexion. Is there nothing of a spring color palette in here?"

I ignore the barb. "Will anyone be joining us?"

"Edith and Geraldine, for sure," she says, tossing her dark curls over her shoulder. Relief floods through me. I haven't been spending as much time with my friend as I should. Ermyntrude continues, "Roslyn was called into London by her mother. Here." She pulls a ruby velvet gown from its hanger and tosses it on the bed. "This one brings out the crimson in your hair. It's so dark you'd hardly know there's any color in there."

I don't point out that her hair is even darker than mine. "But this color is hardly acceptable for church."

She's not wrong, though. It's my favorite dress for a reason. I'm particularly fond of how it also heightens the green of my eyes.

"True." She taps her chin with a gloved finger, eyeing my wardrobe with abject distaste.

"How about this one instead?" I begrudgingly pull out a pale blue dress that will clash horribly with my hair, knowing she will have no complaints. She helps me with the small white buttons up the back, her fingers deft. She's standing so close that her breath tickles my neck as she pins my hair in a demure half-bun.

"Will your brother be at the service?" She doesn't meet my eyes in the mirror as she clasps a golden chain of the sea stones around my neck.

For once, I'm at a complete loss of words.

"Don't play coy with me." Ermyntrude spins me around to tie the laces up the front of my gown. Her face is mere inches from mine, close enough for me to see her pupils flare and smell the wine from last night lingering on her breath. "I know the stories about your mother, and why the Moriartys would prefer them not to be public."

I swallow. "Then why ask?"

"Don't fret. I won't tell anyone. It will be our little secret." She pats my cheek. "So pale. One would wonder if you ever spent any time outside the library."

Yet. She won't tell anyone *yet*.

I pull on my shoes and dust my cheeks with the barest hint of rouge. "Then I expect you already know what church James attends."

Her eyes meet mine briefly in the mirror. "You see me too well, Adler."

Says the black pot. If she had been anyone else, those words would have been a compliment, but coming from her, they are another threat. The way she smiles now raises the hairs on the back of my neck. "I'll meet you outside."

When she leaves, I breathe a sigh of relief as the cogs in my head begin to whir. Perhaps I've piqued Ermyntrude's curiosity and she wants my company to bring some excitement to her life, or has some misguided belief that I can get her closer to James... or maybe she's searching for something else entirely. Regardless, all the prime suspects should be in the church this morning, so I could hardly refuse to accompany her. Also, I do dearly miss Geraldine.

We make our way across campus to Merton Chapel, pressing close to share her umbrella. Normally, I would have been more wary of the thoughts ticking in her too-canny head, but my own mind is still aswirl.

"*When nations are to perish in their sins, 'tis in the Church the leprosy begins,*" James said last night. I haven't the darndest idea what he meant, and it is driving me to the edge of insanity.

Damn him. Having prided myself previously on knowing my brother inside and out, this irks me to no end. Chewing the inside of my cheek, I rack my memory for the source of the quote, but nothing is forthcoming, stirring my temper even more. It's like James knows the exact gaps in my knowledge.

"Where are you, Adler?"

Ermyntrude's high voice draws me from my thoughts. I glance around. "Umm... High Street?"

"No, darling," she says with a laugh like the tinkling of glass. "Where are your thoughts? You were grinding your teeth so loudly you might stir the dead."

If the dead might give me answers, I would continue.

We find our seats beside Edith and Geraldine. The latter greets me with a wide smile, enveloping me in a tight hug.

"Oh, Irene," Geraldine says with genuine cheer. "So glad you could join us."

I open my mouth to ask where Edgar is. The organ begins to ring about the great church, the pews steadily filling with families and their chatter. Ermyntrude has selected our seats carefully, raised above the others and in direct view of James on the opposite side of the chapel. Like the Lady Bedford, my brother has surrounded himself with his retinue. None other than Moran are members of the All Souls cohort, which is hardly surprising. The cohort are his rivals, enemies in the eyes of our father. Only useful as high as stepping on their backs can lift him.

James turns to Ermyntrude, dipping his head in a mocking bow that does little to temper the lecherous grin splitting his face. She blushes, whipping out her fan and flapping it like a hummingbird. He then turns to me, smile suddenly sinister and chin dipping to his chest.

If this is church, then why is the devil here?

When the priest finishes his sermons and the organ's last notes fade into the gold-flecked air, the worshippers finally stir. Around a muffled giggle, Geraldine whispers, "Isn't this the same church where you left those lewd drawings in the Bibles, Ireney?"

I gently pinch her, eliciting another round of muffled laughter. "I would never do something so sacrilegious! I can't believe you would suggest such a thing. Perhaps you're confusing me with Edgar?"

We both know Edgar is too pure and kind to even utter a curse.

Her impish smile matches mine, but it's quickly wiped away by the figure cutting toward us from across the church.

My brother dips into a low bow before us. His friends stop behind him, eyeing each of us ladies in turn. Moran leers at me from over his shoulder, and I suppress a shiver of revulsion. He's been attempting to court me for years.

James's eyes glitter. "You've been remiss, Irene."

"Oh?" Even the single word is scathing across my tongue.

"How you have not introduced me to your lovely companions should be punishable by death." He accepts Ermyntrude's gloved hand, placing a kiss upon its back. "My lady, how did you ever manage to get my sister out of the Bodley?" James brushes a thumb beneath my eyes. "Such dark circles. Having trouble sleeping?"

Seeing too much must be a Moriarty trait.

I refrain from biting his hand. "I'm obviously just having too much fun with my friends."

"Fun? You wouldn't even know the definition of the word."

"Oh, yes she does." Ermyntrude hooks her arm with mine. "We've been communing with ghosts."

Geraldine's and Edith's heads whip in our direction. That's hardly something that should be admitted in church. Geraldine's never been a particularly religious person, though, so she hopefully isn't too scandalized. It's probably why we get along so well.

"Charming." The way Moriarty says it makes it sound anything but. He looks at Ermyntrude, but his body is angled toward Geraldine, easily the more handsome—and wealthy—of the two. "Do you fine ladies have any afternoon plans?"

"Nothing exciting planned, I'm afraid." Geraldine hooks my other arm with her own and gently tugs me away. "We really should be going. The Lady Margaret classes have piled on more schoolwork than we could possibly manage."

Before Ermyntrude or James can argue, Gerry quickly steers me toward the exit, leaving them behind. Her steps are quick and stiff, chin high, and when we pass through the large doors, she breathes a soft sigh of relief.

Geraldine throws a furtive look over her shoulder. "Your brother is such a cad."

I blink, at a loss for words. Ermyntrude gossips with Edith out of our hearing.

"There are very few people whom I actually respect." I look back to Moriarty. "You know that James is not one of them."

Ermyntrude calls out, "Geraldine, darling! I was finally making some headway with that dashing man and you ruined it."

"She should consider that a gift," I whisper, eliciting a vicious giggle from my friend.

We part ways with Ermyntrude and Edith at Queen Anne's statue. I have now crossed the same space twice in less than half a day, now arm in arm with Geraldine. We head straight for the Bodleian and pass a pair of officers, marching in step across the quad.

"How long do you think they will keep the extra security on campus?" Geraldine asks.

A ruby necklace hanging from the pale neck of a passing lady catches my eye. Oh, how I do love pretty things.

"Until the lords are assured that their wares"—I point to her and then myself—"are indeed safe from some sadistic fiends that mean to do us harm."

"But all the deaths so far have been men, and from that All Souls class. Do you think James is worried at all?" Geraldine throws a glance to the stiff backs of the guards.

"I doubt he's afraid of anything."

Students have yet to return in force to Oxford's prime study locale. The tables are blessedly empty, and even the staff are nowhere to be found. I should worry about my own safety, I suppose, and

Geraldine's, too, but I don't believe that the ladies of the Lady Margaret class are the killer's targets.

Leaving Geraldine at a quiet table with a stack of books taller than myself, I go hunting for the librarian to bring me a book on symbols from the stacks. Those brands on the bodies are engraved behind my eyes.

I stop in a puddle of gilded light. The midmorning sunshine filtering through Selden End's high, arching windows is too lovely to ignore. Golden light stains the floor, the sun beckoning me to return outside. I stand a moment, gazing at the birds fluttering past and the leaves drifting by behind the glass. I lean a hand on a table, wishing nothing more than to be a sparrow, the air ruffling my feathers, song spiraling behind me, and oh so very free.

Freedom, a concept unknown despite what it may seem. Here I am, masquerading as a man and living a life of privilege, but I'm not free. Not truly. I can only rise so high and learn so much before reality sweeps me from my feet.

I am a woman, despite this charade I play. A bastard one, too.

Once, I was free. My mother and I had lived with only her childhood friend, Lasho, wandering the world. Elena Adler, a courtesan, a lady of the night sought across many seas for even a night of her company, was driven into hiding by one of her customers, Richard Moriarty. Despite the secrecy with which we had to shroud ourselves, my mother, Lasho, and I shared many adventures. Those years of freedom were too few, and too far away now.

Clouds overtake the sun, filling me with a sudden chill; I turn from the windows about to seek the Bodley librarian again, when a prickling on the back of my neck sweeps my gaze high.

My breath catches. From the second floor, Holmes studies

me. He leans both tanned forearms on the black metal railing, his sleeves rolled back to his elbows and shirt unbuttoned a quarter of the way down his chest. His dark eyes are heavy-lidded, and his jaw juts out in a stern frown. Where there was curiosity in his gaze the last time we met in the library, now something else lingers.

Suspicion.

For whom could you trust less than your mortal enemy? Your mortal enemy's sister, of course.

I ascend the stairs, our gazes locked the entire way. My steps are measured, heels clicking on the floor.

"Sherlock Holmes." With a demure nod, I flash him my loveliest smile. "We really must stop meeting in the library like this. People will start to gossip."

The black of his pupils dilates. "Gossip is the province of the empty-headed."

My gaze drops to the book in his hands, a text about the House of Normandy. Strange, we have no current assignments on it due. I don't let my confusion show. "Are you not afraid of the murderer attacking your classmates?"

"I do not believe it is I that the killer is hunting." Holmes's gaze tracks from my eyes to my lips, and back up.

"How the bloody hell could you know that, Lord Holmes?"

"Because each of the victims is a lord of incomparable wealth and potential power, and I, Lady Adler, am no lord." He takes a careful step back. "Or should I call you Lady Moriarty?"

"And I'm no lady. Not truly." I step toward him again. "And Adler is just fine. There is no love lost between Lord Moriarty and me, I assure you."

A tic forms in his jaw, but he does not move away. "You would dismiss your ties to your father so quickly?"

"Are you particularly close to your father?" A little research, and carefully placed queries around campus, told me that he is, but the deflection feels necessary.

Holmes ignores my question as smoothly as I did his. "What about you and your brother?"

"Half brother," I bite out. "There's no love between him and me, either."

He steps close enough to elicit a small gasp from me, an unseemly noise for the inappropriately small distance between us. But I won't take a step back.

"Oh, I doubt that," he whispers, dipping his face close to mine. "There is no loyalty stronger than that between family."

"You know nothing about me," I say, breathing quickly and scratching at my wrist. When did the Bodley get so cold?

His mouth curls up to the side in a smirk, revealing a dimple beneath his left eye. Aware of the effect his nearness has on me.

"Why do you despise James so much?"

His jaw clenches. "You won't find the answer to that question in any of these books."

"I promise to let you keep your secrets," I say, lifting my chin with a crooked grin to match his, "so long as you let me keep mine."

His smile softens. "Don't make promises you can't keep."

"You've observed me, Sherlock Holmes. But have you truly seen me?" I gaze up at him through my dark lashes. "The distinction is quite important."

Our breath mingles in the chill library air. Any nearer, and it would take only a rise on my toes for me to paint his cheek with the rouge of my lips. The thought makes my heart stumble. Either he does not realize or he does not care. Sherlock Holmes gives not a single damn for propriety or the expectations of society.

"I've observed that your favorite color is red. That, having witnessed you slipping easily between languages, you're a polyglot. The ink stains on both of your hands tell me that you're also ambidextrous." He releases a shuddering exhale. The warm, sweet air of his breath lingers on my cheeks. "And that your favorite scent is lemon. So unlike the other ladies. Do you prefer it because it makes you unique among them, because you believe yourself better than them despite the overwhelming proof that you are not, or because you actually enjoy the smell?"

I open my mouth to slap him with a biting reply, but he barrels on, no doubt seeing as much in my pale face.

"I've seen the way you and your brother glare at each other across the room. How you've never shared more than a handful of sentences in public. You can't stand to be anywhere near him, am I wrong? You use your beauty as a tool, manipulating those around you. I watched you, right over there, manipulating Lord Hayward. Playing him as you would a fiddle. So let me ask you this. What makes you think you're any different from your brother, Irene Adler?"

His dark voice lingers over my name. I take a step back at last, whatever color I have leaching from my skin. We stare at each other a long moment, his gaze daring me to deny his words. Insults and compliments all rolled into one. His eyes flare with a heat to match the fury pulsing inside me.

And matching the way my core stirs with delicious warmth.

"Correct, on almost all accounts," I finally say, refusing to look away. "I am indeed a polyglot. But can you guess which languages I am fluent in and which I merely pretend to know? The ink on my hands is not from writing with both hands, but instead a cracked pen in my bag."

"My favorite color, though, is not red, despite the overwhelming amount of it in my wardrobe." I trail fingers down the front of my dress. His gaze follows the movement, lingering on the soft swell of my breasts. "It's black."

His gaze leaps to mine, eyes widening.

"And the scent in question is Eau de Soleil. I do not wear it to catch attention, or out of favoritism. It was my mother's."

I step even closer, our chests brushing. If he wants to push the edges of depravity in society's eyes, then I will push right back. Holmes audibly gulps. His pupils are so large, his eyes are pure onyx now.

"And I am better than James Moriarty. Do you know why, *Sherlock Holmes?*" My voice takes on a mocking edge as it slithers over his name. "Because I only desire freedom, and my brother would love nothing more than to put us all into cages."

His head tilts to the side, studying me anew. A lock of dark hair falls over his brow and obscures a single eye.

I continue, voice as soft as night, "Don't pick fights you cannot win." I reach up and he goes as still as a statue. My bare thumb brushes gently across the bruise forming on his jawline, left by the back of my head just last night. "You've got a bit of ink on your chin. Just there."

I could lean forward just a hair and our lips would collide.

"Irene?"

We leap apart. My chest heaves as I spin around to face Geraldine, ascending the spiral stairs, her blue eyes wide.

"Gerry!" My cheeks must be burning. "I couldn't find the librarian anywhere."

"He's at his desk...." Her gaze darts between Holmes and me.

I dare a glance in his direction. The heat in his eyes hasn't diminished even in the slightest.

"Let's get back to studying, shall we?" I turn my back on him, putting a sashay into my steps.

"Who was that handsome devil?" Geraldine throws a furtive look over our shoulders.

Sherlock bloody Holmes.

I lead her past the librarian's desk, no longer needing his help. I know where Moriarty and the mystery fellow will meet.

CHAPTER 11

The Treachery of Moriarty

"W̲HEN NATIONS ARE TO PERISH IN THEIR SINS, 'TIS IN THE Church the leprosy begins."

How the devil I hadn't immediately known that Moriarty was talking about the infamous Bartlemas Chapel goes to show that I have too many glass spheres juggling in the air right now. The line is from a William Cowper poem, one of our father's favorites.

Holmes's book about the House of Normandy finally rang the bells in my head. Henry I, not my favorite king—though I prefer him far more than the philandering eighth of that line—used that particular chapel to house lepers more than six centuries ago.

I'm in the midst of pulling Isaac's wardrobe from its hiding place when a knock sounds. Grumbling, I stash the clothes away once more and swing open the door.

Suddenly, I wish I'd just stayed in the morgue.

My brother waits in the hallway, leaning against the wall with a sour expression curdling his normally handsome features.

"Beggars and charlatans aren't allowed on campus," I say, readying the door to slam it in his face.

Moriarty catches it and steps into my room without invitation, gaze sweeping the small space. "Must you always be so rude, Irene? It's no wonder you don't have anyone courting you."

"I thought that was simply due to the fact that you threaten anyone who so much as looks in my direction." I cross my arms over my chest, ignoring the nervous thunder of my heart. "What does *he* want now?"

"Our company, obviously," Moriarty says offhandedly. He opens my mother's box, fingers lingering over the opal necklace sitting atop the emerald velvet interior. He snaps the box shut and moves on to my wardrobe, and I make a mental note to myself to check both later to see if anything is missing.

"Father only willingly spends time with me when he wants something."

"Don't be ridiculous." His smile is twisted and cruel. "There's nothing you have that he could ever want."

His words don't sting the way they would if I actually gave a damn what my father thought of me. James holds one of my amethyst silk gowns to his face, brushing the fabric across his cheek and inhaling deeply. He meets my eye and drops the dress as though burned.

A shiver of revulsion runs down my spine. "Tell him I'm busy."

My brother walks slowly toward me, gaze dripping from my head to toes. I raise my chin and force myself to stand my ground.

When he reaches me, close enough for our toes to touch and for me to smell the amber cologne that lingers in my nightmares, he gestures to the door. "Father will hear no excuses."

My hands clench and unclench at my sides. The threat, though unspoken, is clear. If I don't go of my own volition, he will drag me there by my hair. As he has done so many times before.

If I go with him, I won't have time to change into Isaac's clothes before I go to intercept Holmes. If I know where my brother is, though, I'll know exactly when he leaves for his meeting.

"Let me change before we go." I point to the door. "Wait out there."

I'll need to change into an extra-long skirt to hide the boots I'll wear tonight, and a warm shawl.

As a dean of England's most prestigious college, our father, Richard Moriarty, has a town house just on the outskirts of campus. Dying and shriveled ivy clings to the gray walls, and the rosebushes separating the yard from the road have shed their leaves and petals, nothing more than brown veins and thorns.

Knowing exactly where our father is, I don't wait for the butler, letting myself in without fanfare. Richard Moriarty demanded I be brought to town and properly groomed for my entry into society. He should have known that I would foil his plans for any reputable matches at every turn. Once, when he invited the podgy Lord Percival over for dinner with blatant intentions, I'd made a point to slip, one by one, the rings adorning his porky fingers into his own drink. Without him ever noticing.

Until he choked on them, that is.

Lord Percival survived. My father's marriage plans for us did not.

And I managed to squirrel away a beautiful emerald brooch from his cravat.

I kick the leaves from my boots on the stairs as I climb to the top floor; James sighs from behind me, knowing full well how my brazen behavior irks our father.

Richard's study is all oak bookshelves and plush armchairs, with a large desk overlooking the street below through a window stretching the entire wall. The mahogany desk is clean, not a speck of dust to be seen. His papers are perfectly aligned, his books not dog-eared like mine, windowpanes spotless and iron mullions polished. There's only one portrait in the entire room. Not of me, my brother, or his first wife, James's mother.

Sitting between perfectly aligned and alphabetized textbooks, a small painting of my mother looks down on us all. He had it made after she ran away.

Richard Moriarty stands at the window, hands clasped behind his stiff, ramrod-straight back when we enter. He doesn't turn, doesn't acknowledge our arrival. Oh yes, something has made him very angry today. Shivering, I take a seat, and Moriarty's knee bumps mine as he does the same. I jerk away. My skin has the sharp chill of frostbite beneath my skirts from the quick touch.

One would think that siblings should stick together when facing their most dangerous foe—an angry parent—but I learned early on that James finds me more useful as a stepping stool than an ally.

The dean's breath fogs the window. "I've heard troubling things from your professors, my *children*."

Children. It rankles James to be referred so. His face pulls into a sneer that he quickly wipes away when our father turns.

He and James share the same pale blond hair, thin lips, severe bone structures, and tall, lithe frames. But their eyes, those soulless, hateful eyes, filled with an eternity of ice and wrath, are the most similar of all.

"Is Irene falling behind with her classwork, Father?" James steeples his fingers over a crossed knee.

"You're *both* falling behind!" Richard roars and slaps both palms flat on the desk, making me jump.

"That's impossible," James sputters, straightening as his face drains of color.

"I wish it were so, but *you* rank neither first nor second in your class, and"—our father turns to me—"*your* grades are middling at best."

I'm not surprised about my own ranking—I truly don't give a damn about the Lady Margaret classes beyond the mediocre education and ruse they provide, and more time spent with Gerry—but James's makes my head spin. I can't help the grin that pulls at the corner of my mouth. "Do we get to know who has knocked my precious brother from his gilded pedestal?"

"Sherlock Holmes." A vein pulses in James's neck. I resist the urge to move my chair farther away. "But who else?"

"Some upstart from god knows where," Richard says, turning to face the window once more. "Isaac Holland sits at the top of the All Souls class."

My smile slips. *Keep calm*, I tell myself, acutely aware of the danger I'm in now. Carefully and with genuine inflection, I ask, "Who is Isaac Holland?"

"Just as Father said." My brother makes a noise somewhere

between a growl and a hiss. "A mewling little upstart with nothing to his name."

"Not *nothing*," I say, daring fate. "He's obviously got better grades than you."

James's knuckles blanch as he grips the armrests of his chair hard enough to make the wood groan. I notch my chin high, a wordless dare.

"Says the idiot girl sitting snugly in the middle of her own class." My brother looks me up and down. "Spending too much time socializing?"

Richard turns ever so slightly. "Finally making contacts, Irene?"

"Yes, though I'd prefer to think of them as friends rather than a means for class ascension." I cross my legs and lean back in my chair, drumming my fingers on the armrest as if bored. "Though I guess for Moriartys they are one and the same."

"Careful." Richard turns remorseless eyes to me. "You're a Moriarty just the same as us, but that can be changed. If your grades drop one more iota, I'll withdraw you from Oxford and have you married to the highest bidder before the new year." He points a finger at my face. "Your grandmother might write your checks, but only I can decide your future."

Unless I run away just like my mother did. Despite the hate swirling in my gut, I press my lips together and nod.

"Who in your class have you been spending time with?"

"Just a handful of the ladies." I don't miss the exchange of glances between father and son. I begin ticking the girls' names off on my fingers. "Gerry, of course, and Roslyn Rochester, Edith Blakewell, Maribeth Popkiss, and Ermyntrude Bedford."

"The Earl of Bedford's daughter?" He inclines his head, turning back to the window. "There might be hope for you just yet, Irene."

The butler knocks gently on the door, calling us all to dinner and saving me from having to divulge more about the girls—temporarily. I'm the first to head downstairs, wanting to be out of that room as quickly as possible, but I make sure to leave a single glove on the floor beside my chair.

I stumble when I walk into the dining room and, behind me, Richard demands, "What are you doing here?"

My grandmother, Augusta Moriarty, dressed in a gray and off-white muslin gown and gloves, takes a sip of her soup at the table. Her silver hair is braided into a crown atop her head, revealing pale skin far less wrinkled than any other woman her age.

"Was I supposed to wait for you to stop pretending to be a father before starting my dinner?" Augusta's voice is rough from too many cigars. She waves an irritated hand to the plates. "Sit, sit. I'm famished."

James gives Augusta his most charming smile, stealing the seat opposite her. "Always lovely to see you, Grandmother."

"Your voice cracks when you lie. Like a pubescent boy." She turns, dismissing him, and takes one of my hands as I sit beside her. "I've missed you, my dearest Irene. I begged Richard to let you visit me in Philadelphia, but he's always been such a stubborn ass."

My father coughs, flapping his napkin with too much vigor before draping it across his lap.

"Perhaps over the winter holiday?" I fail to keep the eagerness from my voice. "I'll have some time off between semesters."

"Yes, but not a long enough holiday to make the journey across the Atlantic worth it." She sniffs and resumes slurping her soup.

My disappointment must be written all over my face, because James cannot contain his chortle.

Augusta Moriarty is blue eyed like her son and grandson, but the physical resemblance stops there. Her face is heart-shaped and her figure fuller. Even in her old age, her smooth nose and cheekbones are painted with a smattering of freckles. Mentally, she might outrank us all, too.

Over the fine china and white linens, the awkward silence of dinner is broken only by the gentle scraping of our forks and knives. James's eyes keep turning to the clock above our father's head, but he needn't worry about time. He has an hour yet before he is to meet the mystery fellow. To my intense dislike, my father's icy, beady eyes follow my every movement. James seems to enjoy my discomfort, flashing me a tight-lipped smile over the rim of his glass.

I bare my teeth, knocking my glass against his with much more force than I should. "To a bright school year, in which we will hopefully raise our grades."

I've never felt more vehemently loathed by my brother than I do in that moment.

"Cheers," he announces, raising his glass. "To new friends and old."

"Speaking of new *friends*"—Richard turns to his son—"are you courting anyone at the moment?"

James chokes on his wine. "Not yet."

I hide a smirk behind my napkin that is quickly wiped away when Richard turns to me.

His gaze is cold and calculating, with all the weight of chains. "Irene can make sure to introduce you to Ermyntrude. That would be a rich match."

It would, but Moriarty has long desired Geraldine, who would be much more of a challenge as she cannot stand him. Like the psychopath he is, my brother always does enjoy the fox chase.

"It would be a good match, if James weren't such a spoiled egg." My grandmother sniffs. "Like his father."

I take another pert sip of my wine, though I hate the drink. "They've already been introduced, actually. Ermyntrude finds James to be quite dashing."

My brother's glare would flay a man alive. It's a good thing I'm no man.

"Excellent. I expect you to bring Ermyntrude as your date to the Saint Nicholas ball this solstice." Richard takes another bite of meat, ignoring the clatter of James's fork as it drops onto his plate. I dare not smile, though, as his attention turns to me next. "And you will find a suitable escort as well."

"That's unlikely, but I will try." I bite primly into a piece of steamed broccoli.

"Perhaps Moran," James says around a mouthful of pheasant at the same time Richard says, "It shouldn't be hard for you, Irene, with your mother's looks."

The broccoli suddenly threatens to rise up my throat.

Augusta's fork clatters. "Pray tell me why you insist on pretending to be a man of honor when you chased a woman who did not even want you. Keep up this behavior, and I will name Irene as my sole heir."

Richard reaches for his glass. "It would tarnish our family name to have the daughter of a whore inherit it."

The food is ash in my stomach. I couldn't eat another bite even if I wanted to. My mother's face swims in my vision.

"That *whore*"—I swallow delicately—"was twice the human you will ever be."

My father's knife scratches angrily across his plate, making me flinch. My heartbeat thunders in my ears. I clench my teeth, prepared for whatever lanced words Richard will throw my way.

"I don't think I've ever heard you say something so foolish before, Irene." His furious eyes pin me to my seat.

I raise my chin, nostrils flaring. Daring him to smite me like the devil he is.

"I will die without even a smidgeon of regret for writing you out of the will." We all slowly turn to my grandmother. "For your obsession with Elena was as embarrassing as it was cruel."

Her hands tremble around a wineglass. Augusta may look nary a day over fifty, with her skin hardly wrinkled, but I know of the illness that dogs her steps.

"She accepted my payment quite readily." Richard has the gall to appear bored. He raises a glass of dark wine to his lips, staining them bloodred. "I should have broken her in like the brood mare she was."

The glass is knocked right from his hands. Red wine drips from his hair and the plastered floral wallpaper behind him. Color begins to rise from the base of his throat. My grandmother's fingers, still outstretched toward him, curl like talons. "You are a blight on our family name."

With a trembling hand, Augusta picks up her fork again. "Irene will inherit everything from me, and you nothing."

There it is, the only reason my father keeps a hand on my shoulder, day in and day out. He may yet be written out of Grandmother's will, but society dictates that he can do whatever it is he may see fit with *me*.

My father's eyes are dark with fury. "You will regret that."

Seeing how his face matches the color of the wine dripping from his brow and the wall behind him, I'd say that the decision has been firmly made.

"This is the fault of her mother." Richard's fist slams on the table, making the cutlery sing. "If the woman had just accepted my damned proposal—"

"You'd what?" Augusta demands, daring him to put voice to the violence that has always simmered below his skin.

I'd read the gossip columns years ago, in a fit of curiosity. My mother was an enigma to many, a siren to all. An opera singer by day and courtesan by night. She'd dallied with many men during her year in England, but none had grown quite so obsessive as my father. Three nights. That's all it took before he asked—no, demanded—her hand in marriage. She'd disappeared overnight. My father grew even more obsessed, and like his son, the chase only deepened his hunger. Leading to my mother's death.

For if my father couldn't have Elena Adler, no man could.

Nothing in the column spoke of how dangerous Richard Moriarty could be.

"The woman was right to run from you." She sneers. "How I raised such a disappointment, when you had all the world at your feet, is beyond me."

My stomach roils. I squelch my discomfort with a hearty drink of wine, my throat uncomfortably wet and filled with a sour taste. Standing and tossing my napkin on my chair, I say, "I need to use the powder room."

I tear up the spiraling town house staircase. I want to punch something, anything or anyone, particularly Richard Moriarty and his horrible son.

I don't turn for the privy when I reach the third-floor landing. As silent as a mouse, I dart down the hallway, shutting my father's office door behind me with the softest click. My fingers pass over, without touching, the papers resting on Richard's desk and his collection of inks. The figures in the ledgers are absolutely dismal. My grandmother hasn't been helping out Richard at all. Only me. The thought helps settle my stomach slightly.

His planner sits open in the center, and I glance over the calendar, noting important meetings in red ink, business dinners, and any other times I might avoid my father. Ignoring the books, the quills, and drawers, my focus falls entirely on the stack resting on the desk's corner, on which the names of my All Souls cohort are finely printed.

They're stats about our dwindling number, facts and histories on each of us. Of course my father would draw up such a record, no doubt trying to find weaknesses James can exploit. A small peek tells me that Isaac's is decidedly blank, as I suspected it would be, my mentor keeping all details about me close to his chest. Not that there are any to find about Isaac Holland. A smile pulls at the corner of my mouth. How it must irk my father.

I hesitate over the sheaf of papers with *Sherlock Holmes* at their top. I'm about to give them a quick perusal to memorize it when something itches my nose.

Something sickly sweet and smoky with a hint of floral. I inhale deeply, and my nose is drawn to the center drawer of my father's desk. My hands tremble. Surely he wouldn't notice anything amiss if I simply opened it up.

I slide the drawer open, grimacing when it catches slightly and the contents audibly rattle. My heart thunders loud enough to wake the dead.

Memories, keen as the lancing touch of a whip, lacerate my mind. Of being flogged in the back courtyard until my knees buckled. My legs almost give out again at the thought. Swallowing and throwing back my shoulders, I straighten and continue my search.

I notice nothing immediately remiss and am about to shut the drawer when gilded lettering catches my eye.

There, emblazoned across the top of a velvet box, are two initials.

B and C.

My breath catches. I open the box to reveal six golden seals. One is a rider atop a striding horse, an exact replica of the one branded on Jude's forearm. And there, embroidered into the ruby silk cover of the inside of the box are two words.

Bullingdon Club.

A small creak echoes down the hallway. I snap the box closed and shut the drawer with my hip, bending to pick up my glove just in time for my father to step inside.

"What are you doing in here?" he demands. His eyes travel over the desk, assuring himself that everything is exactly as he'd left it.

"Retrieving this." I dangle the glove before my face, praying that he doesn't notice the sweat beading on my brow.

"You missed your grandmother's departure." He doesn't sound remorseful about his mother's absence. Not even in the slightest.

I feel the barest flicker of disappointment. It is her way. Augusta has always despised farewells, especially since her husband's death. She once admitted to me that she refuses to even say the word *goodbye*, because it might mean a time will come when one doesn't see the other again.

"You should have asked before coming in here." His eyes dart from me to the desk and back again. "You know how I feel about people coming into my office uninvited."

"I'll remember to seek permission next time." I hedge around the desk, leaning against it with my hip to make sure that the drawer is properly shut.

He stops me with a finger on my chin. Angling my face his way, his nail digs into my tender skin as, with a voice as soft as silk, he says, "Make sure that you do."

I can't get out of there fast enough. I scurry down the spiraling stairs, feet threatening to tangle in my haste.

Richard calls down after me, "I've called a carriage for you. Your brother has gone on ahead for another engagement."

I jerk to a halt, catching myself on the black balustrade. "No need for the carriage. I'm meeting with Ermyntrude and Maribeth this evening to study. Maribeth lives but a short walk away."

Richard Moriarty nods. "Excellent. Make sure to boast about your brother."

"Of course, Father," I say with my most saccharine smile. "Ad nauseum."

Collecting my coat from the waiting butler, I step out into the darkening night.

I don't make it farther than the next block when a carriage rolls up on the road beside me. I recognize the crest and horses before the driver even leaps to the sidewalk.

"Come in, child, before you catch a chill." My grandmother's voice is firm.

I climb in beside her after giving the driver directions.

"That codger makes me see red," Augusta says gruffly, shivering. "I should have snuffed Richard out years ago."

I nod in agreement.

"How are classes going?" She leans into me for more warmth.

I know she's not referring to the Lady Margaret ones. "I'm top of my class."

"Good, good. To be expected." She pats my hand, nodding to herself. "James went into the competition with so much ego it's a wonder his back doesn't break beneath it. But I have to ask…"

I wait expectantly as she chews her words, staring out at the dark streets. When she turns to me, her eyes glisten with a fear I've never seen before.

"Must you continue this charade? Leave these old toads behind and join me in America."

My back straightens. "But this would all be for nothing."

"And it will likely continue to be so, once they realize who you are." She grips my hand tighter. "You've proven yourself to everyone who truly matters."

I open my mouth to give her my ready answer, but snap it shut. Augusta sees through all lies.

"I want—no, need—to beat him. I need that seat." I look down at my black gloves. "They've taken everything else from me."

There's no pity on my grandmother's face. "That Moriarty ego will take your life someday."

I hate that there's any part of me that is Moriarty.

"Besides," she continues, leaning back. "They haven't taken *everything*. I'll find you a prince to marry and we will never have to see Richard and James again."

Something about the way her pulse flutters frantically beneath my thumb gives my protests pause. "Is that why you're leaving? To get away from them?"

Augusta inhales deeply. The carriage slows, reaching my destination.

She looks out into the gathering darkness. "Why here? What are you hunting, Irene?"

"A killer, Grandmother," I say with all the petulant frankness of a favorite grandchild.

She releases a long, aggrieved sigh. "Of course you are. Devil take me..."

"I need to stop him before another classmate dies."

"Him?" She peers into my face. "What makes you so sure it is a he?"

"I'm not." I reach for the door handle.

She stops me. "There are some questions better left unanswered. Someday your hunger for answers will dig you an early grave."

When I move to open the door, her grip tightens. She clutches my hand to her lap and her nails dig into the skin under my wrist hard enough to make me hiss.

"Grandmother, what are you—"

"Do not cross him, my darling girl," she whispers. "Or he'll kill you the same as he did your mother."

My entire body goes numb. "There's no proof he killed her."

"I need no proof. He's a son of mine." Augusta Moriarty shakes her head. "If you persist in being a stubborn fool, at least promise me this." She grips my chin—hard—between her long, wizened fingers. "When the time comes, and you need help, don't be afraid to seek it out. Your mother still has friends in these parts."

My breath rattles from my lungs. "How..."

"Go." She shoves my shoulder. "I'll be watching, and you'll be in America soon enough."

In a daze, I climb from the carriage. She doesn't bother to wave as it begins to roll away. When it disappears around a dark corner, reality hits me like a pail of cold water. I have to go back to church.

CHAPTER 12

Bartlemas Chapel

FAR MORE MODEST THAN ITS OXFORD CAMPUS SIBLINGS, Bartlemas sits in a field of dying grass as tall as my knees, a humble, solitary stone building with very few windows and a wooden roof threatening to buckle. The smell of damp dirt, mildewy leaves, and pine is thick in my nose.

As the full moon begins to rise beyond the nave roof, pillowy clouds wafting overhead, I wait for one more person to arrive. My grandmother's parting words tumble through my mind on an endless loop. My father and grandmother have always played cat and mouse with my future, forcing each other's hands. But how much longer will my father allow such disrespect before lashing out?

Augusta must know that Richard Moriarty would find a way to gain favor somehow or get his hands bloody trying.

Two sets of boots crunch softly in the freshly fallen snow. I press behind a bush, watching through the bramble as two men pass.

I strain my neck around the branches and curled leaves. My jaw threatens to drop to my boots as Sherlock walks up to the decrepit chapel. With him is the officer who questioned me after Bertram's death, the young Mr. Watson.

"Really, Holmes?" Watson says, a frustrated edge to his voice. "Just because you hate the man, doesn't mean he's a murderer."

Their strides match perfectly, steps even and quiet. Both men are dressed in black, top hats pulled low to partially obscure their faces.

"I don't think he's the murderer. But he might know who is."

They stop at the gate and look up at the towering Bartlemas Chapel. Clouds settle heavily above the gilded Hunter's Moon and obscure Bartlemas in shadow.

"Not a very welcoming place," Holmes says.

"Do you really think we'll find Moriarty in there?" Watson cocks his head. "Or just a bunch of leper ghosts?"

"I had no idea that you were so superstitious, Watson."

"We should all be, so close to Samhain." I notice, not for the first time, the Scottish burr lilting Watson's words.

"No need to sacrifice a lamb yet. We have a few weeks until the ghosts come knocking on our doors." Holmes turns, peering around the deserted street. I press closer to the shrubs, biting my lip. Even from this distance, in the shadows, I can make out the rise of his brows, but his gaze seems to pass right over me and back to the church.

My mind tosses back and forth over whether to reveal myself to them, tiptoeing between whether it would make Holmes trust me more—or less. On the one hand, he might appreciate having insider knowledge on his number one nemesis. On the other, he will undoubtedly act guarded around me as I have yet to earn his trust and will therefore reveal less than he would otherwise.

I remain pressed behind the bush, breathing deeply into the branches so that my breath doesn't spiral into the air above me and reveal my location. Small snowflakes drift down from above, the first of an early winter. They catch in my hair and on the lads' hats, swiftly melting in the wet grass at my feet.

"What do you know of this place, Watson?"

"This is the least trafficked part of Oxford, the place is near destitute, the ghost stories would deter the average passerby, and a murder here would likely go unfound for many days, or at least until the Lord's Day. I still think we should leave the interrogations to the Scotland Yard."

Holmes merely scoffs.

Watson continues, "They are already on high alert with all the bodies piling up around them."

"Three bodies is hardly what anyone would call 'piling up.'"

Watson pinches the bridge of his nose. "How I've managed to remain friends with you is a feat unto the saints themselves."

"No one would ever confuse you for a saint."

Shaking his head, Watson drops his voice. "One of us 'round the back and the other in the front?"

I nearly bite my tongue off to keep from laughing. Apparently, Holmes's mind wanders in the same direction.

"How forward of you. You haven't even proposed yet."

There's a muffled yelp as Watson smacks Holmes upside the head. "Quit being a prat."

"Is that really what they teach you in the force?"

Watson sighs, running a hand over his face. "Jokes aside, we can't just waltz in the front door."

Holmes gives a curt nod. "It's a good thing that there's no shortage of windows. I'll see you inside."

He dashes around the chapel, leaving a cursing Watson behind. I wait a moment before following Holmes. Hiding behind a tan buttress, I watch as he carefully pries open a window and silently crawls inside. I dart after him. It's too dark to make out much, other than Holmes now dipping behind a pew. On the far side, Watson does the same. But my brother is nowhere to be seen.

I worry the inside of my cheek and continue around the chapel, ducking to make sure that my head doesn't peek into view of the windows. A side door waits on the other side, but my hand hesitates above the handle. Throwing caution to the wind, I open the door anyway. There are lives at stake, after all, and I'd like to believe I'm canny enough to think of an excuse if I'm caught.

Luckily, the door swings open without a hitch. Slinking inside, I press against the wall, my skirts rustling softly in the deep shadows. I'm in a secluded corner of the church, out of sight of the pews, and directly across from a small confessional—from which two pairs of shoes peek.

The air in the chapel is damp, the dark unrelenting. The steepled ceiling is an unending onyx ocean above, shadows reaching long arms down to me like souls from the River Styx. I can almost hear their moaning, the wind rattling the shutters akin to the clatter of bones.

Dragging my gaze away from the black ceiling, and with a careful hand before me should I bump into anything, I slide to a corner and drop onto my knees behind the altar. Whispering comes from the confessional, but I cannot make out the words. I crawl to the end of the altar, not daring to look around.

"And what have you learned about the brands?" Moriarty's voice is muffled behind the red curtains.

"They piece together to make a single symbol."

"A jester could have deduced that. You can't tell me what that symbol is?"

I smile grimly, pleased to have discovered their connection—though unintentionally—before my brother. The cold is so deep in the abandoned chapel that it sinks into my bones. My teeth chatter, and I clench my jaw.

"No" is the curt reply. "But I have learned a rather queer connection about the men."

A shadow flickers in the corner of my eye. I dart beneath the altar's tablecloth just before someone drops where I had just crouched. Even in the dim light, I can make out Holmes's pewter ring. There's a short scuffle on the other side, and Watson kneels beside him. I can make out their shapes in the dim light filtering through the tablecloth.

"What did I miss?" he whispers. Holmes silences him with a shake of his head.

"Who would gain the most from such systematic killings?" James asks.

"You're the genius. Figure that out yourself."

Silence stretches from the confessional. Holmes's fingers curl into a fist.

"You're right," Moriarty finally says, and ice drags up my spine.

"Now where's my pay?" the other man says gruffly.

Another moment of silence passes. There's a twinkle of falling coin from Moriarty's side before the curtain swings open. Holmes and Watson press close to the table and duck lower. Holmes's foot slides beneath the tablecloth, threatening to bump my own. I press as close to the other side of the table as I dare, holding my breath.

Moriarty's boots clip on the flagstone floor as he marches from the chapel, whistling an all-too-familiar tune.

"*The wind blew as'twad blawn its last,*" he begins to sing, whistling some more chords with maniacal glee. "*That night, a child might understand, the Deil had business on his hand.*"

The shutting of the church door behind him steals the rest of the lyrics away. I shake my head. I might not ever be able to read Robert Burns's poetry again without shivering.

"His informant is still in the confessional," Holmes whispers. "We should question him, by force if necessary."

"The law still applies here," Watson says, aghast. "This man still has rights, no matter your suspicions. We've heard nothing to implicate either him or Moriarty in the murders."

"Then he should have nothing to hide." Holmes stands abruptly and strides to the confessional.

Then jerks to a halt.

It crosses the chapel with a mere whisper. My nose wrinkles as something sickly sweet threatens to coat my nostrils, filling my mouth with a sour, cloying residue.

A fog rises from the floor, threatening to encase me. Watson curses and Holmes has become deathly still. I cannot see his face to deduce whether it is panic or curiosity that holds him in place.

"Dammit, Holmes." Watson roughly shakes his friend. "We've overstayed our welcome in this place."

"You know, I think I agree with you for once. But I'm sure this gentleman also feels the same."

Holmes whips the curtain aside and takes a staggering step back. There's a loud thump as something large and heavy falls in front of the table.

A man's vacant eyes stare up at me from under the cloth. I slap both hands over my mouth to suffocate my near scream.

"Unless you want to be an accomplice to murder," Watson says, grabbing Holmes by the arm, "I suggest we leave *now*."

Holmes ignores him and bends over to examine the body. His own starts to rack with heaving coughs. My eyes start to water. I can't hold my breath for much longer.

Watson spins around. "What was that?"

Holmes turns from the body. "What are you talking about?"

"That screaming." He falls to his knees and slaps his hands over his ears.

"Watson?" Alarm pitches Holmes's voice before he coughs again.

"It won't stop," Watson yells. "The whistles, the screams. All of it."

"It must be a hallucinogen." Holmes pulls his friend to his feet. "We need to leave *now*."

They make it all of two steps before he suddenly drops Watson and starts to spin.

"Get it off me! Get it off me!"

I crawl from under the table as Holmes begins to run around the chapel. He careens into a pew, flipping over the back. He's on his feet again, slamming into the wall and then the table, his hands waving erratically in the air above his head. He collides with the altar, threatening to knock the bowl of holy water to the floor.

Unable to hold my breath for any longer, I climb from the table, untie my scarf, and plunge it into the holy water. Neither Watson nor Holmes notice me, both inconsolable. Holmes was right—there must be a hallucinogen in the fog. Taking the drenched scarf, I wrap it over my nose and mouth. I might have already inhaled too much, but it will hopefully keep me from the insanity currently gripping Holmes and Watson.

Scarf covering my face, I yank Watson to his feet and drag him toward the door. His eyes are clenched shut, hands still covering his ears, but he doesn't resist me. Even still, our movements are slow and sluggish. I get him outside and shove him into the snow before running back into the chapel.

Holmes stands on the table, swinging a candelabra. I dip below his wild arms, narrowly missing getting clubbed in the head. The next time he turns, I catch his arm. But he's strong.

I'm thrown backward and my scarf falls from my mouth. Using his momentum against him, I pull him down. He falls atop me hard enough to knock the air from both our lungs.

His eyes widen infinitesimally. *"Petit citron rouge?"*

He's speaking nonsense now. I shove him off me.

His arm thrown over my shoulder, we stagger from the chapel and collapse in the snow. I gasp for air, aware that I have mere moments before the drug must take hold. Without looking back at Holmes and Watson, I sprint for my dormitory.

The walls of the corridor threaten to slice me in half. The stones spring from the wall, flying in my direction. I stagger, step by step, ducking beneath flying stones and soaring doors.

A quicksand pit opens in the middle of the corridor. I barely leap over it in time to not be sucked through. I hear *him* stomping after me, his footsteps heavy and his breath scorching on the back of my neck. His hand yanks at my hair, pulling it from its braid and jerking my head back. I pull away and stumble, at last, into my room.

I slam the door shut and slide down it in a sobbing heap.

Even in the back of my mind, I know this is all a hallucination, nightmares spun by the fog.

Still, his nails drag down the other side of the door. That hateful voice hisses through the wood.

"Irene. Irene. Irene."

I cover my ears with my hands, but I cannot make the whispering cease.

"I will find you."

"No." I shake my head. "No."

"You belong to me, Irene."

The world goes black as I collapse on the stone floor.

CHAPTER 13

Mumely

My mother dances before a blazing fire. Her body undulates, living flame, spinning and rising ever higher. Her hair, dark red like mine, is ablaze in the firelight, the bloodred color striking through the dark curls like embers.

Men toss coins onto the stage, cheering wildly. Her body twists to the strum of Lasho's guitar.

"Santé! Santé! Santé!" the men and women cheer.

My mother's body bends, end over end. She stands on her hands, plucking a stein from the nearest man with her toes and taking a sip. The man grins, raising his fists in the air with a wild roar.

I nurse a mug of steaming cocoa, pulled close to my chest. My young eyes are wide as I take in the mesmerizing scene. I'm barely tall enough to see over the table, and my wild, dark curls are a frizzy cloud about my small face.

My mother throws a wink in my direction.

After another song, Lasho sets aside his guitar. He's a large, burly man, the protector of our family. At least to anyone who looks our way.

In reality, Lasho is more panda than grizzly, coming to find me when he has spiders that he needs killed. Little does he know, I simply put them outside.

He sighs, easing himself into the seat next to mine. "We shouldn't be letting you watch this."

I frown in outrage and bare my little teeth. "Whyever not?"

"Yes, Lasho"—my mother takes a seat on my other side—"why not?"

"You'll give the wee lass ideas." He flags over a waitress. "Deux ales, s'il vous plaît."

"And what's wrong with a mind brimming with possibility?" My mother pushes my fringe from my face with a fond smile.

"Because next she'll be stealing my ale with her toes." Lasho shoves up from the table, making the floor shake beneath his considerable size. "I should have ordered us food, too. One moment."

"May I have a sip, Mumely?" my mother asks, pointing to my mug. When I smile and nod, she slides the drink over. Her eyes shut as she takes a sip, rapturous. "I'll give the French one thing. They know their chocolat."

"A fellow Scot?"

My mother and I both look up in surprise. A man stands at our table, the same that Mother stole his drink from. He clutches said ale to his chest as though her foot might rise up and take it again.

"Tu te trompes," my mother says. Coughing, she falls into the thick French accent she insists we speak with in public. "My grandparents may have been from the Highlands, but I was born in the mountains of Savoie."

The man's mouth curls in a grin. He's tall, like Lasho, but lithe where the guitarist is brawn. His hair, dark and long, is bound at the *nape of his neck. He sets down his floppy hat on the table and takes the seat across from us, unbidden, making my mother stiffen.*

"No need to hide the burr from me, lass. Your man over there"—he nods to Lasho laughing at the bar—"has a French accent laced with only the finest Highland scotch."

My eyes dart between them, brow wrinkled and acutely aware of the tension rippling through my mother. Her knuckles are white, a twitch forming in the corner of her mouth.

She leans back in her chair and says, French accent gone, "What do you want?"

The man holds both palms up. "Just to thank you for the lovely dance. It's been a long, long time since I've enjoyed such a delightful treat." He turns to me. "Will you grow up to be a dancer like your momma?"

I brusquely shake my head. I hate talking to strangers.

Mother rests a hand on my back. "My daughter's dreams are a bit loftier."

"Than yours?" The man's eyes dance over my face before traveling to my mother's. "Or her father's?"

My mother's nails dig suddenly into my back.

"Ow, Mama," I cry.

She snaps her hand back and looks down at me, eyes wide. "I'm so sorry, Mumely. How about you go help Lasho with our food?"

"But I don't want to."

"Don't be rude." She gives me a gentle shove from my chair.

I stand there, clenching my teeth. I could open my mouth and scream. That usually gets me what I want.

The man slides a golden coin across the counter. "Get yourself a pain du chocolat, pet, and some more hot cocoa."

"Je ne suis pas un animal de compagnie," *I snap, but I grab the coin nonetheless.* "Mama says I can only have one sweet a night or I'll ruin my teeth."

"Her accent is better than yours, Elena." *The man seems surprised.*

"We'll make an exception. Just this once." *My mother pulls me close. Her lips tremble as she kisses my brow.* "Now go get yourself a sweet, Irene."

I pull sharply away. My mother has never used my name before. Pouting, I hobble over to Lasho, tripping over my long skirts.

"What does he want?" *My mother's voice trails behind me.*

"Well, for starters, he would like to know how you've evaded him for so long."

Their words fade into the crowd as I climb onto the stool beside Lasho, nearly falling off in the process, and spin the golden coin across the counter like he taught me. The bear wraps a warm arm around my shoulders, laughing uproariously at something the bartender says. I'm asked what I want in return for the money, enough to buy me a month's worth of pain du chocolat *should I so desire.*

My gaze is fastened to that gilded coin. The firelight reflects across its surface, making it seem almost liquid. Even at such a tender young age, my thoughts drift to where the coin came from, and what was expected in return. I wonder if it could buy a room for my mother, Lasho, and I on the nights when we're huddled together in the cold, or bread when our stomachs rumble with hunger. I shouldn't waste such a luxury on sweets when it could bring a smile to my mother's face instead. I look back at my mother, who has her arms wrapped around her chest. The bar is loud, though, the customers rowdy from unspent desire and rage, and I cannot hear what she says.

Lasho pokes me in the ribs, drawing my attention back to the barkeep.

"Que voulez-vous boire?" *she asks, waiting patiently for my order. She eyes my coin with enrapt hunger.*

I turn again and watch as twin tears slide down my mother's cheeks.

"Rien." *I grab the coin with two hands and tuck it in my pocket.*

CHAPTER 14

Life of a Mayfly

I WILL HAVE TO BURN MY CLOTHES.

I also need a long, hot bath.

I awake with my face pressed against the bitter-cold stone floor. Time spun on without me, twisted like Rumpelstiltskin's gilded cord until it wrapped around my neck and dragged me from consciousness and into delirious awakening again and again. I lean up onto my hands and take a look at the mess I've become. The mud on my dress and in my hair has caked and hardened. I grimace at the sludge coating my boots and gloves. My limbs ache as I shove myself unsteadily to my feet, knees trembling. But, more than anything, the pain in my head is sharpest of all. A million little daggers pierce into my brain through my eyes.

I haven't thought of Lasho in a long, long time, though I know exactly where he is.

The bells toll beyond the dormitory, their number stealing the air from my lungs. I have classes today, and my next one starts now. The bells are also much closer than they should be.

I jerk around, the world spinning, to face the window. The clock tower just outside could only mean one thing. There will be no bath, hot or cold, for me.

Because I'm in the men's dormitory.

"*Merde*," I curse, sprinting around the room. I can find no wig or glasses and concealing powder.

I was so focused on making sure that Sherlock Holmes never found out he was sheltering with a fraud, that I hid all my disguises across campus, everywhere but my own room.

A clip of boots outside the room makes my heart stop.

"*Merde*," I curse again. "*Merde! Merde! Merde!*"

I grab a chair and ram it under the door handle. Not a permanent fix, and it will surely be a headache if I come back before Holmes, but I just need time. A glance to the clock, and the window between it and me, and another stream of curses passes my lips.

I fling the windows open, a blast of icy wind licking my cheeks as whatever food remains in my stomach threatens to spill over the ledge. The white ground is at least a twenty-foot drop, and even if I landed in a foot of snow, my knees would no doubt shatter upon impact. Yet it's England in mid-October. There's an inch at best.

A tree, barren of leaves, is a leap away.

I've played this game before. Gambled, and lost.

There's a rattle behind me. I spin in time to see the door handle rise, then fall. The chair screeches.

It's either jump, or lose everything.

The chair screeches again. I leap without thought.

I'm flying across a stormy sky. Lightning arcs above me in gray clouds, a warm breeze making me believe I have wings.

I hit the tree hard enough to knock the air from my lungs. I nearly drop to the ground, but the burning blue sky above makes me grip the brittle limbs tight. My eyes stream from the bitter breeze.

The memory had been so quick, so fleeting. Like the life of a mayfly.

I drop down the rest of the way, heart hammering in my chest. There's no point brushing off the twigs and moss from the tree. I'm still covered in mud. Throwing a glance up to the empty windowsill, I sprint across the green toward the arched entrance in the beige wall.

Anyone could have seen me. The sun is bright, at least thirty windows facing directly into this garden. I pray to all the gods known to mankind that each student, professor, and fellow is in class at this very moment. Like I should be. I turn the corner and jerk to a halt hard enough for my heels to dig groves in the wet sod.

Headmistress Allen, far from the Lady Margaret dormitory, glares at me over crossed arms.

With a formal, written reprimand tucked in my pocket, and Headmistress Allen's promise to notify my father ringing in my ears, I throw my muddy hair atop my head and slam on Isaac's wig. His mustache comes next, ragged and due for a replacement, and then I bind my chest haphazardly. I smear makeup across my face, blending in the fake nose and concealing my faint freckles and the small birthmark dot beneath the corner of my right eye. I'm still pulling on Isaac's boots when I peek around the door. The hallway is clear, my classmates already gone.

I shuffle into class, hiding my face behind a stack of books, Stackton giving me a look for my near delinquency that would shrivel a lesser person. I'm astutely ignored by my classmates as Professor Stackton continues his lecture—well, most of my classmates.

Moriarty's eyes are shards of ice, following me to my seat. I want to turn and stare back, but I don't dare. I wonder if he knows his sister well enough to spot her, even in disguise. And if he could really be a murderer.

From the corner of my eye, I see him turn to face Stackton's loopy scrawl spread across the board, and I finally let myself take a peek at my brother.

He shows zero evidence of his late-night excursion. He's perfectly primped. He wears his favored dark green frock coat atop a black shirt. There are no dark circles beneath his ice-blue eyes, and his golden hair is swept back. His hands betray not even a speck of the dirt that now cakes beneath my nails—despite wearing gloves, I might add. His chin, perfectly shaved, turns in my direction and I return my gaze to the board.

Cold sweat forms beneath my shirt when Moriarty turns in his chair to face me. He wants my attention, because he feels he's entitled to everyone's, and I won't let him have it. As a distraction, I begin to count the heads of our classmates, disheartened by their too-small number.

And a chill sweeps through me to find another missing. My pen clatters to the desk.

Holmes's seat is empty.

When the bells toll again, signaling the end of class, I'm the first out the door.

Thankfully, Holmes is very much alive. I find him in the library, cradling his head in his hands. When I slam my books on the table, he half leaps from his seat, nearly falling to the floor.

"Too many beers last night?" I ask with a forced, light chuckle.

Holmes looks up blearily through his long fingers. "This is a library, Holland. Have a care for how loud your voice is."

The drug must have done more of a number on him than on me. "I'm not loud, Holmes. You're just hungover."

"I don't have a hangover. I've never had one in my entire life," he says, grumbling.

"Then what excuse are you going to use for missing class this morning?" I slide my notes across the table toward him. "I know you said that these are useless, but I find they come quite in handy when you are absent from the lecture."

He looks up, a startlingly beautiful smile splitting his face. "My thanks, Holland."

"Is that the first time you've ever said thanks?" I return the smile, a flatter, crinkled version of the smile I share with others as Irene. "You're welcome."

"But you really didn't have to." He slides the notes back to me. "I did the reading for this class last week."

Of course he has.

"Really basic stuff." Holmes waves at my textbooks. "Do you truly find all of this necessary?"

"Not everyone is inhuman like you," I say primly. Probably too primly for a man. I scratch an insatiable itch on my wrist. "So, if you're not nursing the bottle-ache, why did you miss class?"

He glances around Selden End, devoid of other students. "Because I was..." He bites his tongue. "You caught me, Holland. I had too much to drink."

A harrumph escapes me. Obviously, today is a difficult Holmes day. I spin my notes to face me and open the theology book.

A sniff near my head drowns out the scratching of my quill. I lean away from his looming face. "Bloody hell, Holmes. What are you doing?"

He frowns, canny eyes searching my face. "What is that scent?"

Hopefully the horror doesn't register on my face. Despite wearing Isaac's clothes, I might still smell like my lemon-and-honey wash.

"No idea." I make a show of sniffing myself all over, raising my arms and giving my pits a big whiff just for effect. "I spent the evening with a certain lady last night."

Holmes scrutinizes me, glowering. "Which. Lady."

I give him a name of a lady that he has probably interacted with the least and likely never will. "Ermyntrude Bedford."

He straightens, ogling me with disbelief. "The Duke of Bedford's daughter?"

If I wasn't wearing Isaac's disguise, I'd be insulted. "Apparently, she has a taste for the lesser class. Must give her a bit of excitement to be able to throw it in Daddy's face."

"Do all the ladies of the Margaret class share a laundress?"

"How the devil would I know?" I hope that Holmes isn't so damned nosy that he'll look it up himself. "All ladies smell alike to me."

Holmes clicks his tongue. I continue ignoring him, flipping the pages of my textbook. I have a particular love of this subject. Theology, though I disagree with many of its subjects, fascinates me. There are fewer ways to better understand a person than to learn how and why they pray.

Apparently, I succeed too well at ignoring Holmes. He snatches my quill, ignoring my protests. I could strangle the damn man sometimes.

I hold my hand out expectantly, waiting for him to return the quill once he's finished writing something down, but instead he slides a paper toward me.

We are being watched.

I know better than to look around to see who. Though I can probably guess. My brother undoubtedly sent Moran to follow me. Now that my father revealed that I'm ahead in the rankings, there is a target on my back. Although, there was already one to begin with.

I take the quill back and continue studying. Better to give Moran nothing of note to pass along to my brother, and no reason to follow us. Holmes sighs, thinking I've ignored him and, continuing to read, I let him know what to do in a way that Moran surely cannot understand. My quill taps on my paper and I'm heedless of the ink it splatters.

I tap out an *M*, and then two *E*s, and finally a *T*.

Again and again, I tap out the word until recognition dawns on Holmes's handsome face. He straightens but keeps a blank face, pulling a textbook into his lap and pretending to read. I tell him where he can find me next.

Standing and stretching my arms high above my head, I say

another place entirely. "I'm starving. The lady kept me from breakfast this morning as she was ravenous in a different way. Meet here, then, to compare analyses?"

Sherlock looks as though he doesn't yet understand my choice of words, but he nods anyway. My fake mustache tickles my lip when I force a smile and gather up my books. I have another class to get to in less than thirty minutes and a face to wash off beforehand.

I smell of lemons, my hair still wet from a quick rinse and my curves shoved into an ungodly corset when I arrive—late—to my Lady Margaret class on art history. Though an interesting subject, I have yet to discern its usefulness to a nursing degree.

My tardiness is decidedly—and blessedly—ignored as I slink toward a seat in the darkened rear of the classroom and listen carefully to the lecture. Should I want to stay on my father's good side, I'll need to get my Lady Margaret scores up.

But it's hard to concentrate when the killer could strike again at any moment.

The sigils in the box in my father's desk were exact replicas of the brands on the bodies of the dead. A coincidence, perhaps, but I've never believed in such things.

Everyone on campus knows of Oxford's secret societies, such as the snooty Gridirons and the infamous Bullingdon Club, but only the higher echelons of Oxford's campus have ever been invited to the latter's raucous parties. Isaac Holland wouldn't even be worth their notice. Rumor has it, though, that the club has a soft spot for beautiful women.

"Where's your head at, Adler?"

I look up, startled, but the professor's focus is on the board. The voice appears again over my shoulder. "Late nights getting to you?"

Ermyntrude leans over her notes, raven tresses tumbling over her shoulder, and whispers, "What were you doing out so late last night?"

Damn. I had hoped nobody noticed me stumbling back. "My dinner went much later than I was expecting. I should have accepted my father's carriage, but, as evidence of my ruined boots, I made the mistake of thinking I could walk home."

"How scandalous." Ermyntrude's smile is devilish. "Think of how your reputation would be ruined should our classmates find out."

Warning bells toll in my head. That was a threat if I ever heard one.

I turn to my notes again, my back firmly to her, and say, "I'm sure my brother would be quite upset with whomever started such a rumor."

I doubt my brother would actually give a damn, but Ermyntrude doesn't know that.

As we're leaving the classroom, it's Geraldine, not Ermyntrude, who pulls me aside. Tugging on my sleeve, she whispers, "You should really watch your back with her."

My mouth opens and closes. The words are more warning than threat but are the last I'd ever thought to hear coming from sweet Geraldine's mouth.

Ermyntrude and her gaggle of followers linger in the doorway, watching our interaction from afar.

I nod, taking my friend's hand and giving it a gentle squeeze. "I appreciate your concern, Gerry, but I—"

"No, Irene." Geraldine silences me with a stern look. "You don't know what the Bedfords are capable of."

Nothing that I haven't experienced with the Moriartys, I'm sure.

She drops her voice ever lower. "Where were you last night? You never came back to the dormitories." Her lovely periwinkle-blue eyes are wide. "I had to tell Ermyntrude you were at dinner with your father."

I lift a shoulder. "Well, you didn't entirely lie to her. I was for a time."

"And the rest of the evening?" she presses.

I weigh my words. Telling Geraldine about last night at Bartlemas Chapel would only endanger her in more ways than one. It's not that I don't trust her. It's that I don't trust everyone else.

And I can't lose her, too.

I open my mouth to spew some nonsense about James, when she cuts me off with a bitter noise in the back of her throat.

"Save it, Irene." She drops her chin to her chest. "I've learned well your penchant for secrets."

An ache forms in the hollow of my throat. "I'm only trying to protect you."

With a sad shake of her head, Geraldine turns, but remembers at the last moment to impart a forced smile of farewell for the sake of our audience. "You should join us for tea Saturday evening in my rooms."

I watch her walk away with Ermyntrude, regret swelling in my chest.

CHAPTER 15

Ghosts of Oxford

"How did you find this place?" Edgar whispers from somewhere in the shadows behind me.

We're sneaking around a codgy professor's office, the old badger teaching far, far from here. I lead the way around his desk, to the wall of my desire. The paneling is of plain oak. Blond, boring, and entirely nondescript save for a single black line down the center.

I drag a nail down the line, pressing it into the middle as high as I can reach.

"My mother always told me that the most boring walls hide the most interesting doorways," I say, shoving past the paneling and into the darkened corridor beyond. "See!"

A tiny Geraldine peeks around her brother, bright blue eyes peering into the reaching shadows. "Do you think there are spiders in there?"

"No doubt," I say with a delighted laugh. "Maybe even ghouls and vampires, too."

Geraldine disappears behind her brother's back with a tiny shriek.

"Don't worry, dear sister." Edgar pulls on her hand and tugs her around before him. "I'll protect you." He meets my eyes over her head of piled golden curls. "I'll protect you both."

I can't help the indignance that leaks into my voice. "I don't need you to protect me."

All of eleven and already filled with the precocious energy that would guide me to young womanhood, I dive into the shadows headfirst.

"I'll always protect you."

Edgar's whisper follows me, even now, more than half a decade later, as I stride down a familiar corridor to the office of my choosing.

The halls are blessedly empty, nobody to be scandalized by my ankles. In London, a woman alone would be cause for an uproar, but here, on this blessed campus, I may walk to my heart's desire without shocking the ton. During the day, at least.

The EMERGENCY MEETING that was scrawled across my father's calendar might give me some clues. And wearing my own face, as opposed to Isaac's, might be safer while the students of All Souls are hunted one by one.

Slipping into Professor Stackton's office is a simple matter of picking the lock. It's empty when I enter, shutting the door behind me and carefully turning the lock home again.

His desk is covered with papers as I pass, an unorganized display fitting for a professor. I've come to expect nothing less from any of them except my father. I'm about to walk right past when words written in bright red ink catch my attention. His next exam, so carelessly tossed on the surface of the old oak desk, makes me pause.

It would only take a moment to memorize it. A single glance, and I can be a test ahead of everyone in my class, including Sherlock Holmes and James Moriarty. My victory assured.

That hesitation feels like a damning blow on my soul. A good person, I tell myself, wouldn't even consider cheating. A Moriarty, on the other hand, wouldn't even hesitate to take the answers.

Clenching my teeth, I turn from the desk to the familiar wood-paneled wall behind it. The campus of Oxford is covered in secret staircases and corridors, once used by servants, and now reserved for nefarious people like me. My palm presses firmly against it until I hear a distinct click and it edges open.

I'd discovered this particular passageway as a child when my father brought me with him to work, having not yet hired a governess, and locked me in his office. It took me no time at all to find the corridor's entrance. Geraldine and Edgar joined on many such adventures. We'd pretend to be lost in mazes, dangers around every corner, the ghosts of Oxford waiting with claws bared to capture us in their black webs.

There are no cobwebs barring my path, the dust I expected at my feet instead worn away from a steady tread. Someone else has been using this passage.

The thought fills me with a minute panic. The killer could have been using these passages the entire time. The net with which I toss for suspects grows larger.

The murderer could perhaps not be a student, but rather a professor.

Ermyntrude's warning still lingers in my ears, as does Geraldine's. Too many suspicious eyes and it will be in no time at all that someone notices me trading my skirts for trousers, or even worse—suspects me of murder.

To get ahead of the killer, I have to find out what evidence the school is hiding from everyone else, and what would force them to paint the gruesome acts as suicide.

Biting my lip and listening for any breath other than my own, I continue slowly down the long, dark, twisting hall until I reach the door I desire. Dropping to my knees to peek through the peephole, disguised on the other side as a center rosette, I finally release a long, silent sigh of relief.

The deans of Oxford all sit or stand around Richard Moriarty's desk, wearing matching expressions of disgruntlement. Chancellor Gascoyne-Cecil, thin-lipped, wrinkled, and wearing an expression that perpetually looks as if he's sucking on a lemon, holds court in the center.

He leans forward and his chair groans. "What do you plan on doing, Moriarty?"

"Me?" Richard presses a hand against his chest with a mock expression of shock. "You blame me for the failings of the police?"

"You're the one who came up with the suicide ruse," one dean hisses.

Slowly, like a creeping panther, my father leans forward, planting steepled fingers on his desk. "And you're the one who paid off the coroner."

He looks each of the assembled deans in the eye, his gaze landing last on the chancellor. "Now, instead of pinning blame, we find a way to control it."

Control. My father's favorite word. I scoff softly.

"The Yard tell us that the investigation is still open, at the very least." The chancellor harrumphs, unintimidated by Richard's show. "That damned investigator. It seems they have reasons to believe that the death of one of their own is related to the ones on campus. How the investigator came to that conclusion is beyond me."

A door at the end of the corridor slams shut. I jump, pressing to the door at the same time my head whips in the direction of the noise. My breath catches in my throat. There are no sconces in this hallway, so I can't see beyond the wall of black at the end, and the darkness presses close.

"What of the sigils found on the bodies?" asks another dean, drawing my attention back to my father's study. "Have we discovered their connection?"

"Not yet." Moriarty shoves away from his desk, turning his back to his assembled colleagues. I can't make out his face from my hiding spot, but the tic in his jaw catches in the dim light.

"All the victims thus far have been men," a dean says, drawing a circle in the arm of his chair with a fingertip. "Should we dismiss the Lady Margaret class as a precaution, despite this? Their studies are a joke as it is."

My jaw clenches, just like my father's.

"No." The chancellor straightens. "We need the money their families are providing."

"What of the families of the dead?" my father asks. "How much money can we expect of them now?"

"All were on the verge of bankruptcy anyway." Chancellor Gascoyne-Cecil waves a hand. "Bad investments, from what I've been told."

A tremor of excitement thrums through me. Finally, something new to go on.

"Do you think the murderer is trying to make a statement?"

someone asks. "Why leave the bodies? Make no effort to hide the deaths. He must be trying to say something."

Shaking my head, I whisper, "What makes you so sure the murderer is a man?"

My father turns, seeming to look directly at my peephole. My breath catches in my throat. He couldn't have possibly heard me. I'm about to stand when the air in the hallway drops with a chill. Slowly, I turn as my heart begins to pound against my ribs. I can feel it, as surely as a hand gripping my throat.

A pair of eyes linger on me.

My rational brain clamps down on my erratic thoughts before I can sprint either into the meeting or headlong into the shadow watching me from down the hall. Holding my breath and refusing to break my gaze away from the shadows, I slowly stand. My hands clench at my hips.

From the other side of the hidden door, my father's voice rings. "Whatever we decide to do, the killer is still on the loose, and we must make sure not to force him to break his silence." The church bell tolls in the distance. "Again."

The professors file out of the office behind me, their shuffling echoing through the wall even as I feel that looming presence in the shadows press ever closer. My chest rises and falls with rapid gasps, hands fumbling behind my back for the hidden doorknob. The darkness seems to take another step. There's a click of an oil lamp being shut off behind me, a snap of a door closing.

With a ragged gasp, I fling the door open and stumble through. I don't have a moment to register my luck that the office is actually empty before I'm slamming the secret door shut and sprinting across the office and out into the sunset-lit hallway beyond.

There's a shriek as the door to my father's office is creaked open and the hinges protest.

Shoes slap on the stones behind me in time to a long, running gait. I'm running, too, now, gasping for breath against the constraints of my corset. The air rushes past me, pulling my hair from its careful braid.

Fingers snatch at my dress. I fling myself around a corner and slam into a wall. Warm hands grip my arms.

Not a wall. Sherlock Holmes.

"Easy there," he says, steadying me. "What are you running from?"

"There's a man!"

"In a university? Color me surprised."

"This isn't a joke, Sherlock!" Gasping for breath, I spin around.

There's not a soul behind me. The shadowed hall gapes with emptiness.

My mouth opens and closes, memory and imagination warring within me. I raise a hand, covering my lips. "I could have sworn..."

"Do the ghosts of Oxford frighten you that much?" A small smile pulls at the corner of his mouth.

My cheeks flush what must be a brilliant scarlet as my chest heaves with the effort to catch my breath again, fighting with the corset. Decorum be damned, Holmes reaches out and tucks a loose lock of my hair behind an ear, thumb brushing my jaw and making me shiver.

"I never knew her to be superstitious."

We both jump apart. Moran, my brother's ever-present shadow, ambles around the corner, hands tucked in his pockets. He looks me up and down, grin salacious.

Sebastian Moran. Father has only begrudgingly approved of James's friendship with the son of a minister. Not because he is blind to the usefulness of such a relationship, but because he isn't fool enough to disregard the danger of the insidious nature lurking beneath the man's skin.

"I'm not," I bite out, throwing back my shoulders.

Moran's black, beady eyes dart between us. "Was I interrupting something?"

"No." I resist the urge to bare my teeth. "But I'm sure you'll tell James otherwise, like the good little lapdog you are."

He sneers. "I'm sure he'll love to hear about his sister, skirts raised above her knees and dashing down hallways like a trollop."

I don't even see Holmes move. One moment Moran is leering at me, and the next his enormous head is whipping to the side. The lecher's entire body twists with the movement. He slams into the wall, then crumples to the floor.

Holmes rubs the red knuckles of a curled fist and nods to the groaning Moran at our feet. "Head made of stone, that one."

"Explains why there's nothing in it." I glare at my brother's toady as he climbs back to his feet.

Baring teeth now red with blood, Moran grins. "Your brother is going to love hearing of your new...*friend*."

I take a conscious step away from Sherlock. Not because I'm ashamed.

Because it is safer for him, even if I might have damned him already.

Moran sneers, glancing between us. He steps closer, leaning forward. His breath is hot and rancid against my cheek as he whispers, "Careful, Irene. Don't want to end up like your mother."

My heart stutters to a standstill. With a dip of his chin in Holmes's direction, Moran spins on his heel and saunters down the corridor. Leaving me torn between fleeing for my dormitory or fleeing the country entirely.

CHAPTER 16

A Disingenuous Smile

M<small>Y FIST HESITATES ABOVE THE FAMILIAR BLUE DOOR.</small> Though I pride myself on being able to predict the behaviors of people, my mentor has never been quite so readable. He will be none too pleased to find me on his doorstep. Again.

The door swings open to reveal a wizened professor with more beard than face and spectacles the size of duck eggs.

"At least you had the sense to wear your costume, Mr. *Holland*," Professor Stackton says, huffing. "But not enough to send notice beforehand? What if I'd had guests?"

Before I can reply, he huffs again, giving a cursory glance to the cobbled path behind me. He waves an arm to his foyer. "Well, stop lurking on my doorstep and get inside before someone sees you."

I shuffle across the entryway, mind harkening back to the last time I'd been in Stackton's town house and the last time he'd asked me that exact same question.

His spectacles slip down his nose, suspicion and curiosity twinkling in his eyes. "Now what do you want?"

The man might barely crest five feet high, but he'd always had the canny ability to look me in the eye.

I notch my narrow chin high. "I have a proposition for you, Professor Stackton."

He sighs, dismissing the waiting footman with a jerk of his chin. "Send for some tea, Callum. I expect Miss Adler will be here for quite a while."

Leading me to the sitting room, he gestures toward a floral-patterned love seat. "I should have known you'd show up on my doorstep. The way your eyes perked up at the dinner last night when Richard mentioned the All Souls cohort, and the secret smile you tried to hide behind your glass when your brother spoke of his application."

There's a sharp rattle of china as a maid places a tray of tea and shortbread on the small table between us.

"What are you implying, Professor?" I take a sip of tea.

"There." Bushy brows drawn together in a frown, he points at my face. "That same disingenuous smile. The one thing you inherited from your father."

The comment wipes the grin from my face.

He leans forward, resting an elbow on his knee. "Before you even ask, Irene, I will not sponsor you. As brilliant as you are, All Souls does not accept women."

"But I'm not asking you to sponsor me." I glance to the sitting room doors, making sure that no one lingers on the other side. "I think you should sponsor Isaac Holland."

Stackton sputters. "Who the bloody hell is Isaac Holland?"

I raise a pinky as I take another sip of tea, grin returned. After a moment of silence, his mouth drops open. He leans back in his seat, eyes as wide as the rims of his glasses.

"Before I go on at length about how you're out of your damn mind..."

His hands shake as he takes a sip of tea. The brown liquid splashes over the porcelain rim. He grimaces, reaching into his pocket and pulling out a flask, emptying it into the cup. "I will ask you a single question, Irene."

"Go ahead." *I lean back, crossing my legs.*

"Why do you want to join the All Souls cohort?" *He looks me square in the eye, right into my soul.* "Even if my sponsorship garners you a seat, and if you beat the odds to rise to the top of the class and secure a fellow position, do you really think you can masquerade as a man for the rest of your life?"

I clutch my lip between my teeth. "That was more than one question, Professor."

"Just answer me. Another damned thing you've inherited from your father is your uncanny ability to avoid questions. Don't tell me you give a damn about getting close to the queen." *He rests both arms on his knees now, leaning across the table that divides us.* "What is this about, Irene? Is it to prove something to your father? To your brother? To sabotage his dream of one day becoming a dean?"

He leans back, watching me expectantly.

Sighing, I uncross my legs and set aside my cup. It clatters, betraying my trembling hands. "I'll admit, there's a part of me that would love to watch that cocky, self-important, so-assured-in-his-greatness smile fall from my brother's face. To prove to my father that James isn't the most brilliant person in Britain."

"I will not sacrifice my position to assuage your ego, Irene."

I wave a hand. "Let me finish, you old bat."

"Such flattery will hardly inspire me, either."

"You and I both know that it is a harsh tongue, not a soft hand, that sways you. Or at least that's what Grandmother says."

"I will not be swayed by talk of your delectable grandmother, either."

"I could have gone my entire life without hearing you refer to my grandmother as delectable."

"You're the one who brought her up." Stackton chuckles.

"I want to join the All Souls cohort because I am a woman, not in spite of it, Professor." I look anywhere but at him. "It is exactly because I am a woman that I can hope for nothing. I could take a job in the medicinal field, to occupy my mind at the very least because my father's goal is to marry me to the highest bidder. But whomever I marry will take whatever money I have, whatever I have earned for myself, and it will then be his own. He will even take my name, my mother's name, from me, and it will be forever gone.

"If I succeed, and I most definitely will, this fellowship would be mine alone. I would owe it to no one, and no one could take it from me." I lean forward, unable to keep the begging earnestness from my voice, because it's true. "Isn't that worth living as Isaac forever?"

"Your father will expect you to be married within the year," Stackton sputters, so close to falling within my grasp. "It won't matter should you win or lose, caught or not. You could never hide your fellowship from a husband."

I pull a letter from the pocket at my breast and slide it across the table toward him. "Grandmother has a plan for that."

He doesn't touch the letter, though I know he is dying to. Neither of us says anything for a long moment. His eyes are glued to the letter and my lower lip trembles, entirely of its own accord. When his gaze does meet mine again, he smiles.

"You remind me of your mother."

I blink, mouth falling open. "You knew Elena?"

He ignores my question and leans back. "Let us talk specifics after I refill my flask."

Stackton's gaze is not nearly so warm now, though. He asks, "What do you want?"

"Advice." I don't wait for an invitation, sweeping into the sitting room and plopping down on the familiar floral love seat.

"That's what my office hours are for, Mr. Holland." He follows me into the room, harrumphing with each step, and snaps the door shut behind him. He spins around, pinning me with a shrewd glare. "Now, want to tell me why you disobeyed my strict orders, not least of which was to stay away from Sherlock Holmes?"

CHAPTER 17

The Bullingdon Club

O NE UPSIDE TO PROSTHETIC NOSES IS THAT I CAN'T SMELL A damn thing.

The scents of smoke and ale that normally overpower the Turf are entirely obscured by my mustache and fake nose.

While I wait for Holmes's arrival, I'm second-guessing whether to reveal what I know to him. I have yet to discern why he didn't tell me about the meeting in the church. But this is his last chance to share with me what he's learned. If he doesn't, I take on the Bullingdon Club alone.

I need to find a way to infiltrate the club and see if there's any true reasoning behind the brands, or if they are mere distraction. Someone could be trying to pin the blame on the richest, most powerful men at Oxford.

A waitress slides a bowl of chowder in front of me, and when I look up through the steam, Holmes sits across the table.

He leans back, kicking immaculately shined shoes onto the

table. His too-keen gaze assesses me. "Why do you wear that hat so often?"

"I'm balding prematurely." The lie comes easily. I wave a wooden spoon in the air. "It's a good thing Ermy has a taste for older men."

"Oh, I highly doubt the Duck of Bedford's daughter has a taste for anything other than money." Something I don't care for sparkles in the back of Holmes's eyes.

It takes me a moment to recognize that he *wants* me to feel uncomfortable, to distract him by offering him something more delectable to chew on. Two can play at that game.

"So...was Moriarty happy to see you at Bartlemas?" I take a giant slurp of chowder. My grandmother would be disgusted by my manners right now.

Holmes looks just as appalled. Lip curled back and skin taking on a green tinge, he waves down the waitress. "Were you there, too? We could have all gone to get a drink together afterward."

"Alas, my hands were quite full last night." I flash him the same lecherous grin I've seen on my brother's face too many times.

Holmes takes a prim sip of beer and grimaces. "This stuff is ghastly. I should have ordered wine."

"I'd take a good mug of beer before a glass of wine any day," I say honestly, watching him carefully. "So, what did you learn?"

"I was awarded for my efforts with more questions than answers, and a splitting headache in the morning."

"You and Moriarty toast over too many bottles of wine afterward?" I arch Isaac's bushy eyebrows and take another hearty spoonful of chowder.

"Quite the contrary. I think the bastard drugged me."

I nearly choke on my soup. "That would raise a lot of questions for most people."

I'd come to the same conclusion, but I can't say as much without revealing my own complicity, having dragged his flailing body from the chapel.

A drug that causes intense hallucinations and, judging from my own symptoms, debilitating nausea, acute cerebral pain, and dizziness. Like a hangover straight from hell.

"Someone else was in the chapel last night. Their wet footprints gave them away." Oblivious to the spiraling chain of my thoughts, Holmes continues, "Boots of expensive make. Pointed toe, square heel, size four."

"You can discern all that from half-melted prints?" My shock roots me to my seat. Sherlock must have gone back to Bartlemas, or passed out in the grass from the drug and woke up surrounded by all the evidence my foolishness left behind. "Do you think they were working with Moriarty?"

He shakes his head, his eyes glazed and his focus far beyond the Turf.

"They are not the culprit. Otherwise, they would have left me to overdose on the hallucinogen."

I nod with understanding, perhaps a touch too eagerly. "Moriarty must have other enemies."

"There was a fog that filled the church after Moriarty left." Holmes takes another sip from his beer, lip curling in revulsion. "At first, I suspected nothing of it, my focus entirely on the dead body before me. But then a bat started swooping at my head, and screams rent the air. Then more than bats started falling from the sky, the ceiling of the church broken wide to reveal a black abyss above me. I remember climbing on the table and hitting a man after falling, before I was pulled to the ground. By her."

Shards of ice flood my veins. "By whom?"

"Irene Adler."

The way he says my name, like a lover between the sheets, with more than a hint of malice, makes me shiver.

I hide my reaction around another mouthful of chowder. "Are you sure it was Miss Adler?"

"I would recognize that face anywhere."

Obviously not.

I cough, taking a hearty sip of beer. "But you said that you were drugged? Perhaps she was a hallucination?" In an effort to turn his suspicions even further away, I venture, "Are you sure these were hallucinations at all? Isn't that chapel said to be haunted?"

Holmes looks more disgusted with me than with the beer.

"Maybe they were all ghosts?" I chuckle.

"Do you ever take anything seriously, Holland?"

I level my dripping spoon at him, delighting in the disgust curling his lips. "About as seriously as you seem to be taking this partnership, Holmes. Why go gallivanting after Moriarty and not bring me?"

He's silent for a long moment, swirling the dark ale around and around. "Trust doesn't come easily to me. It never will."

You seem to trust that John Watson, though, I don't say aloud.

"Besides, trusting you would have done little except get you drugged as well." He sighs before chugging the ale down to the dredges. Slamming the pint on the table, he wipes his mouth with the back of a hand. "And leave you wondering if Moriarty is actually the murderer."

I lean across the table, pitching my voice low. "Why would Moriarty search for clues about the murderer if he *is* the murderer?"

Holmes waits for the waitress now refilling his drink to leave before answering. "Maybe to cover his tracks? He killed his own informant, Holland."

My mother would be proud of my acting talents. I can feel my face blanching with shock, and my mouth drops open. "You saw him kill another man?"

"No," he says, pressing his lips in a firm line. "But I saw the body, and Moriarty was the last one in contact with the man."

I lean back. "It's a good thing you're not a detective, because that evidence is hardly damning. Not enough to put him behind bars, at the very least."

Though I suspected as much myself. In order to be sure, I would have to go back to the church and examine the confessional, but returning to the scene of a crime is about as stupid as they come. My footprints are all over that church, as Holmes said, and I have a sneaking suspicion that I've left my scarf there.

"It just doesn't make sense." Holmes plants his elbows on the table, head in his hands. "The pieces are all here, but none fit to complete the puzzle."

"Maybe there's more than one puzzle."

Holmes looks up. "What the devil are you talking about?"

"Maybe not all the deaths are related. The murder you witnessed and those of our classmates. And you being drugged." And my experiment being maliciously ruined, I don't add. Trivial, honestly.

He leans back in his seat, considering the ceiling with a petulant frown. "And what do you have to contribute to this partnership? Have you learned anything yet about the brands?"

I refrain from asking when we had divvied out tasks like schoolwork to be completed during a holiday. My nose twitches beneath the prosthetic. I could tell him what I've learned, but that would risk being left in the dark again. I consider Holmes sitting across from me, dressed in fine navy suede, and another thought crosses my mind. Isaac Holland might not be considered a candidate for the Bullingdon Club.

But the indeterminately wealthy Sherlock Holmes might be.

"Much like these clues, the brands are all pieces of a puzzle."

"Groundbreaking, Holland. I can see why you're among the All Souls cohort," Holmes drawls, rolling his eyes.

My grades are better than yours, bastard. "Can you close your big gob for a single second? It's no wonder you've had zero luck with Miss Adler."

His mouth snaps shut with an audible click of his teeth.

"Now, these brands, they're all pieces of a club symbol. One long lived on Oxford campus."

He's glaring at me now. A muscle in his jaw twitches. "Go on."

"A club known for having the wildest parties and only the richest Brits as members."

"And you know what club this is?"

"It's a wonder how you don't. How did *you* manage to score a seat among the All Souls cohort, Holmes?"

"Oh, blast it all, Holland! Spit it out!"

I grin. "The Bullingdon Club."

"And why, Holland, do you believe that the Bullingdon Club will accept me so readily into their ranks?" Sherlock strides ahead of me, hands tucked into his pockets and red scarf trailing in the morning breeze.

It takes three of my steps to meet a single one of his long-legged strides. I huff, my breath spiraling in the air above my face. He knows full well why the Bullingdon Club would accept him among their number and not me; he just likes to hear me say it.

"Because your family is wealthy, to put it bluntly, and mine is not." I smile beneath my newly trimmed fake mustache. "It definitely isn't because you're a likable fellow."

Holmes is aghast. "I'm a very likable fellow."

I follow him into the classroom, ducking my head to avoid Moriarty's keen gaze.

Holmes turns in his seat to face me and whispers, "How does one even garner an invitation to this club?"

Moriarty's head cocks ever so slightly in our direction.

"Let's discuss this later," I hiss, pulling out my textbooks, acutely aware of the way my brother's eyes flick between us.

Before we part ways after class, Holmes and I make plans to study—and discuss how to infiltrate the Bullingdon Club—that evening in our dormitory. But as I walk toward the Lady Margaret dorms, my head spins with doubts. I should heed Stackton's advice and stay far away from Sherlock Holmes, not simply because he's my steepest competition, but also because the more time I spend with him, the more likely he is to see right through this disguise.

But he's also my surest way into the ranks of the Bullingdon Club. Or at least that's what I'm going to tell myself.

Definitely not because he's one of the most interesting men I know.

No, definitely not.

Shaking my head, I cross the quad's wet grass, an inch of snow still holding on and soaking Isaac Holland's already threadbare shoes. The wind tousles the curls of my wig. I'm tempted to hold the cap to my head, turning slightly to make sure nobody watches, when a figure dressed in forest green disappears around a corner just behind me.

Moran presses on my heels.

I smile to myself, whistling a jaunty tune. I turn in the opposite direction of Lady Margaret. He follows me across the quad and around each building, and whenever I turn, his tall, dark hat slips behind the nearest corner.

Poor fool.

We pass the Centenary Gate and I loop back around, feet well and truly soaked now. Moran pays no heed to where we're at, focused only on not losing sight of me. I cross an outdoor corridor, leaping through the arches with a dark laugh. Moran's pressing closer now.

We're nearly there. I cross a final yard and Moran is so close I can hear his heavy breathing. If he knew where we were, he wouldn't dare follow.

We're a handful of meters from Lady Margaret. I bend, scooping a handful of snow and packing it hard, making sure to collect some rocks and dirt in there as well.

And toss it over my shoulder at Miss Allen's window.

Moran curses. I'm already in the shadows, long from view when the headmistress leans from her window and sees Moriarty's henchman.

"You, again?" Miss Allen curses in not just one language, but four. She waves her arms, leaning so far out her window it's a wonder she doesn't fly. "Wait right there. If you move a single muscle, I'm reporting you to each and every dean."

I'm crouched in a shadowed corner when she bursts from the doorway a moment later.

Lord help the man caught by Mistress Allen.

My cheer rapidly dissipates, however, when I enter the room I share with Sherlock and find two letters waiting for me on my bed. One is attached to a soft brown package. After making sure that my door is locked, I open the letter first.

Thought you might want this back

I don't recognize the scrawl, but I know all too well that it isn't difficult to feign another's handwriting. I set aside the letter and peel back the rough brown wrapping. The breath is stolen from my lungs.

My scarf, stiff with mud, falls to the floor. The sickly sweet smell of Bartlemas Chapel lingers in the woolen threads.

I collapse on the edge of my bed and take up the other letter. This one smells of lavender and is of heavy, expensive paper. My thumb passes over the navy seal, a man astride a horse.

An invitation to the Bullingdon Club's first meeting, in a

chicken-scratch scrawl I don't recognize, either, not at all similar to the first note. No date, time, or location. Below the seal, drawn in blue ink, are three images.

A teacup, a lamb, and a flag blowing in the breeze.

I pick up the first letter and brown packaging paper, sniffing both. The strange fog. The hair on the back of my neck rises. I've smelled it somewhere else before, but don't know where.

CHAPTER 18

Black Embroidered Roses

THREE PRESSING CONCERNS NAG AT ME LIKE KNIFE-SHARP thorns in my side as I sit in class.

First, that scent. I'd smelled it before that night in the chapel, but no matter how hard I rack my traitorous memory, it evades me.

My second concern. What happened to the body that we left in the church? If my scarf was found there by whoever delivered it to my room, and that someone somehow knew that it was mine, I could be a suspect to murder.

I make sure to follow Stackton's erratic notes on the board. I'm on the opposite side of the classroom as Holmes, acutely aware of Stackton's suspicious glare bouncing between the two of us, Moriarty's keen eyes, and Holmes trying to catch my attention by wagging his eyebrows at me every other minute.

I nod when Stackton points my way, my attention focused anywhere but on him, and he knows it. I press too hard on my quill, splattering ink across my notes, and I curse colorfully under my breath.

"Questions?" Stackton's glasses slide down his nose, and he fixes us all with a shrewd glare over their rims. "These concepts too difficult for you all?"

A smarter woman would know when to keep her mouth shut. I raise a hand. "Not too difficult, Professor, though I will admit some slight confusion on my part."

"This should be good," Stackton mutters. "Whatever is there to be confused about, Mr. Holland? The facts here are quite elementary."

I point my ruined quill at the board. "You pointed out that interstitial growth is replaced with appositional cartilage growth after puberty."

"I know what I just said." He raps on the board with a ruler. "I've written it myself."

"Indeed, you have, Professor." A slight smile pulls at my lips. "But interstitial growth still occurs after puberty." Stackton sputters, and I continue, "Even after death."

There is no chuckling in the classroom now.

"Holland is correct." His sharp voice, like a touch of frost, sends shivers down my spine.

Turning in my seat, I meet my brother's glacial eyes before he turns to Stackton, a wicked grin curling his lips. "Our jaws continue growing for our entire life, and our noses, too."

"Are you suggesting that you have more than one nose, Moriarty?" Sherlock says, leaning back in his seat. "One brown, the other where it doesn't belong?"

Moriarty's head snaps in his direction, and though I cannot see his face, the rage emanating off my brother is scalding.

"I will not have my class disrupted by petty squabbles over semantics," Stackton says, voice rising. "You can all thank Mr.

Holland for an extra twenty pages of reading due tomorrow." A collective groan from the class makes me shrink in my seat. "On the differences between appositional and interstitial growth, since my lecture seems to be lacking on the subject."

The bell tolls in the distance, drawing us from our seats. But before the nearest of my number can reach the door, Stackton meets my eyes and says, "Let this be a lesson to all of you."

"How melodramatic, Professor," Moriarty drawls. "I'm sure my father would love to hear about your petty threats."

"I always knew nepotism factored into your acceptance to the All Souls cohort"—Sherlock steps around his desk, stopping close enough to Moriarty that their chests almost brush—"but I never thought to hear you admit it so openly."

"Get. Out!" Stackton slams his fists on the desk. "Get out of my classroom now!"

Moriarty cuts me off before I can leave, bracing a hand on the doorframe. Holmes meets my eyes over my brother's arm.

"Holland," James says, my other name like a tart lemon on his tongue. "I do hope to see you outside of class soon."

"Why would I see you?" I duck beneath his arm and stride down the hallway. I'll be late for Chatham's class—again. Moriarty follows on my heels. "Did we have a dinner date that I'd forgotten about? Just a warning, I'm deathly allergic to strawberries."

"As a matter of fact, yes."

I jerk to a halt and turn slowly to face James. Standing so close to him, I'm daring fate.

I swallow. His gaze drops to my throat and his eyes narrow. "My father is hosting a dinner for our cohort at his town house. You would be remiss to skip it."

"I'll check my calendar," I say with a sneer before spinning on my heel. "But don't wait up for me if I can't make it, Moriarty. I wouldn't want to keep you past your bedtime."

His eyes are blazes of frostbite between my shoulder blades, following me down the hallway. Which leads me to my third pressing concern.

My brother knows that I was in the church with him. Only two men in all of England know that that scarf is mine, a red wool with black embroidered roses, because it once belonged to our grandmother.

CHAPTER 19

The Haunting of the Bodleian

THE FIRST STEP TO INFILTRATING THE BULLINGDON CLUB is, frustratingly, to discern where the Bullingdon Club meets. Over the last hundred years, members of the infamous club have cleared out any trace of themselves from the libraries on campus. I run my gloved fingers over the spines of Codrington's numerous texts. It would take all my life to check every library, every shelf and stack of books on campus. Even batting my eyelashes and sharing my demure smile with all the librarians to turn onto my pressing task had proved fruitless. All leads have come up dry.

Holmes has of course proven useless in this regard. He probably already knows what to do but finds it fun to watch me act a fool.

I glance down to the main floor, scanning the tables that are once again packed with students. The surest way, short of academic research, into the Bullingdon Club would be to follow one of its members.

My suspect browses the shelves, pulling books down and placing them in a neat stack. Carlisle Gillingham jumps when I appear at his elbow, dropping a book. I bend to collect it, making sure that my curls fall over my shoulder, and his scowl quickly falls away when he recognizes me.

Carlisle, a lord about to inherit a substantial fortune, with more land and friends than should be legally allowed. If any of my classmates are members of the Bullingdon Club, he's the most likely.

He's also devastatingly handsome.

"And what have I done to deserve such fine company?" He wets his lips. "You should know that your brother has warned most of us against even speaking to you."

I cock my head and look up at him through my lashes. "But you don't care what my brother says."

"Indeed." He tips the spine of a book. "What can I do for the lovely Lady Moriarty?"

"Irene," I say, too quickly. "You can call me Irene, Lord Gillingham."

Carlisle smirks, as if in on some joke. He reaches out and brushes a curl from my face. "I prefer Irene."

My name on his tongue does not sit quite so nicely as it does on another.

I force a smile. "If you behave like a gentleman, you can continue to call me Irene."

"I'll make note of that." He leans an elbow on the shelf. "If you are anything like your brother, though, you want something."

"Nothing besides your lovely company." I mimic his posture, grinning.

I'm nothing like my brother.

"Well, if it's my company you desire, I can happily oblige." Carlisle's smile widens, revealing dimples. "Perhaps a ride this Sunday on my phaeton?"

If the activities of the Bullingdon Club are as raucous as they say, it is unlikely they occur the evening before classes. "What about Saturday? I have plans with the ladies on Sunday."

He opens his mouth, as though to readily accept, then presses his lips together in a firm line. "Saturday won't work, I'm afraid. I have plans with the lads."

I pout, freshly painted red lips capturing his attention. "We'll resign ourselves, then, to another time. Perhaps the next time we speak, our ledgers won't be quite so full."

Carlisle takes my gloved hand and lays a gentle kiss upon its back. "I'll make sure to clear my schedule."

I turn, dragging my hand along the row of spines as I walk away, aware of his gaze on me with every step. A smile tugs at my lips.

I have the when, now all I need is the where.

Sitting at my desk, I cock my head, examining the map before me. I've spent enough time at the Turf to know that my favorite haunt is not the Bullingdon Club's choice. But that left close to forty different possibilities.

The Bullingdon Club, according to rumor, prefers to meet in establishments of relative luxury, but is banned from most bars, inns, and even theaters. Some places have never even seen a hair of the Bullingdon Club, and others would burn down the entire school should a member step foot in their doorway again. Far too many coins—stolen from James, not mine—slid across counters to chatty bartenders later, and I've narrowed down the list to three different pubs, two taverns, and a single teahouse, and—I check the clock above my bed—with only three hours left to find the one I'm looking for.

Holmes is going to meet Isaac in the library less than an hour for the name of the meeting place in question, and Geraldine expects me at her town house in two hours for tea. Without enough time to slink back to my rooms and change after my meeting with Holmes, I stuff my dinner dress and corset into a small bag that now hangs on the back of my door. I'll have to rush into a lavatory on campus and hope nobody notices a man walk in and a woman walk out. I curse colorfully under my breath and rest my chin on a fist.

There is something queer about the places that have been crossed off, though I can't quite put my finger on what. Which irritates me much more than I care to admit.

The wind rattles my windows, a late-autumn gale that will undoubtedly threaten to tear Isaac's wig from my head. I stand, reaching across my bed to make sure that the windows are fastened shut. A golden head crossing the quad catches my attention, his long, assured strides as known to me as my own.

There's another person I could easily follow who will lead me to the Bullingdon Club's next meeting. My brother will undoubtedly have an invitation, grandfathered in if the seals in our father's desk are any indication.

I could also simply follow Carlisle, but I don't know his whereabouts, nor his schedule. If I am to understand the Bullingdon Club, truly understand their machinations and why their seal is being branded in parts on my murdered classmates, I would need a man inside the club, not just my ear on their door.

I turn back to the map and trace a finger over the places crossed off, falling in a straight line down the page. My hand jerks to a halt.

I turn the map sideways and my mouth drops open. The Bullingdon Club kept their activities strictly to the north end of Oxford. Not a single bartender, manager, waitress, or scullery maid had seen them in southern Oxfordshire.

That leaves only two places left to choose from: a mangy pub or a teahouse. Grinding my teeth, I force myself to admit one terrible, dreadful, annoying thing.

That I might just need Sherlock's help figuring this out.

The crisp November air smells of cedar and nutmeg. Normally, such smells would delight me, but I've been wrestling with a poor stomach for the better part of this week.

Holmes doesn't look up as I march across Selden End toward his table. The wind rattles the tall windows behind him, waving the tree branches beyond so that their shadows flail and twist in the sconces' golden glow. His face is long and gaunt, as if he shares my uneasy stomach.

"You're late," he says, checking the watch hanging from his breast pocket. The hands are made of gold and the face of pearlescent green, with no noticeable wind, and there's an inscription on the back of the case. He snaps it shut before I can make out what it says.

"Some of us have social obligations, Holmes," I say, hands gripping the back of a seat hard enough to turn my knuckles white.

He scoffs, making me rankle, and continues to read. "You are looking too hard, Holland. Did you not see those images at the bottom of the invitation?"

"Of course I did," I bite out, falling into my seat with a huff. "A lamb, a flag, and a—"

"Teacup." Holmes flips another page. "That is where we are to meet."

"That's ridic..." I bite back a growl of frustration.

The Lamb and Flag. A teahouse known for its impeccable decor, delightful cucumber sandwiches, and high-end clientele.

Hopefully, my *friend* understands the clue better than I did.

"Really, Holland? Don't make me regret choosing you as a study partner." Holmes grins crookedly at me.

My nails bite into my palms. I don't understand why this man gets under my skin so easily. What is it about Sherlock Holmes that both intrigues me and infuriates me in equal measure?

"How you have any friends is a feat unto Sisyphus and his boulder," I mutter.

He gives me a tight-lipped smile. "Ask yourself why you're friends with me, and we can perhaps answer your query there."

"I wasn't talking about myself. I was talking about that poor John Watson character." I drag a book across the table and flip it open.

I'm flipping through the pages, teeth still grinding, for many moments before I notice the utmost stillness that has overtaken the entire library. I look up and am immediately slack-jawed. I ease back in my seat, wary of the dark fire in Holmes's black eyes.

"How do you know about my friendship with Watson?" he growls out.

My mouth opens and closes around a litany of excuses. He'll see through them all.

"Was it some kind of secret?" I ask with painfully forced nonchalance, waving a hand through the air.

Slowly, like a panther stalking its prey, Holmes eases from his seat. The sconces in the library are lit, painting his face in harsh shades of black and amber, making his expression all the more terrifying.

If I could melt into the floor, I would. My voice is even further diminished when I ask again, "Was it a secret? Why would it even matter?"

"Because every shred of humanity is a weakness to these people. Something that can be used against us. Are you saying that your carefully blank background is not purposeful?" When I don't—*cannot*—respond, he plants steepled fingers on the table and leans across. "So, I'll only ask once more. How do you know about my friendship with John Watson?"

I open my mouth to do what I seem to do best—lie. He eases farther forward, the sconces flickering and bathing his face in shadow.

That's not the sconces. I leap to my feet. Holmes is jerked back by two black-gloved hands on either shoulder, a bag thrown over his head. I spin around, leaping for the entryway. Something cracks into my temple, and I sprawl to the floor. Someone chuckles from above. The ghosts of Oxford must take delight in this.

A black canvas bag slips over my face and I'm jerked back to my feet. Cold words whisper in my ear.

"The Bullingdon Club has come to collect."

CHAPTER 20

A Bloody Initiation

I'M GOING TO MISS MY TEA WITH GERALDINE.

Someone claps and a deep timbre cuts through the air. "Are we ready to greet the new recruits, lads?"

I'd let them lead me blind through the streets of Oxford, memorizing turn after turn, each river we crossed over and the way the shadows deepened through the black bag over my head when they turned us down alleys. Holmes is at my elbow, stumbling occasionally as our captors take no care to help us over sidewalks or lumpy cobblestones.

Finally, a bell tinkled above, and we were led through one doorway, then the telltale gust of air told me that we passed through another.

I will my shoulders to not tremble. None of these men would show their fear. Irene Adler might see the strength in acknowledging each emotion, but to these men... any bare-faced emotion on Isaac's is a weakness.

I've heard all the stories imaginable about the infamous hazing of the Bullingdon Club. Swimming up the Thames. Breaking into the chancellor's house. Stealing test rubrics.

Streaking across campus.

If they demand I do anything wearing less than a shirt and pants, I'll have to quit this game. But that will no doubt elicit their curiosity. And the curiosity of young, self-important men is perhaps the most dangerous of all.

The trembling is uncontrollable now. A heavy arm drapes over my shoulder, guiding me along. Feeling my furious shaking, a man chuckles in my ear.

"Scared, Holland?" he whispers. I recognize the illustrious accent as Carlisle's. "You should be."

I clamp down on the fear with a viselike grip.

The fear held me for long enough, though, for me to lose count of my steps and fail to mark the direction I'm led. I recognize immediately when we're in a new room, the space suddenly warmer and the air smokier. Sweat slides down my spine, making the corset pinch my tender skin. Hands clamp on my shoulders and force me down onto a wicker chair. My knee knocks someone's in the chair beside mine. The bag is ripped away.

The sudden brightness makes me blink. A large room with blue-painted walls, lit by a dozen sconces, greets my watering eyes. There's a large oak table in the center, around which four men sit with black canvas bags on their heads, beside another four like me without. And standing, a dozen or so men surround us. Their brocades are unbuttoned, beer sloshing on their fronts and the floor.

"Here they are!" Carlisle's grin is both wicked and lovely as he swaggers around the table. Gone is the suave gentleman who wooed Irene.

A few of his pals chuckle in a corner. Avery Williams, another of my cohort, steps into the room, his dark hair curling atop his pale collarbone as he sloshes beer onto the floor.

Oxford's finest.

Avery drips more beer onto the shoulders of the lad sitting at the table before him. He jostles for the fifth position in All Souls and, despite the mess he's making, the shrewdness of his green eyes betrays him as the most sober one in attendance. Making a mental note to watch him carefully, I shift my attention to around the table.

My throat clenches, suddenly dry. Edgar Hayward stands behind a hooded figure, arms crossed over his chest. Disappointment is a frog lodged in the back of my throat. Geraldine would have a fit if she knew of his involvement with the club. Beside me, the silver filigree of Moriarty's jacket catches the light, as does the family ring on the middle knuckle of his right hand, an onyx eagle blazoned across it. I blink again, and his face is clearer, his grin bared for all here to see. To his left, shoulders hunched and recognizable despite the hood over his head, is the burly form of Moran. Across from us sits Holmes and, to his right, a hood is ripped away to reveal a figure entirely unexpected.

His wrists bound behind his chair, familiar gray uniform crumpled, John Watson strains against the hands pressing him firmly down, a gag bearing into his mouth.

The Bullingdon Club laughs hysterically. They clink their mugs together, downing the last of their beers. Holmes's face is a blank mask.

Carlisle slams his mug down on the table before Watson. "Time for a show, lads!"

My trembling begins anew. I'm all too aware of the worn corset stays keeping my curves hidden, the clip that digs into my scalp and just barely keeps my wig in place, and the sweat dripping down my temples, threatening to wash away the makeup concealing the small birthmark below my eye. Moriarty sneers at the men around him, nose upturned. "Did you manage to drink any of the beer, or did you just spill the entirety of it down the front of my finest suit?"

Avery's fist, quick as a viper, lashes out. It catches my brother across the jaw. His head snaps to the side. I flinch, heart thundering in my chest.

"Took the words right out of my mouth, Moriarty," Holmes says, looking to each man standing around him, likely memorizing each of their faces. He only barely meets my gaze before turning next to Carlisle, now leering above me. He's rewarded with a similar blow. Holmes spits blood onto the table and asks, "Do you regularly beat each other, or do Moriarty and I just have faces that beg for it?"

"My handsome face begs for it, Holmes." Moriarty leans back, and I roll my eyes. "You, on the other hand, just have to speak, and anyone within hearing distance longs to knock the legs right out from under your chair."

Edgar releases the gag from Watson's mouth, and he's already roaring before it falls to the ground.

"What do you bastards want with me?" He's loud enough to make the windows tremble.

"What the bloody hell are you doing here?" Holmes asks, aghast.

"I could ask the same of you," Watson retorts. "Where the hell are we?"

James and I must not have been the only ones to notice the

familiarity between Holmes and Watson. Either when he came to class to question me with the inspector, or perhaps when Bertram's body was found in the library. Or perhaps even another time I wasn't privy to. The club no doubt has spies in every corner of Oxford.

"The lair of the Bullingdon Club." Holmes rests his head against the back of his chair. "The Lamb and Flag, to be precise." He looks to Carlisle. "If you include the location on the invitation, why are the bags over our heads necessary?"

This elicits another punch. He'll be lucky to keep all his teeth by this meeting's end.

"We have brought you all here today, along with the most valuable people in some of your lives," Carlisle says, grinning crookedly, "to prove your dedication to the club."

Carlisle circles the table until he's behind Watson, and rests his hands on the officer's shoulders. He doesn't care if Watson recognizes him, remembers his face or name. Such is the prize of power. Watson could sooner arrest the queen than Carlisle Gillingham, easily the most powerful student at Oxford.

His gaze falls to me, and his smile widens. "Now you." He points at my face, making my heart trip a beat. "You were accepted into the All Souls for some reason. Not your wealth, nor family. Our spies can learn nothing about you save your name. A file so purposefully empty must be hiding something."

I bite my tongue, a snarky response itching to leave my mouth.

Holmes's nostrils flare. "Could Holland's invitation perhaps have been because he's top of our class?"

It takes everything in me not to turn and stare. How could he know that?

The door is kicked open and a servant stalks into the room... bearing a tray of raw meat.

Intestines hang from the silver platter, dripping blood on the wooden floor. Flies swarm the carcass. The stench turns my stomach.

Plates and elegant silverware are set before the men at the table. One member walks behind them, scooping heaping spoonfuls of the vile meat onto each of their plates. One of the invitees sitting closest to me heaves. Edgar, bless him, turns a sickly shade of green and covers his mouth.

"Will that be all, Lord Gillingham?" the waiter asks, a small smile curling the corner of his mouth.

"Are you enjoying this?" I demand, then snap my mouth shut.

"No, my lad." Carlisle claps the server on the back and tucks a handful of notes in the man's breast pocket. "I've left a tab open at the Red Negligee on Southside. Treat yourself and the fine owners of this establishment to some treats. Courtesy of the Gillinghams."

A brothel. I've heard the Red Negligee name only once, when some of my classmates had been crowing one morning before class about a "delightful" evening there. With a grin, the server leads his coworkers from the room.

"What the bloody hell is wrong with you people up at that school?" Watson's face is a particularly dark shade of magenta. He shoves his chair away from the table.

Avery shoves it right back in, mugs and plates tinkling from the brute force. Crystal glasses are set before each man, filled with a liquid too dark to be wine. Carlisle straddles a seat at the end of the table. He raises one glass for a toast.

"To the club, and those brave enough to join us."

"To the Bullingdon Club," Avery says, thin-lipped smile reminding me of a snake. "May our enemies quiver in their saddles and our arrows find their tainted throats. Where the blood runs true and the bonds may never die."

No doubt they're talking about their bloodlines. These men are vile. Any number of them could be killers.

Disgust turns my stomach, and not just from the rotting meat on the table.

"Enough chatter—let's get the games started," my classmate Robert Lancaster says, practically drooling at the idea of torturing us.

My heart leaps into my throat, but Carlise points to Holmes. "Gag him if another smart-ass comment comes from his mouth."

Holmes has the gall to waggle his eyebrows.

Glass still raised, Carlisle continues, "The rules are simple. Answer our questions, and you're rewarded with a drink. Refuse, and you must serve your companion his dinner. Once the plates are cleared, we learn who amongst us has the balls to join us."

It's an effort not to scoff. I'll never understand why men hold up their testicles, easily the most sensitive, weakest parts of their bodies, as a torch of strength.

Avery turns to a man at the end. "My lad Jenson, your father has been raking in quite large sums as of late but has called in the majority of his ships to dock." He claps the lad on the back hard enough to sting. "Tell me, how is it your father is so impossibly wealthy without the manpower out there to amass it?"

My brows draw together. What a curious question. Why would

Avery, or even Carlisle, with more wealth than God, care about Jenson's ships?

After a moment's hesitation, Jenson reaches for the crystalline glass. "My father has the pockets of the East India Company. Much of their business is done at his direction because of the ears he has in the palace."

My mouth pops open. The man just gave up his own father.

Just when my mouth couldn't drop any lower, Avery waves a flippant hand. "How can we entrust our secrets to you if you won't even keep those of your family safe? Take Jenson out back and let him stew for a bit while we decide what to do with him."

Jenson is dragged kicking and screaming from his chair through a door at the far end of the room. His howls of disbelief are firmly silenced by the slamming of the door.

"Now, Holmes." Carlisle shifts in his chair to face him once the door clicks shut. "Tell me where I can find the blueprints for your father's latest invention?" Holmes's face turns a sickly shade of green, and Lord Gillingham continues. "You know, the one your father brought to the palace just last week."

Holmes presses his lips in a firm line, and Carlisle's eyes drop to the plate before him.

"If you won't answer me," he says, "you'll have to feed your dear friend."

These fools. To kidnap an officer proves they either have shit for brains, or they're drunk on power and wealth.

Watson struggles against his binds once more and says exactly what I'm thinking. "You are all idiots to apprehend a member of the Yard, during an active murder investigation no less. When my superiors hear what you've done, they'll have all your families dragged behind bars."

His head is forcibly whipped back, and his eyes are so wide, the whites shine in the candlelight.

Carlisle thrums his thumbs on the arms of his chair. "The club has eyes and ears everywhere. As well as hands in many pockets. How do you think we knew where you'd be? Who you've been talking to? Were you not the least bit suspicious when your fellow officers, ones who have never given you the time of day before, invited you out for drinks tonight?" He chuckles, the corner of his mouth curling. "Is having Sherlock Holmes as a companion so middling that you were willing to overlook the queer nature of such an invitation?"

Watson's glare could flay a hare. "Holmes, cut me loose and let's leave these bastards behind."

But Holmes's gaze has likewise dropped to the plate before him. His hand inches toward the silver spoon.

"Holmes?" Watson's eyes are suddenly pleading. "Cut me loose. Why are you even with these men?"

His friend takes up the spoon, scooping a heaping portion of blood and raw flesh. "You couldn't even begin to understand, Watson."

"Try me." He bares his teeth, pulse throbbing in his neck.

"You couldn't begin to understand," Holmes says again, voice wooden. "Because you are nothing more than a commoner, and commoners deserve to eat filth."

Before anyone can blink, he shoves the spoon toward Watson's mouth. John flings himself backward. His chair crashes to the floor.

The wood shatters beneath his weight. One arm free, Watson spins to release the other.

All the air rushes from my lungs in a great gasp. The men in the room are too distracted to take note of the decidedly feminine note, thankfully, as they drag Watson to his feet. He doesn't go without a fight, though. His free hand swings, fist catching Carlisle's jaw. A lot of muffled cursing amid a scuffle ensues, silverware clattering and a plate shattering, but my focus is solely on Sherlock Holmes. A tic forms in his stubbled jaw, but his face is otherwise unreadable.

Watson's knees slam the floor beside his friend, his face red as he glares daggers at Holmes. Blood drips from the corner of Watson's mouth onto his uniform.

"You rutting bastard," Watson yells, before his mouth is forcibly opened. Robert presses fingers thick as sausages into his cheeks, peeling back Watson's lips and revealing his teeth. Watson struggles again against the hands that hold him down. He violently convulses, shoving himself up from the floor. He roars, "You're no friend of mine!"

Holmes jerks back as though slapped. Watson spits blood at his feet.

His efforts are rewarded with a punch. Watson's entire head whips to the side, blood spattering the hardwood floor. Holmes's normally tan skin has taken on a sickly pale.

Carlisle, plate raised high, brings it crashing down onto the back of Watson's head.

He collapses to the floor. He's so still, I bite my cheek to keep from calling out for help. Carlisle claps Holmes on the back with a loud whoop. "Well done, mate. Welcome to the Bullingdon Club."

"This is vile, Carlisle." Edgar moves to check Watson's pulse. Geraldine's brother shares his sister's golden curls and pale skin, which have blanched impossibly further. "Surely we can think of another way to test their mettle."

"Weak stomach, Hayward?" Carlisle shakes his head.

"Perhaps I just don't believe that this will inspire the loyalty in our recruits that we desire."

Something dark shutters behind Carlisle's eyes. "If you really feel that way, then you can follow Jenson out the door."

Edgar looks to each of the other members, eyes beseeching. But he elicits no feeling from any of them. With a resigned shake of his head, he turns for the door. His hand rests on the handle, and he turns to the Bullingdon Club. "What madness have we plummeted to?"

There is no doubt in my mind that Shakespeare wrote of madness when he said, *"What a piece of work is a man."*

When Carlisle's back is turned, his focus on the next club hopeful, Holmes reaches a shaking hand down to his friend's—former friend's—neck and breathes a sigh of relief. No blood pours from the back of Watson's head, and his back rises and falls, albeit slowly. Just knocked unconscious.

Carlisle's grin is acid-laced when he turns to Moriarty. "Are the rumors true? Is Irene really the daughter of the courtesan Elena Adler?"

I clench my jaw to keep my mouth from falling open.

James barks a laugh. "Truly? You could ask me anything and instead you inquire about my sister? Might as well cut my binds and end this charade now, because if you wanted to know about Irene, all you had to do was ask."

Carlisle waves a flippant hand. "Irene's parentage is only the start of our questioning. I simply want to make sure I'm not rolling in the mud by courting her."

Sherlock hisses between clenched teeth.

My brother's icy eyes dart from him to Watson's limp form, and then to Carlisle and the door Jenson was dragged through. "I'm trying to understand your logic, Lord Gillingham. Truly I am. Either I tell you my father's secrets and get punished for it, or I don't, and dear Moran here will eat pig guts for it."

"Sounds like you understand me completely."

"What I don't understand, then, is why I should do either, or even with candor."

"He never intended for Jenson to be a Bullingdon Club member," Holmes says. "He just wants the valuable information we have."

Moriarty purses his lips. "Did you really think that Oxford's brightest scholars would not see through your pitiful plan?"

Carlisle plants his hands on the table, glaring at both Holmes and Moriarty before turning to me with an unimpressed look. The floor threatens to swallow me whole.

A burly young man rushes into the room, bearing a tray laden with overfull steins and pipes. "Ready to get rowdy, boys?" He slams the door shut behind him hard enough to rattle the glass of the window.

"You're a wee bit early," Robert says, waving a hand to the mess on the table and the men still sitting in chairs. "We haven't finished serving these lads dinner."

The door opens again, a man in a pressed suit striding through the doors. "Milord."

Avery wraps a long arm around the elderly man's shoulders and turns him toward the others. "Lads, this is Howard Ainsley, owner of this fine establishment."

Mr. Ainsley gives the younger men a broad smile. "As future members of this esteemed club, let me welcome you now and tell you that, should you ever have need of the Lamb and Flag, our doors are always open for you."

It's not just the servants in this place. It's the whole damn establishment.

"Christ's sake," the one with the tray curses, sliding it down the table and knocking plates to the floor. "I don't give a damn who that old codger is. I'm ready to get pissed."

Carlisle strides around the table to Moriarty, pointing a finger at Watson's limp form along the way. "Someone take out the trash before you get too deep in your cups."

Holmes doesn't even protest, only taking a long dredge of the beer handed to him. He doesn't watch as Watson is dragged from the room.

"Blimey, that one put up a fight," mutters the burly man.

Carlisle claps a hand on Moriarty's shoulder. "Don't think you've skipped our inauguration, Moriarty. You may not have the blood we prefer, but the power and potential are there, mark my words."

My brother's smile is so cold it could freeze hell. "And what of the spy?"

My heart skips a beat.

"Spy?" Carlisle asks.

My brother leans in my direction. Cold realization swells in my chest.

"Yes," Moriarty drawls. "The one in this very room."

Carlisle looks to each of the men around the table. His gaze lingers on Holmes, and then finally me. His brows narrow, mouth forming a question.

The door slams open. Men all around me yelp and yell. Officers stream into the room, followed by the wizardly Inspector Gregson. Between two fingers, he holds up my invitation.

"Sorry we're late, lads," Gregson says. "My invitation only just arrived this afternoon."

CHAPTER 21

A Scorpion's Sting

Those of us at the table had our binds cut and were escorted from the premises before we could hear the questioning Carlisle and the other club members received from the Scotland Yard.

With my invitation, anonymously mailed to his office, I included a drawing of the Bullingdon Club brand, which Inspector Gregson—wise man that he is—no doubt used to put two and two together, matching with the brands on the bodies. Or, at least I hope he did.

He was at least smart enough to deduce the location from the symbols at the bottom of the invitation. Unlike me.

Many seats in class are empty today, but this time not on account of bloodshed and murder. All known members of the club received week-long suspensions. Their punishments would have no doubt been more severe if half the deans of Oxford were not also Bullingdon Club members themselves, and their spies in the Yard must have been paid. Heavily.

Holmes also hasn't attended his classes for nigh on five days. The tip of my quill taps against my desk, splattering ink across my notes, but I give it no mind. My attention wanders, yet again, to the empty desk beside me. I refrain from chewing the inside of my lip, an Irene habit, not Isaac's. What if the Bullingdon Club deduced our plot and disposed of both him and Watson? Even worse, what if Holmes actually chose to become a full-fledged member?

I don't even hear the bell ring, my attention so unfocused that I hardly notice as my classmates start packing up their notes. I don't follow them from the classroom, though. Instead, I stop at Stackton's desk.

"Yes, Holland?" He doesn't turn from the chalkboard. "If you want the lecture again because you were too busy daydreaming, you're sorely out of luck."

I set the box I've pulled from my bag on his desk and open it with a click. Stackton finally turns from the board. When he sees what I've stolen from my father's desk, he hurries to the door, shutting it firmly and pulling low the blind.

"Don't tell me someone as lowly as Isaac Holland elicited an invitation from the Bullingdon Club." He pulls the box of silver seals across the desk toward himself. "Or worse, their ire."

"Yes to the former." I cock my head. "Hopefully not the latter, though, not yet."

Stackton arches a single, bushy eyebrow.

"I know where they meet and can provide a detailed report of their hazing methods," I say, itching distractedly at my damned wig. "And a list of their current members, recruits, and alumni."

It had taken no time at all to dig up that information once I drew together a list of the men I'd seen in the Lamb and Flag, though I'd yet to discern how they were connected to the murders. The Scotland Yard has been frustratingly mum with the press about the club. No doubt their silence was paid for with blood money.

With a great, heavy sigh, Stackton sits in his chair and rubs a hand across his face. "I'll have to report this information and it will no doubt leave a target on your back. Are you prepared for that?"

The image of a bloody spoon rising to Watson's red face flickers behind my eyes. "I can weather this storm just fine."

"No doubt you believe so," Stackton says, closing the box with a soft click and tucking it in a desk drawer, "but whether you actually can is yet to be determined."

"Your unerring faith in my abilities is inspiring, Professor."

He merely *harumphs* in response. I slide the piece of paper with the damning report, three names purposefully absent, across the desk, and leave him to process the information on his own. Cutting across the green to the library, though, I cannot ignore the feeling that a dagger's tip presses between my shoulder blades, waiting to be rammed home.

The ghosts of Oxford, should they exist, seem to be working overtime to haunt my excitable classmates. Their whispers fill the halls, of ghosts and demons peering over their shoulders. The Lady Margaret dormitories are nearly all vacant, gathering dust and cobwebs as students flee for safer pastures. Or at least until the killer is safely behind bars.

Personally, I think they aren't actually that superstitious. They likely just miss the everlasting balls and parties of London.

Head ducked to deter the cutting wind from stinging my eyes, I stomp over to the building next door. Officers stop me, asking for the seal we must all now carry that proves we are students, before letting me pass.

We each have a cubicle for our mail in the Clarendon Building. I rarely ever visit mine on account that Isaac Holland never receives any. There is no reason to write to Isaac Holland, because Isaac Holland doesn't exist.

But my reason for crossing the airy threshold of the tall building is twofold: retrieve an exam for which I haven't seen my marks yet and also hopefully run into Holmes doing the same.

He's not here, and his cubicle is nearly as empty as mine. Nearly. When I pull the folded exam from my mailbox, I give a little start. A small envelope leans against the back. Curiosity plucks through me like harp strings, and I flip it over.

The blocky scrawl and familiar stamp on the wax seal fill me with a thrum of trepidation. The rider astride a horse.

You have yet to finish your initiation.

The Bullingdon Club would like to meet with me.

They leave directions across campus, back to the Queen's Chapel. One murder has already happened there, so what would the odds be of another happening so soon? Hopefully, the odds are in my favor.

The details on the club won't be published for another day, so at least they won't be hunting for my head quite yet.

I cut across the green, the sun rapidly setting behind me, and quicken my steps once I reach the ancient doors of the chapel and swing them open. Ghosts wail on the wind down the long, narrow hallway and through the shuttered windows, begging to be let into the holy space. I ignore them, my steps echoing across the chapel. I didn't expect the Club to just be sitting in the pews, heads bowed in prayer or eagerly waiting my arrival, but the fact that only a single other soul sits in the room is mildly disappointing. And concerning.

A flicker of caution whispers in my chest as I take in the hunched figure sitting in the very front pew, head bowed over her knees. Her shoulders heave around sobs. Her head snaps up when I get closer, black hair tumbling down her back, and she leaps to her feet, face obscured in the shadows.

The air is knocked from my lungs when a click echoes throughout the chapel.

Slowly, I turn. My palms are now slick with sweat as I stare down the barrel of a silver pistoleer.

My heartbeat thuds like an anvil in my own ears. A figure cloaked in red and shadow, face obscured by a heavy velvet hood, aims for my heart. Every instinct in me screams that a man hides beneath that cowl. He raises the gun higher.

I act without thinking. His pointer finger tightens on the trigger just as I fling myself in front of the lady. Her scream rings at the same time the gunshot goes off. I crash into the pews.

There's a burning in my side. Like a scorpion's sting, it blossoms and grows, flowing across my abdomen like the blood now pouring from the bullet wound. The woman screams again, fleeing. With vision stained red, I look up as the cloaked figure disappears through the doors.

Leaving me to bleed out on the chapel's floor.

CHAPTER 22

The Red Negligee

MY HAND LEAVES BLOODY FINGERPRINTS ON THE WALLS. The image, though already blurred like looking through red-and-gray mesh, will be forever imprinted upon my mind.

"Always apply pressure," Lasho once told me. *"Stop the bleeding, otherwise you will die before anyone has a chance to even look at your wound."*

My palm presses hard into the hole in my abdomen, making me cry out; I continue my stumbling walk across the city. The stars flutter above like a thousand fireflies, like the ones from the stories. They whisper and buzz, telling me all their secrets.

"There better not be a speck of dirt here," my father hisses. *"Or I'll take out the belt again."*

I stagger for a glance at the bloody wall, wondering blearily if I should stop and clean it. Richard will be so cross. My back will ache for weeks from his belt. The earth spins beneath my heels and the wall disappears.

I lurch from one alley to the next. Whispers of drunks and

catcalls of carriage drivers follow me down each darkened street. The buzzing grows, and the mesh seems to tighten more and more around my eyes.

"*Mumely*," my mother whispers. "*Trouver le nid.*"

My knees give out and I hit the ground hard enough to make them sing. They cry like the last notes of an opera, ringing on and on until the darkness swallows me whole.

Sweet smoke tickles my nose. It makes my eyes water beneath their sealed lids. I reach up to wipe away the grime sealing them shut, and a sharp hiss echoes in my ears. It takes me a moment to realize that the sound came from my own lips. The pain in my abdomen is a mere echo, thanks to a drug no doubt, but still very much there.

"Don't move," says a gruff voice in the darkness. "You'll rip the stitches and bleed out all over my bed."

That voice, so warm and familiar, itches the back of my neck like a heavy jumper. I cannot place it; I need to see who it belongs to. I rub again at my eyes, and large hands suddenly envelop my own. I pull my fingers from his, tracing the back of his hand until I land on a smooth patch of skin around his enormous wrists.

"Lasho," I say, though the name comes out more like a croak.

He tips some warm water down my mouth, and I eagerly drink the blend of herbs and honey. They flood my chest with delicious warmth and push the pain in my stomach back just a little bit further.

"Little one," my old protector says. "Always getting yourself into trouble."

"I wish we had met again under better circumstances."

A giggle rings from beyond the darkness. I sniff again. Roses and incense greet my nose. Another girlish laugh, followed by dark chuckles and sloppy noises that can only mean one thing.

"A brothel." I laugh bitterly.

"No need to be all prim and proper about it. You were born in one, remember?"

"Yes, in the Americas." Where we stayed until one of Richard's men found us, and we caught the first ship to Italy, and then Germany, and finally to France. "As thankful as I am for your diligent care, hopefully nobody saw you carrying Isaac Holland into the Red Negligee."

Lasho coughs. "Actually, you found me here."

"*Trouver le nid.*"

"The nest." I chuckle, making me grimace. My eyes finally open to reveal red and black silk hanging amid wisps of gray incense from the ceiling above. "Mother always said you flocked to little chicks to protect."

"Why did you wait so long to visit, Mumely?" Lasho's voice is gruff with pain, a far different kind than is racking my midriff as we speak.

To protect you, I do not say.

Instead, with a voice as cold as ice, I say, "I've been busy."

He's not fooled. "Is it because you feel that I failed you and your mother?"

"Is that how you feel?" I arch a brow.

"Yes," he admits.

Silence stretches long arms between us. As he eases me into

a sitting position, Lasho holds out another cup of tea for me to cradle. I take sip after sip, the pain receding further and further, and I consider the man sitting across from me. I haven't seen him since that fateful night in northern France. He's aged significantly in those twelve years. His black hair is threaded with great vines of silver and white. There are more scars on his cheeks and arms, making a face that would otherwise be warm and welcoming a bit fearsome. He's lost much weight, replaced by hard muscles, no doubt needed to throw customers through the brothel's door.

"Why did you follow me to Oxford?" I ask, voice thick from the pain, both in my gut and in my heart.

"I made your mother a promise." His teeth clench a moment. There is no energy in me for a barbed reply about how he already broke that promise. "How did you know I was here?"

I take another sip. "My mother taught me how to keep track of those I care about."

He waves to me, dressed now in only a black silk sheet, disguise left somewhere either on the street or in another room. "What got you in such a mess, Mumely?"

"Don't call me that," I snap. "Ever."

Pain temples his brows. "What happened, Irene?"

"I've made many enemies." Another sniff. That sickly sweet smell seems to be everywhere. "What is that god-awful stench?"

"The herbs in your tea." Lasho nods to the cup in my hands. "Boss uses it to ease her clientele. Gets them to open their purses a bit more. It also eases pain."

I consider the liquid before me and want to pour it on the ground. "What else does it do?"

"Sleep will hit you soon. Your dreams will be vivid," Lasho says, even as my eyelids start to grow heavy. "The alternative was to let you suffer."

"I might have preferred that," I admit, words slurring. Warm hands tug the cup from my grasp as the back of my head hits my pillow and sleep claims me once more.

My mother rocks me in her arms in a wicker chair before a roaring fireplace. The sweat on my brow is from the medicine doing its trick outside of this dream, but I still cling to the folds of my mother's dress as if it were real.

"Don't leave me," I beg, tears slipping down my cheeks.

My mother kisses them, one by one. "Never."

"Promise?"

She continues to rock back and forth, the flames in the hearth bathing her eyes a bright gold. Her lips press into a firm line and her arms tighten infinitesimally around my waist.

"Promise?" I demand again.

"What have I told you about making promises you can't keep?" She kisses my brow to soften the words. "There are some dark things in this world, Mumely. Things that would stop at nothing to control me. Control you."

"Like what?" My voice is that of a high-pitched child.

"Not what. Whom." She pinches my chin sharp enough for the depths of unconsciousness to finally lessen their hold. The fire dims, the last sparks spitting toward us, and answering sparkles of pain dance up my side. "He will destroy you."

Dawn wakes me, reaching bright fingers through the one window to pry my eyes open. Lasho is where I last saw him, resting his elbows on his knees across from me with a dark expression.

Who will destroy me? Who was my mother trying to warn me about? James... Or Sherlock Holmes?

"Remind me to pay for the room," I say, voice cracking. A chuckle, and I'm coughing around my next words. "Or rather, my brother's purse will pay for it."

"No need." He holds up another cup before my mouth, but I turn away with a pinched noise and lips.

"No. No more drugs."

"It's a broth," he says, Scottish burr thick. "Just turmeric and garlic."

"Fine," I bite out, accepting a spoonful to ease the dryness of my throat. The pain in my abdomen is still present, but nothing more than a dull throb. "I see you haven't lost your healing touch."

"A blessing the wound was only minor. You still lost a fair amount of blood, though." His eyes are wet. "What happened?"

"I was shot."

"Obviously. By whom?"

I shake my head. "I don't know."

It could have been anyone. Moriarty. Holmes. Someone from the Bullingdon Club. My list of enemies is nearly as long as I am tall.

"Well, best you find out before their aim improves. Thankfully, the bullet only grazed you."

"I don't know if they were aiming for me." I think of the other woman in the chapel, crying.

"What kind of mess have you gotten yourself into?" Lasho asks.

I lean my head back with a sigh. "The kind only an Adler can get themselves into."

"Your mother—" he starts.

I cut him off. "My mother is dead."

Silence rings throughout the room. There are no sounds beyond. The working hours of the brothel are long past. Finally, I ease my feet from the bed, wincing with each labored breath it takes to do so.

"I should leave. My absence will be noted, and my father will be told within the hour." I wince again as the room spins. Why are there four Lashos watching me with varying expressions of concern? "How long was I asleep for?"

"Two days."

I curse. "I missed my classes. I'll fall behind."

"Damn the All Souls to hell!" Lasho roars, climbing to his feet. "You could have died!"

"I would rather be dead"—my voice rises to match his—"than a slave to my father any longer!"

Lasho jabs a thumb toward the wall. "You think that school can save you from him?"

"No," I say, sneering.

There's a tentative knock on the door behind him, and a muffled voice asks, "Everything all right in there, Louis?"

"Fine," he says, voice losing that sharp edge.

The muffled sounds of shuffled footsteps edge past the door and are lost in the building.

"How long have you worked here, *Louis*?" I ask, though I already know the answer. I learned of his whereabouts days after he landed in England.

"Four years." Lasho sits back down, the stool groaning beneath his bulk.

I force my next question out. "Why?"

My old friend hangs his head between his hands with a great sigh. "You know why."

More silence, broken now only by the steady ticking of the watch on his bedside table. The time on its face fills me with another thrum of anxiety.

"I should go." I ease to my feet, reaching a hand to the bedside post for balance when the world tilts beneath my heels. "Where are my clothes?"

"You should rest." Lasho's hands land on my shoulders, but I gently brush them away.

"No." I brusquely shake my head. "People will notice my absence. My father will start searching for me."

He can't find me here. He can't find Lasho.

Finding a folded pile of my clothes, freshly laundered, I gingerly dress. Each muscle in my body protests mightily. I move toward the door, willing my body to ignore the pain and exhaustion dragging my steps. When I ease it open, I nearly slam it back shut. A man sucks at the neck of a barely clothed woman right outside. He grunts, and she giggles, and I barely have time to make out their faces before they tumble through the opposite door.

"A regular here," Lasho whispers from behind me. "Seems to keep this whole place afloat with his bottomless pockets."

I shrug. "Who am I to judge a man for knowing what he wants?"

Taking another step into the hallway, I bite back a hiss as the small movement sends shock waves of pain up and down my side.

Lasho's brows knot with worry. "Will you come back?"

The begging note in his voice cracks my heart.

But to potentially lead my father here. To him.

Never.

I don't answer, instead slipping down the dark hallway like a ghost of my own past.

I don't find Holmes. Rather, he finds me.

That night, I'm nursing a particularly large mug of dark ale and a perpetual burn below my ribs when he jerks away the chair my feet are resting on. I hiss, resisting the impulse to clutch my wounded side. The mood in the Turf is already loud and raucous, so none notice my sharp exclamation as beer spills down my doublet.

"Bloody hell, Holmes." I dab uselessly at the growing stain with my hat. "What a waste of ale."

"And what a waste of life you are."

The cold, lethal hiss of his voice stops me. My hand pauses its gentle dabbing. "Pardon?"

I flinch when he slaps both palms on the table and leans across toward me. I angle my face away from his, but can only go so far back. The cold wall of the pub presses against my back as Holmes's face inches toward mine.

"This is done."

"Pa-pardon?" I ask again.

I want to ask if Watson is recovered, and if their friendship is repaired, but Holmes's wrath no doubt answers those questions. Even more, I would give anything to be able to rip away this disguise and prove to him that we fight the same battle, duel with the same foes. I grip my mug tighter to keep my fingers from pulling away my wig.

"This." He jabs a hard finger into my shoulder, sending a twinge of pain into my abdomen. "This partnership. It's done."

I blink. "But why?"

"Because of the sacrifices I've had to make to keep this ruse alive," he says, voice ragged. "You don't deserve any more explanation than that."

"It was all worth it, Holmes," I say. "Our classmates are being murdered. *They* could come for us next."

He sits suddenly, cradling his head in his hands. "The Bullingdon Club had nothing to do with that. They are all useless excuses for human life, but they are not guilty of murder."

"You don't know that."

Holmes jerks upright and cuts a hand through the air between us. "I do. Now that I am a member, I know all their names, and they all have alibis the day of Bertram's murder."

"And what of at the time of Davies's murder?" I demand. "Wilson's? They can't all have alibis."

"Leave it," Holmes says between clenched teeth. His entire chest heaves, his breathing ragged and hands clenched into fists. "They may be mad. They may deserve to rot in hell for all eternity, but they are not murderers."

"The odds are just too—"

"Damn the odds."

I leap to my feet. "What of the All Souls? What if they murder to get closer to the queen?"

He swipes the beer from my hands and flings it at the wall. The mug shatters. The air and noise in the room are all sucked away.

The silence is deafening. I stare, gaping, as my beer trickles down the wall. We have the attention now of everyone in the pub. The barkeep has paused his polishing, fist and rag still in a mug. The waitress is over-pouring a beer, but neither she nor the patron notice.

"You." Trembling, he leans back, jaw clenched. "You are no better than him."

Shivering, I dare to ask, "No better than whom?"

"I would have never accepted the club's invitation if it wasn't for you. Watson should have never been dragged into this." He shoves away from the table. His chair crashes to the ground, and people begin moving about the pub once more. Their idle chatter is more urgent now, forced, as they still listen to us with a single ear.

Sherlock trembles with rage, his jaw clenched so tight a tic forms. If I were Irene, I'd reach a hand up, brushing it away with a tender thumb as I gazed up at him through my lashes and asked for forgiveness.

As Isaac, I force myself to stay the course, despite everything screaming in me that I am going down the wrong path.

"If I noticed your friendship with the officer, of course someone else would," I barrel on. "Why are you so protective of him? What is the sacrifice of a friend if it means saving our classmates?"

Even before I finish the sentence, I recognize my own stupidity. Instantly, I would do anything to eat my words.

The anger falls away from Sherlock's face, but the cold, almost empty expression in its place is somehow even worse.

"You don't give a damn about our dead classmates. Not a single care for the Bullingdon Club and the evils they inflict. No, you only care about the All Souls and ensuring that you live long enough to see yourself to the top. You wouldn't understand, because you don't have a single friend here." He shakes his head with a dark chuckle. Voice a ragged whisper, Holmes shreds my heart, my very soul, into disparate pieces. "You are no better than Moriarty."

All further words are stolen from my throat. I can only watch as he storms from the Turf, leaving a gaping absence in his wake.

I should have argued with him, drawn up a lie to defend myself. Not because he's correct, that I hunger for the seat above all else, but because, deep in my soul, I know my desire to find the murderer stems from something perhaps worse.

Because it is a question I don't immediately know the answer to.

It is a long time after he leaves until I catch my breath again. There's a steady thunder in my ears, and only vaguely do I recognize it as the pounding of my own heart. When the waitress slides me my bill, there's an added charge for the broken mug.

CHAPTER 23

A Single Good Lord

A VIOLIN SINGS THROUGH THE HEAVY WOODEN DOOR. ITS notes are melancholy and lovely, the kind of song one would expect to play in a father's mind when he gives his daughter away at a wedding. I rap my gloved knuckles gently on the door and the music immediately slows. There's no answer.

There's been nothing in the papers of the shooting in the chapel, but also blessedly no more murders. Either the mystery woman hasn't told anyone of the shooting, or the Yard wants to keep this facet of their investigation under wraps.

Nothing yet of the Bullingdon Club and the names I've revealed.

And nothing of Sherlock Holmes. His parting words to me are like a scab I can't stop picking at. Even as I think over them, I want to scratch at my wrists.

I'm no better than a Moriarty.

Because, despite how hard I fight against it, I am a Moriarty. The same blood flows through my veins, and perhaps the evil with it.

The owner of this room hopefully believes otherwise.

I knock again; the music dies softly.

I rest my forehead against the cool wood. "It's Irene."

Still, no answer beckons through. The hallway behind me is silent and, thankfully, bereft of any of our classmates.

"There's nobody with me," I say, my voice low and pleading.

Still nothing. I sigh heavily through my nose and turn on my heel to leave. I'm just about to pass the corner at the end of the hallway when the door creaks open.

Geraldine's curls are a frizzy halo gilding her head as she peeks into the hallway. "You should be in class."

"Shouldn't you, too?" I stop, resting a hand on the flagstone wall.

She doesn't answer, merely returning to her room. She leaves the door open. Just a smidge. I accept the begrudging invitation, shutting the door softly behind me. My movements are stiff with pain, but I hide it behind a tentative expression, as if I am merely hesitant to bother my dearest friend.

Geraldine stands in the middle of her room, hugging herself in a thin, white silk nightgown. Her room is just a smidge smaller than Ermyntrude's but would still manage to dwarf mine. A cushioned chaise sits before an unlit fireplace, across from her white-painted boudoir. Her cheeks are pale and blotchy, her eyes red-rimmed.

"Well, don't just stand there staring at me, Irene," she snaps. At her elbow sits a violin on the table. "What do you have to explain?"

"I missed tea," I say, trailing my finger through the dust on her desk.

"You did." Geraldine clenches the frilly lace hem of her nightgown, notching her chin high. "What was so important that you couldn't even have the decency to send a note? Not even in the *days after*. You never even returned to the dorm."

"My brother...I followed him."

She crosses her arms, waiting for me to continue.

"I had to know what my brother was up to that night," I say, hands trembling. "You share my distrust of him."

She looks away. "If I ask you why, will you answer honestly?"

"I owe you that at least." I walk to the window, where a green lawn, dotted with patches of winter-browned grass, stretches below. "I am investigating the death of Bertram and his classmates. Though I have no love for James, I would rather not see him killed. I worry that my brother might be next on the murderer's list. Or even perhaps myself."

Not entirely true, but not entirely a lie, either. This game of half-truths and misdirection might spin a yarn too knotted to be undone.

"Why do you dislike James so?" Geraldine has come to stand next to me, her breath fogging the weathered glass.

I press my lips in a firm line. Perhaps a bit more truth will loosen up the knots.

"He is made of the same poison as our father." I take a deep, steadying breath and grab Geraldine's hand. "You may not have heard before that I lived with Augusta Moriarty until I was fourteen. Or so my father's story goes. I didn't start living with my grandmother until I was eight."

"Your *father's* story?" Geraldine, face somehow paler, pulls back her hand. "You mean the stories of what he did are true?"

Lips trembling, I nod. "I am the bastard daughter of opera singer and courtesan Elena Adler"—I take another deep breath—"and

Lord Richard Moriarty. He had her murdered and brought me from France against my will."

The color drains from my friend's face. Her hands, trembling uncontrollably, curl into fists.

"Why didn't you ever tell me?" Geraldine's voice balances between disbelief and anger.

"I was forbidden." I look out through the frosted windowpanes over the quiet city of Oxford.

"You've broken rules before."

"Right." Such as the costume currently hidden in my room.

Geraldine faces me, all the while one of her long, elegant nails drags through the frost. "Why did you not trust me?"

"I was born in secret. My mother traded in secrets. Secrets are as much a part of me as my hair and eyes." I place a hand over hers and pull it from the cold. "Perhaps that is the curse of being a Moriarty."

With a sigh, I say, "I've spent too many years running from the truth to ever know what it is. My father grew obsessed with Elena, even more so when he learned she was pregnant. My mother asked for nothing, only his silence. She'd witnessed his cruelty, and the malice that lingers in all Moriartys. So she fled England, thinking he would return to his wife, James's mother." Silence drifts between us. It's heavy, a weight on my tongue. But not as heavy as the iron crown that is the title of Moriarty.

"Go on." Geraldine reveals nothing in her face.

"Little did my mother know, the hunt only made my father hungrier and, the longer she evaded him, angrier." Tears slip down my cheeks. "My father decided that, if he couldn't have my mother, nobody could."

He had her killed.

My hands tremble as I turn my back to face her and pull my hair atop my head. "There. Do you see it peeking out from my neckline? There should be a pale, silver line. We've been friends long enough that surely you've noticed it before."

I jump when her cold finger touches it. Her voice shakes as she asks, "What is this from?"

"A favorite pastime of James's was locking me in my room." I swallow, my throat painfully dry. "One time, when our father went to Paris, James locked my door while I was sleeping. I screamed, I wept. I threw the furniture at the door. But no one came for me. I didn't eat for four days."

Geraldine gasps softly, and I turn to face her, to show her the tears sliding down my cheeks. "I tried climbing out the window. There was a tree not far from its ledge, and I thought that I could reach it if I leapt far enough. I was mistaken."

Flashes of that night rain through my mind. Of my wild leap despite the hunger draining me whole. Of my fingers glancing across the branch and my wild tumble to the ground over a dozen feet below.

"James blamed the accident on my trying to run away, which"—I incline my head—"I had been known to do on occasion. He claimed that I'd thrown a tantrum, and that he was punishing me by locking me in my room. Father didn't believe me when I told him that I had been locked in my room for days. James had scared the servants into silence, their word the same as my brother's."

This was but a minor offense from my brother in comparison to the other torments. I don't tell her that this isn't the only scar on my body from my brother, nor do I mention the many other scars I will bear with me forever in my mind.

"You poor thing," Geraldine says, wrapping her thin arms around me. I grimace when her hip bumps the bullet wound, but she doesn't seem to notice. "That horrible man will get what's coming to him in the end."

"And despite it all, I don't wish him dead." I gently extricate myself from her hug.

A gentle knock on the door makes us both jump.

"Can I enter, dear sister?" Edgar's face peeks around the door and lights up when he sees us. "Oh, you have company." Without waiting for Geraldine's approval, he marches into the room, chest puffed up.

He shares his sister's fluffy, gilded curls and porcelain skin, the kind of hair and complexion most women would kill for. But the honest earnestness of his features, the complete trustworthiness, would deter even the devil from ill thought. The only member of the Bullingdon Club to speak up against their vile actions.

He offers me a low bow. "Irene Adler. I dream of the days when you grace my presence."

"All these years we've known each other, and I've never heard such a lie." I laugh and curtsy. "The pleasure is all mine."

Geraldine looks between us, a small smile blossoming on her face.

Edgar takes my hand and places a soft kiss upon its back. "So good to finally see you again."

My cheeks warm and I dip my gaze demurely, remembering keenly why I left his name from the list I'd given Stackton. When I look up again, his gaze is just as earnest, if possibly more so. I have to admit that he would make a match much better than I could possibly hope for when he finally proposes.

I curtsy again. "Well, I hope you have the courage to do so from now on. I will leave the two of you."

Edgar opens his mouth to protest, but Geraldine stops him with a hand on his arm. She nods, a silver twinkle in her eye. "Shall we make plans to study this evening, Irene?"

I return her nod. "I'll return after tea."

The violin picks up its lovely song, trailing me long after I leave the dormitory.

CHAPTER 24

Oxford's Dirty Laundry

OXFORD'S DIRTY LAUNDRY
DECEMBER 1, 1872

Oh, how the gentry squander their potential and power.

Coming from a credible but anonymous source, the notorious and yet never publicly outed Bullingdon Club is finally brought to light. Members ranging from Parliament's most esteemed council and the royal gentry themselves are among the Bullingdon Club's prestigious ranks. But, it seems, even the rich and fabulous must stoop to the level of court jesters and hooligans. The *Daily Bugle* is even privy to their names, which you'll find below....

CAMPUS IS AFLUTTER WITH TALK ABOUT THE ARTICLE, AND still none mention the bloody mess left behind in the Queen's Chapel. Perhaps someone cleaned up after I fled to Lasho, especially when they came back and found my body missing.

My normal seat in Stackton's class is taken by the time I hurry in. A frown pulls at my brows, but I take a seat in the back without question. No time to make a fuss. Sherlock has returned to class, I notice, sitting many rows in front of me and likewise not in his normal seat.

My frown remains, an itch forming at the base of my spine.

My suspicions are confirmed when the classmate in front of me, Avery Williams, spins in his seat the moment Stackton's back is turned. He plucks the quill from my hand and snaps it clean in one movement, turning around just as the professor faces us once more.

My mouth drops open.

"Do you have a question, Mr. Holland?" Stackton glares at me down the rows of students.

"No, sir." I dig in my bag for my nib pen.

When I straighten, pen in hand, the paper has been swiped from my desk. Grumbling, I reach for the spare paper in my bag, still-healing wound in my side hitching with the movement. Irene's fluid, French notes sprawl across the front of the page. Sighing through my nose, I flip over the page and begin taking notes. Throughout the hour, though, my classmates—all Bullingdon Club members—turn in their seats to stare at me. Their gazes are neither malicious nor wicked. Instead, even worse, they're carefully blank.

When the bell tolls in the distance, I reach for my sheet of notes. Black ink splashes across its surface, raining on the back of my hand. Avery's bag continues its swing as he pulls it across his shoulders.

"Blast it, Avery," I can't help but snap. Now both sets of notes are ruined.

"Sorry, Holland." His hyena-like smile says that he is anything but apologetic.

"What's this?" Stackton has shuffled to the back of the classroom. Seeing the mess, angry red blotches start to form on his cheeks. "May your clumsiness teach you a thing or two, Holland. You will clean this mess up immediately."

Without hearing a word of argument, he turns and walks to the chalkboard. My classmates chuckle around me and a blush starts to form under Holland's fake mustache and nose. I voice no argument. Too much attention has been drawn to me today.

I bend, ready to wipe the desk clean with my own sleeve, when a cold hand grips the back of my neck. I grit my teeth.

"We know what you did," Avery hisses into my ear. His friends have circled round, blocking me from Stackton's view. "We know the names that have been left from your *list*."

My entire body tenses. "I don't know what you're—"

"Don't bother lying." He shoves me down, hard. My knees buckle and I collapse to the floor. "We found your report before the professor could give it to the deans."

Avery's fingers grip hard enough to leave bruises, his nails piercing my skin. I bite my tongue to keep from crying out, my pain sure to betray my disguise. With his free hand he rips the hat from my head. My heart thunders in my ears, wild like a stampede of horses.

"Best watch your back, Holland," he says. "The Bullingdon Club's memory is long."

"What's going on back there?" Stackton demands.

Robert Lancaster shoves me back down, taking my nib pen with him for good measure. "Mr. Holland dropped his pen, and I was collecting it for him. Seems the poor lad is all thumbs today."

Through the crowd of men around me, I can make out Stackton's clenched jaw, but he nods and turns again to the board. Once his back is turned, there's a tiny crack above me, and pieces of my pen litter to the floor.

Chortling, Avery and Robert lead the men from the classroom. Holmes and Moriarty have not moved from their desks. Moriarty shakes his head, ever so slightly, before following the others. Holmes's eyes travel over my ink-stained hands and broken pen. His face is unreadable, and he offers me nothing before following the others.

My thoughts are a tumbled mess as I pack up my belongings and get to cleaning the ink from my desk. I use my own hat to wipe it clean as best I can. Getting the stains from my hands will be an even larger concern, that and the Lady Margaret class I'm currently truant from.

I'm obviously being watched. If the foiled experiment in the library was any clue, so was the scarf in my dormitory and now my movements as Holland to and from classes. All signs lean toward my assailant in the chapel. I could adopt a third persona to lead my watchers on a merry chase, or I could simply limit my movements as Holland to the main campus and find a new place to change my disguise.

But all that would be meaningless if someone already knows my secret.

Stackton has finished packing up before I'm done cleaning. He takes one look at me and shakes his head.

The ink stains on my hands take an hour of vigorous scrubbing to remove, and even then, shadows of it still linger beneath my fingernails. I'll have to be especially careful to wear my gloves at all times when out as Irene until the ink finally washes away.

Alone in my dormitory, I've spread a large piece of paper across my desk. I've chosen my dorm in the Lady Margaret wing, far from the wrathful Holmes. I don't trust him not to turn me in now if he ever discovers my dual identity. Hair tucked out of my face in a tight bun and my last nib pen clenched between my teeth, I consider what I've written so far.

Perhaps *written* isn't the correct word to use here.

I've drawn a large tree, with branches that swoop and cross and splay even smaller branches from their tips.

The Bullingdon Club tree.

On tiny limbs, I've written each of the member's names, tracing their family lineage back to the original members. Carlisle's family extends all the way to the tree's roots, the Haywards, too. Bertram's family has a long history in the club, as does Davies's, though Jude, the other victim, does not. A soft huff of impatience escapes me.

And there, a low-hanging branch, but a branch nonetheless, are the Moriartys. Their place on this tree all due to my grandmother.

My father must have been a member of the club, as evidenced by the seals in his desk, so James's surprise at being invited must have been feigned. Holmes, on the other hand, has not a single family member on the tree.

His family's meteoritic rise to wealth is nothing short of extraordinary. A story the gossip columns speculated about to no end.

I draw a few empty branches for families I haven't placed yet, for surely they're waiting for me to discover them. I will have to find more traces of the symbol around campus because, for now, I can find no possible connection between the murders and the club other than the brands. I refuse the idea that Holmes was right and I am being led on a merry chase.

I let the paper dry before rolling it into a long cylinder and shoving it up the sleeve of one of my jackets.

There's a soft knock at the door, making me jump, and a letter slides beneath the frame. A crowned lion rampant reflects in the red wax upon its back. With a sharp knife, I pry the letter open and unfold it.

Dearest Ireney,

I greatly enjoyed our chat the other day, and have dearly missed spending time with you these cold autumn months. Strangely, despite sleeping down the hall from you and the other young women of Lady Margaret, I have never felt more alone. Perhaps that is the ghosts speaking, perhaps the fear I feel for the murderer no doubt lurking in the shadows. Thank you for your honesty. I've found that most ladies have half your truthfulness. Would you please bring my brother and me joy by joining us for tea next week, December the 8th?

*Your friend,
Gerry*

P.S. Don't tell Ermyntrude. We wouldn't want her to be jealous.

I cannot contain the smile that pulls at my lips and the fluttering in my stomach.

I quickly draft my response on the letter's back, sealing it with my grandmother's crest and smiling so wide it hurts my cheeks. Before leaving, I carefully check my hair, my face, and dress for any signs of Isaac Holland. I pull on my maroon jacket, excitement shaking my fingers as I pop each onyx button into place.

My smile falters when I swing the door open.

"Has anyone ever told you that even the brightest days are darkened upon your arrival?" I ask, my voice laced with sweet venom.

James cocks his head. "Quite the opposite, actually."

"Don't lie. It's unbecoming."

He catches my wrist before I can pocket my key. "Those are curious ink stains."

My heart lodges in my throat. I've forgotten my gloves. "I've been a bit careless lately."

"And truant from your classes." Moriarty's eyes bore into mine.

My face is the image of profound boredom. "Are you monitoring all my movements, James?"

"As all good brothers should." His smile is wolfish.

"No one would dare confuse you with a *good brother*."

"Nevertheless." He plucks the letter from my other hand, the Hayward crest glimmering in the ink seal still clinging to the envelope. "I want you to bring me to whatever it is the lovely Lady Hayward invited you to."

"Could you be any more desperate?" I snatch my hand and the letter away. "You have been attempting to court Gerry for almost as long as I've known her, and she has never shown a lick of interest in return."

"No heart is truly made of stone. I have faith the lovely Lady Hayward will eventually be swayed." He catches my chin in my hands, pinching tight enough for a gasp to escape me.

"You're hurting me," I say with another gasp. My heart hammers, loud enough for even the ghosts of Oxford to hear.

"You will bring me to whatever it is Geraldine invited you to, or I'll tell the deans about your indiscretions."

"Indiscretions?" I shove him away, sucking in a large breath. "What madness are you talking about?"

He snatches up my ungloved hand. "I know what you've been up to, *Mr. Holland*."

Time seems to still. My stomach is frozen in a viselike grip, and yet I could puke my entire breakfast up then and there. My voice tremors as I say, "I don't know what you mean."

"Do not play games with me, Irene," he says, voice a low hiss. "I'm not Holmes, willfully ignorant to all that he deems below him. I've known since the moment you walked into class." He steps close, crowding me against the cold stone wall. "If you do not help me woo Geraldine Hayward, I will expose you. I will expose Stackton, too, while I'm at it."

He takes a step back, straightens his suit, and puffs out his chest. He pats his head, assuring that his hair is smooth and, ever the image of a placating brother, says, "Now come along, Irene. Let's get your letter posted and visit Father. We both know how he feels about tardiness."

CHAPTER 25

His Weakness

I CANNOT FOCUS ON THE PAGES BEFORE ME. THE WORDS BLUR together as tears threaten to spill onto the text.

My brother knows and has possibly always known, if his word is to be believed. He could expose me at any moment.

The once blessed solitude of the Bodleian has become nothing short of a curse. My thoughts are aswirl. Fear focuses my vision to a single point on the page, keen and sharp like the long edge of a knife resting against my spine. I know all too well what Moriarty does to the people who displease him.

A cold draft tugs at my long skirts. They feel as thin as tissue. Shivering, I flip errantly through the pages with little hope that I'll absorb any of their knowledge.

"If that's how you study, it's a miracle you've learned anything."

My head snaps up.

Holmes leans against the doorframe of the reading room, considering me. Black curls artfully fall over his brow. His deeply tan skin reflects in the flickering lamplight, shadowing his features, though I can still make out the small smile pulling at his lips.

I gesture to the seat across from me. "If you have a better method, Mr. Holmes, I insist you teach me, then. Work is the best balm to sorrow."

"I cannot agree with you more." He crosses swiftly, taking the offered seat and folding his elegant hands in his lap. He's dressed much nicer than I've ever seen him before, in a charcoal frock coat and trousers. He flips open a timepiece, then clicks it shut again.

"Going somewhere special this evening?" I ask, returning my attention to the book before me.

"Just dinner with"—he hesitates—"friends."

"You have friends?" I arch an eyebrow, giving him a teasing grin.

His eyes catch on my bloodred lips, pupils flaring. "I used to."

"*We* could be friends," I say, flashing him what I hope appears to be a genuine smile.

He inhales sharply. Silence, comfortable despite the tense nature, stretches between us, broken only by the scratching of my pen and the whisper of my turned pages. His eyes on me, on my hair, cheeks, and pale chest peeking through white muslin, are like the gentle touch of a fingertip.

He sighs heavily, leaning back in his seat and resting a booted foot on his knee. "If I hadn't known otherwise, I would have never seen the family resemblance between you and your brother."

I swallow, and his gaze follows the movement with the intensity of a lion watching its prey. "If I thought your fascination with my face had to do with my brother, I would have begun wearing a mask."

His face reveals nothing. "Are you not already? Always?"

I notch my chin high. "How did you even learn about our… ties?"

He sniffs. "He mentioned you in class."

A lie. I query again. "What did James have to say about me?"

"That, when you're with your friends"—he sniffs again—"you spend like your purse has no depths."

Another lie, and I pocket his tell for later. Smiling to myself, I flip another page. "Now you know my weakness, Mr. Holmes. Whatever shall you do with it?"

"I could think of a number of things." This time, his gaze travels leisurely from my head to clavicle. Heat stokes in the pit of my stomach. I snap my book shut.

He slides it away from me, considering the title, *Méthode de Nomenclature Chimique*.

"Curious texts the Lady Margaret class is having you read." Holmes's eyes bore into mine. "In fact, I've heard that the classes they force you to attend are nothing short of elementary. Something this text most definitely is not."

"Must you always use so many words to arrive at a single point?" I ask, a tad too tartly.

"Interesting, then, that this exact text was assigned to the All Souls cohort just last week." Holmes taps a finger on the thin pages, and I try to keep my expression blank. "Do you always go out of your way to prove that you're smarter than your brother?"

I can't help but smile. He's so close to the point he must taste it. "I have nothing to prove."

He watches my lips intently. "I couldn't agree more."

I straighten, suddenly hot despite the persistent autumn draft.

"Though, you're right. The Lady Margaret classes are a tad too slow for my liking, so I've decided to jump headfirst into a text that might even be a bit too difficult for me. I keep getting stuck on the complex chemical substances section. Care to explain it to me?"

"I could, but you and I both know that you understand it perfectly." His dark eyes twinkle. He leans forward, planting an elbow on the table and his chin in a palm. "If the work is not difficult for you, then what truly ails you, Miss Adler?"

Adler, not Moriarty. The way he says my name, like letting a good scotch laze upon your palate, floods me with more warmth.

"Like you, I have dinner plans this evening," I say, pursing my lips. "And they are not with friends. In fact, they are with someone I would rather never see again."

Curiosity flickers for the briefest moment behind his eyes, gone in an instant.

He turns his gaze toward the ceiling, a small yawn parting his lips. Another way to hide his feelings. "You mean to tell me that the irrepressible Irene Adler hasn't designed an excuse yet to not attend?" He turns to me again. "Maybe you're not half as clever as I thought."

The challenge ripples through me like the call of a hunting horn, and I climb to my feet. "And are you, too, unable to come up with a sufficient excuse?"

He mimics my movements, standing as well, and his answering grin stirs heat in my core. "As much as I loathe to admit it, I have no excuses to not attend this dinner. In fact, I very much have to."

"Are there lives at stake, Mr. Holmes?" I turn around the table.

"When the rich and powerful are involved, Lady Adler?" Holmes walks toward me. The heat returns at the sight of his very tall, very lean body towering over me. "There are always lives at stake."

"Wouldn't have thought that you were the type to rub elbows with those sorts of people." I find it hard to breathe with this man so close. So within reach.

"And I never thought that you were the type of woman cowed into submission, let alone a dinner with someone you don't like," he replies brusquely.

"It's not that simple."

"It's never that simple, but that doesn't mean you and I aren't clever enough to think of exceptions."

We stare a long moment, eyes unabashedly searching each other. Our faces, our bodies, hands and shoulders. His eyes travel my neck, across the curves of my breasts, the birthmark below my eye, before lingering on my lips. Mine graze his tan chin, and his fingers lift to touch the shadow of a beard there, as though my gaze is strong enough to feel.

I cannot help but wonder what it would feel like for his lips to press against my neck as mine kiss his jaw. My heart skips, and I suck in a sharp breath.

He leans forward, so close his breath warms my cheek and, in a voice like black velvet, whispers, "Make them regret the day they made Irene Adler do anything she didn't like."

Our eyes meet, separated only by the mere inches of difference in our height. My mouth opens slightly. I could ease forward just the tiniest amount on my toes and graze my tongue on his lower lip.

He leans backward, and cold floods through me. I blink dully as he stalks to the doorway.

He pauses and cocks his head without looking back at me. "Especially if that person is James Moriarty."

Dumbly, I stare at the doorway for a long moment after he

leaves. My pen, stolen from my father's desk, spins between my fingers as my lips purse. I'd once thought of freedom as a bird in flight, myself akin to a bird in a cage. I may not be free yet, but this bird can still sing.

"You look lovely, Irene," Geraldine says, kissing each of my cheeks. She looks me up and down, eyes wide. "That color suits you perfectly."

I shift uncomfortably, musing over my friend's compliment and my oily swirl of thoughts. If I hadn't already missed one dinner with my friend, I would have perhaps let my anxieties run wild and missed this one, too. I'd be continuing my search, sans Holmes this time, for the murderer.

With a demure smile and tongue as heavy as iron, I force a reply to Gerry. "Thank you. I saw this dress in the shop window and couldn't resist."

I had also bought it, full price, on my brother's credit. The color, a pale ivory that was in fashion last year, does not suit my rosy complexion and dark garnet hair, but the cut accentuates my figure to its best advantage. Something I note Edgar has noticed.

His cheeks are bright red as he nods. "My dear sister is correct. That dress looks ravish—I mean, beautiful on you."

I kiss him lightly on each inflamed cheek and accept the seat he pulls out for me. "You're too kind."

Geraldine calls over a waiter to ask for her favorite blend of Earl Grey. With her attention elsewhere, Edgar leans over to whisper, "I was being completely honest, Irene. You're looking especially beautiful today."

I dip my chin with a demure smile. "Thank you, Edgar."

He reaches across the table, then hesitates, his hand hovering over mine. "Have you already picked out a dress for the Saint Nicholas Ball?"

The Saint Nicholas Ball. I'd almost forgotten. It's less than a few weeks away.

"Is the school still truly hosting that party? With all that's happened…"

"The Bedfords have volunteered their estate," Geraldine pipes up, gaze bouncing between us with a growing smile.

"Oh." I cough, snapping out my white napkin to spread across my lap. It doesn't surprise me that Ermyntrude wouldn't dare let a few deaths get in her way of a party. Not after seeing the delight and eagerness with which she delved into our séance earlier this semester, so soon after Bertram's murder. "Then no, I haven't picked a dress out yet."

Geraldine sits up straighter. "I'd be happy to help you pick out a dress. I know exactly the color to bring out that hidden bordeaux tone in your hair."

"Perhaps red, or even black?" The hunger in Edgar's blue eyes is unmistakable.

"So out of season, though!" Gerry protests.

Edgar ignores her, scooching his chair closer. His gaze is earnest and eager. "Would you save your first dance for me, Ireney?" He does take my hand then, rubbing his thumb over the back with a tenderness I don't deserve. "It would mean everything to me."

My mouth opens and closes, words lost to me for once. I should accept him with all the eagerness of a newborn fawn. Lord Edgar

Hayward is the catch of the ton, a dear friend, and would dote on me for the rest of my—hopefully—long life.

"Yes," I say, the tremulous edge to my voice not forced. "Of course."

He gives my hand a squeeze and leans back with a smile so bright it could outshine the very sun.

"I'm so glad Edgar finally got the courage to ask you. He's been hounding me to do it for him for *weeks*," Geraldine says, practically glowing with happiness.

He blushes, and it makes me adore him all the more. "I don't believe in hiding my feelings, but I will admit that your lovely face, Irene, could make even the bravest man tremble."

A voice in the back of my head says that he would dote on me... and that I couldn't stand it.

He says to me, "James mentioned that he might join us."

Geraldine's aghast face turns toward me. "Did he change his mind?"

I snap open my menu. "He's otherwise occupied."

Geraldine opens her mouth to say something, reconsiders, and closes it, but the look she gives me says plenty, that I'll hear all about this later. Fair, but I'm sure it will be nothing compared to the earful I'll be getting from James.

"I've heard that the whitefish here is perfection on a plate," I say, raising a gloved hand to signal the waiter. "Shall we find out?"

Moriarty doesn't bother to knock before storming into my Lady Margaret room that night. I'm seated at my boudoir, running a brush through my hair when he storms in, and the only acknowledgment of his arrival that I give him is a slow rise of my eyebrows. "I hope you weren't late to dinner. Ermyntrude was so happy to receive your invitation."

"I'll make you pay for this. I looked like a fool," he growls, stomping toward me. His face is a startling magenta, and spittle flies across the room with his words. "I should have returned the favor."

"You always look like a fool." A shiver of fear runs up my spine. I give no indication of it, though, merely continue to brush my hair. "But our father will be pleased with you nonetheless."

He stops just short of reaching me and spits out, "What?"

"Father." I roll my eyes and repeat, "Will be so pleased with you. Classes addling your head, James?"

"You do that plenty." Moriarty takes another measured step. "What did you tell him?"

"That you had dinner plans with Ermyntrude, and I with the Haywards." I wave a hand in the air. "Rubbing elbows with the wealthy and lofty and all that."

His hands land firmly on my shoulders, and the shiver that runs up my spine is impossible to ignore. Between gritted teeth, he repeats, "What did you tell Father?"

"Just that we're finally doing what he's been asking us all along." I try to shrug from his grip, but he holds me firm. "Geraldine's brother is likely to propose to me within the week, and Ermyntrude would accept a proposal from you in even less time."

"I'm not marrying that trollop," Moriarty says, his words lashing like a whip. "You know very well my designs have always been for Geraldine."

"And *you know very well* that Gerry despises you."

He ignores the sleight. "And you don't give a damn about Edgar. Never have. Not really. His head is too full of fluff for your taste. He's not clever enough for a Moriarty."

My heart stills just as my eyes meet his eyes in the mirror. "Geraldine has no interest in you."

He lurches forward and snatches the brush from my hand. It splinters against the wall across the room.

With an effort to keep my body from trembling, I say, "I must remember to charge my new hairbrush to your account the next time I go shopping with Geraldine."

"Make sure to impress upon her my affections, then," James hisses.

"We can't court siblings from the same family, James. Imagine how the people will gossip." I hold a pearl earring up to my ear, consider my reflection with pursed lips, and put it back. "White really doesn't suit me."

"Irene." The calm in his voice is like a sheet of cold water. "Did you forget that I hold your seat in the All Souls class in the palm of my hand?"

"Even if I had forgotten, I doubt you'd allow my lapse in memory for very long," I say with all the tartness of a spring lemon. "But you wouldn't want to ruin your own chances, now, would you?"

His hands slide up from my shoulders, wrapping icy fingers around my neck. "What are you talking about?"

He squeezes, drawing my breath tight.

"The only way you could secure that seat is if you beat Isaac Holland through merit, not by forcibly removing him," I force out, meeting his pale eyes in the mirror. "They're not going to be so impressed if you come in second to Sherlock Holmes, and even less impressed if you would have gotten third without ripping the mask from Isaac's face."

His grip is almost imperceptibly tighter, making me wince.

My next words tumble out on a great gasp. "You can't beat Sherlock Holmes without me."

Moriarty releases me with a jerk, and I fall forward into the boudoir. Pain lances up my side from the bullet wound, making me bite back another gasp.

Sneering, he says, "I don't need you, or anyone, to take down Sherlock Holmes."

I rub my throat, eyes watering. "Is that why Holmes was accepted into the Bullingdon Club and"—it hadn't been hard to figure out that the dinner Holmes was being forced to attend tonight was for the club, and that the only reason Moriarty would be free to force himself into mine with Geraldine was because—"you were not?"

"Come again?" James comes to stand beside my chair and rests a hand atop my head, fingers digging into my hair. He tugs on the dark locks until my head is pulled back as far as it will go, baring my neck completely.

"Have you not noticed yet that all the All Souls professors are Bullingdon Club members, including our father?" I swat his hand away and turn to face him. "Are you hoping that nepotism will secure you that seat as well? Especially after you failed initiations night."

"I don't owe you any answers. Isaac Holland failed that initiation as well," James says, voice low. He cocks his head. "Is that why you notified the authorities about their little gathering? To keep them from asking secrets you couldn't answer?"

"How astute of you." I give him an exaggerated roll of my eyes, cocking my head just as he did. "I needed answers. Granted, I was hoping the Yard would wait at least a few moments more before storming the castle. Why did *you* accept their invitation?"

"Answers. The same as you. The Bullingdon Club means nothing to me, anyway. Only the All Souls seat." James walks about my room.

He pauses at my pillow, fingers splayed across the white cotton. Moriarty's teeth could cut like a knife with the smile he gives me. "And you think that you can break Holmes?"

"I know his weakness."

My brother goes as still as a statue. "I'm all ears."

Another shiver courses through me, this time from toes to the top of my head. "Me."

CHAPTER 26

A Rosewood Pipe

I STAND ON MY FATHER'S DOORSTEP, DRESSED IN THE FINEST dress I could find in my closet. My hands clench and unclench at my sides, feet tapping the white stone steps. Raucous laughter rumbles through the door, the evening well on its way. I raise a fist gloved in white silk, and then drop it again.

I should sit this dinner out. It's far too risky. Holmes—oh, Holmes, I can't believe I sold him out to my brother like that—is already too close to the truth. Moriarty only needs one misstep on my part to sell me out, and my father—oh, lord. My father is going to kill me.

Stackton is sure to be here, and he will flay me alive once he sees that I've disobeyed his direct order to not attend. Which, if I'm being honest, just made me want to attend all the more. The answers I might get from attending would be helpful, but would it be worth tumbling this tower of cards?

But Father will, and I'm not exaggerating, kill me.

"I can't do this," I say under my breath, turning on my heel.

And nearly bowl into Holmes. "Oh, I'm sorry, sir."

He takes a step back, chuckling. "Can't do what, Lady Adler?"

On my father's doorstep, the man is devastatingly handsome. His dark curls shine in the shimmering lamplight, painting the sharp panes of his face in shadow and gold. Sherlock's dark eyes, so depthless and knowing, carry an intelligence that stirs a hunger inside me.

Heat rises up my chest. I pat down my front, searching desperately for some excuse. "Eat dinner here tonight. My father's chef is a ghastly terrible cook."

Sherlock misses nothing. "Did you forget your pocket mirror or something?"

"Are you implying I need a mirror?" I give an awkward laugh and scratch at the inside of my wrist. Thinking fast, I say, "Just a token. I carry it everywhere with me, but must have left it in my dormitory."

He cocks his head to the side. "I've never noticed a token."

A flush threatens to rise up my neck. I spin on my heel to rap on the blue-painted panels.

He murmurs, "You really shouldn't have come without an escort."

I turn ever so slightly. "To my own father's house?"

"It's unseemly."

I scoff. "As if you give a damn about that. As if *I* give a damn."

He leans forward and, stealing my breath away, whispers, "There is also a murderer still at large."

The door swings open, my father's disgruntled and disapproving butler giving us both a wary once-over, and I'm saved from replying to Holmes by being ushered inside.

Holmes is correct. There is a murderer still running amok, and he could very well be in this room. In fact, it's the only reason I'm attending this damned dinner.

The All Souls cohort crowds my father's parlor. Sweat beads on the footmen's brows, likely not from the many lit candles, but from the wealth and power emanating from a single group of people. As if they, too, understand that they are in the presence of the Grim Reaper. Because any of this number could be the one swinging the scythe. I feel like a fool to ever believe I'd be able to discern which one tonight.

Edgar is notably absent, but Carlisle Gillingham is in attendance, rubbing elbows with the chancellor, all raising a toast to the impending winter holiday. Holmes is surrounded by our classmates, who stare daggers into his spine. None seems even the slightest bit afraid. None seems concerned about their mortality.

Dean Moriarty laughs and toasts with a group of them; my classmates flock to him, and my brother is on the opposite side of the room with his own entourage.

And I, with a glass of champagne, stand alone between them all.

Stackton's gaze meets mine for a mere instant, and he flushes such a dark maroon that I genuinely worry for his heart. Sputtering, he storms from the room, leaving a squall of confused professors and students in his wake. Holmes raises an eyebrow at me, and I astutely ignore him, looking for that curious fleck of dust in the bottom of my glass. I know it's there somewhere.

At least I wasn't fool enough to show up wearing Isaac's clothes. James, with that assured, cocky smile I've grown to know and despise, swaggers over. He leans down to whisper in my ear. "Rather brave of you to show your face here."

Flashing my brother a close-lipped smile, aware of at least a dozen pairs of eyes on us, I reply, "Wouldn't miss it."

"Irene," says a deep voice behind me. "I wasn't expecting you this evening."

Cringing, I turn slowly to face my father. His gaze sweeps me from head to foot.

"James insisted I make an appearance." I raise my glass in my brother's direction. "So many eligible bachelors in a single room."

"Don't sell yourself short, Irene," James says, gripping my shoulder. Hard. "You could catch the eye of any of these men even in a crowded pub. Like the Turf."

"Am I supposed to know where that is?" I raise my brows, face the image of sincere curiosity.

Dean Moriarty ignores his son. "I've been told that your grades are continuing to slip, Irene. And that you were recently truant from a number of classes."

"I was," I say, nodding. Sweat beads and drips down my spine, despite the discernible draft weaving through the room. "I was ill."

"With what?" My father's lip curls.

"A stomach bug, sir. I must have caught it while out to dinner with the Haywards."

I throw my friends' name out there like a bone for a hound, hoping my father will latch on. Perhaps the hunt for husbands is more important than my middling grades.

Dean Moriarty chuckles, eyes like cold obsidian. "Irene. I thought we discussed what would happen if you failed to bring your grades up."

"I'm sorry, sir." I bow my head. "I promise to never be truant again."

Nodding to himself, Richard returns to his other guests. James glares at me before marching over to his friends.

"That was too close," he whispers as he passes.

I snatch another glass of champagne from a passing servant and take a hearty gulp, steeling my nerves. I can do this.

I ignore the classmates glaring at me as I walk by. Moriarty and my father are deep in conversation with another professor, one from some absurd history course or another. "Monarchies Throughout the Centuries," or something. Slipping away, I take a deep, steadying breath.

I seek the company of the sole person who can calm my fears.

The library is easily the largest room in the house. There are many nooks and crannies perfect for hiding, ones I frequently used when escaping my brother. The book collection is extensive, stretching two stories high on worn shelves. The chemistry books hiding in the dark corner, untouched by the light streaming from the window, give me pause. And fill me with revulsion.

Dean Moriarty first came to Oxford, so many years ago, as a student of chemistry.

Like myself.

I don't care to consider how alike my father and I truly are. That would take me down a rabbit hole from which I could not climb.

I ignore the dusty texts and go straight to the portrait hanging above the room's sole fireplace, of Elena Adler.

My mother's face is just as I remember. I have her hair and skin and am reminded of such every time I look into the mirror. Our lips are the same, flush and a ruby red so bright I have to dash

Isaac's with powder every time I don his disguise. But she was slender where my curves linger, her chin rounded where mine is sharp, and she does not share my birthmark below the right eye.

Her smile, too, is so unlike mine. Witty, clever but not cunning, friendly and not forced. Despite being a courtesan, she was more of a lady than I could ever aspire to be.

"She is lovely, is she not?" I say to the darkness.

"I've seen lovelier."

Not even a trickle of surprise goes through me. I'd sensed Holmes the moment I walked into the room. Our souls seem attuned to each other.

His scent of stables and smoke harangues me as he slowly walks to my side, gazing up at the portrait. "An almost exact likeness of her daughter, save a few things."

"More than a few things," I say too quickly.

"Why are there no portraits of James's mother?" Holmes asks.

"Father never requested one made of her." I shrug. "Elena was an opera singer by day, a well-known adventuress"—my mouth quirks to the side—"by night. According to the rumors, it was love at first sight for Richard Moriarty, despite his pregnant wife at home. His obsession scared her, and she fled the country." I don't like the way Holmes's eyes burn into my face. "Or so they say."

The depths of my father's depravity were never shared on a gossip rag, rather across dinner tables. Many men admired Elena Adler, but none coveted her so much as Richard Moriarty. In the end, that obsession came at the cost of her life. Tears prick my eyes, and I brush them brusquely aside with the back of my wrist.

"My parents never mentioned it." Holmes inclines his head. "But we had not nearly so much money then."

My hands clench at my sides. "Which story do you believe?"

"I don't know which to believe, and perhaps that is exactly how you would like me to think." A small smile pulls at his lips.

I bite the inside of my cheek to keep from returning that smile.

"Have either of you considered that both stories are wrong?"

We both spin around. Dean Moriarty's hulking frame crowds the doorway. My father's face is shadowed, making it unreadable. A tremor of fear skitters up my spine.

"Would you care to correct us, then, Professor?" Holmes asks.

"I would not," he says, voice hoarse. He pins Sherlock with his icy gaze. "Were you invited up to the library?" He turns to me. "I hope I have not raised you to be so uncouth, Irene."

Before I can open my mouth, Holmes says, "James invited me up here, sir. Lady Adler just happened to be here."

Admiration rockets through me unbidden. Throwing James under the wheels of the metaphorical carriage is usually my expertise.

"And what is it my son wanted to discuss with you?" Dean Moriarty asks, voice laced with condescension and disbelief. My father's face is unreadable in the dim light, but I would know that tone anywhere.

Holmes either doesn't notice or doesn't care. "To discuss our research without the other students overhearing. Although, between us lads, I think it was truly only an excuse to get away from those stuffy old prats out there."

"Right." My father says the word like it disgusts him. "Well, my son should have known that this room would be closed for the party." He indicates the doorway. "I have to ask you to leave."

It wasn't a question. Rather an order.

I follow Holmes from the library, acutely aware of my father trailing my steps and of how very observant he has always been.

"Pardon me," I say, stepping aside to let my father past, cradling my stomach. "I find that the breakfast I ate this morning is not sitting well with me, either."

"Still feeling ill, Irene? Why did you bother attending this dinner when you weren't even invited?" Revulsion curls my father's lips. "Use the washroom on the second floor. If any of these boys sees you looking even the faintest bit ill, your worth on the marriage mart will slip."

With a nod and no argument, I dash up the stairs, ignoring the painful hitch from my still-healing gunshot wound and aware of my father's eyes burning between my shoulder blades.

Once safely ensconced in the washroom, surrounded by the familiar floral wallpaper, I rest my hands on the edge of the sink and take a deep, steadying breath. The cool porcelain beneath my palms is a balm against my frayed nerves. I will not let panic seize me. I will not let my fears keep me from solving this mystery. I will not let my doubts keep me from claiming that All Souls victory. Meeting my eyes in the mirror, I whisper, "You're still here."

This isn't for a seat in the All Souls. This is for the lads who were killed—I believe by the Bullingdon Club.

I inch the door open and take a peek down the hallway. Shadows stretch from one end toward the stairwell, threatening to chase me back to the party below. But I'm drawn across the hall, and my fingers land on the polished door to my father's office.

Picking the lock is a simple feat when I pull out one of the clips holding my curls in place. Making sure to lock the door once more behind me, I clench the clip between my teeth and get to work.

The meetings and classes blotting out the dates on his desk calendar are enough alibis to assure me that he is not the Bullingdon Club member committing the murders. On the underside of my wrist, though, I write each date down to verify later. My father, as I well know, is not above nefarious actions. He has nothing to gain from murdering my classmates, however.

I make easy work picking each drawer's lock, popping open one after another until the entire thing is wide open for me like the yawning mouth of a lion. There are no secret drawers in the desk; my father is too confident in nobody snooping around it for that.

There's a letter from my grandmother dated from a fortnight past. Her illustrious scrawl dances across the page before my eyes. My lips curl into a wry smile. My grandmother's letters never cease to bring me happiness—especially the venom-laced ones she sends my father.

Richard,

You know how much I despise having to write these words. I will no longer fund your child's education, nor will I fund your…habits. Irene's ship will stay its course, but James's will have to find a new captain. I cannot abide by the stories I've heard about your behavior, and his. They leave much to be desired in a civil society, and I've obviously done neither of you any favors in paying to further these unsavory endeavors. Give Irene my regards and tell James to wipe that frown from his face.

Augusta

So, she's finally cutting my father off.

What "unsavory endeavors" finally inspired that bold move? And my brother, though more wicked and twisted than a viper, must have finally bared his fangs wide enough for Augusta to see.

With pursed lips, I flip through the handful of papers in the desk. I find nothing until my fingers graze the back of the drawer and bump something hard. Frowning, I pull out a curved rosewood pipe. I'd never noticed my father smoking before. Perhaps a newer habit? But the scent wafting from the pipe is so unlike the normal scents from a pipe and yet gallingly familiar. Bringing the pipe to my nose, I take a careful sniff.

My vision immediately begins to fragment, cascading around the corners of my eyes like looking through a kaleidoscope. I blink quickly and the image disperses.

I shove the pipe into the back of the desk and take a step back, breathing hard. Whatever laces that pipe is no mere recreational smoke. Could this be the unsavory habit my grandmother mentioned?

Shaking my head, I slide the drawer shut and turn my attention to the others. I flip through documents, immaculately organized by date, and sigh when I find nothing important. There's a clip of heels down the hall and I still, hand hovering over the stack of letters. The gait, uneven and slow, is the familiar tread of the Moriarty butler, Reddington, and I return to snooping. He's not allowed in the office.

After closing and locking up the desk, I turn my attention to the shelves lining the study. There are no knickknacks or memorabilia in my father's study. As England's most prized mathematician, he has neither the patience nor interest in material things.

Instead, the shelves are lined with textbooks. Without looking, I already know that the top shelf is lined with old maps, some dating back hundreds of years, and not a few of Oxford campus.

There is the one painting, though.

My mother's sad smile mirrors my own as I walk over to the shelves. She wears Victorian lace, a white that I could never do justice, and her hair is pulled up in a braided crown. Her throat, long and graceful, is bare save a simple necklace with a pearl locket. My mother never took it off, even during performances. She even wore it to her grave.

Her ghostly hand seems to rest on my shoulder, and I whisper into the deepening shadows, "Give me a sign, Mother. Where can I find the killer?"

"No, sir." Reddington's voice wafts through the door of my father's study, making me flinch. "I haven't seen anything in the hall."

Cursing under my breath, I dive for the curtains. My father's footsteps pound toward his study. The lock clicks.

"But we'll miss dessert, and you know how much I love your chef's shortbread." Stackton's consoling voice echoes in the tall study.

My heart thunders in my chest hard enough to bruise a rib.

"I don't trust that gutter rat," my father barks. "Why didn't he show his face tonight? Where did you find him anyway?"

They're talking about Isaac.

"He's my nephew, as I've told all of you before, and I pray to God he's studying, as all these lads should be." Stackton sighs heavily. His shuffling gait passes right by the curtain I'm pressed behind. "You're not going to lecture me on nepotism, are you?"

Dean Moriarty makes an indistinguishable noise. There's a

click from the desk and the sliding open of his drawers. My grandmother's letter burns a hole in my pocket. If my father notices its absence now, I might as well guillotine myself.

"Let us return, Moriarty," Stackton says. He stops just before my feet. "To your black heart's desire, you can pester and embarrass the boy all you like in class, just to prove that your son is better."

"I don't need to prove anything." There's a click from somewhere in the room.

"Who is that?" There's only one painting in the room for Stackton to ask about.

"Irene's mother," the dean answers flippantly.

"Not James's as well?"

Stackton has no idea that there's not a single likeness of that woman in the entire house.

"Adelia meant nothing to me." Another click.

Stackton coughs. "Well, then. Onto more pressing matters. Should we double the officers on campus to appease the gentry? The university could not withstand another semester without their pocketbooks."

I can feel the weight of my father's skepticism even through the heavy curtain. There's a small groan from his chair as he stands and walks over to the window. I hold my breath and silently will him to not look my way. One look to the right, in Stackton's direction, and his gaze will cross my hiding spot.

"No," Dean Moriarty says, continuing to gaze out the long panes of glass. "We will find the killer soon enough."

From this angle, his nose is hooked like an eagle's beak. There's a soft patter of rain behind me but I can still damnably hear my own breathing. I clench my trembling fingers and jaw shut.

Stackton's steps echo as he walks around the desk to the other side of the window. "I think Holland will surprise you both."

My father chuckles. "Unlikely. Nothing surprises me anymore."

He shifts on his heel, and I bite my lip. But he's looking at Stackton. From here, I can see the threads of silver peppering his blond hair and the port-colored mole below his ear. "Shall we return to the party?"

"Only if you promise me another glass of your excellent brandy."

"That can be arranged," Dean Moriarty says, voice rough like gravel.

I wait long after the lock on the study clicks again and their steps echo past the stairs before returning to the party. I grab a glass of champagne to hide my burning cheeks and sweaty brow as I take a turn about the crowded room.

My brother veers in my direction, no doubt with some insult waiting to pounce from his tongue. I spin, ready to avoid him, and come face-to-face with Stackton.

His smile is forced when he says, "So glad you could attend, Irene."

What he truly wants to ask is *What the devil are you thinking by coming here?*

My fake smile matches his. "It would be rude not to attend."

I needed to find answers.

Silence stretches between us. Red fury blots his cheeks.

So low that I struggle to hear over the chatter of our classmates, Stackton says, "You are a bloody fool."

There's not even a flicker of surprise in me. I should have known better than to attend this dinner.

"Better than a dead fool." I swallow but keep my smile plastered on my face. "Why do you think I wore a dress instead of a suit?"

One of my classmates passes, and the professor raises his glass. "Have you tried the brandy? It's really quite exquisite."

"You needn't bother with a charade here," I say, raising my own glass. "These peacocks are too busy preening for the deans to give a damn about our conversation."

"And you should care much more," he snaps, all pretense gone. He hides his furious trembling behind another sip. "You really think they aren't watching our every move? Trying to read what our lips are saying? You're a blasted, arrogant fool, Irene Adler. Just like your father."

The words have the effect of a slap across my face. My breathing turns shallow, and I bite my cheek to keep from spitting back.

Heedless or uncaring to the turmoil he's stoked in me, Stackton continues, "The moment they found out Holland's rank, they started watching you. The moment you turned in that list, you put a target on your back. The moment you stepped into your father's office, he sniffed you out like a damned bloodhound caught on a scent."

"You really shouldn't tell me what topics you'll discuss in class next, Professor Stackton." I sniff, turning to the milling crowd around us. To everyone, we look like we're simply having a philosophical discussion.

"I no longer endorse Isaac Holland."

My gaze snaps back to him. "What?"

"I withdraw my support for your candidacy." Stackton nods, frowning. Shock shudders through me. "Yes, I will withdraw my support on Monday. You will still have your seat, but you can no longer hide behind me like a child behind their mother's skirt."

He grips my shoulder, giving it a firm squeeze. "Do not take it personally, Irene. I have known you since the day your father brought you to England. I've seen your stubbornness only grow over these many years. I just cannot continue to stand by while you let it drive you to risk your life."

After he leaves me, I stare into the bottom of my glass for a long time, swirling the golden liquid.

CHAPTER 27

A Matter of Dignity

The King's Colours flaps erratically in the breeze above me, and the first hints of winter whisper under my boots as I scurry across Merton Field to class. My books are tucked under my arms, and my breath fogs before my face, threatening to frost Isaac's glasses.

I can't help but feel a pair of eyes glued to the back of my neck. The corridors are eerily quiet as I moan with each step, *"Run, little girl. Run, run, run!"*

"Superstitious madness," I whisper to myself.

Gaze firmly glued to the floor, I bustle past my classmates to the back of the classroom just as the door slams open.

With the hounds of hell on his heels, Dean Moriarty strides in and slams a textbook on the desk, making us all jump. But none so high as myself. We're not supposed to take my father's mathematics class until the spring semester, by which time I was hoping to test out.

"Professor Stackton has asked for me to replace him today." My father picks up a piece of chalk and immediately starts scribbling formulae across the board. "I have neither the time nor patience for fatuous questions, so please keep up."

As if sensing my dread, James turns to me. His crooked smile is laced with vinegar and poison.

I force myself to sit behind the tallest student in our cohort, Robert Lancaster, a lord from the heart of London's elite. The equations my father scribbles are difficult, but not impossibly so. I get to work on solving them, one by one, knowing not to wait for his instruction, and Moriarty does the same. The dean despises very little more than having to explain what he wants.

"Well?" he barks. "What are you waiting for? Do you all need me to hold your pen as you write these down? I thought we chose scholars, not children."

Noses pressed firmly to their notes, my cohort begins their first class under Dean Richard Moriarty.

Some of my classmates have no previous knowledge to draw from, though, and sit there dazedly watching my father. Holmes dives into solving the problems, but of course has no need to write them down to do so. His lips move as he repeats the formulae under his breath, merely scrawling the answers. Brilliant ass.

The wind howls down the corridor outside the classroom, covering the incessant scratching of pens. I will my focus to remain on my own pen as Dean Moriarty stalks up and down the lines of desks.

He pauses next to Holmes, peering over his shoulder at the answers—the only thing he's written—on his sheet. He stops beside James, a sneer curling his lips. I quickly return my gaze to my own paper when he starts in my direction.

Despite the chill, sweat drips down my spine. My head is suddenly insufferably hot beneath Isaac's wig and my lips clammy under his fake mustache. My father treads closer and closer until he's right beside me, then stops. Astutely ignoring him, I continue my furious scribbling.

His breath is hot against my neck when he leans down. "Number four is incorrect."

My pen screeches across the paper. A giant inhale echoes from around the classroom.

"Better to take the time to properly solve a question than to work too quickly and get everything wrong." Dean Moriarty straightens, and nobody could confuse the smugness on his face. "Use your classmate Mr. Holland as an example, class, of how not to be a student. You will all likely go far, but upstarts such as he must accept that brilliance is only found in a certain social class."

Earned by the wealthy and powerful, he fails to add.

Chuckles escape my classmates. My face burns a brilliant scarlet. Dean Moriarty continues walking down the row. I drop my gaze back down to the paper, pen raised to cross off the equation and try again, but my hand stays above the paper.

I should be quiet. I should keep my mouth shut. I should not say a single word.

"*Draw no undue attention, for they cannot know what you are hiding.*" Though no longer my mentor, I should still heed Stackton's advice.

My mouth opens and my voice damns me. "Professor."

His pale eyes pin me to my seat as surely as if lanced. My shoulders threaten to bow beneath the weight of that heavy, judgmental stare. Meek Isaac would swallow his own words and beg for forgiveness. My mother seems to speak through me when I say, "Actually, my answer for number four is correct."

Holmes's brows rise as high as his hairline, and the glare my brother shoots me would back down a lesser man. I am no man, though.

"Did you hear that, class?" The smile on my father's face is smug. "Little Holland thinks he is smarter than a dean of Oxford with more than thirty years of mathematical study under his belt."

Carlisle, not one to miss an opportunity, says, "I believe I heard him say '*I am the smartest one here,*' but feel free to correct me, Professor."

"No need." He turns and starts walking toward the front of the classroom. My classmates watch me, waiting to see if I'll bite my tongue or put my own neck in the lunette of a guillotine. I open my mouth, tempting the reaper's scythe.

"Mr. Holland is likely correct, Professor Moriarty."

Shock splashes over me like a wave from the frigid sea. Slowly, I turn to see my brother now rising from his seat. He continues, "The way you've written the formula on the board is incorrect. You should have written the first half with a closed interval, not an open one."

"That's Dean Moriarty, to you," our father says with a snarl. His gaze snaps to the board where, sure enough, I'd automatically assumed he meant to write a closed interval. When he turns back to his son, the look he gives him reminds me of the darkest days of my childhood. The simmering, lethal fury in his eyes shutters.

"Be that as it may"—his nostrils flare—"only fools question their superiors."

"Better to question a superior," I say, voice deep and low, "than to blindly follow one to my folly."

Dean Moriarty turns to me, leveling me with the full might of his ire, the effect like taking a pan of baking grease to the face. Hopefully he doesn't see how the tailoring of my suit might not hide my hips, or of how the makeup on my face might be smudged and reveal the birthmark below my eye. Or perhaps recognize the eyes and lips I share with my mother, things no amount of makeup could hide. I tip my chin high, glaring down my nose at the man who ruined my life. Daring him to discover my secret.

Before he can retort, though, my brother speaks up again.

"Where would England be if we so blindly followed our rulers?" James asks, still standing. "We would be no better than the serfs."

A tic forms below my father's right eye, twitching so badly I wonder if he's on the verge of an aneurysm. With a parting glare that promises words later, Dean Moriarty turns to the board. Wordlessly, he writes an impossible list of equations and reading for us.

"Bring these to my desk by tomorrow at noon," he says, answered by a chorus of groans from my classmates. "Or remove yourselves from the All Souls cohort."

My fellows turn in their seats to glare at me, but none are so angry as my brother. While my father may turn him upside down with a verbal lashing later, James will chew me up and spit out the pieces. He didn't save me from our father's ire out of brotherly affection.

He did it because my secret is his to use when it is most advantageous, and he didn't want our father to discover it just yet.

Which begs the question: When will he tell everyone?

Night settles upon Oxford like a dark fog, and the men's dormitory is almost entirely empty, most of the male students having long fled to their country estates and London townhomes, no longer comfortable with spending time in this city.

When I shove open the door to my dorm, I find the floor plastered with newspaper clippings. Leaked images of the bodies.

Even more surprising is Sherlock Holmes, sitting on my bed.

"Do you think it's a warning from the club?" Holmes asks, waving to the papers.

"I think it's the murderer." I bend and pick up one, the front page a giant picture of Bertram's body hanging from the library window. "They want our fear."

I sweep past all the images and sit at my desk, the stack of texts tumbling from my arms. "What are you doing here, Holmes?"

"I live here, too."

"You haven't stepped in this room after dark since that night we visited the mortuary."

"Fine, if I'm being honest—"

I scoff.

He continues, ignoring the sound. "I want to resume our partnership." He folds his hands over his stomach and leans back, watching me begin to number the left side of a piece of parchment. "Academically, at least."

I chuckle dryly. "Tripping yourself on Dean Moriarty's homework?"

Silence stretches between us, broken only by the scratching of my pen. I let it, refusing to break before that pompous ratbag.

"I'm sorry, Holland."

My head snaps up and my jaw drops.

"It was wrong to compare you to Moriarty." He leans forward and plants his palms on the table. His eyes, so dark I cannot read them, bore into mine. "And to blame you for the actions of the Bullingdon Club. We are nothing but pawns to all of them, when we really should have been working together to make them regret playing games with us."

We methodically conquer each of my father's assignments one by one. Our minds work brilliantly together, his methodical, mine creative. Where I cannot find the answer, he can, and the holes that he overlooks I am quick to notice.

"That was a queer... tête-à-tête in class earlier." Sherlock gives me an indecipherable look, kicking his feet into the air and stretching across my bed.

"Get your shoes off my pillows, Holmes."

He ignores me. "What did you do to stir Dean Moriarty's ire?"

I release a long, beleaguered sigh. "I had the gall to rise higher than his son in the ranks."

He frowns. "Then why would his son defend you?"

I don't like the way he examines me.

"Perhaps it had less to do with defending me than the act of standing up to his father." I shrug, returning my attention to the endless list of equations. "It was probably a matter of dignity."

"I very much doubt that," Sherlock mutters.

Before I can resume my studying, his voice stops me. "I'm truly sorry... Holland."

I continue writing, shoulders curled inward. "I know. No need to repeat yourself."

"For being angry with you like I was." I lift my gaze as Holmes drags a hand over his face. "It's not your fault the club is so vile, nor did you force them to partake in such terrible acts."

"It was inevitable, really." I straighten my jacket. "That the rich and powerful would play such games, when they gamble with people's lives as though they are nothing."

"I lied before," he says. "I haven't entirely ruled them out."

"You believe one of them could be complicit in the murders?"

"Not just one. All."

I blink behind Isaac's glasses. "What made you deduce that?"

"Deductive reasoning." He nods to himself, straightening his jacket.

I mirror his nod. "Exactly the nonanswer I've come to expect from you. Perhaps you could be useful for once and clean up the mess on the floor?"

"Would you agree to resume our partnership if I do?" There's no mistaking the hopefulness in his voice now.

"I'll consider it," I allow.

Quick as a whip, Holmes leaps from my bed and starts crumpling all the pieces of paper into balls, tossing them one after another into the small, unlit hearth. Every so often, he glances up at me, working away on our assignments, but doesn't press further.

Eventually, I give in to my curiosity and dare to ask, "Has your friend forgiven you yet?"

He straightens and pulls out his pocket watch, glances at the face, and then tucks it away. "Friends are for fools."

Hurt flashes through me, and I attempt to tamper it down. I'm not his friend. I'm using him like all the others.

A Moriarty through and through, I think bitterly.

"Why do you think they did not accept James? His father is a powerful figure on campus. He could take the slight personally."

"You're more likely to catch a weasel asleep than see James Moriarty be concerned about petty *slights*." Sherlock sneers, light from the lamp partially shading his face. "That ratbag has far too large an ego to ever be concerned with what anyone thinks of him."

I cannot argue with him, nor am I given the chance to.

"Glad to hear you think so highly of me, Holmes."

Both of us jump, spinning to find James leaning against the doorframe.

"Why are you here?" Holmes bites out. "Shouldn't you be tucked into bed?"

"Didn't you hear the bells?" Moriarty points a finger to the ceiling and cocks an ear.

They ring, no rhyme or reason, no specific number to announce the time. Loud and clear, they announce for all something ominous and foreboding. The blood drains from my face.

Holmes whispers, "There's been another murder."

I must be as pale as a sheet. "Who?"

My brother's smile is greasy enough to butter bread. "Edgar Hayward. Geraldine's brother."

A pained noise escapes me. Holmes's gaze whips in my direction. I grip the arms of my chair to keep from falling out of it. A heartrending assortment of emotions rain through me.

My voice cracks. "You're lying."

"Why would I lie about that?" My brother looks at me with something akin to disappointment before turning again to Holmes, whose skin has taken on a deathly sheen. "His body was found just outside the Bodleian, in fact. It will take a long time to remove the blood. Anyway, the Yard is searching the campus for suspects. As you two are the only men still residing in the dormitories, I'm sure you'll be at the top of their list for questioning." His grin is both wolfish and wicked. "Again."

James dips his chin and turns on his heel, leaving me and Holmes to stare at each other, the abject horror on his face likely mirroring mine. Too late, I remember someone who likely feels worse than me.

Geraldine.

CHAPTER 28

His Golden Hair

THE GHOSTS OF OXFORD TRAIL MY POUNDING FOOTSTEPS. The Scotland Yard patrols every shadow and stalks every hallway. With a single stop to grab a nightdress from a hidden nook, I avoid them all, dashing across green and cobblestone road, tearing free my costume as I go. The wound in my side blazes with the fires of Dante's inferno as I toss the pieces of my disguise, tussle up my hair, wipe the makeup from my face, and rub my eyes extra hard to make them red-rimmed.

Sure enough, officers are loitering in the doorway of the Haywards' Oxford town house. I shove past them. They're heedless of a woman in their midst, having no doubt resolved themselves that a woman could never be behind these gruesome murders. Taking the stairs, I sprint up them, two at a time, and dash down the familiar corridors. At the end, on a small window seat, they interview a sobbing Geraldine.

Officers huddle together and whisper around her. Arranging

my face into my best I-can't-believe-it's-true look, I tiptoe toward them.

With a face pulled taut with regret, John Watson turns to face me. "You need to return to the dormitories, or better yet your family's home, Miss Adler. An officer will escort you."

"Please tell me this is all a grand charade." My pleading expression is far from an act.

I want to beg him to tell me it is all a lie, that my brother is wrong.

"I'm sure the school will share that information with you in time," he says gently, reaching an arm out to guide me away.

Fast as an adder, I duck beneath it and dash down the hall. Ermyntrude sits beside Geraldine with an arm wrapped around her trembling shoulders. Ignoring the protesting officers, I kneel on the cold floor at my friend's feet and rest a tentative hand on her knee.

"Gerry?" My voice shakes of its own accord. There is no false pain in me where my friend is concerned. "What happened?"

I hate to ask. I know damn well what happened, and thinking of Edgar's sweet, cheery face fills me with shame. I can only imagine what Geraldine must be feeling.

"He's dead," she sobs through her hands. "My brother is dead."

Even with prior knowledge, I threaten to crumble beneath the tragedy of it all. Unbidden, tears stream down my cheeks and a sob escapes me.

"How?" My voice cracks around another wrenching sob. "That can't be true."

I don't believe it. This must all be some wicked game my brother plays. These officers are all his pawns. Edgar's lovely face swims in my mind. His tousled golden hair and endearing, honest smile.

"That's what we're here to find out." John Watson steps behind me, pad of paper and pen ready. "Where have you been this evening? What brought you to this house tonight?"

"Sleeping. Where else would I be?" I say, affronted despite the lie. "My brother brought me the news."

He frowns imperceptibly, just the slightest narrowing of his brows. Hopefully the officers didn't knock on my door before I got here....

"And how did you know Edgar Hayworth?"

"I..." The answer escapes me. "I..."

"Irene has been a friend for many years," Geraldine says, dropping her hands to reveal swollen red eyes. "And my brother loved Irene for all that time."

"How poetic," Ermyntrude whispers.

Something akin to guilt eats at me in the pit of my stomach. I'd never thought of Edgar in that way, never with such romance. Ermyntrude's gaze bores into me, but I refuse to meet it.

Lip trembling, Geraldine turns to Watson standing above me. "Why would anyone kill Edgar?"

"We're still trying to figure that out." He hesitates, shifting from foot to foot. "There is no doubt now that these murders are related."

"Then why haven't you fools learned anything in months?" Ermyntrude snaps. "Once my father hears of this, he'll—"

She's interrupted by the arrival of Lord Hayward, Geraldine and Edgar's father. There's a sudden commotion at the end of the hall. He roars for answers as the officers all crowd around him. I take Geraldine's hand, cold as ice, and give it a gentle squeeze. Words of comfort escape me, for once at a loss of what to say.

She seems to sense as much, giving me a small nod before cupping her face in her hands once more. Ermyntrude rubs her back, glaring at me as though all of this is my fault.

And I wonder if it very well could be.

CHAPTER 29

The Orchard and Bend

THE EARLIEST BUDS OF SPRING GLAZED THE TREES OUTSIDE my room with pale green and pink. If I wanted, I could smash a window and reach through the mist toward them. Songbirds trill, begging me to escape my newfound prison. With a tiny huff, I turn from their taunts and slam my bottom down on my bed.

Tantrums had gotten me nowhere, and begging had fallen on deaf ears.

I'd only been allowed to leave my room three times in the ensuing weeks since arriving at the Moriarty estate on that dark winter morning. Once, for dinner with my father and brother, abruptly ended when I flung my soup in Richard's face. The second, when led around the garden and promptly paddled over the lip of a fountain for my insolence. And the third when I flung myself from the window.

My arm was in a sling, the back of my neck carefully stitched up, and my windows firmly nailed shut.

I'd given up hope of ever leaving again when Reddington abruptly swung open the ornate doors of my room. In strode Augusta, not yet so wrinkled, with piercing pale eyes that pinned me to the bed.

"I've heard from my son that you're quite the menace," she says, striding toward me. "That you listen to no command and have no wisdom but your own." Her lips pull into a pale pink smirk. "That you're a Tasmanian devil in human flesh."

I raise my tiny chin, staring down this woman I have yet to meet or know, daring her to bring out the monster lurking inside me.

"That"—slowly, she sits on the edge of the bed beside me—"your mother failed to bridle the Moriarty in your blood."

"I'm no Moriarty," I say, voice cracking.

"You are," she replies without emotion. "But that doesn't mean you can't have friends."

Taking my good hand in hers, she tugs me to my feet. Mutely, searching for any escape, I follow her down the long halls of Moriarty's town house. She leads me down the sweeping, spiral staircase to the foyer, where the doors hang open and let in a cool breeze.

Three figures stand in the entrance. My grandmother, followed by the Lady Hayward, walks into the sitting room and leaves me with the two perfect children.

Geraldine looks exactly like a doll, with her porcelain, unblemished skin and Botticelli gilded curls. Edgar could be Eros, likewise perfect and serene, and not a day older than twelve. While the Moriarty servants have all looked at me with a mixture of revulsion and fear, the Haywood siblings are merely curious.

"You're Irene Moriarty?" young Geraldine asks with an imperious voice.

"Adler." My face pulls deeper into a frown. Both siblings raise their pale brows in question, and I elaborate. "Irene... Adler. I'm no Moriarty."

"That's not what my momma said." Geraldine raises her chin.

"But Father said she would go by Adler," Edgar tells his sister, but his gaze never leaves mine.

"I'll never go by Moriarty." I can feel the telltale pricking of tears behind my traitorous eyes.

"As you shouldn't." Geraldine sports a petulant frown. "They're a bunch of ratbags."

"Gerry!" Edgar scolds.

She ignores him. "What happened to your arm?"

I think in vain for an excuse for the sling across my chest and come up empty. "I tried to fly."

"I tried to fly once." Geraldine flashes an adoring smile to her brother. "Edgar caught me before I could fall."

"I could catch you next time," Edgar says eagerly, bright blue eyes boring into mine. He steps forward and places a hand over his heart. "It's what a friend would do."

With my head slightly bowed, I look up between the two of them. "I've never had a friend."

"We can be friends." Geraldine takes my tiny hands in hers. "The three of us. Forever."

"Forever," Edgar repeats with a smile as bright as a summer dawn.

Despite knowing the word as impossible, my young heart still wants it to be true. So, I grip Geraldine's hands tighter and say, "Forever."

The wind outside screams and rattles the shutters. I find no solace in sleep. Sweat coats my body beneath the scratchy wool of my coverlet. I toss and turn, kicking the blanket from my bare legs and imagining it is a face bathed in shadow, a portrait without an object. The faceless murderer who haunts my every step and taunts my every waking moment. Who stole from me a man I could have grown to love if I had ever given him a chance.

Gnawing on my nails, I leap from the bed and storm over to the desk. I cannot tumble down that rabbit hole. Not yet.

My mind becomes as methodical as Holmes's. First, I finish the last of my homework due to my father as the night ever gradually turns to gray.

Then, taking out my crudely drawn tree of Bullingdon members, I hang it on the stone wall. Beside it, I hang a blank sheet, take up my last nib pen, and begin to write.

Their names come to me like whispers in my ear. First there was poor Bertram Elmstone, found in the library. Then Jude Wilson and Hugo Davies quickly followed suit with their untimely demises. And, last, I write Edgar Hayward.

The pain in my chest is like a manacle around my heart, squeezing tighter and tighter as I scratch his name across the sheet. Despite the years full of memories with Edgar, laughing and blushing and dancing in midnight gardens, that is all I feel, and perhaps that makes me a monster. I should be devastated at the death of one of my oldest friends, but all I feel is a lingering pain and a single-minded drive to find who did this.

I could have never loved him as much as he loved me. Perhaps I'm selfish for never returning his affections in such an ardent way. Or perhaps I'm heartless after all my family has put me through. Or, even worse, perhaps it is simply the Moriarty in my blood.

I will find Edgar's murderer.

For Geraldine and Edgar and the forever she once promised us both.

My friend shooed all of us, Ermyntrude included, from her room many hours ago. I'll check on her this afternoon.

The cold stone floor burns into my feet as I pace back and forth, considering the two sheets before me. Looking at the long, splintered branches of the Bullingdon tree, I take up my pen and begin to write once more, noting the families and lineages of the deceased.

Bertram and Edgar being cousins, I draw a line between them. Next, I draw a line from Hugo to Edgar, both related to the Earl of Arundel. Hugo and Jude were also distant cousins, one the son of a viscount and the other the nephew of the Duke of Bedford, Ermyntrude's father.

I purse my lips. Glancing between the lines on the two papers. Ripping down the Bullingdon Club sheet, I hang it before my fireplace. The fire burns bright, illuminating the lines like beacons. On top of the sheet, I pin the other.

I blink, mouth popping open. "Oh."

The lines perfectly match. All have family, extended or otherwise, that were once members of the Bullingdon Club. But that can't be the reason behind their deaths.

Someone wasn't killing merely members of the All Souls cohort, or members and enemies of the Bullingdon Club, because those three things are all one in the same—they're killing the members of the ruling class, reaching right up to the highest echelons of nobility.

And all these dead heirs were, like herding sheep to slaughter, brought to the same place: the All Souls.

But who is killing them and what do they have to gain?

A pounding on my door makes me jump.

"Irene," James bellows. "I know you're in there."

I look around for a place to store the papers. But with the ink still wet and the sheets so large, none are forthcoming.

"Did you forget that I have a key?" There's a scuffing of feet on the other side of the door as he must fumble in his pockets.

With a grimace, I rip down the papers and crumple them up, tossing them into the fire just as the latch on my door turns.

I glare at my brother as he marches into my room. His chest is puffed up. "I've just come from Geraldine's rooms. Poor woman is quite a mess, but I think I've stirred up some light in her life."

My lips curl. "The only feelings you could stir in anyone are revulsion and fury."

"No need to be so sour with me, dear sister." He looks to the fire and back to me, eyeing the fresh plumes of smoke. "What were you doing? Don't you have to put on your ridiculous disguise soon to make it to our father's office in time to turn in your work?"

Damn. He's right.

Though I won't admit it. I cross my arms and baldly lie. "I've already turned it in."

The way he rolls his eyes says just how much he believes that. "Well, don't let me keep you. I've offered to take Geraldine to her country estate for the next few days in our family carriage."

"How uncharacteristically gentlemanly of you," I say with a smile so sweet it could choke. "I can only wonder what you have to gain from it."

"Are you so blighted by Edgar's death that you're taking it out on me?" He clucks his tongue. "I'm sure you'll find some other lord desperate enough to court you."

I only respond with a glare.

"I'll see you in class." He tips his hat, turning to leave. "That is, if they don't cancel them. Edgar's death has caused quite the uproar. The deans have let this go on for long enough. They've even reined in the clubs. No more parties until the killer is caught."

"Clubs?" As in plural? "Not just the Bullingdon Club?"

"The Bullingdon Club and the Gridirons." James scoffs. "You truly do only pretend to know everything, *Ireney*."

"Don't call me that," I bite out. Only Gerry and Edgar can use that name. "Where were you at the time of Edgar's death?"

He turns slowly, smile gone. "At the Turf with Moran. Plenty of witnesses. Why? Am I a suspect on your list?" He points to the smoldering ash where my notes roast in the fire. "Time to stop playing at detective, Irene, or you'll find yourself on the top of someone else's list of victims."

I cross my arms. "Is that a threat?"

The bastard merely shrugs.

He slams the door shut behind him and, damn it all, I barely have enough time to pull on my disguise and dash across campus before my father can give me the boot from the All Souls cohort. I'm leaving his office after dropping off my work when I walk headfirst into Holmes.

He grabs me by the shoulder. "We need to talk."

Oh, bloody hell. "We talk every day, Holmes. Can I not have a single moment of peace?"

He steers me from the building. "Let's get a pint."

"It's not even noon."

"A pair of them, then. Each." He marches across the courtyard, not waiting to see if I follow. "This cannot wait."

After Holmes downs the contents of at least three pints, he claps his chest and stares me down. I sit across from him in the corner of a crowded pub. His eyes flick warily to the patrons milling about.

"I cannot carry on my charade with the Bullingdon Club," he says unceremoniously, resting his feet on a chair. "They're meeting next at the Orchard and Bend, this evening. I won't join them."

My eyebrows rise. "Why the hell not?"

He inclines his head. "I just cannot stand their stupidity and brazen disrespect for others."

I must be hearing things. "Edgar—our classmates are dead and you won't attend a meeting because you *can't stand stupidity?*"

"No. Well. That, too." He tries to win me over with a crooked grin that only makes me angrier. "I am their lapdog. A toy for the rich. They lead me on with their merry games, but they have no inclination toward keeping me as a member of their club. Only the nobles have that *privilege.*"

The way he says the word emphasizes how very far from a *privilege* he believes it to be.

"But that's just it, Holmes." I slap a hand to the table, failing to keep my voice to Isaac's low, male tenor. "The murders are related not to the club, nor to the All Souls cohort. They're all nobles, related to one another."

His eyes go vacant; the cogs whirl in his head.

I continue, "Though the club might not be ordering these murders, they sure as hell are complicit. We only need a few meetings more, just a smidgeon of information to find out which among them is an accomplice."

"We have no proof that they are actually complicit."

"Hence why we must forge on."

He shakes his head. "I don't need to attend their damn meetings. We can learn this another way that doesn't involve me swallowing my dignity."

"Your dignity has enough ego to stomach it, I assure you." I lean back, fixing him with my sternest glare. "This is worth it."

"Then sacrifice your own neck for all I care," he says, waving a hand through the air.

"It's no wonder Lady Adler won't give you a moment of her time," I say between clenched teeth. "You're absolutely incorrigible."

"Using her to inspire something in me won't work, Holland."

"It won't?" I cross my arms. "Did you know that Edgar Hayward was courting her at the time of his death?"

His feet thud to the floor. Whatever emotions I would have been able to read in his gaze are shuttered out. Now I am as cruel as my brother, manipulating Holmes as James manipulates me.

My throat tightens. "She must be feeling ghastly right now."

Sherlock swallows. "I will not go to another meeting."

"Then I'll go and spy on them."

"You can't go alone," he says firmly.

We hold each other's gazes. "This was never about stopping murders, was it? For you, this was about making sure that you're not the next target."

"Don't you dare lecture me, Holland," he hisses, pointing at my chest. "This was never about stopping the murders for you, either.

This was about a question you couldn't stand to not know the answer to."

My heart thuds hollowly in my chest. Sherlock Holmes sees me more clearly as Isaac Holland than he ever could Irene, and it kills me.

Throwing a pair of coins on the table, I march from the pub without looking back.

Isaac's disguise still firmly glued to my poor face, I inch from shadow to shadow, creeping down Oxford's streets to the Orchard and Bend.

As I'm crossing the bridge over the Cherwell, pulling my jacket high to hide my face, a thought hits me like the gong of a drum.

Only a few more turns, and I'll arrive at the Orchard and Bend. Just past this very bridge. The last place I saw Hugo before he died. Hugo Davies had lodging in town, not campus, so why had he come to this bridge at all?

"Might as well kill two birds with one stone."

The papers said that Jude's murder occurred on the corner of Alfred Lane and St. Johns on the other side of the bridge, toward campus. The buildings on the corner arch high into the night sky, dimming whatever light from the moon I had hoped to use for my snooping.

I know from my snooping in the morgue that Jude was stabbed in the abdomen. There is no way, despite what the Deans of Oxford and newspapers suggest, that the wounds could have been self-inflicted.

Why would the newspapers lie, or had they been fed false information? And why haven't the people who found Jude's body reported the true nature of his wounds? Can someone in the Yard not confirm these blatant untruths, or has the Bullingdon Club paid them for their silence?

Too many questions. Not enough answers.

I slap a gloved hand against the stone wall and bend down to examine the stones, grateful for the flickering lamplight. No trace of blood remains after all this time, of course. I should have come straightaway if I wanted those kinds of clues. But, from the sketch in the tabloids, Jude had been found slumped over, chin drooping against his chest, and exactly on the corner.

The stench of smoke permeates the air, burning my nose. Someone had either surprised and stabbed him just as he made the turn, or perhaps he had been walking with someone he knew, and so he had turned to face them just as the knife pierced his gut. The brand on his body connected his murder to the others on campus, at the very least. Or perhaps a false ruse. I sigh heavily, clenching and unclenching my hands.

The time of death had been just past midnight. Three hours after I had last seen him at the Turf. Doubt rises in me like a cold wave. It is unlikely that it actually took Jude that long, though drunkenly, to walk from the Turf to this spot. So where had he gone in that time, and why would the Yard lie to the press about it?

More questions. Still no answers.

Had I still been on the Yard's list of suspects, it would be incredibly hard to find an alibi. All the murders happened within spitting distance of where I, as Isaac Holland, had been only hours before. Either the murderer was trailing my footsteps, or they were working overtime to frame me. Obviously, neither thought is comforting.

I scrunch my nose, trying to remember what lay on the map between the Turf, the Orchard and Bend, and campus. Nothing noteworthy comes to mind. Another sigh escapes me as I continue down the cobblestone road. A puzzle I will have to piece together later.

The Orchard and Bend is a white building, a moon on the dark street, as I round the next corner. My steps immediately slow, despite the people milling to and fro in the early evening. Not a single unaccompanied lady, save myself technically. Still, the front door just won't do.

Much nicer than the last establishment I bore witness to the club's antics in, the fine dining restaurant boasts the most prestigious clientele and steepest prices. I avoid a beggar sprawled across the ground in the back alley and peer through a window. Nothing but a dark room greets me. I try another room, but only see diners enjoying their overpriced meals. Cursing colorfully under my breath, I try the third and final window, a long, narrow slat carved into the brick wall. There's no one, but I can see a set of carpeted stairs.

I weigh my options. I could go inside and pretend to be a customer, before dashing for the "water closet." But there would be too many witnesses.

I could also try to sneak in the servants' entrance. Biting my lip and ignoring my thundering heart, I ease open the back door. I creep down the long hallway, keeping an ear on the bustle behind the kitchen door. The door opens and I straighten, plastering a confused look on my face.

The waiter stops before me and asks, "Looking for the lavatory? It's just up the stairs."

He points and I give him a grateful smile. "Thanks, lad."

On the next floor, I follow new sounds. Raucous cheering comes from the end of this hallway, behind a single door at the very end. Carlisle's unintelligible voice booms through the red-painted wood. My heart is loud enough to stir the dead now. There are no windows for me to hide behind. No friends downstairs I can pretend to have come to meet. If I'm caught now, I've as good as signed my own death warrant.

I try the handle of the door beside and find it unlocked. Easing the door open, I step swiftly inside the unlit room.

The sounds in the next room suddenly dim. Pressing my ear against the wall, I hold my breath and wait for Carlisle's voice to greet me.

A blinding pain flashes in the back of my skull and the world crashes into darkness.

CHAPTER 30

Teeth Stained Red

I'M SO COLD, MY BONES THREATEN TO SPLINTER. LIGHT PIERCES my heavy eyelids. Blearily, I blink to a lantern swinging before my face. The chill comes from an open window behind me. My jacket's been ripped off and my feet are bare. The back of my head still stings, and blood drips down my neck.

"I never expected the lad to weigh so little," someone beyond my sight muses.

"Not all of us have fathers to pay for our every meal, Gillingham," I say around a mouthful of cotton. If they still think I'm a lad, then I'm lucky enough that they haven't noticed the binding around my chest, nor, judging by the breeze against my bare neck, has my wig been ripped off.

But it's only a matter of time.

They've taken Isaac's glasses, so I squint as though I struggle to make out the figures standing around me. "Is this really necessary?"

"You tell us, Holland." Carlisle's voice greets me from the back of the room.

I sigh. "When the porter told me that the lavatory was upstairs, I had no idea I'd have to relieve myself with my hands behind my back. Any of you lads want to help me out?"

I'm rewarded with a punch across the jaw that snaps my head to the side. My teeth sing and blood fills my mouth. There's a sharp sting in my side, and warmth begins to trickle down my abdomen. The bullet wound has torn open.

Spitting blood at their feet, I grimace. "That was definitely unnecessary."

Robert Lancaster steps into the light, rubbing the knuckles of his pale hand. I bet his skin is so soft, the bones so weak, that the lord hurt his hand more than my face. Entitlement makes these boys weak, inside and out.

Carlisle scoffs, stomping forward. "You've been watching us from the moment you stepped onto Oxford soil, haven't you?"

"Truth be told, you only caught my eye when the bodies started piling up around campus." I notch my chin high, glaring at them all. Up close, I can recognize all their faces, and all come from unimaginably powerful families. If I ever make it out of this mess, Isaac Holland will forever have a target on his back. If he didn't already.

With little else to lose, as they will discover my identity soon enough, I say, "Why did the club have those lads murdered? How could their deaths possibly benefit you?"

Carlisle's skin turns an ungodly shade of red, and his teeth are bared. "You think that we had those men killed? Are you insane, Holland? Why would we kill our classmates?"

I shrug. "To get the top seat?"

"You think I give a damn about that seat?" Carlisle barks a

laugh. "None of us have need of it. Many of our parents bought our seats in the hope that we would win and gain access to Queen Victoria's court."

There is no lie in Carlisle's voice, try as I might to find it. "I don't have a daddy to fill my coffers like you do."

The lanterns overhead sway, back and forth, painting all their faces in darkness and then shades of amber and then shadow again.

"Interesting that you should bring up fathers." Carlisle crosses his arms, reclining against a table. "We could find nothing about yours, and Professor Stackton has been predictably mum. Care to educate us?"

"Isn't that what you're attending Oxford for?" I bare blood-stained teeth. "An education?"

I don't even see Robert's fist before it snaps my jaw to the side. The glue attaching my fake mustache slides, exposing half my lip.

Panic pours down into my core like a river of ice.

Carlisle lurches forward. "What is this?"

Sweat pools at the base of my spine, drenching my suit despite the cool breeze sweeping through the open window behind me.

"It seems that Isaac Holland has more to hide than we thought, lads." Carlisle stops before me, reaching toward my face. His fingers graze the whiskers of my mustache.

The lights snap out. Darkness blankets us.

"Bloody hell." The sounds of stumbling echo throughout the room. Carlisle orders, "Someone turn the blasted lights back on."

My arms snap free, binds cut. Warm arms wrap around my

chest, and before I have time to cry out, I'm tumbling backward out the window.

"Perfect timing, Holmes," I gasp.

Sherlock tugs me farther down an alleyway. "Those rats will have the torches lit and pitchforks raised to chase us down at any moment."

I jog after him, bare feet slapping the cobblestones. We turn around a corner, and he presses himself flat against the brick.

The pain in my side hitches, making me stumble into the wall beside him. "You should get out of here before they catch you, too."

Holmes smiles crookedly. "Oh, I have no doubt they know exactly who is to blame for their spoiled fun. I just don't want to leave them a direct trail for where to lay their retribution."

I spare him a curt nod before peeking around the corner. Each step feels as if a knife slides between my ribs. The blood flows heavily now, staining my shirt and pouring beneath the band of my pants. The alley is empty, our exit assured. We flee down the street, taking haphazard turns and leaving a random path behind us that only a bloodhound could hope to follow.

When we finally reach the outskirts of Oxford's campus, we stop. I'm gasping, hands clutching my stomach. I pull my jacket tighter to hide the red stain growing across my front. Tonight's sleep will be absolute hell.

Holmes looks hardly winded. His normally tan face, marked white in the pale moonlight, is pulled into a wide smile. "Is now a bad time to tell you 'I told you so'?"

Blearily, I notice his jacket stained with mud and worn, ragged pants. "You"—I point a trembling finger at his chest—"you were the beggar outside the restaurant."

"Watson lent me the pants. A bit tight around the waist."

He looks me up and down. His brow pinches, smile slipping. "What did those bastards do to you?"

He reaches for the bloodstained shirt, and I slap his hand away.

"Nothing." The movement makes me gasp. Gritting my teeth, I lean against the cold wall. "Just an old wound."

"An old wound that is about to become a deadly wound if you don't staunch the bleeding."

Sherlock reaches for me again. I try to move away, but the world tilts beneath my feet, and before I know it, I'm falling into his open arms.

"You're nothing but skin and bones, Holland." He grunts. "A pigeon weighs more than you."

He sets me down, ever so gently, and I don't have the strength to resist. I've lost too much blood, too fast. All the stitches must have torn.

"Don't, Holmes," I say between gritted teeth. "Just help me to the dormitories and I can sew myself back up."

"You'll likely bleed out before we even reach Radcliffe." His hands find my midriff and, before I have time to cry out, rip open my shirt, sending buttons soaring. "Holland, I—"

He stills.

The only sounds in the alleyway are our labored breaths. They curl in the air before us. His dark eyes, barely visible in the dim light, jump to my face, landing on the askew mustache, and widen.

The corset is a blaze of crimson across my middle. Holmes finally sees me for all I am.

"I said I'd tie the stitches myself." With the last of my strength, I stand.

The world slips beneath my feet and I tumble into the darkness.

CHAPTER 31

A Bed Full of Dresses

THE HEADACHE I AWOKE TO HOURS AGO IS NOTHING compared to the blinding pain that rips behind my eyes with every twitch of my muscles. Grimacing, I roll over, expecting to shove myself up from cold cobblestones.

Instead, my arms tangle themselves in sweaty sheets as my hands press against a fluffy mattress. I jerk upright, then immediately groan, falling back to the bed while clutching my side.

"Christ," I hiss between my teeth.

"Your wound was ripped open completely," says an awfully familiar voice from the shadows. "I had to stitch it without anything to ease the pain. Whoever originally stitched your wound had a clumsy hand, but did an effective job at least."

"And you're suddenly an expert at treating wounds?" I roll over onto my side to face Holmes, sitting once more on my bed.

He's placed me on his own, resplendent with softer blankets, fluffier pillows, and a much more comfortable mattress.

"I see your family spared no expense when it comes to furnishing the bed you never use." I roll onto my back with another groan, reaching for my wound. My hands brush against bare skin and I jerk upright once more. Shirtless, pantless, and without a single piece of Isaac's disguise. My horror grows exponentially.

"No, no, Watson is the expert at treating wounds." His eyes dance as he watches me come to realize that I am almost entirely bared for him to see. "But I am an expert in chemistry, botany, mathematics, and"—his gaze travels slowly down my body—"human anatomy."

With blazing cheeks, I pull his sheet up to cover my chest, though he's at least returned my bind to give me some modicum of modesty.

"You're not surprised," I say, gambling a little bit. "How long have you known?"

He doesn't hesitate to answer. "Since your father's soiree. You and Holland share the same tell." His gaze drops quickly to my hands and back up. "You scratch at your wrists when you're lying."

He's been reading me all along, just as I have him.

"Are you going to report me?" I can't help the tremulous edge to my voice. I'll beg if I have to.

Holmes has the gall to look confused. His dark brows draw together, jaw dropping open slightly. "Why the bloody hell would I do that?"

"To get the top seat." I shrug, making the sheet fall slightly. I hurry to pull it back up, but not before Holmes's gaze drops and his mouth snaps shut. "To humiliate the Moriartys."

Holmes raises his eyes to mine. Black to green.

"You seem to take great joy in making your brother's life miserable all on your own. And I'd prefer to win that seat on merit. I know a worthy adversary when I see one." He shares a small smile.

I stand, making Holmes inhale sharply. The sheet hangs before me, and even though I still wear my undergarments and the binding across my chest, I could be naked before him for all the intensity he watches my every movement and every breath.

"Well," I say, suddenly finding it hard to breathe. "Could I have some privacy?"

"Oh!" He leaps to his feet, dropping his gaze to the floor, the wall, the windows, anywhere but me. "Yes, yes! I'll leave you to get dressed."

"Good," I murmur, too softly for him to hear as he flees for the door.

Because nigh is the perfect time to continue making my brother's life miserable.

It gives me no small amount of joy to see that my dormitory is nicer than James's. Even colder than his bedroom at the town house, not a single shred of his personal life takes up any space in the dark room. Making no care to hide my presence here, I rip open the blinds, filling the room with pale morning light.

The bump on the back of my head still aches, the light doing nothing for the pain behind my eyes as I search his shelves. My movements are stiff, every breath tugging at Sherlock's stitches and the bandage I placed sloppily over them. The pain is a welcome distraction, though. Now that Holmes knows my secret.

The mathematics textbooks on the shelves don't stand out to me, nor the Gaspard Monge biographies taking up an entire shelf. I drag a finger across their spines, marveling at how a young man so devoted to privacy and image could let an entire inch of dust gather on the books' surfaces.

Taking a pen from my brother's desk, I twirl it between my fingers and crumple, in the most unladylike fashion, into his chair. With my other hand, I bite into a ruby-red apple just as the lock clicks and James swings the door open.

He doesn't react when he sees me, merely raises his eyebrows.

"How did you get in here?" He doesn't take the seat across from mine.

"I have a key, of course." I take another bite of the apple. Loudly.

"I don't have time for this nonsense, Irene. What are you doing here?" He slams a pile of papers on his desk.

"Why haven't the deans canceled classes yet, brother?" I set the pen down with a click. "Surely the lords must be in an uproar, watching Oxford bumble about. No doubt they have pulled all their children from harm's reach."

"Right now, the focus of their ire is on the Scotland Yard," he replies curtly. "For it is their fault that the murderer still is on the loose."

"Who do *you* blame?"

He hesitates, mouth a thin line.

I lean forward. "You don't know, do you?"

"Did your latest adventures with the Bullingdon Club not give you any more clues? Those arrogant fools couldn't even hide a pin in a haystack."

"Careful, brother"—I lean my head back—"one might think

you were jealous. After all, it's common knowledge that you failed the initiation, and Sherlock Holmes did not."

"Get. Out. Now." He marches around the desk, and a moment of fear lances through me when he yanks me to my feet. I gasp as pain flashes through me. His fingers are scalding through the fabric of my sleeves, nails digging into my arms. "Before I tell Father all about your game."

"Oh, please." I rip my arm away. "That is hardly a threat. You would have done so weeks ago if that threat bore any weight."

He shoves me hard enough to make me stumble. I catch myself on the firm oak door.

"What were you doing in here, Irene?" he asks.

I stand straighter. "I truly wanted to know if you've learned anything about the murders."

"The Yard will find justice where it awaits."

"Were you always so callous and cruel?" I raise my chin. "Or only when Richard cast aside your mother?"

"Silence, Irene."

"Or perhaps it was relief you felt," I say between bared teeth. "So you would no longer have to face her scorn?"

The slap he deals me is hard enough to fling me to the floor. Blood fills my mouth, iron lacing my tongue. I stand slowly, pulling a handkerchief from my pocket to wipe the liquid seeping from the corner of my mouth.

"I'll give Grandmother your regards," I say acidly, turning and leaving.

To no avail, I knock gently on Geraldine's bedroom door the next morning. Silence greets me through the heavy wood. Not even a stirring of music fades into the hallway. The Hayward town house is as quiet as a cemetery.

I see myself out, slipping past the staff as easily as I did on my way in. I hit the quiet street, clutching my wool shawl tight around my shoulders.

"Irene, darling! What are you doing out there?" I look up to Ermyntrude hailing me from her carriage. It slows as it passes, coming to a stop. "You'll catch a devil of a cold walking around in this weather. How unseemly, too."

"I was hoping to visit with Geraldine." I press my lips into a firm line, hugging the shawl closer.

Her smile curls. "Want to write a message that I can bring to her? I was going to visit after she returns on Monday."

"Returns? Return from where?" I already know the answer before the question finishes tumbling from my mouth.

Ermyntrude answers regardless. "She and her father left for their family estate this morning."

"Already?"

"It's what her father feels is best." Ermyntrude opens the carriage door and beckons me into the warmth. "Join me for the morning. The girls and I are picking our dresses for the Saint Nicholas Ball."

I'd almost forgotten about the ball. I was supposed to save my first dance for Edgar. The memory causes my stomach to swoop. With arms curled around my waist, I step inside.

Ermyntrude pats my shoulder with the tips of her fingers. "Don't fret. I know just the colors to bring light to that snowflake skin."

Her family's Oxford town house is only a handful of blocks away. Withering vines creep up the painted white exterior, framing wide bay windows and climbing the black iron fence separating the small front garden from the sidewalk. Without waiting to see if I'll follow, Ermyntrude leads the way inside and up the cobalt staircase.

Frowning, I let her guide me to her room. Every piece of furniture is weighed down under dresses of all designs. Silk, velvet, satin. Black, ruby, emerald. Cut low and high. They pile as tall as the four-poster bed frame on which many of them rest. Maribeth holds a gaudy orange dress up to her chest. As I draw closer, I notice her eyes are foggy and unfocused.

"Might I recommend this one instead?" I take the dress from her and hand over a lovely green satin one.

"You have such excellent taste, Irene," Ermyntrude says, handing me a brimming glass of wine.

"Coming from you, that is a compliment of the highest regard." I set aside the glass and pick up a silk peony gown. "Where are Edith and Roslyn?"

"Their parents have called them back to town until the ball."

Like most of the students. I drag my finger down a length of black velvet. "Because of the murders?"

"Precisely." With a saccharine smile, Ermyntrude lifts a garish monstrosity of purple and white tulle. "This would look lovely on you."

Liar. Forcing a smile, I say, "I have one with the tailor as we speak, using red silk that Geraldine helped me pick out."

"Oh, poor Gerry," Maribeth says, hiccupping and reaching for my glass. Her eyes brim with tears. "And poor Edgar."

"Edgar was courting you, was he not?" Ermyntrude snatches my glass from her and shoves it back into my hands. "You must also be devastated."

"I must confess that my heart is quite adrift," I say without forethought, as I am not lying. Though not devastated, my mind has been elsewhere these last few days. Perhaps that is why I was so easily captured by the club.

Ermyntrude watches me, cocking her head. "I had no idea you cared so much for our dear Edgar."

Our Edgar. Her little reminder that Edgar belongs—belonged—to a class entirely different from my own.

No, I did not care for Edgar as much he did me, nor as much as I should have. And the guilt of that will forever trail my steps.

Snow falls steadily outside, cascading down to carpet the grass. It is unlikely this snow will melt anytime soon. Even with Ermyntrude's fire blazing, my breath curls in the air next to the window. I look out at the stretch of white lawn, swirling my glass of wine but never taking a sip.

She notices. "Are you not thirsty?"

I grimace. "I prefer not to drink so early in the day. It fogs my head too much to pay attention to my classwork."

"But we don't have any assignments due," Ermyntrude says.

I might not have any work due, but Isaac has more than I can handle right now. I set the glass down. "Perhaps not for the Lady Margaret class, but my grandmother has hired separate tutors for me. I have a lesson in only an hour, actually." The lessons my grandmother unknowingly provides were the excuse Stackton and I agreed upon should anyone notice my absence while I attend the All Souls courses.

"Your grandmother?" Ermyntrude's dark eyes narrow in on my own. "Augusta Moriarty?"

"None other."

She drags a finger across the small table between us, stepping close. "Are you very close with her? Is your brother?"

I force a laugh. "More so I than him, actually."

There, a flicker of disappointment is in her eye a moment and then gone.

"Why such curiosity about my family, Ermyntrude?" I ask, turning fully to face her. "Designs on James, perhaps?"

She inclines her head. "I admit that I once found your brother to be quite alluring. I was drawn to him as Helen was to Paris."

Or Narcissus to his own reflection.

"But," she continues, "I have turned my attention to a far greater prize."

"Now who"—or what—"is that?"

Her smile is coy. "Wouldn't you like to know."

Yes, obviously, or I wouldn't have asked.

Swallowing a sigh, I check the buttons of my dress. "I'm afraid, as fun as this has been, that I must depart. My Italian tutor is waiting."

"Well, I hope your Italian tutor is more handsome than mine." Ermyntrude looks to Maribeth, collapsed in a fit of giggles on her bed and surrounded by piles of silk and tulle. "Mr. Regio has this obnoxious mustache fit for a schnauzer."

Forcing a laugh, I let it trail me as I depart, eager to leave that suffocating room. Maribeth doesn't even look up as I leave. My smile drops quickly to a frown, and I hail a carriage to campus.

CHAPTER 32

A Rare Luncheon

I wait in the shadows for Stackton to arrive before walking into the classroom, not trusting my classmates to not beat me to a pulp the moment I walk through the door. Their gazes skewer me nonetheless. Stackton ignores me and immediately begins writing notes on the board. Distractedly, I take a seat in the front of the classroom, closest to Stackton, and begin copying his notes on how to deduce drug overdoses in a corpse.

Holmes throws me looks throughout class, trying to catch my attention time and time again. I ignore him.

I'm standing, bags packed before the bell has even finished its last toll at the end of class. Hurrying to Stackton's desk, under my breath I say, "A word, Professor."

His hand hesitates over the pile of papers before him. After a moment, he gives me a small, barely perceptible nod. Loud enough for everyone outside to hear, he says, "If you insist on walking me to my office, you may. But I'm afraid there is nothing you can say that will make me reconsider."

Before I follow him from the classroom, it is impossible to miss the simmering fury in Carlisle's face from the row of desks. And the bald confusion on Holmes's.

Once the office door is firmly shut behind us, he turns and says, "I thought I made myself abundantly clear, Irene. Our partnership is over."

My lips tremble of their own accord as I lock the door. "If my life means anything to you, please reconsider."

Stackton's office is littered with piles of books and papers on every surface. There's nowhere for me to sit, but I have no desire to do so.

"I believe that someone is systematically killing off the members of the ruling class," I say.

"Cut right to the chase, now don't you." Stackton's skin has blanched a deathly pale. "But only the members of the All Souls cohort, correct?"

"At first I thought so, and perhaps it was some psychopath's design to win the competition through devious means." I start to pace. "The Bullingdon Club, though not removed from my list of suspects... I don't believe any of them are fool enough to implicate their own members by branding the bodies."

"How did you learn about that?"

"Trust me when I say that you would prefer not to know."

He falls heavily into his desk chair. "Irene. You are like a grandchild to me. I cannot stand by while you risk your life. Please don't think that me allowing you to come with me to my office means that I am encouraging this ill-minded detective work."

"Oh, no. I don't think that." I shake my head but continue my pacing. "I only wanted to walk with you to your office to avoid being murdered by the club."

He sighs, a great weary heave that shuffles the papers on his desk. "I thought you said that they weren't on your list of suspects?"

"They're not. But they caught me spying on them, and they're onto Isaac's deception."

His face lands in his palm. "For the love of Christ."

"Don't be so melodramatic." I shake my head. "They don't know yet who is masquerading as Isaac." I grimace, adding, "But Sherlock Holmes may now realize that I am hiding breasts under this costume."

Stackton sighs wearily enough for a thousand tired souls. "Leave the hunting to the police, Irene, and get on with your education."

"Not until I catch Edgar's killer."

"And what are you hoping I can do about it?" He shoves a pile of papers from the desk, sending them cascading to the floor. "I told you not to stick your nose where it didn't belong."

"Well"—I incline my head—"I was hoping you would at least pretend to be my sponsor again. So that I have an excuse to walk with you to your office after class."

Face a startling shade of purple, he jabs a finger in my direction. "Your grandmother will be so angry with you when she hears of the trouble you've been stirring."

"Quite the contrary." I flash him a devilish smile. "I think she'll be rather proud of me."

"Oh, off with you." He waves a hand in my direction. "There's a door behind that paneling there. Take the second r—"

"Second right and then third left to Professor Hoddor's office, correct?" My smile widens as Stackton's face flushes a wonderful magenta. "I've seen my father's old maps from when he was a student."

"The devil with you," he mutters, snapping open a book and refusing to meet my eyes.

His furious muttering chases me down the long, dark passageway to my next class.

I return to the scene of the original crime.

No longer able to use the Bodleian under Isaac's guise, I'm wearing a green velvet dress that highlights the dark ruby curls falling down my back. Standing in the history section, my gaze sweeps the room from corner to corner, searching every last nook and cranny for clues.

There are none. Not even a drop of blood remains on the windowsill from which Bertram was once splayed.

The murderer keeps spinning me in circles, causing me to chase my own tail and run down an endless maze. The Bullingdon lead may have been fruitless, but at least it scratched off a few names on my list.

Humming softly to myself, I'm so focused on searching for answers, I almost don't notice the clip of a heel at the end of the row behind me.

Without turning, I say, "It's rude to walk up on a woman unannounced, Mr. Holmes."

"Only if they're indecent." His hands are clasped behind his back and his eyes focused on my face. "How did you know it was me?"

How to tell a man that I've memorized his scent. "Lucky guess, I suppose."

He nods, but his eyes express his disbelief all too clearly before they drop to the textbook hooked under my arm. "Curious. What would a Lady Margaret student want with a book from the advanced chemistry section?"

"No need to continue playing along with that charade, Holmes."

We stand far closer than propriety allows. Heat, despite the chill of the library, swirls between our bodies. His gaze, like the touch of a feather, rests on my collarbone. His hand reaches tentatively across the space between us.

"What are you doing up here, Holmes?"

Carlisle's voice makes us both jump. He strides down the line of tables and books, smug grin plastered across his face. I don't know how I ever thought him handsome. Now all I see is smarmy arrogance in the pale, severe lines of his broad face.

"I was just asking the Lady Adler the very same thing." Holmes's voice is rife with irritation.

Carlisle ignores it, though, and turns to me. "So, Lady Adler, I have a proposition for you."

"Oh." My mouth pops open with surprise, though I suspect I already know what he will ask.

"Would you care to attend the ball with me?" In a gallant display, he bows low, arm tucked behind his back.

After seeing his and the club's behavior, there is nothing I would want less. But a charade is a charade. The ball is *this* week? Where has the time gone? "I would love to."

"Excellent." He snatches up my hand, placing a kiss upon its back. "Shall I send a carriage for you this Saturday?"

"No," I say, struggling not to stutter. Refusing to meet Holmes's gaze, I force a thin-lipped smile. "That won't be necessary. I promised Geraldine and Ermyntrude that I would take a carriage with them. It is at Ermyntrude's estate, after all."

"Shame," Carlisle says, cocking his head. "It would have been lovely to have a moment alone with you."

What a revolting thought. I swallow my shudder. My cheeks are burning as he walks away. Holmes coughs, though I could have never forgotten that he was there.

"You shouldn't let him talk to you like that," he says, glaring daggers into Carlisle's retreating spine. "It's not proper."

"You and I can hardly discuss propriety after our recent... interlude in the men's dormitory. Besides." I shrug with forced nonchalance. "He's a lord. They can do whatever they want. He'll get his comeuppance eventually. They always do." Fighting a grimace, I turn slowly to Holmes. "Forget I said that."

"On the contrary, I rather like the honesty." He smiles and something warm stirs in the hollow of my stomach. "I only regret that I did not ask you to the ball first."

"Next time, Sherlock Holmes. Next time." I rest a gloved hand against his cheek. "Perhaps I'll save you a dance."

Taking another book I need from the shelf, I turn without sparing him a second glance. Because if I did turn to look at him, I don't trust my body to not do something I might regret.

Carlisle may have to wait to attend the ball with me on his arm, but I cannot resist the temptation to make him look like an utter fool before then.

Like a mouse quick to dive for the food in a trap, he responds swiftly and eagerly to my invitation to luncheon the next day. My dress, a lovely blue satin, accentuates my figure. I make sure my cheeks are pinched to pink perfection, my dark curls artfully arranged on top of my head to bare my long, pale neck.

He blinks slowly when he arrives at my door to pick me up. "Lovely as always, Lady Moriarty."

I don't care to correct him. His mistake is to my advantage this time. Demurely, I smile. "Where are we to dine this afternoon?"

The question is unnecessary. I paid his maid to tell his valet what my favorite restaurant is. Or, at least, what restaurant I want him to think is my favorite.

"Let it be a surprise, my dear." He offers his arm and leads me to his sleek black victoria.

The ride passes quickly, Carlisle's flatteries endless and my flirting easy. These games have always been too easy for me, perhaps a gift from my mother, but right now it is to my advantage because no one would suspect that Richard Moriarty's demure, bastard daughter is actually the wolf in sheep's clothing.

When we pull up outside the Lamb and Flag, it is a struggle to keep my smile from turning devilish. Clapping my gloved hands, I exclaim, "Oh! I love this place! How did you know?"

He shrugs, placing a hand on my hip as he leads me inside. "I remembered spying you here with the ladies."

I gaze up at him through my lashes. "You are *so clever*, Lord Gillingham."

He coughs, hunger roiling beneath his eyes. At the best table, he pulls out my seat for me. "Please. Call me Carlisle."

I accept an offered menu. "That would be too forward, sir."

"And yet you have told me to call you Irene."

"Only if you behave like a gentleman." I soften the words with a coquettish smile. "How did you get James to agree to this luncheon?"

"He hasn't the slightest," Carlisle says, snapping his napkin out before draping it across his lap.

Oh, I'm sure that ass knows exactly where I am.

Carlisle leans across the table, caressing the back of my hand with his thumb.

Swallowing bile and retracting my hand, I ask, "And how fare your studies, Lord Gillingham?"

Carlisle's smile is positively carnal. "Are we not close enough now to move on from such mundane topics of conversation?"

"The All Souls cohort is anything but mundane to me," I say, arching a brow. "Your classmates are all anyone talks about."

His smile disappears. "Is that so?"

I nod. "In fact, the Lady Margaret class is rife with rumors of ghosts and sadists among your cohort."

He chuckles. "Are those two not the same thing?"

"I think some ghosts might take offense to that question." I finish my tea.

"Would you care for a glass of wine?" Carlisle waves over a waiter. "Your father won't mind, will he?"

I dab my lips with a napkin. "Though your offer is kind, and indeed my father won't mind, I must be honest with you."

"Yes?" His smile widens. "A rare thing from a Moriarty."

I roll my eyes. "I haven't the taste for wine."

He leans back. "I love a woman of surprises."

Our plates of food arrive, covered with stainless steel serving covers. Clapping his hands, Carlisle reaches over to first lift my cover, revealing an array of tea sandwiches and fresh fruits.

"Isn't this a bit much just for afternoon tea?" I hold his gaze. "You didn't have to go to all this trouble."

He tucks his napkin in. "No trouble at all."

Carlisle reaches for his fork as the servant lifts his own cover, then he roars. He slams his chair back from the table, and it crashes to the floor. He's on his feet in an instant.

"What the hell is this?" Carlisle demands.

I leap back from the table. Silverware clatters to plates. People around us scream. I take a trembling step back myself. My gloved hand covers my mouth, eyes glued to the plate before me.

Blood runs from the pile of raw meat before us, staining the white tablecloth. Flies immediately begin to swarm the dripping carcass. People scream and flee. I curl my lips, baring my teeth as I glare up at a stammering Carlisle.

"Is this some kind of joke, *Lord Gillingham?*" I pitch his name high for everyone in the restaurant to hear and throw my napkin down on the table beside his plate. "Is this meant to be an insult?"

"Why the devil would I serve myself raw meat?" Carlisle's face has flushed a dark red.

"You picked this place to eat." I point to the gaping waiters. "You even told them when and what to serve.

"My brother will hear of this," I say, leveling him with every ounce of hatred and venom I can muster. I bark over my shoulder, "This establishment and your family name will never outlive this shame, Carlisle Gillingham."

Ignoring his protests, I spin on my heel and stride from the Lamb and Flag.

It'd been easy to bribe a kitchen maid to tamper with Carlisle's plate, and even easier to find her a job with my grandmother. With a list of names she had given me in hand, I sent the job references of every unhappy employee in that restaurant out to the surrounding restaurants. The others, those who had found joy in the Bullingdon Club's inflicted suffering, would have to find new jobs on their own.

But the owner, whose idea I had learned it was to feed raw meat to the club inductees and had found such satisfaction in it, might never run a restaurant again.

I hail a carriage, and it isn't until it's clattering down the street to Oxford that I let a smile form on my lips.

My smile disappears, though, when I walk into my room.

James sits on my bed, one leg draped over the other. "I took a gamble today, dear sister."

"Have I ever told you just how much I despise you?" Sighing, I unbutton my jacket. "What did you gamble?"

"Whether or not you would be in this room, or the one you share with Sherlock Holmes."

My hands still. "And what made you decide to stalk me here?"

"Because he now knows what you hide beneath those trousers."

How he managed to learn that is beyond my comprehension. Words, for once, escape me.

"Cat got your tongue?"

"Oh, go back to staring at yourself, James."

"Good evening to you, too, Irene." His smile is smug. "Or

should I say a bloody good evening? However did you manage such a scene?"

I sniff. "I haven't the slightest idea what you're talking about, James."

In one smooth motion, he's on his feet. I flinch despite myself.

Striding over to me, he says, "Deftly done. Humiliating Carlisle at the same restaurant he tortured the club inductees. No doubt you want me to tell Father, so he'll be righteously angry on your behalf?"

"I was hoping he would find out on his own, as he does with all things, but if you want to speed up the process, I won't complain." I pull the pieces of Isaac's disguise from their hiding spots throughout the room. "Is this all that you were looking for?"

He steps closer. "How did you learn of Father's involvement with the club?"

Because of the seals in his desk, I don't say aloud. Instead, I say, "Newspaper clippings here and there." I wave a hand through the air. "Why do you care?"

"Because you're putting your nose where it doesn't belong."

"That's the pot calling the kettle black." I snatch up a pair of trousers and hold them to my waist. "Are you done 'putting *your* nose where it doesn't belong,' or must I continue to tolerate your company?"

"I've come to ask a favor, actually," he says, walking toward me. He drags his hand along my boudoir. "The Duke of Bedford's daughter. I need you to secure for me a dance with her at the ball."

"Ermyntrude?" I blurt. "But she's ghastly."

"Why would you care if I romance her, then? Afraid for my virtue?" His smile is impish, and I want to smack it from his face.

"I couldn't care less, honestly." I shrug. "Though, the Bedford ship may have sailed. You spent too much time chasing after Geraldine, to no avail."

"You could say that I've had a change of heart." He frowns, examining my hairbrush—which I bought using his money. "Is this new?"

"You broke my last one, remember?" With a long, weary sigh, I ask, "Why the sudden interest in Ermyntrude?"

"What's not to like in a lady as lovely as she?"

"And as rich." I sniff. "Why should I help you?"

With a diabolical smile, my brother pulls a letter from his breast pocket. "Because if you don't, I'll make sure that this letter never finds its way to our grandmother."

My throat is suddenly painfully dry. The letter of recommendation for the kitchen maid at the Lamb and Flag. "How did you get that?"

He starts walking toward me. "You wouldn't want this affronted scullery girl to go to Lord Gillingham with your treachery, now, would you?"

I jerk a chair between us, legs screeching in protest on the stone floor. "I can at least get you a dance with Ermyntrude." I hold out my hand for the letter. "Now give it back."

He tucks it back into his pocket. "Not until I have that dance."

Gritting my teeth, I say, "Fine."

"Now that we've come to an accord"—James's smile is all gentility—"I will share one hint with you."

I bite my tongue, waiting, and cross my arms.

"The seals you stole from our father's desk"—he crosses the room, grabbing his top hat—"those were never his."

"Don't lie to me," I snarl.

"Why do you think I did not get grandfathered into the club? My father was never a member of the Bullingdon Club. He's always been loyal to their rivals, the Gridirons. Such a lack of thoroughness in your sleuthing will get you lost, Irene. Those seals actually belong to your beloved mentor, Professor Stackton. Or should I say, former mentor."

"What?" My knees threaten to buckle.

"I believe you're familiar with the expression *checkmate*." He tips his hat and swings the door open. "Have a good evening, Irene."

CHAPTER 33

The Mask Falls

I SAAC'S EXAMS ARE A BLUR. THEY CASCADE THROUGH MY MIND, falling one after the other, until my final exam in Stackton's class. I fly through them all except the last. I stumble over the words written before me, the cause of death I'm supposed to deduce from a few mere clues. I can hardly focus on the exam when the man who sold me out to the Bullingdon Club sits in the front of the classroom.

Stackton nearly leaps from his seat when I slam my textbooks in front of him after the exam. "What in God's name, Irene!"

"You knew," I say, turning and slamming his office door hard enough to make the windows rattle. "You knew that the Bullingdon Club would hunt me down and flay me alive for turning them in. You knew, because you're the one who reported me to them."

He leans back, face unreadable. "I did warn you."

"Did you also tell them *why* I was chasing their tails?" I demand.

"Of course not." He pulls a stack of papers toward him and a pen from within his desk. "Now, if you're quite done interrogating me, I've got tests to grade."

Before he can blink, I swipe the papers, pens, and books from his desk. They fly across his office as I slam my fists down. "Why would you betray me like this?"

Stackton leaps to his feet and roars, "To save your bloody life!"

The air steals from my lungs. I stagger back, blood draining from my face. "You did no such thing."

"I did, damn you." He points a long, crooked finger at my face. "I stopped their digging. They're foolish, rich men, Irene. They thought they'd had the answer to their problems handed to them on a golden platter. Why would they think to look at what was glued beneath it?" He plants both hands on his desk. "What do you think they would have done had I not revealed you to them? They would have pulled up every single piece of history on every single student at Oxford. The lads of the Bullingdon Club are wealth and power incarnate. They would have learned that Isaac Holland doesn't actually exist. That your name is not actually Isaac Holland. That your classes are perfectly aligned with the Lady Margaret class. How long then do you think it would take them to figure out who you truly are?"

"Judging by the tests littering your floor, even then they wouldn't have the wits to figure it out."

Now it is his turn to slam a fist on the desk. "This is not a joke, Irene. If they found out who Isaac Holland truly is, your reputation would be ruined. Not even Augusta could protect you then."

He releases a heavy sigh, shaking slightly as he sits back down. "I never should have agreed to this foolish charade. Not only has your reputation been put in danger, but so has your very life. And for what? You've accomplished nothing."

My lower lip trembles. "That's not fair. I am doing great in my classes, and I've nearly caught—"

"The murderer?" He cuts me off, shaking his head. "No, you haven't. This killer still runs circles around you."

"How would you know?" I cross my arms over my chest. "I'm closer than the blasted force to finding them."

"Oh? Pray tell." He leans back, crossing his arms. "Who is your prime suspect?"

I open my mouth, then snap it shut. He knows damn well that, without the club in the running, I have none.

"That's what I thought."

"Do *you* have a prime suspect?" I level him with an icy glare that could freeze a lesser man's soul.

"I do not." He stands, placing his palms on the desk and matching me, glare for glare. "Because that is not my job. I am a professor. You are a student. Leave the sleuthing to the Scotland Yard, Irene, and attempt to salvage what you can of your studies. If you do not give up this foolishness, I will write your resignation letter and give it to the chancellor myself."

Taking the passageway from Stackton's office and dropping off Isaac's disguise, I roughly rub the powder from my face and storm across campus. Tears blur my vision as I stumble back to my rooms. My dress is crooked, the ties only half done up. My hair is a mess, and no doubt I will be the talk of Oxford. *That Moriarty's daughter is a trollop.*

The ladies I pass in the hall give me curious looks, but I ignore them all. I should be going to the library to reread some chapters before my next exam, but all I can think of are the faces of the men who were murdered and how I failed to save Edgar.

"Get ahold of yourself, Irene," I mutter to myself as I slam the door behind me. I didn't start this. I didn't murder Bertram and Hugo and Edgar, nor the others.

It was some faceless specter, taunting my every foolish attempt to catch him. Whoever it was, they outwitted me.

No doubt they knew someone would sneak into the morgue to examine the bodies.

I jerk to a halt. The air rushes from my lungs in one long, ragged breath.

Someone did know I would sneak into the morgue.

Ripping down a map I have stashed in my closet, I unfurl it on my bed, so impatient that an edge catches on my thumb and slices it open. Hissing, I throw a book on each corner and take a step back.

Only one other person had known I would be in the morgue that night. Only one other person had been coming down from the upper floors of the Bodleian the afternoon of Bertram's death. One person who had also been witness to Hugo's drunken behavior at the Turf the night of his death. One person who was toe to toe with me for the All Souls Fellowship. Whose family mysteriously grew in wealth, fortune, and standing, seemingly overnight.

I'd seen his address at the top of his file while snooping in Father's desk. Though his home address is in London, he is currently living in a flat during the week. I trace a finger on the map, landing on Alfred Lane. The same street where Jude had been found murdered.

Shock, cold and gripping, lances through me. I take a step back from the bed, curling a fist over my rapidly beating heart.

Sherlock Holmes.

CHAPTER 34

Eden's Papaver

GERALDINE SITS ACROSS FROM ME IN THE ROLLING CARRIAGE, staring blankly out at the darkening world beyond. The silence stretches on for the hours it takes the carriage to pass through the city and into the countryside. I take her gloved hand in mine and give it a gentle squeeze. Even through the fabric, her fingers are like ice.

"Where do your thoughts lead you, friend?" I ask.

"What a silly question," Ermyntrude says from beside me, scoffing. "Whatever else could she be thinking about?"

"If you're referring to my brother"—Geraldine's voice is sharp—"then you're mistaken. I was actually thinking about the ball." She turns hollow eyes on us both. "But my endless thanks for your reminder of my dead brother who cannot attend."

Ermyntrude sucks in a sharp breath.

"My brother said that he took you home to see your parents," I say, and Ermyntrude's face whips toward me. "I hope he wasn't too much of a bother."

"It was kind of him," Geraldine says, returning her attention out the window. "Not everyone is full of ill intentions, Irene." She softens the blow by leaning over. "You look lovely tonight. My brother would have been in complete awe."

Unbidden, my eyes begin to brim with tears. "Thank you."

I don't mention how it seems that I cannot trust anyone these days. How all my allies have suddenly shifted into possible enemies. How she is the only pinnacle of kindness left in Oxford.

And she is so impossibly lovely this evening. Geraldine wears a black dress with a tulle skirt and tapered sleeves.

Silence once again settles around us until Ermyntrude suddenly claps, making Geraldine and me jump.

"We're home, ladies," she says, a giddy edge to her voice.

I pull the curtain aside. The sun hasn't set completely yet, spilling the rolling fields beyond with ruby and gold.

I blink. That cannot be right.

"Flowers?" Astonishment grips me, my jaw dropping. "In winter? How is that possible?"

Ruby heads sprout from the blanket of snow, facing toward the setting sun.

"Eden's Papaver. My father harvested the seeds himself from his travels." Smugness practically radiates off Ermyntrude. "They prefer the cold. Almost like snowdrops."

"But red." Even Geraldine's voice is tinged with awe.

Like blood.

"Father is very proud." I turn to see Ermyntrude's brilliant smile. "They're of the poppy family."

"Incredible," I whisper.

We pass down field after field of endless scarlet until we clatter up to Woburn Abbey, the Bedford estate. My jaw threatens to drop again as I take in the spectacular sight. Shimmering white walls reflect gold in the last of the sun's rays, the glare in the tall windows blinding. Even from inside the carriage, I can see that, through the windows, the walls are all beautiful, with floral wallpapers, and the balustrades artfully carved.

A hundred carriages descend upon the estate. Gravel crunches beneath shined boots. Skirts swish and swirl up the pristine white marble steps. Snow cascades down around us, reflected in the golden light spilling from the abbey. Taking each of us by the arm, Ermyntrude leads our trio inside.

Almost immediately upon stepping through the wide doors do I miss the haunted halls of Oxford. The grandeur here belies the stiffness of which the entire evening will surely radiate. The servants are mute as they take our jackets.

Ermyntrude's father greets us at the bottom of the stairs, and it takes all my strength to keep my brows from rising up to my hairline and mouth from popping open. I've seen this man before, in a darkened corridor that smelled of sweet smoke and echoed with delighted giggles and exaggerated moans. His pale lips had been pressed into the neck of a woman just as they tumbled through a doorway.

"My dears," the Lord Bedford says, looking much less disheveled than he had in the Red Negligee, his dark eyes sweeping over us from shoes to hair. He dismisses me entirely, attention focused solely on Geraldine. "A pity your father could not join us."

My friend's face hardens. "He is still in mourning, sir." She dips a curtsy. "Thank you for inviting me to your lovely ball."

His gaze follows her as she hurries away. Haunting music swells up the grand marble staircase, chasing Geraldine's and Ermyntrude's steps as they hurry up, then down the hall. I stay back, though, running a gloved hand along the ebony balustrade.

The red silk of my skirt drags behind me. I am a rose among the sea of summer-colored gowns. The bodice is beaded with black to match the lace gloves that reach past my elbows. My hair is arranged artfully on top of my head, leaving bare my long, pale neck. The neckline dares propriety, giving just the barest glimpse of my skin, as well as my ruby-and-black-pearl necklace. When I move close to the chandeliers and lamplight, hints of red shimmer in my hair.

The colors are so out of season, but I don't have a care in the world. Because they are the colors Edgar picked out for me, and I would give anything for him to be able to see me now.

My classmates watch me, but I pay them no heed. I walk through wide French doors into a domed hall. The light from the glass chandeliers above is cold and fragmented. Servants swirl around me bearing overladen trays of champagne and hors d'oeuvres. A quartet sits in the far corner, filling the ballroom with lilted song. Lord Bedford obviously spared no expense.

A dance has already started, frilly skirts swirling across the cobalt marble floor. I accept a glass of champagne from a passing servant but do not take a sip. My classmates quickly pair off, some disappearing into curtained alcoves, while others join the waltz. Geraldine sits alone in her black silk frock and watches the dancing with a forlorn gaze.

I offer her my glass. "A pence for your thoughts?"

"It would be a wasted pence." She accepts the drink and takes a long dreg. "You know exactly where my mind is, Irene."

I take the seat next to her. "Well, that's not entirely true. There are a number of places it could be. It could be on the dance before us."

"Don't insult me."

My mouth pops open and I lean backward. "Or, it could be on your brother, who I wish dearly was here."

"Do you?"

My head snaps in her direction. "Do I what?"

Her eyes bore into mine. "Do you truly wish he was here?"

I take a deep breath before answering. Laying a hand on hers, I say, in all honesty, "I truly do."

She searches my face for a long moment, her periwinkle-blue gaze stripping away any lies and deceit. "He loved you."

I inhale sharply. "I've long forbidden myself from entertaining romantic relationships with men above my station. I never even considered Edgar, believing it would be foolish."

She turns again to the dancers, patting my hand and pulling away.

My brother saunters toward us, threatening that peace. Ignoring me, he bows low to Geraldine, sweeping an arm behind his back. "May I have this dance?"

"You may not," Geraldine says, prim as a peony. She raises her chin, though softens the blow with a smile so diplomatic it could rival the queen's. "I'm afraid I left my dancing spirit back at Oxford."

James gives me a look that could curdle milk and extends his hand for me. "Irene, may I have this dance?"

I barely resist the urge to slap his hand away. "Only if you promise not to ruin my shoes."

"Well, I bought them, so that would hardly be wise."

He leads me around the dance floor. His hand rests on the small of my back, and my stomach roils with revulsion. Despite his best efforts, James's dancing is rough, like the jerking of a serrated knife, as he takes me for a turn.

"Have you decided which of the girls you wish to romance?" I ask curtly. I cannot get enough space between us. "Or are you set on Geraldine again?"

He twirls me fast enough to make my head spin. "You know very well that I have set my sights on Ermyntrude now. Have you secured a dance for me yet with her?"

I scoff. "I would *never* help you."

He chuckles, his breath hot against my cheek. "How easily you forget that I hold your future in my hands. Do you want me to give Carlisle that letter?"

"What letter?" I smile sweetly up at my brother. "You mean the one I hand-delivered to Grandmother last night? Or the one that is currently ashes in your fireplace?"

His hand curls into a fist at the base of my spine, his smile frozen in place. "What?"

"Did you think I would sit idly by while you threatened me?" I allow him to twirl me once more. "If this is a game of chess, James, you sacrificed your queen prematurely."

The music reaches its crescendo at the end of the hall. It must take all of James's self-control not to make a scene. "You have made a serious mistake, Irene."

I arch my chin. We join the lines of dancers. He bows low to me, and I make sure to toss him a playful wink when I curtsy. "The only mistake I made was letting you bully me for all these years."

I lose him among the crowd of departing dancers, searching the chairs for Geraldine. She's not where I left her.

I search the ballroom. Pairs dot the dance floor, skirts twirling high enough to give scandalous glimpses of ankles. By the refreshments, the professors and deans crowd, chortling merrily. My father, though no doubt in attendance somewhere, is not among them. He likely thinks himself too good for them. Many professors watch my Lady Margaret cohort hungrily, stirring disgust inside me. Lecherous old bats.

Out of the corner of my eye, I spy Carlisle making a beeline toward me. I march for the curtained alcoves, dipping behind a pair of tall lads along the way. There's no sign of Holmes yet, though I hardly expected him to attend. Ermyntrude is surrounded by an army of men, which my brother joins. Maribeth giggles with a classmate on the edge of the dance floor, eyeing a pair of lads on the other side.

"Have you seen Geraldine?" I ask her, searching the crowd in vain for my friend's golden head.

Maribeth merely shrugs. "Didn't she arrive with you?"

"I was preoccupied," I say.

"That's a lovely dress," the girl with Maribeth says, eyeing the red silk. "Brave of you to wear a color so out of season."

I ignore the attempted slight. "So, neither of you have seen her?"

They both shake their heads, much more focused on the dancers than on me. I shouldn't be surprised. Without Ermyntrude and Geraldine around to boost my status, I am nothing but a lowly daughter of a dean.

That doesn't impact how the men view me, though. Moran watches me as if I am a juicy cut of lamb, and he a wolf. The other men are not so different, their gazes hungry as I flee the ballroom, searching for both Geraldine and a moment of respite from the crowd.

The hallway is much quieter, though muffled giggles and whispers can be heard from the dark rooms beyond. Geraldine wouldn't have snuck off with a lad. I continue down the hallway, which is lit by three great crystal chandeliers.

I pass the final chandelier, where two white doors await on either side of the hallway. Both are closed and greet me with hollow silence. I reach for the handle of the one on the left, and find it locked. Too many people mill in the hall for me to pick it open, so I turn to the right. The handle turns easily, and I slip into the dark room.

Sweeping windows fill the far wall, but shelves with leather-bound books reach toward the ceiling on all the others. I run a hand along the dust-laden tomes, walking idly toward the windows, where, sitting on a bench, Geraldine stares forlornly out at the falling snow.

She doesn't look up. "If you've come to ask me to rejoin the party, you'll leave disappointed."

"Then would you mind if I simply joined you here?"

She waves to the seat beside her, and I sit as gracefully as I can without wrinkling my dress.

After a long moment, she finally speaks. "Edgar was so looking forward to this ball. He had even come out to the Bedford estate to help Ermyntrude's father arrange carriages for everyone."

"Edgar was quite the dancer."

A small smile parts her lips. "He was."

"So was my mother." There are no lit torches in the library, the room only lit by the moon peeking through the clouds. "The best dancer I've ever seen."

She turns slowly to face me. "Someday, perhaps when I am feeling not quite so adrift, would you tell me more about her? Your mother, I mean."

"Of course." My eyes trace the gentle fall of her hair down her back. "What was Edgar studying?"

A soft laugh escapes Geraldine, turning her gaze to the high ceilings. "He knew what you were studying without me having to tell him."

"That's unfair." I return my gaze to the snow falling outside.

I can feel her eyes searching my face. Another moment of silence passes before she says, "He was studying botany. Merely a curiosity. Father wanted him to take his place."

I meet her eyes. "Has your family been close with the Bedfords long? You never mentioned Ermyntrude before."

"Very." She nods, her lips puckering slightly. "Though I admit that our fathers haven't spoken in quite some time. Edgar was hoping to mend that fence, so to speak. The offering of our carriages and horses was meant to be the olive branch."

"Did your father decide not to offer his horses?"

Geraldine shakes her head. "He even called Edgar a fool for offering them up. I hope he's regretting his harsh words right now." She releases a heavy sigh, brushing her skirts. "I've had enough talk of Edgar. I cannot cry here where everyone will see me. Let's find ourselves some dancing partners as distractions."

Before leaving, though, she rests a hand on the library door and turns to me. "You wouldn't do anything to hurt me, Irene, would you?"

"Why would you ask me that?"

"I ask because"—she swallows—"everyone I love dies."

And before I can say another word, she turns and throws open the door.

CHAPTER 35

To Waltz with Brilliance

I FOLLOW GERALDINE FROM THE LIBRARY WITHOUT ARGUMENT. Just as we emerge into the hallway, the door opposite slams open. She jumps, and I steady her as Carlisle, Roslyn, and Edith stumble out, followed in quick succession by the gangly Robert Lancaster and a smug-looking Ermyntrude.

While the others stumble down the hallway back to the ballroom, clearly too deep in their drinks, Ermyntrude sashays toward us, grinning wickedly.

"They've clearly been having too much fun," she says. Her gaze darts between me and Geraldine. "What have you two been up to? Something wicked, I hope."

"Sorry to disappoint you," Gerry replies tartly, looking anything but apologetic. "We simply wanted to take a quick respite from the dancing."

"What were *you all* doing?" I ask, unable to quell my curiosity.

"Indulging in my father's finest," she says, holding a gloved finger up to her lips. "If you promise not to tell anyone, I can share with you as well."

Something snaps in Geraldine suddenly. She straightens, peering around Ermyntrude. "Will it take my mind off of my brother?"

Grinning, Ermyntrude waves us inside. "It would be my honor to distract you."

I follow both ladies into the room, though I have no desire to temper my mind. Ermyntrude shuts the door behind me, rolling the lock home with a soft click. Immediately, though, my feet catch on the rug.

Lingering in the air, as sharp as an adder's teeth, a scent lingers. I cannot place it, but it stirs the edges of my memory.

The study is brilliantly lit with oil lamps. All the furniture is rich mahogany. Above her father's desk, a family portrait watches me with oily eyes as I cross the Persian rug to the chaise below. I don't sit, however, instead letting my gaze continue to sweep the room.

Ignoring the mundane questions Ermyntrude asks Geraldine, I surreptitiously look over the desk. Papers, unorganized, litter the surface. The royal seal graces the corner of one, but I cannot make out the writing as it is under a stack of notes. My fingers inch to peel away the papers and take a peek, but Ermyntrude's gaze bores into my spine, watching my every move with a hunter's focus. I am the mouse, and she the hawk.

In a gilded frame, a large map of Oxford stretches across a wall of Lord Bedford's office. I step close, looking it over. The campus, the ancient streets, even the Bartlemas Chapel are all drawn in painstaking detail. I cannot help but feel miffed as I look it over. That map would have been incredibly helpful as I chased down the Bullingdon Club this semester. My gaze lands on the Lamb and

Flag, tracing the steps from there to campus, when it catches on something curious.

A dotted line, faint but undeniable, mars the map's surface. It follows roads, quartering the town of Oxford. I trace it with a gloved finger.

Ermyntrude steps up behind me, her breath warm and sweet against my ear. "My grandfather drew this map himself. Isn't it remarkable?"

"Astounding. I didn't realize that your family had such strong ties to Oxford."

"We're all graduates of Oxford." Her finger traces the dotted line, brushing mine. "Grandfather's even one of the founding members of one of their most notorious clubs."

I blurt, "The Bullingdon Club?"

She cackles, startling me enough to make me jump. I back away from her and the map as she continues to convulse with laughter.

"Those idiots?" She shakes her head. "No, my family founded the Gridirons."

Unlike the raucous infamy the Bullingdon Club seems to revel in, the Gridirons are a smaller, more exclusive club, not prone to the wild debauchery of their Bullingdon peers.

Increasingly uncomfortable, I walk toward the liquor cabinet beside the desk and let my gaze just barely pass over the papers again. Notices from the royal treasury and from the East India Trading Company. Curious.

"Your father has exquisite taste in scotch," I say, turning and reaching for the cabinet.

"He has exquisite taste in everything."

Ermyntrude hovers somewhere behind me, dimming the lights

as she floats about the room. My hand stills above the cabinet's ivory handle.

There, behind a crystal decanter of amber liquid, peeks a familiar velvet box. The same as Stackton's, with the Bullingdon Club seals.

"What year is this one?" I reach into the cabinet, prepared to sneak a glance at the box's contents.

But why would Lord Bedford have a box of the Bullingdon Club seals if he was a member of the Gridirons?

"Oh, I didn't invite you in here for whisky," Ermyntrude says.

I spin around, hand dropping to my side.

She holds aloft a pipe. "This will ease all your worries."

"I thought you were offering spirits." I take a step back, box forgotten. "I've never enjoyed the taste, I'm afraid."

Geraldine quickly rises, hooking her arm in mine. "I'm afraid I must decline, too."

"You cannot." Ermyntrude's face falls, though something shifts in her eyes. "It would be rude to refuse."

"Then let it be a stain on my reputation," I snap.

Ermyntrude's glare could flay a man. We flee for the ballroom, a dance ending just as we walk in, partners dispersing to mingle at the drink tables and cushioned chairs. Geraldine leads us to the last empty pair of chairs, accepting an offered glass of champagne along the way.

She shakes her head, taking a sip. "I've known Ermyntrude for years, and it was not until quite recently that she became so uncouth."

I incline my head, thinking of the few times I had seen her

before starting the Lady Margaret class. My grandmother had forced me to attend only a few social trivialities. A handful of dances, an opera or two. Ermyntrude had been in attendance each time, a haughty little thing with her nose perpetually in the air. "Why the sudden change?"

Geraldine sighs, the air fogging her glass. "Her father has been in dire straits, as of late. He lost a shipment out to sea recently, and quite a few business partners needed it. My father included."

I wave a hand to the opulent ball around us. "At first glance, one would hardly notice."

It irks me to admit it, too. I like to pride myself on seeing through facades, and here I find none.

Curious.

The night seems full of endless surprises.

She opens her mouth to reply, then instead whispers to me from behind a hand. "Carlisle Gillingham is making his way over to us right now."

"Hopefully he asks you for a dance," I say with a sniff. "And not I."

"Unlikely." Her smile is genuine and wicked all at once. "I once dumped a glass of wine on his head."

My jaw drops. "You did *what?*"

She stifles her giggles behind a gloved hand as Carlisle comes to stand before me. He bows low, a gallant show.

"May I have this next dance?"

"You may not," I say tartly. "I've already promised it to another."

Fury—likely no one has ever refused him in his entire life—sparks behind those cerulean eyes. He demands, "To whom?"

I rack my brain for an excuse, a name, anything to avoid having his slimy hands on me.

"To me," a deep voice says.

We all turn, and it is an effort to keep my face still.

Sherlock nods to Carlisle before holding out a hand. "The Lady Adler has promised this dance to *me*."

CHAPTER 36

Dangerous Assumptions

T*HE MUSIC SEEMS TO DIM, MY HAND MOVING OF ITS OWN* accord to accept his outstretched one. Sparks race up my arm at his single touch.

With a dancer's grace that even my mother would envy, he leads me to the dance floor. He places a hand at the small of my back, holding the other aloft, and the waltz starts. My eyes are impossibly wide, my mouth hanging open. His dark gaze bores into me, looking past all my facades and deep into my soul.

"Your dress," he says, gaze roving the red silk. "It suits you."

"Is that meant to be a compliment?" A small smile, despite myself, pulls at the corner of my lips.

He chuckles. "Of the highest order."

Sherlock leads me deeper into the maze of spinning dancers. His scent, his warm hands on my body, the way his eyes refuse to leave my face. It all stokes the fire growing inside me.

But could he be a murderer? I ask myself, squelching those embers.

I gaze up at him through thick lashes, refusing to turn away. He twirls me, then pulls me in close enough for our hips to brush, and our chests to collide.

"Either you are much more concerned with social graces than I thought," he says against my hair, "or it is my turn to unsettle you."

I turn to watch the dancers around us, looking anywhere but that knowing gaze. "Neither. Simply lightheaded."

"You're normally a much more practiced liar, Irene Adler," he whispers. His gaze darts to my lips.

"Do you always speak such nonsense, Mr. Holmes?" I flick my eyes up to his.

He spins me out, then pulls me in. Our chests brush, breath intermingling for a single, heart-stopping second. My mouth snaps shut around a swallowed gasp.

"You are quite a remarkable actress," he says, voice low. "The hair, the scents, the handwriting. I never got to tell you just how amazed I was with your act. That you fooled an entire class into genuinely believing you are a man."

A warm blush rises in my cheeks, but I keep my lips firmly shut. I am keenly aware of how all eyes in this ballroom seem to follow us.

"You truly thought of everything. You even covered up that lovely birthmark beneath your eye." He looks me up and down. "You had me fooled for the longest time. However did you manage it?"

"A magician loses all their power once they reveal their tricks." Over his shoulder, my eyes meet James's. I raise my chin, but my voice is soft when I say, "My mother. I learned my tricks from my mother."

"She must have been an incredible woman," he says, everything in his face promising sincerity.

"Will you still keep my secret?"

He leans close, lips brushing my ear. "Depends on what other secrets you are keeping from me."

So much for his honor, and for wanting to beat me to the All Souls seat with his own mettle.

I inhale sharply and say, "You think you see everything, William Sherlock Scott Holmes"—his breath hitches—"but you fail to observe the very things that reveal your own tricks."

"I have no tricks."

"Like me, you're not a terrible liar. Quit pretending otherwise."

He leans backward with a frown. "I may be many things, but a liar is not one of them."

"Oh, you definitely are a liar." My skirts brush his legs, filling me with traitorous, delicious heat again. "And you're right. You're many other things as well. What was it Mr. Watson called you? *A prat?* Yes, that's quite fitting."

"You were there. In the church."

I nod. "Yes, not a figment of your imagination."

"You followed me?" His eyes widen.

"Don't insult me. I managed to solve that riddle just fine on my own." I sniff. "Just as you had."

"You were there already. With your brother." His dark eyes are unreadable. "The murderer."

"Just like you are many things, so is my brother," I reply acidly. "And though I have no love for him, I will not let you accuse him of murder." I bare my teeth. "Not when the true murderer holds me now."

H stumbles for the first time, face going slack. Triumph, glorious and burning, fills me.

"Do you deny it, Holmes?" His grip is loose, and I take the reins, my turn to guide him around the dance floor. "You were upstairs at the time of Bertram's murder. Your apartment is just above where Hugo was found. You're the only student lobbying for the fellowship other than James and me. We're the only ones who actually need it."

His hand is a fist now, curled above the small of my back. "You're making dangerous assumptions. You're twisting your facts, Irene, to suit your theories."

"Am I?" Defiance arches my chin high. "You could have tampered with evidence while we were in the morgue. You said so yourself that the Bullingdon Club is innocent. What if that's because you knew all along?"

He chuckles, a low, dark sound. "There are many admirable qualities about you, Lady Adler. Your wit, beauty, and talent high among them. But your overconfidence will be your Achilles' heel in the end."

The music reaches its crescendo in the distance, and he dips me low enough to steal my breath. Hands gripping me firmly and face just above mine, he says, "I am not the murderer you are looking for. I believe your brother murdered our classmates, and your confidence has made you blind to that fact, blurring any possibility that the murderer is right behind you without your knowledge."

"Nothing, not even confidence," I say honestly, "could ever have me falsely defend that man."

My eyes meet Moriarty's over his shoulder. My brother's lips are pulled back in a hideous grin.

"Why not?" Holmes pulls me in one last time. "You two are much more alike than you would like to believe."

The song ends, and we take our turns dipping to the ground before each other. Fury coils deep in my belly like a snake, but within me rests something else. Something I care not to examine.

Doubt.

I open my mouth to continue our verbal sparring, but a hollow scream pierces the air. Everyone stills, the air sucked out of the room.

I wrench around, gaping, as Edith throws herself through the ballroom's double doors.

"He's dead!" she yells.

People begin to scream around us, everyone rushing for the hallway. Wordlessly, I follow the crowd, aware of Holmes pressing on my heels. James has disappeared in the bedlam. I find Geraldine among the fleeing partygoers and latch a hand around her wrist. I can't lose her, too.

The closer we get, the louder the moans, the sobbing, the muffled curses rise. Screams rend the air as ladies and men alike flee Woburn Abbey. I shove through the throng of horrified people. What I find, though, takes my breath away.

In the library, splayed across the cushions Geraldine and I had been sitting on only moments before, is the body of Robert Lancaster.

His shirt is ripped open, baring his daggered chest. The blade remains, driven to the hilt in his stomach as blood pours in narrow rivulets. There is no brand, no lingering stench of burnt flesh. But, like all the others, his face is split in an expression of abject horror.

Sherlock steps up beside me. His gaze sweeps the corpse before he turns to me and says, "What a way to ruin an otherwise delightful evening."

CHAPTER 37

A Great Mind

WHOEVER WAS FOOLISH ENOUGH NOT TO FLEE WHEN THE body was found is forced to stay behind for questioning. Myself included.

Officers swarm the ballroom, and where once the air was filled with music, now relentless whispers fill the space. The Scotland Yard's officers move from student to student, peppering each in turn with the same insipid questions. There is no tact, no logic behind their questioning. I have no doubt that if the murderer has not fled, they would already have their answers prepared.

Arms folded across my chest, I fling myself into a chair with a heavy sigh and await my turn. Geraldine comes to sit beside me, face blanched like milk. She must be thinking of Edgar, and if he was found in a similar manner. I reach out to grab her hand, but she jerks away.

The movement isn't missed by my brother, standing across the ballroom. He leers, before turning to the officer—Watson, I realize with a start—walking up to him. I cannot read the officer's lips well enough to know what he asks my brother, but James's answers are clear enough.

"I never went into the library."

"I hadn't spoken to him at all this evening."

"I was there"—he points to a table littered with spilled champagne glasses—"when he was found."

Watson's face, normally cordial from my limited experience with the man, is pulled into a severe frown as he moves on to question Moran. Another officer steps in front of me, blocking my view.

The very same one who questioned Isaac Holland about his glasses months ago. The elderly inspector leans down with a grimace as his knees mutely protest.

"Lady Irene, correct?" he asks me. When I nod, he continues, "I'm Inspector Gregson. We just got done interviewing your father back in Oxford." He looks down at his notes, caterpillar brows scrunching. "He mentioned you were quite close with Professor Stackton."

"Yes, though I hardly see how that's relevant," Ermyntrude snaps over my shoulder.

I jump, having not heard her slither over, but otherwise ignore her. I nod again. "I am. He is an old friend of my grandmother's. What does Professor Stackton have to do with this? Is he a suspect?"

"No, no, no," he says, shaking his head. "Has news traveled so slowly?"

Now I want to be as rude as Ermyntrude and demand he reach the point immediately. "What are you talking about?"

"The death here was not the only one this evening." His icy eyes see right through me. "Professor Stackton was found dead in his office."

I ease back in my seat, face slack. A gloved hand grips mine, the voices around me falling to a dull roar, but all I can see is Stackton's face staring down at me.

He was so disappointed in me when I saw him last. I was nothing but a nuisance, an abject, utter failure.

Inspector Gregson's eyes see too much. "I see you were much closer to him than I previously realized."

"No." I straighten, snapping my mouth shut with a click. "I've just seen and heard of too much death lately." A lie, too fluid and easy to make me a good person, slides between my teeth. "I'm reminded of my mother's death."

"Oh, Irene," Geraldine says, dropping to a knee beside the inspector. "I am so sorry."

She shouldn't apologize. But whoever murdered her brother and Stackton will.

Tears, unbidden, rise and fall from my eyes. I let them roll down my cheeks. Let these people think they are tears of sadness, when in reality a storm brews inside me. I will make whoever did this pay.

"We will find his killer." Inspector Gregson looks among Geraldine, Ermyntrude, and me, his gaze lingering on me the longest. "I promise you that."

Across the room, Holmes is being questioned by his friend. He shakes his head, words unintelligible from this distance. I should have learned to read lips, not dance. Carlisle Gillingham is being questioned by another officer just beside him, his normally handsome face aflame, beet-red to the point of steam coming from his ears.

He yells, "This is an outrage! Why am I being questioned? You have absolutely zero reason to suspect me!"

And he's correct. With Robert's death, the Bullingdon Club and all their members have fallen far down my list of suspects. Again.

But, once again, at the top of my list, Sherlock Holmes rises. The man whose friend both Avery Williams and Robert Lancaster beat to a pulp.

I flick my gaze back to Inspector Gregson. He still watches me, waiting for me to say...what, I don't know.

"In Professor Stackton's office, we found a number of things. Letters from your grandmother, notes on his latest protégé, and, most curious, a set of seals."

I blink, despite none of those things being unexpected.

"Any idea how the old bat was connected to the student murders?" Ermyntrude asks, leaning forward, eager for any morsel of gossip she can share with her flock.

The overwhelming urge to slap her flashes through me. I tuck my curled fists beneath the silk of my dress, staring down at my knees.

"No connection as of yet," the inspector says, still watching me. "But we hope to find one soon."

And no doubt they will discover the hidden passageway from Stackton's office, where I've been hiding Isaac's disguise. How long until they put the supplies I left behind in both the Bodleian and Queen's Chapel, and there in that passageway, together? Any of the students could link that jacket to Isaac Holland, and my notes as well.

A clock ticks above me, signaling the countdown until my ruse is up.

Just then, the doors at the end of the hall slam open, another contingent of officers swarming the ballroom. Their uniforms are freshly pressed, a stark contrast to the Scotland Yard's wrinkled and worn shirts and trousers.

"What is the meaning of this?" Inspector Gregson demands, face mottled.

The closest officer holds up a badge. "This murder is now under the jurisdiction of the Luton Borough."

"This is an outrage," the inspector says, slamming his notepad shut. "You're going to destroy any evidence that we might have gathered."

"And let you ruin another of our investigations?" The officer sneers. "Here at Woburn Abbey, the murder falls under our jurisdiction. Besides, all here have borne witness to how you've been bumbling your own investigations. Catch the Oxford killer yet? Or has he still managed to give you the slip?"

Inspector Gregson grinds his teeth, looking like a camel about to spit.

"This is outrageous," Ermyntrude says, stomping toward the Luton officer. "Not only are your officers contaminating the crime scene, but you're causing a fuss for nothing. The Scotland Yard is perfectly capable of catching the killer."

"Lady Bedford, correct?" The officer points a pale finger at Ermyntrude. "Yes, we're well aware of your family's tendency to call on the Yard to clean your messes."

Ermyntrude bares her teeth like some sort of feral cat, about ready to bite the man's finger. "What do you dare imply?"

I want to ask the same question. Curiosity piqued, I lean forward to hear better, but the officer is stopped from replying by a loud shout from the hallway.

"Sir." An officer of the Yard jogs toward Inspector Gregson. "We've found something."

The army of officers can do nothing to stop the swell of academics as we all rush for the library. They form a wall where Robert's body still lies undisturbed, but the area surrounding him is now a mess. Tables are overturned, chairs flung aside. In their haste to discover clues, the Scotland Yard has ruined the most central of evidence: the scene of the crime.

The Luton officer knows it, too. He snarls, "You fools."

The lights in the room are dim, painting faces all around me deep in shadow. A window behind where Robert lies swings open on a winter breeze, carrying inside fat, white flakes of ice. Beside me, Geraldine rubs her arms.

"Not all clues are lost," a Yard officer says. He points to the space between the wall and Robert's body.

Both Inspector Gregson and the Luton officer step forward. I hold my breath as they lean over the body. Pulling out his pen, Gregson reaches carefully behind Robert and pulls up a watch with gold hands and a pearlescent green face.

I turn just as Sherlock's face drains of blood.

Standing beside me, he begins to vigorously pat his chest and pockets. "That's impossible."

Inspector Gregson peers at the face and reads the inscription aloud.

"*My dearest Sherlock, to a great mind, nothing is little. Love, Violet.*"

My heart skips, stutters, then comes to a halt. As one, everyone in the room turns to face the man with the most brilliant mind in all of England. Holmes doesn't even protest as an officer steps forward with iron cuffs, and raises his wrist for the man to bind them.

Watson steps forward, blanching. "What are you doing? That's not enough evidence to arrest this man."

"Don't let your friendship blind you." With white fingers, Gregson grips Watson by the shoulder.

The young officer's mouth opens and closes like a fish. "Let me find more evidence. Let me prove his innocence."

"I'm afraid—" Gregson waves to the surrounding crowd and says, so low I can barely hear, "if I do not arrest Holmes now, we will have much more blood on our hands tonight."

He speaks the truth. Fury, riotous and tumultuous as a spark, threatens to alight this whole crowd like a living flame. Even if I wished to speak in Holmes's defense, my words would fall on deaf ears.

He's dragged from the library as Watson looks helplessly on. I hold my tongue, the cogs in my head falling together.

For all my ego and brilliance, I couldn't have been more wrong about Holmes.

His watch couldn't have fallen behind the body at the time of the murder.

Because I had felt it in his pocket when we danced.

CHAPTER 38

The Framing of Sherlock Holmes

Someone framed Sherlock Holmes.

Ermyntrude sends Geraldine and me back to Oxford ahead of her, though it isn't until the sun creeps above the horizon, filtering dawn's early light across the red flowers on the Bedford estate, that we finally put Woburn Abbey firmly behind us. If Geraldine speaks, I hear nothing.

Stackton's face floats in the periphery of my mind, a haunting specter that refuses to release me. I chew my lip relentlessly, gazing out the window of the carriage.

I remember nothing of climbing the college's stone steps, nor collapsing, fully dressed, on my bed. The spiders lurk on the ceiling above me, taunting me for my inferiority—and my inability to save anyone.

My mother. Edgar. Stackton. And though I held no love for them, I couldn't even save my classmates. Even Sherlock, what feelings I have for him I can't hope to place, I couldn't stop him from being dragged to the gallows.

My corset burns into the bullet wound and drags me from my tumultuous thoughts. I rip off my dress, letting the fabric pool on the cold flagstone floor, and dig into my wardrobe for a dressing gown.

Taking a handful of my clothes with me, I collapse. Sobs rack my chest, the cold floor stinging my bare skin.

I allow myself only a few moments of self-pity before climbing to my knees, rubbing my eyes brusquely with the back of my hands, and beginning to clean up the mess I've made.

My grandmother would be ashamed. My mother would be doubly ashamed. Even in our darkest moments together, Elena never cried.

I gather my clothes first, returning them to the wardrobe. My hand roughly brushes against the blank paper I stashed in there among my clothes. Again, the paper slices into my palm. Hissing, I rip it from my wardrobe and throw it on the floor. I suck the wound, the blood intermingling with the tears now drying on my face. I grab up the paper, prepared to toss it into the kindling fire. My hand hesitates above the beckoning flame, though.

With quill in hand, I lay out the paper on the floor to draw a new tree.

I trace a finger around the tree's branches. Bertram, Hugo, Jude, Edgar. Just a handful of the names on the tree, but each rising to the highest branch.

Jude's name stands out amongst the rest of the victims. Frowning, I take the paper to my bed and spread it wide. Jude's father was a baron, his family located somewhere north near Wales. Chewing my lip, I step close to the bed, knees knocking into the wooden frame. Not nearly so esteemed as Carlisle's or Ermyntrude's family, but high on the ladder, so to speak.

I'm so close to the answer, I can almost taste it.

A fist pounds on the door, making my heart leap from my chest. *The Scotland Yard couldn't have deduced my secret identity already.*

I crumple the tree and throw it into the fire, calling to the door, "Who is it?"

Did my voice just crack? Oh, blast, my ruse is nearing its end.

"Geraldine!" My friend's voice is barely a squeak, though the tremor of fear is undeniable. "Please let me in."

I do so, and she rushes into the room, dressing gown trailing on the stone floor. She paces and gnaws on her thumb. "I have something important to tell you."

"Oh?" I hug my arms around myself, cold despite the blazing fire.

She does the same when she turns to me, face the color of ash. "I think the murders are connected, Irene."

"Why do you think that? Did someone tell you?"

I wait with a semblance of patience as she gnaws on her thumb and paces a bit more before collapsing on the edge of my bed. She shakes her head, refusing to meet my gaze. "It feels like heresy to say it out loud. I've known the family my entire life, but the murders keep lining up like cards, all falling, one after another."

My focus narrows. "What family, Gerry?"

"Please don't think I'm mad," Geraldine begs, continuing on. "Her father has long been in dire financial straits. She would never tell anyone, though. Edgar told me...just before he...he visited their estate to refuse their use of our ships." A sob escapes her.

"When Robert was found dead, I remembered that his father, Lord Lancaster, wouldn't loan them the money they needed."

"What family?" I repeat firmly.

"I can't say, Irene." Her lower lip trembles as she finally looks up at me, pale face framed by a mess of golden hair. "Oh, it cannot be true."

I blink, entirely at a loss for words.

It all clicks into place, the pieces of the puzzle coming together of their own accord in my head.

"The Bedfords," I whisper. "You think Ermyntrude's family is responsible for killing all those men."

CHAPTER 39

Feminine Wiles

"B<small>UT WHY KILL</small> H<small>UGO</small>? B<small>ERTRAM</small>? S<small>TACKTON</small>?" I <small>SHAKE MY</small> head, coming to sit beside her. "And why frame Sherlock Holmes?"

The one piece of the puzzle that doesn't quite fit.

She shrugs. "Maybe he's in on it, too? I've never trusted that man. Too many secrets."

I look to the closet, where my pants hide from Geraldine's view.

I chew the inside of my cheek a moment, before I say, "He was framed. The watch. It was in his jacket while we danced."

She turns sharply toward me. "Why didn't you say anything?"

"Fear? Shock? I don't know," I say, but not out loud do I add, *Perhaps some part of me agrees that he has too many secrets, and doubt, my ultimate vice, suffocated my voice.* I return her gaze. "But I will make it right."

The disbelief in her face is what ultimately inspires me. I take her hands in mine and look her directly in the eye. "Gerry. As my oldest, dearest friend—"

"Your only friend," she interrupts.

I can't help but grimace. "I am about to trust you with something that can ruin my life forever."

Despite the tears still clinging to her dark lashes, her eyes are as hard as steel. "Go on."

Standing, I move to the closet. Every fiber of my being screams to keep my secrets, to keep myself safe. But perhaps if I had been honest from the very beginning, more lives would have been safe. Stackton might still be alive. Sherlock Holmes's neck wouldn't be headed toward the gallows.

I pull the pants from the closet and hold them up for her to see.

Geraldine slowly stands. "Why do you have your brother's trousers?"

I refrain from sighing. "They're not Moriarty's. They're mine."

She waits for me to elaborate.

"I've been dressing as a man for the last three months in order to attend the All Souls cohort." I notch my chin high. "I am just as smart as those men, if not more so. I go by the name of Isaac Holland and am not ashamed."

Silence stretches between us, as thick and dark as tar.

Slowly, she says, "You've been dressing as a man...all this time...in order to go to school?"

I nod. "Yes."

"You've been lying to everyone, including me, in order to win the All Souls Fellowship?"

Hesitantly this time, I nod again.

"You've been pulling the rug from underneath everyone, in order to foil your brother's chances?"

"Not for him. For me." After a moment, I add, "Though proving he is the lesser sibling is quite nice."

A smile splits her face, as bright as daylight. "Brilliant, Irene Adler. You're just brilliant."

Relief soars through me as she pulls me into a great hug. She whispers into my hair, "Thank you for entrusting me with this."

I return her hug, gripping her tight.

"Now that you've proven you're the cleverest girl in England…" She withdraws, holding me at arm's length and staring me down. "What are you going to do to stop the next murder?"

They say that hindsight is a rare and elusive breed. Lurking in the shadows of the Metropolitan Police Headquarters, I have to agree.

Geraldine is going to meet me in Ermyntrude's room tonight to search for any clues left behind. But first, I need to retrieve Sherlock Holmes. We really should have planned out this prison break beforehand. But at least I'd had the foresight to grab the local paper. Scanning for recent arrests, a small smile pulls at my lips.

I smear the rouge on my cheeks and paint on my eyelids. The green gown I borrowed from Gerry highlights my figure and brings out the emeralds in my eyes. Tears form at the ready, partially obscured by the black gauze veil hanging before my face, and I stumble through the doors with my handkerchief pressed beneath my nose.

Officers of the Yard stop and stare as I march for the front desk, sobbing with each step. The building is filled to the brim with officers, each haggard and marked with dark circles beneath their eyes. Christmas season inspires the unruliest behavior, it seems, as I step past disorderly men and women being led to their cells.

I stop before the front desk with a great sob, coughing softly into my handkerchief, and the officer sitting there looks up. His brows draw together in concern, though they linger on my heaving bosom. "Everything all right, ma'am?"

I shake my head wildly. "My godfather." Another sob. "You've arrested him."

He drops his pen. "May I ask for his name and what we've arrested him for?"

"Lord Grey," I say, pouting. "For disorderly behavior. Our family is so scandalized."

And hopefully this Lord Grey isn't one of the prisoners being pushed around out here, nor his family members any of those standing along the wall.

"Please just let me see him one last time."

The officer holds his hands out, placating. "I'm sorry, ma'am. I'm not sure what you want me to do. We can't bring you to see him. He should be released in only a few days."

Surreptitiously, I pull a stack of notes from my purse. "My mother has sent this donation to the force. Please take me to my father, so that I can at least see him."

"Your father?" His gaze sharpens, and my stomach twists. "I thought you said Lord Grey was your godfather?"

I glance to the papers on his desk and away from his too keen eyes. "Yes, yes. My godfather." I lean forward, giving him an ample view of my chest. "My real father died many years ago, and Lord Grey has been more of a parent to me than my real father ever was." A single, solitary tear slides down my cheek. "He always has a hard time around the holiday season."

He considers my face, then his gaze falls, back to my bosom.

Men can be so predictable.

My hand falls on his own, inciting a blush to rise in his cheeks. "Please, sir, help me, and I'll do anything I can to thank you."

The officer coughs, raising his eyes from my chest with considerable effort. "Well, I guess I shall permit you to speak with him, but I cannot accept your mother's bribery. He must remain behind bars until my superiors see fit."

"Yes, of course." I nod vigorously. "I would ask for nothing more."

He snaps his hand away as though burned. "Let's go before I reconsider."

I let him lead me deep into the station, among the labyrinthine sprawl of cells and cement walls. I dip my chin to my chest, following on the officer's heels. From my understanding, the prisoners considered dangerous are kept from those that are simply disorderly, and I'm assuming far apart. Where this officer takes me, I must go to the opposite end to find Holmes.

He stops before a door, pulling a set of keys from his hip to unlock it before leading me through. Other officers give us curious looks as we pass. I trip on my shoes, falling into the officer. He catches me, giving me a concerned look, but doesn't ask questions before leading me on.

Before we reach the cells, however, I stop dead in my tracks. He turns on his heel, giving me an impatient look.

"Having second thoughts?" he asks, eyes narrowing. "It is rather unusual of a lady to be seen in these parts."

His concern for my reputation is almost endearing.

I give him a quick shake of my head. "No, it's not that. Umm…" I dance on my toes. "I am rather afraid to ask this but…"

"He won't be with any murderers, ma'am," he says, puffing out his chest. "And should any of them make any uncalled-for movements, I will see to their punishment."

How gallant. I resist rolling my eyes. "No, it's...uhm..."

"Yes?"

I dance some more. "Can you take me to the ladies' room, please?"

As with all men when presented with the functions of female anatomy, he snaps immediately to attention. I let him lead me to the water closet, careful to hide my smirk. He stops at a door and, voice rife with hesitation, asks, "Do you need me to wait here for you?"

His superiors would be infuriated to hear him even ask, but I know he would rather brave their sharp teeth than deal with anything to do with a woman's bits.

"No need." I point to the end of the hall. "Would down there be more comfortable?"

Nodding fast, he speed walks to where I pointed and astutely puts his back to me.

Dipping into the ladies' room, the cogs in my head begin to whirl anew, formulating the next steps in my plan. I pull the keys I plucked from the officer's hip out of my sleeve and hold them up before my face. Time for the second act.

With his back turned to me, it is easy to avoid the officer and dart through door after door until I arrive at the closet I'd seen on our initial foray into the station. I grab a uniform from the rack and switch clothes, pulling the ever-trusty fake mustache from my purse when I'm finished donning the pressed clothes.

My heart pounds in my chest, making it difficult to punch the buttons through their holes, and dotting my lip with sweat that makes it hard for the mustache to grip. Fear, true and tremulous, grips me like a vise as I march down the hall to the cells.

I reach the cells and ignore the prisoners' jeers as I pass.

"So tiny that one could be a snack," one says.

"Too small to be a snack," says another, looking me up and down with black eyes. "I could snap that one like a toothpick."

Another presses his pockmarked face against the rusty bars of a cell. "I'd like to give that a try."

I pass cell after cell, searching for the one that holds the incorrigible Sherlock Holmes. I come to another door, this one locked as well. After unlocking and swinging it shut behind me, I turn and slam into a firm chest. Arms reach to grip my narrow biceps.

Officer Watson looks down on me, eyes narrowed. "I don't recognize you."

Panic flutters in my chest. I open my mouth to give a name not my own.

"That's no officer." Both our heads snap toward the end of the hallway, where Holmes leans against the bars of his cell. His arms drape between the bars, and he points a long finger at me. "That's my classmate Isaac Holland."

He gives his friend a smug smile. "Or as you also met her, the Lady Irene Adler."

CHAPTER 40

The Ripper of Oxford

WHEN PRESENTED WITH DANGER, EVERY LIVING CREATURE reacts to the situation with a natural physiological response, commonly known as fight or flight.

I choose the latter.

Panic seizes me. I rip my arms from Watson's grasp and sprint down the hallway. His footsteps pound behind me. I grasp desperately at the handle as the prisoners hoot and holler on the other side. A large hand reaches over my shoulder and holds the door firmly closed.

I spin, ready to punch the man in the jugular. Predicting my movements, Watson catches my fist. He bends it back, tearing a cry from my throat.

He grunts. "I've been punched by enough gentry in the last few months."

Fist behind my back, he drags me down the hallway and slams me into the bars of Holmes's cell. A sharp pain in my side reminds me of the ever-present bullet wound that is too slow to heal.

"Not twelve hours and already planned an escape, Sherlock?" Watson asks.

"Gentle with the lass," Holmes says, eyeing the bruise already forming on my chin. "And I had an escape plan formulated the moment I stepped through that door. This one came of her own accord."

His voice drops so the other prisoners cannot hear. "Here to seal your brother's plan, Irene?"

My brother would never be foolish enough to get caught, I don't say aloud, deriding myself. Out loud, I say, "No such luck. I doubt he's had a single thought about you since you were dragged away from the party."

"Then what are you doing here?" Watson demands.

I bare my teeth and damn myself. "To free Sherlock Holmes and prove his innocence."

Holmes's brows rise as high as his hairline. "Just yesterday you accused me of murder," he says, attention fixed on the bars of his cell. "What changed your mind?"

"Would you believe that I simply had a change of heart?"

"I'd believe in fairies first." He sniffs, turning his attention to Watson. "What are you waiting for? Give the lady the keys and get me the hell out of here."

Watson releases me, his face stern. "You know I can't do that. No matter how innocent I believe you are."

No matter, I don't say aloud. *I have keys of my own.*

"What if I could prove Holmes's innocence?"

"Then you can do so at his trial," Watson says firmly.

"Did I mention that my dear friend here is a stickler for the rules?" Holmes leans his head against the bars. "Even when it is to the detriment of his fellows."

· · 349 · ·

Watson pinches the bridge of his nose. "My father warned me about you."

"You and I both know that the gentry that has so eagerly pummeled you will not allow Sherlock Holmes a fair trial." I raise my chin. "Give me twelve hours with him to prove his innocence, and if I fail, you can have the esteem of bringing both of us back in handcuffs."

Watson stares me down, the kind face from our first meeting replaced by one as cold and still as stone. I weigh how to sneak Holmes my set of keys so he can formulate his own escape when Watson releases a long, heavy sigh.

"Eight hours," he says. "You get eight hours before they have all our necks."

I reach for the lock hanging from Holmes's cell.

"But you two will have to find your own way from the Yard." He straightens his jacket and reaches a hand inside the cell. "Sherlock, give me the keys you stole from my pocket. They won't believe me if I tell them you took them from me."

Rolling his eyes, Holmes tosses the keys to his friend. "Fine. Any brilliant ideas, Adler?"

Grinning widely, I hold my own set aloft. "Steps ahead of you, Sherlock. As usual."

Watson said that he will meet us in an hour. To prove his innocence, he must make an appearance among his fellows while we escape. Getting Sherlock a uniform of his own to change into as we rush from the Yard is no small feat. We spend many breathless moments crowded against each other in shadowed corners, standing so close that heat cascades over my body like fireworks.

Swallowing any feelings whatsoever, I take the lead, not risking him leading us into a pitfall. Across the foyer, I make sure to keep my head ducked, and Holmes does so as well. I wonder if they can hear the rapid pounding of our hearts, and if Poe was actually onto something when he wrote the "Tell-Tale Heart."

I don't let myself even breathe until we're at least a block away from the precinct, and it all comes rushing out in one great gasp.

My eyes are wide and my heart in my throat. "We're going to prison."

Holmes looks hardly fazed. "Only if we don't prove my innocence."

"How can you be so nonchalant all the damned time?" I demand, my voice rising.

Now he looks worried, glancing this way and that, down the abandoned alley we've stopped in to make sure nobody heard my outburst.

He catches my chin, holding it firmly up so that our eyes meet. "If you want to leave, Irene, I would not be offended. You have proven your worth enough at this point."

I hold his gaze a moment longer. "I owe it not just to you, but to Edgar and all the others to find the killer."

He nods, dragging a thumb over my lower lip. "Then let us go. We only have seven hours and thirty-four minutes left before Watson places me back in handcuffs."

Of course he's counting down the minutes. I let him lead me through the city, ducking our heads whenever people pass. Thankfully, few people are on the streets. We pass a paperboy and I pay him for the latest news.

Holmes's face is plastered across the front page.

THE RIPPER OF OXFORD

I turn the page, hoping to learn who painted Holmes as the villain of this story when another face, painted in black-and-white, stares at me from the paper.

ISAAC HOLLAND, UPSTART AND MURDERER?

The article tells an elaborately woven tale of my murderous exploits, of Isaac's falling-out with Stackton, and even my jealousy at not being accepted into any of Oxford's hidden societies. None of it is necessarily a surprise—I had known they would come after me eventually—but what does make my jaw drop is a name mentioned toward the end.

> Placed under house arrest just this morning, the Lord Carlisle Gillingham is also a prime suspect. Though the Luton Borough is keen to keep their secrets, the *Gazette* has learned that the rebellious lord has a stockpile of knives and weapons in his town house off campus. He is currently being held for questioning.

Wordlessly, I hand the paper to Sherlock, watching as his face falls.

Holmes crumples the paper and throws it down an alleyway.

"The echelons of Oxford wasted no time putting targets on our backs. The murderer must no doubt be among them if they want the spotlight so quickly turned. But the inclusion of Carlisle among the suspects is especially interesting."

"You and I have a very different definition of *interesting*." I feel hollow. "Where are we going?"

Sherlock glances skyward, watching London's dreary skyline. "Once they notice my absence, they will no doubt go to my family home to search for me. Who knows how long before they learn that you are at fault for my escape. Watson told me that they found some of your disguises near Stackton's office."

"I will admit that I had that same thought." I puff out my cheeks before releasing a big breath. "So where exactly are we going?"

"The one place my mother, lord bless her, doesn't even know about."

"Which is?"

He grins. "My second flat."

I blink. "Is that supposed to mean something?"

He crosses his arms but keeps walking, turning the corner. "For a lady who no doubt prides herself on knowing everything about her classmates, you seem hardly fazed to learn there is more to me than you know."

"I never assumed to know *everything* about my classmates," I say, raising my chin and following him.

"But do you deny that you have an inflated sense of self-worth?" He laughs, making my imaginary hackles rise. "That you believe yourself to be the brightest student at Oxford?"

I stop, glaring and silently willing myself not to punch him square across the jaw. "I do deny it. I have never thought myself to be the smartest student at Oxford. But just because I'm not the most intelligent, does not mean I am less than my classmates. Just like how knowing that I have a measure of brilliance does not mean I have an inflated sense of self-worth. Where ego and self-confidence are lauded among men, women are often told to hide their talents and are chastised for their pride. I will not apologize for knowing my worth."

I'm breathless by the time the last word tumbles from my lips. I place my hands on my hips, daring Holmes to insult me again.

Finally, he says, "You're a remarkable woman. Don't let anyone dare make you question your worth, Irene Adler." He waves to a set of stairs behind me. "Welcome to 221 Baker Street."

We've reached a narrow town house of mottled pale blue-and-gray stone. Shutters in dire need of a paint job cover the windows, and the ivy creeping to the room should have been trimmed back years ago. The door, a royal purple, is the finest part of the exterior, complete with a brass knocker in the shape of a cat's derriere.

"Classy," I murmur as he leads me up the stairs and through the door.

My eyes sweep the messy foyer, landing on the jackets thrown across the floor, and gadgets resting on every surface within reach. "No wonder you keep this place a secret from your family."

"If I had known you were going to be so disparaging, I would have left you on the doorstep."

"No, you wouldn't," I reply with a smug smile. "Do you not employ any servants? Someone who could perhaps do some laundry?"

His skin turns a smidge brighter red before he starts up the stairs. "I will find a change of clothes for us both."

I take a turn about the room, snooping at my leisure. There's not a place to sit, every surface covered with random trinkets. Shelves curved from the weight of hundreds of papers and gadgets surround me in the sitting room. I peer into the murky depths of a fish tank to try to discern what animal it holds. No answer forthcoming, I turn to the one table in the room and begin flipping through the pile of papers on its surface. I hold aloft a curious design, a charcoal drawing resembling something between a kite and a fork. "What is this?"

Holmes, appearing in the doorway, rushes across the room and snatches away the drawing. "None of your business."

Raising my eyebrows, I continue my blatant snooping, picking up various gadgets of all shapes and sizes, their materials ranging from branches to copper. "Are you a bit of an inventor?"

"An aspiring one, if nothing else." Sherlock watches me carefully. Draped over an armchair, he holds a pair of brown breeches and a jacket. "My father is the inventor. Holmes Industries. He hopes to bring the name to every household."

Some unnamed emotion flickers in and out of his voice, be it distaste or ire I cannot say.

"So that's what our classmates refer to when they call you an upstart," I say, more than ask. I knew that his father was a businessman, but had not yet looked deep enough into his backstory, I'm embarrassed to admit.

I pick up a metal plate, barely the size of my palm. "What's this?"

I turn it over, revealing a poppy flower painted white atop its back. I press on a leaf, and the plate snaps, folding over into a half fan. I nearly drop it when Holmes snatches the curious thing from my hands.

"This one doesn't have a name yet," he says, tucking it into his jacket pocket.

I take the clothes from his arms without comment and begin to undo the buttons of my shirt. I peel it away, revealing the corset beneath that binds my breasts tight as a fist. Once the pants fall away, the dressing gown I wear beneath falls to my feet as well. In the lamplight, the dress leaves very little to the imagination.

I look up at Holmes, whose mouth has fallen open ever so slightly.

"What?" I ask, my face the image of innocence as his face blushes a vivid shade of magenta. "Don't pretend now to give a modicum of interest in my decency."

Mouth pressed firmly closed, he turns on his heel and marches from the room.

Smiling to myself, I pull on the new pair of clothes, tossing the uniform in the corner where it blends right in with all the other dirty laundry.

Before I can call out to Holmes and tell him that I'm decent once more, the front door slams open. I jump as Watson storms into the room, more furious than I've ever seen him.

"You have seven hours left, Holmes, before I'm forced to turn you back in," he yells, before turning to me. "And don't think I won't turn you in as well."

"Touché." I shrug, piling my dark hair atop my head and pulling on a black bonnet. "They will have to find me in order to arrest me, though."

His eyes trace my jaw, and he rubs his own. "My apologies for the bruise. It's been a rough couple of months, but that is no excuse for treating a lady as I did you."

"A lady can murder as easily as a man," I reply, my voice icy.

"Nevertheless." He continues to eye the bruise. "Make sure to put a cold compress on your face when this is all over."

I don't mention that the bruise is the least of my wounds I've accrued over the course of this hunt.

"Do you believe Gillingham is behind the murders?" The way Watson looks at me, as if he actually values my opinion, fills me with warmth despite everything.

I shake my head. "He was framed, as Holmes was. The Bedfords are behind it all."

Realization and horror, in turn, dawn on Watson's face. Holmes returns to the room, throwing me a furtive glance as if to assure himself that yes, I am actually dressed. In his hand he has a long tube of paper.

"Yes, I've heard all about their financial difficulties," Holmes says. "Ermyntrude's father begged mine for a loan, not so long ago. My father nearly took him up on it, but the way they disparaged our lack of nobility snipped the deal. Mycroft wouldn't have let him loan out money anyway. That bastard is such a tightwad."

"Mycroft?" I ask.

"Sherlock's jackass older brother," John explains.

"Their club tried to recruit me before the murders even began," Holmes says, thumping his palm with the tube.

"Not more of that Bullingdon Club nonsense," Watson says, throwing his hands in the air. "I did not let you escape prison just to chase a wild goose."

"Not the Bullingdon Club," Holmes says, unfurling the paper across a crowded table. Gadgets threaten to poke holes in it, pressing up against the back to create mountains on the Oxford map stretched before us. "The Gridirons."

"Of course," I say softly. "They likely framed the Bullingdon Club."

"A red herring we too easily fell for." Holmes nods. He jabs a finger onto the map where Bartlemas Chapel stands. "The chapel sits on Gridiron land, not Bullingdon."

Watson crosses his arms and nods. "The man they found there had ties to Lord Bedford. Apparently, he was their coach driver some years ago."

"What a poor detective you would make, John."

"Will you shut up, Holmes?"

"The clubs, the secret societies, the brands, and the church. It was all a ruse." Their heads snap in my direction. I cradle a fist above my heart. "They're killing the heirs."

Holmes stares at me blankly for a mere moment before rushing to a bookshelf and carrying back a heavy tome. He drops it on the table, and the map no doubt tears beneath as he opens up the book to a family tree similar to the one I drew.

He grabs a pen, circling the names of our dead classmates, one by one, until nearly all the branches are marked up. Only a handful remain.

Silence, deafening and still, fills the room.

"It's not for money," I whisper. "It's for power."

Watson's jaw tightens. "Gillingham would be next in line to the dukedom."

I shake my head. "Carlisle may be vile, but he isn't nearly clever enough to pull off this scheme." I raise my chin. "In fact, the one who would benefit the most from this plot is likely not involved at all. The Bedfords have been murdering the heirs of any family that would keep Ermyntrude's brother, George, from succeeding the dukedom. They were on the brink of poverty, if Geraldine is to be believed."

"A lofty goal, but unlikely," Holmes says softly, turning back to the book.

But Watson has taken a step back from the table, his skin as pale as the moon. "She's right, Holmes."

We both turn to stare at the officer.

"My father was there, on the Bedford estate. The night he died."

"That's where he died?" Holmes's face is unreadable.

"That's what he just said." I lean closer. "Why was your father visiting the Bedfords?"

"The family reported a disturbance. Someone broke onto the grounds." He presses his lips together a long moment before continuing. "Whoever it was, they killed my father."

Sherlock turns slowly toward me. "Is your memory so fine, Irene, that you remember that cadaver Professor Stackton had us examine in class?"

I don't have to ask him which one, though there were many. "The one whose time of death had been only hours before."

"That was Watson's father." He closes his eyes for a moment, and when they open, they are dark and sharp as an obsidian blade. "He must have seen something he wasn't meant to. Something the Bedfords couldn't afford the Yard learning about."

"The flowers," I breathe.

"I'm so sorry, John," I say, reaching out and gripping his cold hand.

He squeezes my fingers.

Holmes slaps a palm on the paper. "Well, that might just make getting the answers we need a fragment easier."

Watson looks up, grimacing. "Why do I suspect I will not like the next words that tumble from your mouth?"

He shrugs. "Perhaps. Perhaps not."

Sneaking onto campus in ladies' clothes is surprisingly easy for Sherlock Holmes. He follows, gingerly lifting the hem of his skirts until I slap his hands away.

"A lady would allow her hem to be ruined before her reputation."

He sniffs. "Must get blasted expensive ruining gowns on a daily basis."

"Not when you have access to your brother's credit." I don't miss his smirk. "Where did you find that dress anyway?"

"It's my sister's."

"Fits you perfectly."

"I'll take that as a compliment."

"As you should."

His long black hair is bound on top of his head, artfully arranged to appear like a tight bun and decorated with pearl bobby pins. Add in a dash of blush and some dark powder to his eyelids, and he's gorgeous. But, just in case, I still lead Holmes down the secret passageways instead of tempting fate in the main corridors.

"These damn shoes pinch my feet. Couldn't I have worn something that fits properly?"

"Even ladies' shoes that are the correct size hurt, Holmes." I peer around a corner to make sure nobody waits. "Beauty is pain."

"How uncivilized."

"You have no idea."

When we reach the Lady Margaret corridor, I don't lead him to my chambers, but instead Ermyntrude's. I can only hope that she is still at home. The door swings open the moment my knuckles rap on the heavy wood.

Geraldine's eyes widen from over Ermyntrude's shoulder, but I spare her barely a glance as I swoop inside, hugging the Lady Bedford tight.

"Oh, you poor dear," I say, resisting the urge to dig my nails into her arms. "You must be exhausted."

Her room is as bright as winter will allow, blinds pulled back to reveal a white sky and fireplace blazing. On her boudoir sits a single silver box, lid askew. It is the only thing out of place in the entire room. Everything else untouched.

"Not too tired. Where have you been?" She looks me over suspiciously before turning to Holmes behind me. "And who is this?"

Sherlock's rouge-painted lips pucker. "Eunice Featherington."

Ermyntrude blinks once, twice, then frowns. "I've never heard of you."

"You've been introduced to all thirty-one million of England's population?" Sherlock replies tartly, his voice high-pitched.

I refrain from grinding my heel into his toes, but Ermyntrude doesn't miss a beat.

"No, but I have met everyone of *importance*."

I should have left Holmes back at his damn town house.

Before he can steep us deeper in a pit of tar, I step in front of him, blocking Ermyntrude's line of sight. "Ignore Miss Featherington," I say. "She never knows when to shut her mouth. I wanted to see how you were doing after the bedlam last night."

Ermyntrude waves a hand through the air. "Oh, I'm fine. My father is having a devil of a time. Police are all up in his business."

"Seems like a common thing for them to do this year." I give my eyes an exaggerated roll. "They questioned me for what felt like hours after I found Bertram's body. They didn't question *you* at all, did they?"

"Not in the slightest, actually." Ermyntrude flounces over to a settee, falling back on the seat with a great sigh. "My father took the brunt of their questioning."

"And Edith," Geraldine says.

"Oh, yes. Poor dear. She was the one to find the body."

"How did she find him?" Holmes asks, voice a touch too deep.

Ermyntrude's gaze skewers him, her nails digging into her palms. "Haven't the slightest."

A lie if I ever heard one. I sit at the edge of her seat, forcing her to move her feet. "Where is poor Edith now?"

"Sleeping." Ermyntrude turns to the fire, hands clenched tight. "She was exhausted when she returned from my estate."

"I almost envy her." I lean back, closing my eyes. "I haven't slept in well over a day. I could use a good tonic."

I peek at a frowning Holmes. If my suspicions are correct, John's father wasn't killed by a heart attack. Or, at the very least, not by itself. The abject horror on the man's face, the paralyzing fear that would keel a man over. I can remember only once feeling that way.

When I inhaled the tainted fog in Bartlemas Chapel.

If I am to prove that, I must try the sedative I believe Ermyntrude has been using all along.

"So blatant, Adler." Ermyntrude walks to the silver case. "If you wanted a sedative, you could have just been forthright."

She pulls out a pipe, already stuffed with a browned herb of some sort. Even from where I sit, the smell wafts over to me. Sickly sweet and musky. Just the same as my memory of the Bartlemas Chapel. Of the herbs used at the Red Negligee, where her father is a frequent guest. Of her father's office, where that same pipe once was.

Sherlock crosses in front of me before I can accept her offer and extends a gloved hand for the pipe.

"I could use a whiff," he says with a girlish giggle. "It's been a hard day."

After a moment's hesitation, Ermyntrude begrudgingly hands him the worn pipe.

I can feel my eyes boggling out of my head as Holmes brings the pipe to his mouth and takes a giant toke.

His eyes immediately begin to dull, words slurred as he says, "Oh my! I thought this would be nothing more than my father's weak tobacco." He coughs, the sound horrifyingly male. "This is much stronger."

"Well, your father is not my father." Ermyntrude takes the pipe back with a small smile. "We grow the leaf on our very own estate."

My mouth falls open. "The Eden's Papaver."

Ermyntrude blinks, perhaps realizing that she had said too much, before turning and returning the pipe to the silver box. "None other."

I take Holmes's hand, giving it a tight squeeze. "Well, we really must be leaving. Geraldine, do you still want to see that dress my father bought for me?"

Geraldine leaps to her feet. "Oh, yes. I—"

"I would like to see it, too." Ermyntrude cuts her off, walking swiftly to the door.

Geraldine's mouth opens and closes, fishing for an excuse to keep the woman away.

"You cannot," I say. Ermyntrude's head snaps in my direction. "You'll spoil the surprise my brother has for you."

The lady's eyes shutter a mere moment before a cold smile splits her lips. "I do love surprises."

"Then I'm sure you have no wish to ruin this one." I take Geraldine's hand, my other still gripping Holmes tight, and drag them both toward the door. As I'm leaving, I call over my shoulder with forced sweetness to save face, "Tea later this week, Ermyntrude?"

Her reply is soft. "Of course."

And I cannot help but feel that she sees right through me.

CHAPTER 41

To Dance with Death

I lead Geraldine and a rapidly fading Holmes down the secret passageways of Oxford, ignoring both of their questions as panic slowly begins to overwhelm me. The corridors are empty, the classrooms filled with nothing but ghostly whispers. Winter's draft chases our heels down the dark corridors until we arrive at Stackton's office at last.

It isn't until I see his desk, the papers I had thrown aside only days before still littering the floor, that a sob escapes me. But it is the only ounce of remorse that I allow myself to feel. I shove Holmes into Stackton's chair and pry his eyelids open.

"What are you doing to him?" Geraldine asks, peering over my shoulder. "Why is he wearing a dress? What was in the pipe?"

"A very, very powerful narcotic," I tell her. Holmes's eyes are bloodshot, his breathing shallow. He mutters something under his breath that I do not understand. "I have no doubt that that was a much more potent dose than a human body can handle."

With a sweep of my arm, I knock everything on Stackton's desk to the floor. "Help me lay him down."

We each take one of his arms, slippery under the gauzy dress fabric. His fingers twitch and he continues to mutter under his breath. His eyes dart around the room and his nose begins to weep. Once we have him leaning against the far end of the desk, Sherlock decides to start screaming.

"Unhand me, you brigands!" he roars, flinging Geraldine aside.

She collapses in the piles of papers and ink. I avoid his swing and slap a hand over his mouth. His teeth clamp down on my fingers, pulling a yelp from my own lips.

"I will not dally with you rats any longer! Release me from your ship!" He continues to roar.

Before his screams can bring everyone on campus to us, I curl my fingers into a fist. "Sorry for this, Holmes. This will be much easier with you unconscious."

Fire lances up my arm as I slam my fist into his face. He thumps backward onto the desk.

"Did you kill him?" Geraldine looks aghast, her skin deathly pale.

"Just forced him to take a wee nap." Leaning forward, I rest my face against his chest. It rises and falls steadily, his smell filling my nose as I listen for his heartbeat. There, faint, and steadily dropping, his heart thumps against my cheek. I wipe the sweat gathering on my brow with an impatient hand and sigh before saying, "We have to keep his breathing steady, and that is almost impossible with him in these fits of a panic attack."

I search the office for what I need. "Ermyntrude somehow knew that she was one of my suspects. She has been trying to get me—and you—to try that poison for a long time. No doubt her wine is laced with it, which is why the girls all act like mindless fools when she begins pouring."

"That night with the séance. The ghosts Edith saw." Geraldine raises a trembling hand to her mouth.

"Not ghosts. Drugs." I tear the hem of Holmes's skirt with a grimace, using the shreds to bind his legs and arms to the desk. "A small dose, no doubt, but enough to keep the other girls continually wanting more while blaming the side effects on the wine."

"But why?"

"You were the perfect candidates for the test trials. The Bedfords are in dire financial straits, correct? What if this drug was meant to get them out of such a pit? And when your brother refused to let her father use the Hayward fleet? They killed him to keep the plan a secret."

Geraldine wraps her trembling arms around herself. "Why would they even want our ships?"

"To ship the drug to the Americas, no doubt."

Ignoring Geraldine's gasp behind me, I glance about Stackton's office. "Find me Stackton's pipe and his scotch. I believe he kept the pipe in a hollowed-out book."

She looks up at the hundreds of books on his shelf. "Any idea where to start?"

"Try Vesalius," I say, pressing the back of my hand to Holmes's forehead. It is clammy. "If not there, try *Anathomia Mundini*. Those were his favorites."

"Good guess." A pipe and a bag fall from the first leather-bound book she pulls down. "And the scotch?"

Absently, my focus mostly on keeping Holmes's breathing

steady, I wave to Stackton's desk. "Top drawer on the left, in his ink pots."

"That seems like a recipe for disaster." Geraldine brings both the ingredients over. "What do we do with these?"

"Watch his breathing." I straighten. "I need to make an opium syrup."

"An opium...that seems counterproductive." Her eyes are wide, almost dazed.

"Laudanum would have been better, ironically, but Stackton loathes—loathed the stuff, so you won't find any here." I open the door to my passageway, one of the many places on campus where I hid my chemistry equipment. "It will keep him steady by stirring muscle contractions throughout his body, raising his blood pressure until the nasty stuff Ermyntrude gave him is out of his system. The hallucinations aren't the problem now that he's unconscious, though I suspect that wasn't the case for some of the other victims. The horror on their faces. The things they must have seen." I shake my head, garnet hair falling before my face. "Basically, the coca syrup keep his breathing steady and make sure he coasts on the high so that he doesn't fall into a respiratory depression."

"Other victims? You think Ermyntrude killed all those men with this drug?"

"Not with it." I grimace. "Well, at least one of them. Monitor his breathing and I'll explain."

Geraldine rushes to his side.

I open the window. With a tentative peek to make sure nobody is watching, I scoop the snow from the sill and place it in one of my beakers. "An inspector was found dead on the Bedford estate a few months ago. They blamed his death on cardiac arrest, but the man seemed perfectly healthy."

"Be...beer," Holmes mutters, eyes fluttering a moment before he loses consciousness once more.

"Yes, they also blamed his death on alcohol. Stay asleep!"

Good god, this man is astonishing. And a pain in my ass. I would slap him if he wasn't on the brink of death.

"I'm guessing they hit the poor man with a dose heavy enough to instill hallucinations that caused cardiac arrest. Each of the victims had the look of absolute fear about them, as well. The amounts she puts into the wine must be minimal, and the smoke released in Bartlemas must have been a heavier dose, but less deadly because it filled up the entire church."

"Bartlemas?" Geraldine asks.

"Yes, I followed my brother there when I thought he was responsible for the murders."

"How long have you been investigating this, Irene?"

"Since I found Bertram's body in the library." I open Stackton's bag, tipping around the white powder with pursed lips. "I'm going to have to guess on this dosage, though."

"What happens if you give him too much?" She leans over my shoulder to take a closer look and her jaw drops. "Is that—?"

"Erythroxyline. Also known as coca." I tip the bag and sprinkle the powder over the snow, setting the flame below the beaker alight. "A tea might work best. I'm afraid something too concentrated, like a paste, might be too strong for him."

"But why my brother?" Geraldine asks. "He would never willingly take a drug like that."

"I don't think Edgar was slipped this drug."

The snow melts above the ardent flame, pooling as the cocaine mixes into the liquid and disappears. Before the powder can begin to cook, I cut the flame and pour the mixture into the mug Stackton always used for tea. "I've seen its like in both gas and liquid form. A curious drug.

"Like Stackton, I think Edgar was a victim of prescience." My face has hardened, scowl forming between my brows as I swirl the liquid around. "They both knew too much, and the Bedfords couldn't allow that."

I rest my cheek against Sherlock's warm chest and ignore the rapid thundering of my own heart. His heartbeat is slower than I'd like and his breathing too shallow.

"We must be quick." Clenching my lip between my teeth, I hoist him up, gasping at his considerable weight despite his slim frame. Resting his head between my breasts, I nod to the still-steaming mixture on the table. "I'll hold open his mouth. You pour."

A panicked look fills Geraldine's eyes, like a deer looking down the barrel of a rifle. "We could kill him, Irene!"

"And he'll die either way if we don't try," I snap. I pinch his nostrils closed, forcing his mouth open. "Pour!"

Geraldine grabs the steaming mug, hands shaking so hard liquid splatters on every surface. But there's just enough left to spill into Holmes's gaping mouth. He chokes, gagging, but I slam his mouth closed and hold it still until I feel his throat constrict around the liquid.

His eyes flutter open, meeting mine. A question—or accusation—lingers there a moment, then gone as he falls back into unconsciousness.

I push his dark hair from his sweaty brow and set him back down on the table as gently as I can. Pressing my lips against the hollow of his throat, I allow the smallest sigh of relief when his heart skips a beat.

"He'll be fine," I say, brushing the sweat from my own brow. The panic recedes like a tide, leaving me bereft and hollow.

"How can you know already?" Geraldine's voice is a piteous screech, her hands gripped in the folds of her dress.

I walk to the window, grabbing another ball of snow. "Because his heart recognized the feel of my lips."

She blinks when I hand her the dripping snow, commanding, "Wipe his brow with this occasionally and continue to monitor his breathing. I will go find him some men's clothes. I have some that might still be hidden not too far from here."

My mind roars like a typhoon as I dive into the labyrinthine sprawl of Oxford corridors. I should stay and make sure Holmes rouses, but time is not on my side. His face, clammy and lifeless, floats in my vision as I scour the hallways.

I dip into an empty classroom, everyone gone for the winter holiday. In the back, another door sways, hidden by a long, maroon curtain. I pull open the cupboard and pull free the clothes I have stashed, but my mind isn't hovering over the fact that the pants will be three inches too short for Holmes, nor that the shirt will likely be tight across his chest.

I'm thinking of Ermyntrude, the little minx who outsmarted me the entire semester. I thought for so long that it was one among our own cohort, someone seeking to take the top seat. But none of the rich bastards had need of it. I pinch myself, berating myself for not seeing Ermyntrude's connections to each of the dead sooner.

Each of them, save the very last.

Professor Stackton.

What could Ermyntrude have to gain from killing an old anatomy professor?

CHAPTER 42

A Steady Heart

"It just doesn't make any sense," Geraldine says, voicing my own thoughts as she paces the disheveled remains of Stackton's office. "I've known Ermyntrude since we were little girls. I cannot believe she would actually murder someone!"

"Desperation makes monsters of us all." I take Holmes's wrist, assuring myself that his pulse remains steady. He shouldn't be out for too much longer—hopefully.

"Maybe her father put her up to it? I've never liked that man."

I blink. An itch forms on the back of my neck.

"Perhaps he was responsible for some of the murders," I muse. The answer rests on the tip of my tongue, taunting me. I wave to the shelves around us. "But it still doesn't explain Stackton's death. Neither of them have a reason to kill him, unless he deduced their secrets. But how did he do so, and how could they have known if he did?"

"Perhaps the deaths are unrelated?" Geraldine bites her lips.

"Or perhaps they are more related than Irene would care to admit."

Relief soars through me. I leap to my feet, a soft gasp escaping my lips. "Sherlock?"

"None other." He coughs. "What the bloody hell did you do to me?"

"I saved your damn life," I say, a smile rising to my cheeks despite myself, patting his arms, his chest, anything to assure myself that he is really, truly, okay. "How are you feeling?"

"Like I've been skewered by a javelin," he says, coughing again. "Or did you want me to describe my symptoms?"

"I can very well guess those on my own." Without thinking, I swoop down and press my lips to his cheek. "I'm so glad you're alive."

A blush has risen to his formerly pallid skin. "All thanks to you, I'm sure."

"And Geraldine." Remembering myself and blushing as deeply as he, I step back. I wave to my friend, who stands awkwardly on his other side, gaze flicking between us.

"I merely assisted." Geraldine gathers another ball of snow from the sill. "As I'm sure you know, the Lady Margaret classes are quite wanting."

"What inspired you to take Ermyntrude's pipe?" I demand, accepting the snow and dabbing it on Sherlock's forehead.

Silence hangs heavy between us for a few moments. His face mere inches from my own, I can see him chewing his words for a moment, his nostrils flaring, before he finally says, "Because, loathe am I to admit it, I knew you could bring me back from the brink. I didn't trust myself to do the same for you."

His eyes never leave mine. My heart tumbles in my chest,

constricting as though wrapped in a viper's grip. I barely register as Geraldine leaves, whispering that she will keep watch outside the office.

My lips tremble. "Don't be so dramatic, Holmes."

He stands, swaying on his feet. I catch his waist on reflex, his muscles hard and warm beneath my palms.

"I am many things," he says. "Dramatic is not one of them."

Insults, tart replies, both dance on the tip of my tongue. And they are all swallowed by the kiss he steals from me.

His mouth covers mine, so warm and flushed with spices. I can still taste the tonic on his tongue, and it colors my eyesight with stars. He deepens the kiss, taking my hips roughly in his big hands, and I gasp against his lips. A moan, low and guttural, claws from his throat at the sound. More, I want more, but I can't. Not now.

I tear myself away. "We can't."

He opens his mouth, but I cut him off. "Now, what did you mean about the murders being related?"

He grimaces, rubbing his raw lips. "Think about it, Adler. Who has to gain from both the murders and would rise in the ranks? Who would benefit the most, other than yourself, from putting me in prison?"

His name passes my lips with a whisper. "James."

Sherlock nods. "I know he's your brother, and that there must be some part of you, no matter how vehemently you deny it, that would want to protect your kin, but you must see it."

"He's been keen on courting both Geraldine and Ermyntrude for months." I incline my head. "Ermyntrude fancied him as well. And he was there in the chapel when that man was murdered."

He nods again. "And he's been third in the All Souls cohort. All he would have to do is ruin your ruse, once I was kicked out, and he would ascend to the top."

"He must have been the one to shoot Isaac Holland," I say breathlessly.

I ignore his aghast expression. "If my brother is the one who shot me, he must have done so to take out a challenger in the competition. It still doesn't explain why he would frame the Bullingdon Club, though."

"Ermyntrude's grandfather was one of the founding members of the Gridiron Club."

"Her father could have worked with James to set them up to lead us off the scent."

"They must know we're onto them by now." Sherlock sits back, crossing his arms. "They will have planned out our trail."

"Or maybe we're using the wrong pieces to complete this puzzle," I snap.

"That's your denial speaking," Sherlock says. He accepts the clothes I hand him with a look of distaste. "It has to be Moriarty, but not in the way that we think."

I chew on my fingernails and start pacing the room. "But how do we catch him?"

"We find his and Ermyntrude's next target. The next branch on the tree."

I blanch, as though doused in a cold wave of ocean spray. "Geraldine!"

I sprint for the door and fling it open. Panic claws up my throat, seizing me.

The hallway is empty.

CHAPTER 43

Her Beloved

W E STORM ACROSS THE CITY, BARELY TAKING THE TIME to make sure nobody sees us. Damn my reputation when Geraldine's life hangs in the balance.

The front door of the town house hangs open, no butler or maid waiting to greet me as I rush up the stairs to find the door to Geraldine's room already ajar when I fling it open. I jerk to a halt, mouth gaping and chest heaving. Holmes stumbles behind me.

"Bloody hell," he mutters.

Ermyntrude sits at Geraldine's boudoir. "I thought you might come here."

The blankets of the bed are in disarray, the image of a restless sleep; the blinds are flung wide. Amber coals smolder in the hearth, and Geraldine's lovely dress for the ball lies in a crumpled pile beside her closet. Silver bullets dot her boudoir.

A chill sweeps over me, freezing me to the floor.

"You were going to make this look like a suicide," I say, not a question.

"So clever, Irene." Ermyntrude stands and turns to face me, her elegant black dress sweeping the floor.

"Where has he taken her?" My throat is raw, holding back tears and the roar clawing from my lungs. "Where is Geraldine?"

"But not so clever as to figure out that," Ermyntrude says, voice as soft as velvet.

"He wouldn't bring her to campus." Holmes is a warm wall at my back. "Too much death there already. Too many things that already paint you as the villain."

"Correct." Ermyntrude cocks her head, then whips a gun from the folds of her dress. "But too late, yet again."

My heart stills. Holmes sucks in a deep breath.

"You see"—Ermyntrude walks toward us, keeping the gun trained on my forehead—"the only things standing between me and my wealth are my father's gambling habits and"—she pulls the hammer—"Geraldine Hayward."

"Your fathers are both gentry." I raise my chin, keeping my eyes fastened on hers. "Take one out and the other is sure to rise in the monarchy's favor. Why not kill Lord Hayward instead?"

She shrugs. "Good things come in time, I suppose."

"She's leading us in circles," Holmes says, cursing under his breath.

With a voice as quiet as silk on skin, I ask her, "Why the dukedom? Why bother with this murderous charade at all? Are you really so hungry for power that you would stoop to murder?"

Ermyntrude tips her head back, glaring up at me.

I continue, "Is it worth the blood staining your hands, or is it something more?" My voice rises with each word. "Who has twisted you so much that you would do this?" It drops again to a whisper. "Our hearts are not born black. They are made that way."

She cocks her head. "My beloved says that monsters lurk in us all, and it is better to feed them than to wait for them to bite."

The nail drives home, her words an anvil.

"Your beloved," Holmes says. "Moriarty?"

"None other."

I want to run for the window and fling my guts up. The same monster lurks inside of me.

"You—you both conspired together. To kill my classmates. And you"—I swallow the bile rising in my throat—"you killed Edgar."

"I kept my hands bloodless for as long as I could, but when my father invited him out to our estate, he saw the flowers." She looks to Holmes, smile widening. "Very impressed that you managed to withstand such a heavy dose."

"As you said," Holmes bites out, "Irene is very clever."

"Is she clever enough to withstand a bullet?"

I already have once.

She squints, aiming. "Let's find out."

A shot rings out and I scream. Ermyntrude ducks, the bullet piercing into the wallpaper behind her. Holmes sprints across the room and kicks the gun from her hand.

"Bloody hell," she snarls.

Watson stalks into the room, his own gun aloft. "I was wondering what was taking you so long, Holmes."

"Who the bloody hell are you?" Ermyntrude screeches.

"I'm John Watson," John says simply, as though it is the most obvious thing in the world. "Reach for that gun and I'll blow off your hand, lady or not. Tie her up, Holmes."

I stride for the bed and rip off the sheets. Sherlock helps me shred them, and we use the pieces to tie an irate Ermyntrude to her chair.

I brace my hands on each arm of the chair and lean into her face. "Now, where is Geraldine?"

"Why should I tell you?" Ermyntrude spits, and I swing my face to avoid the spray.

"Your game is up." Holmes almost sounds bored. "Nobody will believe it was a suicide now."

"But who would they believe murdered her?" Ermyntrude rests her head against the back of her chair. "The lady tied up in her own room, or the two students wanted for murder and the officer who freed one of them from prison?"

My heart stutters. "Damn you, Ermyntrude Bedford."

She cackles, and I turn to resist punching her square in the jaw.

"Where could Geraldine be?" My fingers pass over the bullets on the boudoir without touching them. I resist the urge to crumple to my knees.

Holmes is silent, methodical even, as he walks slowly about the room. I want to scream at him to hurry, to say anything, to rage against my friend being taken from right under our noses.

But Holmes isn't here, not mentally. Again, he is gone from my reach. Not from drugs this time, though.

"Of all the bloody times to be silent. No witty comeback, Holmes?" Watson mutters under his breath.

"Better silent than so loud I cannot think." He rubs his temples. "Perhaps we wouldn't be worrying about where they took Geraldine if Irene had not picked the most obvious place on campus to heal me?"

I turn, slowly, to face him. "Excuse me?"

Holmes waves to Ermyntrude, indignant to the waves of fury coursing through me. "Lady Bedford knew who you were. Who you really were. Did you really believe she hadn't figured out your connection to Professor Stackton by now?"

"Forgive me for coming to the best place to save your life," I say, my voice rising to a piteous screech.

"Perhaps we should be focusing on the matter at hand," Watson says.

Ermyntrude laughs again.

"You couldn't bring me to one of the many little rooms you've claimed for your experiments all over campus?"

"You're the one who ruined my mercury heart." I stride over to him, jabbing a finger into his chest. "And you can thank me later for bringing you to the most obvious place to save your bloody life."

He merely looks me up and down, eyes lingering on my lips.

"Imagine you dying like Edgar because of that damnable woman." I wave my hands through the air, turning so he cannot see what must be a devastated expression across my face. Tears fall down my cheeks. "Like Edgar."

Holmes stills behind me. My own breath catches, hands curling into fists.

"Like Edgar," I repeat. I spin around, facing Ermyntrude. Her face pales. "Moriarty will take her to Edgar's grave."

Ermyntrude is as white as snow now, a cold sweat forming atop her brow.

"Where a mourning sister would take her life," Sherlock whispers.

I point in Ermyntrude's face. "No doubt you would have done something similar had we not interrupted you earlier. Time to take Geraldine away from campus, to unlink these murders from those like us who are connecting the dots."

"We'll take my carriage." Holmes strides for the door, and I follow as though the bats of hell swoop at our heels. "We must get to the Bedford estate straightaway."

"The Bedford estate?" I jerk to a halt. "We haven't the time. We need to go to the graveyard."

"It's a ruse, Irene." Holmes sighs in frustration, pinching the bridge of his nose. "They don't have to kill Geraldine. They have to kill Ermyntrude's own father if they want to ascend to the highest echelons of society. James Moriarty knows exactly where we are, what we've found, and where we are going next." He jabs a finger at the bullets. "They are five steps ahead of us. Lord Bedford will squirrel away the drugs, sealing their fortune. And if Lord Bedford were to meet some mysterious end in the near future? Imagine the power that your brother would come into with Ermyntrude as his wife."

"Ermyntrude wouldn't have her own father killed," I say, looking to the witch in question. "Her brother would inherit anyway."

"This is too easy, Adler," Holmes says, shaking his head. "Can you not see that? That is why Ermyntrude told you of her father's involvement with the Gridiron. Why they left breadcrumbs asking each of the murdered for money only weeks before their deaths."

Ermyntrude chuckles from behind us, making me gnash my teeth.

"Get her out of here," I snarl, whipping around to face Watson. "Why haven't you taken her to the Yard?"

"Because we don't have enough evidence." Watson nonetheless strides to the bound Ermyntrude. "But I can arrest her on charges of carrying a weapon with malintent."

Sherlock waves an impatient hand through the air. "She'll just claim self-defense. Leave her here while we stop her father—at the Bedford estate."

"To hell with Ermyntrude's father, trap be damned." I march for the door. "I will save my friend even if it means falling right into it."

"Moriarty will have a gun, if he is actually there." Holmes steps in my path. "How do you plan to stop a bullet?"

I raise my chin. "I will find a way."

He and Watson leave me, seething and breathing hard enough to strain the stays of my corset.

Ermyntrude watches me. "You should know that I will scream the moment you leave. They'll be hunting you again soon enough."

"Not if you're incapacitated." I spin around, searching until I find exactly what I need.

"No," she yells when she spies the pipe I hold aloft. "No! That will kill me."

"What didn't kill Holmes shouldn't kill you." Using the smoldering ashes in the fireplace, I light the pipe and stride to the bound Ermyntrude. "Have you felt its effect yet?"

She shakes her head, crying now so tears spill down her front. "Please, Irene."

"Don't worry," I say with a bitter smile. "I won't dose you with as much as you did us."

I puff into the pipe and fill the air between us with black smoke. She coughs wildly as I cut the binds on her arms. Careful to hold my breath, I don't let the fury simmer for a moment longer. I slam the door shut behind me as Ermyntrude begins to moan. So like the ghosts that roam Oxford's corridors.

It will be a long while before anyone finds her.

CHAPTER 44

A Grave Mistake

My hand stays curled in a fist, pressed against the roof of the carriage. I cannot hasten the journey to Holywell Cemetery any faster.

My anxiety, keen as a string around my heart, begs me to go faster, to hurry, not dawdle. Perhaps Holmes's absence is felt more keenly than I will let on. His steadiness needed when my nerves threaten to ribbon my very soul.

I drop my hand to the folds of the black muslin dress I had no time to change out of. For Geraldine, I will do anything to save her life. My failure to catch the killer cost her brother his life. I will not do the same again.

I leap from the carriage before it turns the corner down the last street to Holywell. Clouds crowd the forlorn skies above the cemetery, blocking the moonlight from the gray sea of crosses and headstones. As quickly and quietly as I can, I stride for the trees lining the cemetery. As I near, I slow my steps as much as I dare, my boots crunching softly in the fresh, untouched snow.

"Let me go!" Geraldine's voice cuts through the chill night.

My breath catches, lips clenching around the cry I long to yell out to her that I'm here. I press the leaves of a branch away with a gloved hand.

In nothing but her shift, Geraldine braces a hand against Edgar's headstone, and her breath curls high in the cold night air. Even from a distance, I can watch her tremble, but from cold or fear, I cannot say.

For the barrel of a pistoleer is aimed directly for her heart.

The same silver gun that nearly took my life.

In the dark, I cannot make out the figure's face. He is tall and his hair too light, even in the darkness, to be mistaken for anything other than blond.

James.

He cocks the trigger wordlessly. A sob escapes my friend as she looks down the barrel.

Before I can stop myself, I scream, "Stop!"

The gun flashes, bullet biting the tree branch above. A startled yelp escapes me, and I drop to the snow. James marches toward me, gun trained on my head.

"Run, Geraldine!" I yell.

His arm swings the pistoleer toward my friend, and she screams, diving behind a gravestone just in time. A bullet cracks into the stone like a bolt of lightning. I crouch low beneath the snow-covered boughs.

Wordlessly, he stomps in my direction, keeping his gun trained on the gravestone Geraldine cowers behind. Silent as a mouse, I creep along the shadows until I'm pressed behind another tree. James trudges toward me, his breathing hard.

The snow is falling harder now. In the dark and through the white haze, I can barely make out my brother. His movements are given away by his laborious breathing. The pistoleer rings out again, biting the frozen ground at my heels.

Tossing caution to the wind for my friend, I yell out again, "Run, Geraldine!"

I feel the sting of the fourth bullet before I hear the lightning shot of it leaving the gun. My shoulder burns, the bullet slicing right through and planting itself in the tree behind me.

Gasping, I grab at my shoulder and grit my teeth against the unbearable sting. Hauling myself behind another tree, it takes everything in me not to cry out.

"I can smell your blood," he says, words barely heard over the roar of pain pressing down on me.

Warm blood seeps through my gloved fingers, dripping down my back and front, accelerated by the rapid thundering of my heart. I force myself to breathe slowly, in and out. My fingers tremble, though, as James steps up to the tree I hide behind.

Hopefully, Geraldine has taken my brother's distraction to flee. But dimly, an itch in the back of my mind tells me she has not. Likely too paralyzed with fear to do so much as move from the grave she hides behind.

My blood staining the snow has ruined my brother's ruse. Any policeman who comes to investigate will know that there had been foul play here. That Geraldine hadn't come to take her own life.

And James will want revenge.

Best to give him the show he wants and buy Geraldine more time to escape.

I crawl toward the graves, my movements masked by the dark

night and fall of snow. But as I reach the first line of headstones, the snow begins to slow. I'm no longer cloaked in winter's white shawl.

I climb on unsteady legs and turn to face the trees, raising my chin high.

Moriarty strides from the line of trees, gun trained on my chest. But it isn't James who glares down at me. I reach a trembling, bloodstained hand for balance on the nearest grave.

My father cocks the pistoleer. "It's a shame it had to come to this."

CHAPTER 45

Never Trust a Moriarty

S NOW EDDIES AROUND US, SLOW AND SOLITARY WHITE FLAKES that land on my nose and hair. My lips tremble with every breath, and the pain threatens to buckle my knees.

"You're right," I say with a small grimace. I'm losing feeling in one of my arms. "Such a shame I had to ruin yet another of your parties."

"Especially when—*again*—you were never extended an invitation to begin with," Richard Moriarty says, lowering the gun slightly. I daren't hide, though. I'm not faster than a bullet, especially from so close. "Geraldine is just a necessary casualty."

I raise my chin. "The Yard is already on their way to the Bedford estate."

He inclines his head and raises the gun again. "Pity. We'll see if they make it there and back in time. You and Sherlock Holmes have been too late each time." The barrel of the pistoleer is a dark, bottomless abyss aimed between my eyes. "Just as you are now."

"You were the one in the Queen's Chapel." I meet his eyes,

forcing him to hold my gaze. "You nearly killed me, and before that in Bartlemas. You released the gas. Killed that man. I thought it was James, but—"

"James has always been a thorn in my side." Richard sighs. "He's been suspicious from the very start, and as soon as I heard that he'd visited the bodies, I knew he would keep digging. I couldn't leave any loose ends for someone to find. Imagine my surprise when I watched you run from Bartlemas."

I cannot hear Geraldine. I dare not turn to see if she still lingers.

How could I have been so blind, distracted by my singular hatred of my brother that I forgot the true enemy before me?

"Why?" I choke out the word, so like the heroes in my favorite stories, begging for answers before the villain steals their final breaths. "What do you possibly have to gain?"

"The same as my dear Ermyntrude." His smile is as slick as an adder's, filling me with revulsion. "To ascend to the dukedom." He squints, staring down the barrel at me. "But you already knew that. You're asking for Lady Geraldine's benefit should she escape."

I swallow, my throat painfully dry. Geraldine, thankfully, doesn't make a sound behind me.

"You're right," I say, voice rough. "I did know that. What I cannot figure out is why Stackton. Why murder your own friend who stood no chance of ascension?"

"You can thank yourself for his death."

My father scratches his chin with the barrel of the gun. "He knew too much. In protecting you, *Isaac Holland*," he says my false name with a sneer, "and abetting your snooping, he figured out what you failed to. That it was I who orchestrated the murders of your classmates."

"Too bad Ermyntrude will be rotting in a prison cell soon enough," I bluff. "We captured her just an hour ago."

"My soon-to-be bride will find a way out of that cell," Richard says, not even a hint upset at my words.

"You framed Carlisle rather than murdering him outright. Why?"

"If our ruse was discovered by Stackton, others were sure to follow. You're an example of that." He shrugs again.

Silence drifts between us, broken only by my shuddering breath. Somewhere behind me, Geraldine is as silent as the dead around us.

"James knew you had seduced Ermyntrude," I say aloud. Not a question.

The snow has stopped falling, the clouds parting to illuminate the cruel smile on my father's face.

"I will admit that I'm proud of you," my father says, for the first time in my life. He squints, aiming. "For figuring it out. Your rivalry with James did blind you in the end, though."

"If you're going to murder the ladies, best get on with it, then."

Hope arcs through me, and my father whirls.

Sherlock Holmes doesn't even give the gun a mere glance. "The Scotland Yard is on the way, so if you're hoping to murder three people, cover your steps, and make an escape, best to be quick about it."

My father sputters. His deathly facade begins to crumble away.

I cough. "He needn't bother."

Richard spins toward me again and demands, "Why?"

"Because a pistoleer only has four shots." His eyes widen for the barest second before I leap across the space between us.

We collide, crashing into the snow. His chest is bumpy with more weapons beneath his coat. If Geraldine hasn't sprinted to safety yet, I pray she takes the opportunity now. He grips my wrists, clenching with bared teeth. I fight against his hold, but my wounded shoulder and abdomen have left me with minimal movement on that side. He easily tosses me aside. My back hits the corner of a headstone.

"Irene!" Holmes sprints across the cemetery, a blur in the corner of my eye.

"No, Sherlock!" I only have time to cry out a warning before my father whips another pistol from his breast pocket.

A shot cracks the air. Silence fills the graveyard.

My father staggers to his feet and growls, "I should have killed you years ago."

His face is wild, a monster and wolf rolled into one. His hair wet, blond wisps slashing his long forehead, his eyes wide and white in the moonlight. The gun shakes, trained on my heart.

I cannot stand, the pain in my shoulder dragging me to the earth. I slide down stone, eyes glued to the weapon.

"Goodbye, *Mumely*." He says the nickname with a wicked sneer. "Give your mother my love."

"Dean Moriarty!" Holmes leaps to his feet again and tosses something between us. It gleams, silver in the moonlight. My father shoots, the bullet biting into stone as Holmes dives behind a headstone.

The metal plate he tossed slides across the snow between us. The same metal plate with poppies engraved on its surface that he hid from me. I only have time to squeeze my eyes shut before it snaps open like a fan.

And nothing happens.

"Damn," Sherlock murmurs from somewhere to my right. "That was meant to be more exciting."

I ease my eyes open to watch as my father steps toward the device.

He reaches for the metal plate. "Your family, Sherlock Holmes, really amounts to nothing."

The plate hisses.

Gas fills the air around my father's face, and he roars. I duck my head and plant my face into the snow.

"What the devil is this?" The plate crashes into a stone beyond me. My father stomps through the snow. "What did you do?"

His steps suddenly slow, feet dragging in the snow.

"Elena?"

Slowly, I lift my dripping face. My father stares at a now-standing Sherlock. Richard's mouth gapes, eyes blinking rapidly. Holmes marches forward, face determined.

"Elena, please," Richard trips over his own feet, falling backward. "I meant you no harm. It was only a warning!" His voice rises with each word, until the last is a piteous squeak.

Eyes wild, Richard raises the pistol once more, aiming at Sherlock's chest. His hand shakes, finger dancing over the trigger. "No, don't hurt me!"

I throw myself into his arm just as he squeezes the trigger. Sherlock ducks.

The bullet goes wide, flying into the night. The gun soars, knocked from Richard's grip.

Now my father meets my eyes, tears spilling from his own. "Please, Elena. I would never hurt her."

"So many lies, Richard." I raise a fist, ready to knock my father out cold.

Another shot splits the night. I feel the thud of a bullet hitting its target before anything else. Blood spreads beneath the palm I have splayed across my father's chest. It soaks through my gloves, as warm as the dying heart inside him.

He releases a final shuddering breath and says, "Please forgive me, Elena."

The light in his eyes goes out, leaving two horrible gray discs staring up at the moon.

"Why did you kill him, Holmes?" I demand, easing myself away from my father's body. "We should have brought him to the authorities."

"Sherlock didn't kill him. I did."

My head whips around to see James pointing a still-smoking gun directly at me.

CHAPTER 46

A Smoking Gun

"James?" His name is a mere croak from my lips.

Sherlock frowns at my brother as though he is nothing more than a mere annoyance. "How did you know we would be here?"

"Figure that out for yourself, Holmes," James says. He considers me for a moment, then lowers the gun. "Just be appreciative that I got here when I did."

There's a thunder of feet behind him, and from around the corner a group of men comes running. An entire battalion of officers, John Watson among them.

"Oh, Irene!" Geraldine sprints toward me, blond curls streaming behind her. She drops to the snow, reaching a trembling hand for my arm.

The gentle Watson runs to me first, ignoring the prone body on the ground. He drops a bag beside his knee. "You're wounded."

"Indeed," I say with a grimace. "Though not nearly as bad as my father."

Watson looks to the body of Richard Moriarty and stiffens. "I'm afraid he is beyond saving." He turns to me, kind eyes probing my face. "But you already knew that."

He may have been my father, but Richard Moriarty caused me—and my mother—nothing but pain. I give Watson a curt nod, moving stiffly so that my back is to the body.

"I found this list in my father's office," James says to Inspector Gregson, pulling a piece of paper from his breast pocket. "Of all the victims, their places of death, and the Lady Hayward's is at the bottom. I had to stop my father before it was too late."

Watson looks between us but doesn't say anything.

Sherlock kneels in the snow beside him, looking me over. "Any other wounds Watson should know about? Did you hit your head at all?"

I shake said head, gritting my teeth before saying, "I forgot you had an interest in medicine, John."

He peels my jacket open to look at my shoulder, the wound still covered by my dark dress. "I wanted to become a doctor, but my father would never allow it. When he passed this fall, I felt it was best to follow in my father's footsteps. Do as he pleased, even if posthumously."

He tears the shoulder of my dress, and a gasp escapes me. "My apologies."

Between tears, I say, "Tell me more to distract me from the pain. Do you not think your father would want you to do as you've always wanted?"

Watson's gaze flicks to Richard's prone body. "Like your father?"

Holmes is silent, glancing between us with an unreadable face.

"Like my mother," I say. I don't make another sound as he cleans and stitches my wound.

"If I could go into medicine"—Watson meets my eyes after placing a bandage over the wound—"I would."

Geraldine is now being questioned by the officers. I can only hope she uses some discretion. It would be best if she didn't reveal that I'm the one who freed Holmes from prison.

"What was that metal disc? The one you threw between my father and me?" I ask Holmes.

From his jacket pocket, just far enough for me to see, he pulls the disc out, then tucks it once more out of eyesight. "A little contraption my sister and I have been working on for a couple of years. A bomb that dispels gas, rather than firepower. Much more subtle, with less boom. When we were in Ermyntrude's room, I took a small pinch of the drug she used to intoxicate me. It managed to incapacitate your father quite nicely."

I look between him and Watson. "Did you stop Lord Bedford in time?"

"I did." Watson puffs out his chest. "I stopped his carriage before he could even leave home. Busted the drugs he was hoping to cart as well."

Holmes's face is unreadable. "I realized, as you did, that they would expect us to chase after the Gridiron red herring."

"So many red herrings. William Cobbett would have been impressed," I say with a grimace, leaning back against a cold gravestone. It's a balm against my burning shoulder. "My father never expected us to come after Geraldine. Just Ermyntrude's father."

"Because he never realized that you were the one hunting him." Holmes's dark eyes are unreadable.

"But why would your brother shoot him?" Watson asks, pressing the back of his hand to my forehead to check for a fever.

"That"—I look to my brother, relaying his heroism for another officer—"is a mystery for another day."

James meets my eyes over the officer's shoulder and there, I see a flicker as the new head of the Moriarty family smiles.

CHAPTER 47

All Souls Triumphant

Holmes, Watson, Moriarty, and Adler. Like children awaiting a scolding, we crowd the benches outside the chancellor's office. Guards are positioned on either side of the chancellor's doorway. A marquess and a former All Souls Fellow, Robert Gascoyne-Cecil is rumored to be a prickly bear of a man.

Indeed, judging from the roaring echoing through the thick wooden doors of his office, we are all about to brawl with a beast.

Isaac Holland is no more. My ruse is ruined, my mentor dead, my title bloody, and my reputation in tatters. My hands tremble. I still them by gripping the folds of my dark skirt, still stained with my father's blood. They sat us outside the chancellor's office while officers, lords, and deans argue a scant five yards away.

"You've really made a mess now, Irene," my brother drawls. He leans back, resting his head against the flagstone wall and crossing his ankles.

"No more so than you," Holmes says, lazy drawl matching my brother's. "You've been digging as long as we have. Perhaps longer."

Watson looks nervously between Holmes and the guards watching us from the doorway. "Perhaps we should save this talk for later."

Holmes ignores him. It must be a common thing, because Watson merely rolls his eyes when Holmes says, "You killed your own father, Moriarty. Without batting an eye. No matter how much of a monster your father may have been, you must have felt something watching his life drain away."

"I felt nothing," James says with a sneer.

"'What strange phenomena we find in a great city, all we need do is stroll about with our eyes open. Life swarms with innocent monsters.'"

All heads snap toward me.

"Or so Baudelaire once said." My voice cracks as I continue, "A monster begets monsters. And my brother"—I meet James's icy gaze—"is no different."

He arches a brow. "Careful, Irene. You are a Moriarty, too."

"No," I say. "I am an Adler."

The door swings open and slams into the wall, making us all jump.

Inspector Gregson, eyes twinkling, waves us inside.

And I feel, not for the first time in the last twenty-four hours, that I am walking to the gallows.

I'm seated between James and Sherlock in an uncomfortable wooden chair. It creaks as I take my seat, but all eyes are already pinned to me. In a room with the most brilliant people alive, I am still the main attraction. The lion in a circus.

Keenly aware of the blood and mud speckling my pale neck, I raise my chin. "What fate does the judge, jury, and executioner hold for us?"

Chancellor Gascoyne-Cecil mutely regards me with thin lips and stern eyes.

It is a golden-haired lord who breaks the silence, his face familiar, but I cannot place it. "You're not being tried for murder, Lady Irene." He cuts a stern glance to the other men in the room. "Of that I assure you."

"But that won't save you from being expelled from Oxford," one dean cuts in, sneering at the blond lord.

"Indeed." The chancellor coughs, drawing all attention to himself. "If it were ever to get out that a woman managed to parade around like a man, in our very school, for months, we would be the laughingstock of England, a joke to the world."

"Then perhaps," I say cuttingly, "you better choose your next words wisely."

Silence, pungent and heavy as sewage filth, seeps into the room. Everyone holds their breath.

Finally, the chancellor asks, "Are you threatening me, Lady Adler?"

"Merely holding you accountable, Chancellor. Holding *all of you* accountable." I hold the gaze of each man in this room, including James and Sherlock. "A woman did dress as a man and take part in your prestigious All Souls competition. Professor Stackton knew the entire time and still saw fit to mentor me. Because he saw my potential. I was ahead of everyone in that competition, and I will not pretend otherwise simply because I am a woman."

"You also held chemical experiments all over campus, led a hunt for a killer, and undermined the authorities at every turn." The chancellor stands slowly, bracing large hands on his desk. "You also broke a man out of prison."

Watson, to my right, seems to slide deeper into his own chair.

"I also caught the killer," I say, voice soft and cold as fresh snow. "I stopped the murder of Geraldine Hayward when not a single member of the Scotland Yard could do the same."

"Actually, my dear sister"—Moriarty stands, cutting me a smile that freezes my core—"I am the one who caught the killer."

"You. Did. Not." I grit out, standing as well, and pointing a finger stained with blood—our father's blood—at his face. "You just took the credit by killing him."

"And how were you handling it, Irene? Did you actually manage to catch him, or was he about to kill you and Holmes both?"

I sneer but have no cutting reply. For once, I am at a loss for words.

The chancellor looks him up and down. "Oxford is indebted to you, James Moriarty. Even if it came at the cost of a dean, your own father, we are eternally grateful to see the end of this trail of death."

"You're not afraid, then," Holmes says, speaking up at last, "of him following in his father's footsteps?"

"Would I really murder my own father if that was true? I put an end to the murders on campus. I am the one who put the Ripper of Oxford to rest." James covers his heart with a hand, his face of such absolute sincerity that anyone other than myself could hardly believe him of anything else.

Yes, I do not say aloud. *You would murder your own father if it was in your own interests.*

But I cannot voice such a thing.

"And so," the chancellor continues, easing himself back down into his seat, "we will not forget this justice you have brought to us."

"However." He levels me with a cold, granite stare. "Neither can we forget all that you have slipped past us, Lady Adler. How you have threatened the very foundations of this school with your weaselly ruse."

Truly? These bastards are more offended that I outwitted them than that one of their own committed multiple crimes of the highest order? Angrier about me pretending to be a man than James committing patricide?

The chancellor takes up a pen, and with a single stroke on the paper before him, he slices my heart in two, signing his name on a document still fresh with wet, black ink.

"You are forthwith expelled from Oxford."

"That's not fair," I say, stuttering slightly. "Cut me from the All Souls cohort, if you must. But not the Lady Margaret class."

"The Lady Margaret class that you are failing?" His dark eyes spear me to my seat.

"Only because I was excelling above everyone in the All Souls cohort," I say, voice rising with each word. "All the while fighting for my life, and the lives of my classmates, too, I might add."

I clench my teeth. Moriarty practically glows, glee barely contained. Watson looks pained, his face pale and drawn. The devil only knows what will come of him now. He will no doubt be forced to leave the force after helping me break Holmes free from prison.

"For which we couldn't be more grateful," the golden-haired lord says, cutting in. He looks me up and down, his blond hair peppered with silver, and blue eyes hauntingly familiar. It is just as I realize where I recognize him from that he speaks again. "You saved my daughter, Lady Irene, for which we all owe you a world of favors. Lord James Moriarty's heroism aside, he would not have arrived in time to stop your father from shooting Geraldine. Just as Oxford failed to save my son from being murdered on these very grounds."

Lord Hayward turns to the chancellor, a marquess and therefore his inferior, and places his palms on the desk. "I implore you to reconsider."

Chancellor Gascoyne-Cecil, to his credit, shows no emotion save a slight trembling of his lower lip. He looks from Duke Hayward to me, and to the men crowding this room.

Finally, he says, "I cannot rescind Lady Adler's expulsion."

"Whyever not?" Lord Hayward waves a hand to the paper before the chancellor. "The ink has yet to dry."

The chancellor coughs, then continues, "But each man in this room will be sworn to secrecy. The Lady Adler's reputation will not be ruined. Her exploits will be forgotten. She is free to move up the ranks of society by any other means."

"And you can laud James as a hero to distract the world from realizing that one of you"—I level a finger, pointing it in his face—"was the murderer all along."

This is not to save my reputation, but Oxford's. I have outsmarted each man in this room, made them run circles around one another. If it ever got out, they can consider themselves ruined.

I drop my hand. "You may not take me back, but I do have one request."

"And what makes you think we will deign to even listen to said request?" The chancellor looks me over with distaste, ignoring the simmering Duke Hayward towering above him.

"Because if you don't listen to what I have to ask, I will ruin all of you and this very school. My reputation be damned, I will tell everyone what I did, what conspired beneath this roof, if you don't listen to me now."

The chancellor has the good sense to pale. After a too-long moment of heady silence, he finally nods.

"I will go quietly from Oxford. You will never again have to hear my name or Isaac Holland's again, taking rightfully what is mine, the brightest student Oxford has ever known, if you give my seat to someone else who deserves it."

The chancellor waves an impatient hand to Holmes. "Holmes needn't worry about losing his seat. His place here was never in question."

Because he's a man, he doesn't need to add.

"Not Holmes." I turn and point to a stunned John. "John Watson deserves a place in your medical school."

The chancellor and deans all sputter now, Moriarty among them. Watson's jaw slowly drops as a grin splits Holmes's face.

"That is absolutely, unequivocally absurd," one dean says.

Another shouts, "Don't let this woman boss you around."

"You're insane," the chancellor finally says.

"The only insane thing here," I yell, pointing to the doors, "would be letting me walk out of here without making a promise that you will admit that man to your program. Just because he's not a lord, doesn't mean he doesn't deserve a place at this school."

More sputtering ensues, some bland denials and refutes.

Finally, Duke Hayward says above the din, "You will admit that man, and I will pay for his tutelage."

Silence fills the room once more.

"But..." Watson's voice is feeble, wobbly even, as he says, "I work for the Scotland Yard. I don't have time for both work and studies."

"That will be no problem," Inspector Gregson says, speaking up for the first time this meeting. His smile over the steepled fingers on which he rests his chin is genuine and yet crafty all at once. "For your involvement in Holmes's prison break, you can turn in your badge after this meeting." He softens the words with a small wink. "It's what your father would have wanted."

I turn to Chancellor Gascoyne-Cecil, glaring down at him with as much righteous fury as I can muster. "Do we have a bargain?"

He stares up at me, eyes full of hatred and disgust. For he, a marquess and the chancellor of Britain's greatest university, was outsmarted by a girl less than a third his age.

Finally, he says with great effort, "We have an accord."

The room erupts with protests, but he ignores them all, holding my gaze.

My love for Oxford runs deep, and it will break my heart to turn my back on it and my education. I still have faith that this beautiful world with infinite possibilities will move beyond their backward ideals and will stride into the future. Someday.

Inspector Gregson walks me to my dormitory in the Lady Margaret wing, leaving Duke Hayward with Watson to square out his future, and Holmes and Moriarty to deal with the deans and chancellor in my wake.

Gregson is silent as we stroll, letting me take in the last of Oxford I may ever see again. I breathe in deeply. The beautiful old stones, the trees with branches bowing beneath sleeves of snow.

The cobblestone paths and worn flagstone floors. Even the ghosts seem to whisper their goodbyes, my hair pulled from its braid to curl in the soft breeze.

"What will happen to Ermyntrude?" I ask as Inspector Gregson holds open the door of my dormitory for me.

"Unless the lords continue their meddling in legal affairs, she will hopefully be staring at the wall of a cell for a very long time." He considers me. "You gave us quite a chase, Lady Adler."

"I'll take that as a compliment," I say with a soft laugh.

He only nods, whiskers tickling his nose as he smiles. "I will leave you to pack your own things while I hail a carriage to take you home."

I stop him before he can leave. "To my grandmother's, please. I cannot go back to Lord Moriarty's house ever again."

He leaves me to pack my few belongings. This is the first time I've packed my own things since I was taken from my mother, and the act of pulling bags from beneath my bed and piling my belongings in them swells my heart.

"Your dresses will be ruined if you don't fold them properly."

I spin to find Holmes leaning in my doorway, watching me with an unreadable expression. He has a bag of his own slung over his shoulder.

"Did they expel you, too?" I nod to the bag.

"No." He chuckles. "My father has paid enough tuition to make them overlook murder."

I bark a laugh.

"Too soon?" He smiles, eyes crinkling in the corners. He drops the bag on the bed. "No, this stuff is all yours. Chemistry equipment, some of your disguises, and everything left in our dorm."

I've always prided myself on my ability to read people. But he surprises me, again and again.

"Oxford will be infinitely darker with you gone," he says, striding toward me. He takes the dress from my hand and folds it, eyes never leaving my own.

"I had no idea you could fold laundry. I thought you only knew how to toss it on the floor." I take the garment from him with a crooked smile.

He pokes my unwounded arm, sending sparks of warmth throughout my chest. "Would you prefer your brother was here to help you?"

Silence stretches between us.

"Don't let him win," I eventually whisper, my gaze dropping to his lips. "Don't let James take that All Souls seat."

"I make no promises." He drags his gaze away, turning to the clothes. "Our antics may have sealed my fate. Even if I perform better than Moriarty, his act in the eleventh hour, killing his own father, has secured his place at this institution for a very long time."

"His plan all along."

"Likely so."

We work in pained silence, packing the last of my belongings methodically. Finally, I reach for my jewelry box and flip open the lid. I look over the baubles, the tokens I've received from my grandmother and pieces of my mother that I have cherished. I take out a single ring, gold with a ruby nestled in a wide band.

"Where will you go? What will you do now?" Holmes asks, desperation leaking into his voice.

As though he knows he might never see me again.

"The Americas." I brush my hands over my skirts, to stop them from shaking more than anything else. "To travel with my grandmother to New Jersey. It was where I was born, did you know that?" I give a rueful shake of my head. "No doubt she has lofty plans to marry me to a crown prince from Poland or something else equally ridiculous."

He steps forward, brushing my dark fringe from my eyes. "You'd have any king, emperor, or god wrapped around your finger."

My gaze catches on his lips again. "I don't want a king, emperor, or god."

I step close and balance on my toes. I brush a single, soft kiss against his lips. He inhales sharply but doesn't pull away.

Stepping back, I take his hand with mine. I place the ring, my mother's all those years ago, in his palm and press his fingers around it. "You'll see me again, Sherlock."

We stare at each other, our breathing suddenly heavy.

A cough in the doorway snags our attention. Watson knocks tentatively on the wooden frame. "Gregson sent me to help you with your bags."

They help me carry the few bags I have, one strapped over each of their shoulders.

"Thank you, Lady Adler," Watson says as we walk. "For what you did for me in there."

"Don't let Oxford chew you up. They think of themselves as wolves." I throw a wink to Holmes and give Watson a wide smile. "But they are more bark than bite in the end."

"Not all of them," Holmes says, thoughts no doubt on my brother.

"You'll make an excellent doctor someday, Watson. I can barely feel the wound on my shoulder already." A lie, though it is no fault of his. I'll feel that gunshot for many years to come, and not just physically.

They lift my bags onto the back of the carriage, which I note has the Hayward coat of arms, and Watson leaves us to our goodbyes.

"In town, you'll find an old friend of mine. A family friend, really." My hands clench. "Can you tell Lasho something for me?"

"Anything," Sherlock says earnestly.

"Tell him where I'm going." I nod, more to myself than him. "Yes, tell him where I'm going. I'll have Grandmother prepare a room and position for him in the house."

"Irene...," Sherlock says, taking my hand and easing me up into the carriage.

"I know." I give him a small smile. The ghost of his lips still lingers against my own.

The coachman moves to shut the door of the carriage, but I stop him by bracing my good arm against it. "Good luck, Sherlock Holmes. My brother's mastery lies in mathematics, but in humanity, he is useless. He is too conceited, too assured. Use that to your advantage."

Across from me, a newspaper carefully folded in his lap, Lord Hayward pulls the door shut the moment Holmes takes a step back. He knocks on the roof of the carriage, and the horses whinny outside, setting us all into motion.

Lovely gold hair, just like his children's, falls before his brow. Lord Hayward looks me up and down, smiling crookedly. "You made real asses of all those men in there."

I return his smile. "They did that to themselves, really."

Considering me, he slaps his knee gently with the paper, the Moriarty name blazoned across it multiple times in vivid black ink.

"I have a proposition for you, Lady Moriarty."

"Oh, pray tell?" My brows rise, curiosity and excitement dawning within me. "And please, call me Adler."

I throw one last glance through the window. As the carriage rolls down the street, Sherlock Holmes stares after me. As though, should he take his eyes away, I will disappear forever.

But, watching the streets of Oxford blaze by, I know that is not true. I may not have won the All Souls seat, but I will still win the game.

England has yet to see the last of Irene Adler.

John Watson, James Moriarty, Sherlock Holmes, and Irene Adler were created by the late Sir Arthur Conan Doyle, and appear in stories and novels by him.

Acknowledgments

Despite *words* literally being my job, I always struggle the most with the acknowledgments. How do you tell every single loved one in your life that none of this would be possible without them? That each and every single one of my friends and family had a guiding hand in the creation of these books?

I want to start with my agent extraordinaire, Amy Bishop-Wycisk. Irene wouldn't be here without you; she wouldn't have the voice she has long deserved without your hard work and advocacy. Thank you for being the best agent I could have ever asked for.

Thank you, Mike Whatnall, Lauren E. Abramo, and the DGB team for paving the way on this publishing journey. I would have never made it this far without you all.

To Little, Brown Books for Young Readers and the NOVL, thank you for all your support and for taking a chance on me. To Nikki Garcia and Milena Blue Spruce, editors extraordinaire, for all your hard work and patience. Infinite thanks to the incredible support team behind the scenes—Andy Ball, Annie McDonnell, Martina Rethman, Jenny Kimura, Sasha Illingworth, Starr Baer, Andie Divelbiss, and Savannah Kennelly. I couldn't have gotten this far without all of you.

To my cheerleaders across the world, my greatest champions and best friends I could have ever asked for: Lis and Natalia, Autumn and Guapo, Molly and Jeannie, I love you all so very much.

Infinite thanks to Tola, for his very particular wisdom and skill set. Holmes owes you his life. Literally.

To my family, in both Alaska and Vermont, my staunchest cheerleaders since the day I was born. Especially Monkey, Mum, Scott, and Dad—I owe you all the world.

These acknowledgments would be incomplete without a shout-out for my furchildren, Momma and Tuff, who keep my lap warm at all times, my floors dirty, and my heart full.

And, last but never least, to Zach I owe an ocean of thanks and mountains of love.

Steven Rennie

CLAIRE M. ANDREWS

was raised in both Alaska and Scotland, but currently lives in Vermont. When not writing, she can usually be found outside, swimming, skiing, or hiking across the state's famous Green Mountains. She is the author of *Daughter of Sparta*, *Blood of Troy*, and *Storm of Olympus* and can be found on social media at @cmandrewslit.